Tender Vow

What Others Are Saying about Sharlene MacLaren and *Tender Vow*

Sharlene MacLaren delivers yet another heart-tugging story in *Tender Vow*. As Jason and Rachel cope with grief and loss, their faith is tested, even as they grow more and more dependent on each other. Every aspect of this richly woven tale—from the picturesque vistas of the tourist haven to the deeply emotional, elemental scenes—will draw readers in and not let them go until they add *Tender Vow* to their "keepers" list!

—*Loree Lough*
Best-selling author of more than 74 novels,
including *Beautiful Bandit*

Yet again, Sharlene MacLaren pens a story that digs deep into the heart, revealing the healing powers of love, faith, and grace. This is a book you won't want to put down, by an author you can trust to deliver insight, along with a few fluttering hearts.

—*Roseanna White*
Senior Reviewer, The Christian Review of Books
(christianreviewofbooks.com), and author, *A Stray Drop of Blood*

Tender Vow takes readers into a skillfully written and inspiring novel that shows God's gentle hand as He guides the characters toward healing—and love. Once again, Sharlene MacLaren captivates her readers with a book that satisfies the heart. This is a book you'll have a lot of problems putting down!

—*Penny Zeller*
Author, *McKenzie* (book one in the Montana Skies series)

Be prepared for a heartwarming journey into healing and forgiveness that guarantees to touch your life. Sharlene's books always deliver an entertaining message. *Tender Vow* will reach straight to your core.

—*Denise Casemier*
Book reviewer, thusfarthelordhashelpedme.blogspot.com

I am totally captivated! Sharlene's characters are so lifelike. As they converse, I feel like I am in the same room with them. Her books have also challenged me to be more compassionate to those around me. There is only one drawback—whenever I complete one of her novels, I end up missing the characters I've grown to know and enjoy! You won't be disappointed with *Tender Vow*, and you'll probably find, like I did, that you can hardly wait for Sharlene's next release. I just wish she'd write faster!

—Marilyn Hontz
Speaker and author, *Listening for God* and *Shame Lifter*

Tender Vow

Sharlene MacLaren

**WHITAKER
HOUSE**

TENDER VOW

Sharlene MacLaren
www.sharlenemaclaren.com

ISBN: 978-1-60374-098-2
Printed in the United States of America
© 2010 by Sharlene MacLaren

Whitaker House
1030 Hunt Valley Circle
New Kensington, PA 15068
www.whitakerhouse.com

Library of Congress Cataloging-in-Publication Data

MacLaren, Sharlene, 1948–
  Tender vow / by Sharlene MacLaren.
     p. cm.
  Summary: "Grieving the tragic death of her husband, John, and struggling with the pressures of single parenting, Rachel Evans looks to God for the strength to accept help from others, like her brother-in-law, Jason—especially when their long-ago love is rekindled"—Provided by publisher.
  ISBN 978-1-60374-098-2 (trade pbk.)
  1. Widows—Fiction. 2. Single mothers—Fiction. I. Title.
  PS3613.A27356T45 2010
  813'.6—dc22
                                              2010024538

2 3 4 5 6 7 8 9 10   **WJ**   16 15 14 13 12 11 10

DEDICATION

To my precious, longtime Bible study girlfriends (in no particular order): Becky, Leesa, Sandy, Terri, Margie, and Jan, who always lift me up to the Father in amazing ways, especially when those deadlines loom. I cherish and love you more than you will ever know!

PS: Your food always tastes so much better than mine!

Prologue

I cy breezes whistled through the trees in Fairmount Cemetery, prompting the faithfuls gathered there to pull their collars tighter and button their coat fronts higher, as the tent that had been set up for the occasion did little to protect them from the elements. Just two days ago, northern Michigan had experienced a warm front, unusual for late November, but today's temperatures made a mockery of it. Twenty-nine-year-old Jason Evans shivered, no longer feeling his fingers or toes, and wondered if the numbness came from the dreadful cold or from his deliberate displacement of emotion. He still couldn't believe it—it was only five days after Thanksgiving, and his brother, John, just two years older than he, was gone. *Gone.*

As Pastor Eddie Turnwall from Harvest Community Church pronounced the final words of interment, sobs and whimpers welled up from the mourners. His mom's guttural cry among them gouged him straight to the core. Jason's dad pulled his wife closer while Jason placed a steadying hand on her shoulder. His girlfriend, Candace Peterson, stuck close by, her hand looped through his other arm. His sister-in-law—John's widow, Rachel—stood about six feet away, clinging tightly to her father and borrowing his strength as tears froze on her cheeks. Her coat bulged because of her pregnancy of eight months, and Jason worried that the added stress of her grief might send her into early labor. Meagan, John and Rachel's three-year-old daughter, was the only one oblivious to the goings-on; she twirled like a ballerina until Rachel's fifteen-year-old sister, Tanna, bent down to pick her up. *If she knew the significance of this day,* Jason thought, *she'd be standing as still as a statue.* What a blessing God kept her shielded—at least, for the time being.

"And now, dear Father, we commit John Thomas Evans into your hands," Pastor Turnwall declared. "We know—"

"No!" Rachel's pitiful wail brought the reverend to a temporary halt. In the worst way, Jason wanted to go to her, but he had his mom to think about. Mitch Roberts supported his daughter, whispered something in her ear, and nodded for the reverend to continue. Pastor Turnwall hastened to a finish, but the last of his words faded in the howling winds.

At the close of the brief ceremony, many of the mourners stepped forward to give the family some final encouragement. Jason went through the motions, nodding and uttering words of thanks. While he longed to linger at the bronze casket, the weather made it impossible, so, as the last of the small crowd left the tent, he followed, Candace's quiet sniveling somehow disarming him. He didn't have the strength to comfort her, especially since she'd barely known his brother; she barely knew his family, for that matter.

"Are you all right?" Candace asked in a quavery voice.

"I'm doing okay," he muttered, his gaze pointed downward as they walked along the frozen path. How could a person explain how he really felt on a day like this?

In front of them, mourners scattered in various directions, heading for cars covered by a thin layer of freshly fallen snow. Despite the cold, Rachel walked with slow, faltering steps, sagging against her father. Even from ten or so feet back, Jason could hear her mournful cries. The sound made his chest contract.

Without forethought, he left Candace to her own defenses and raced ahead to catch up with them.

"Rachel." Breathless, he reached her side. "I'm so sorry."

"Jay." She turned from her father's supportive grip and fell into Jason's arms, her sobs competing with the sighing winds.

They stopped in the path, and he held her sorrow-racked body, feeling his eyes well up with tears. Through his blurred vision, he noted both families halting their steps to look on. One of Rachel's girlfriends took Meagan from Tanna and headed toward one of the cars. "Shh. You can do this, Rachel," he whispered. "Think of Meagan—and your baby."

"I—I c-can't," she stammered, her voice barely resembling the confident tone of the Rachel he'd known as a kid, when he and John would argue over who was going to win her in the end. Of course, it'd been John, and rightfully so. And not for a second had Jason ever begrudged him. They fit like a glove, Rachel and John.

"Sure, you can," he murmured in her ear. "You are Rachel Evans, strong, courageous, capable—and carrying my brother's son, don't forget." He set her back from him and studied her perfect, oval face, framed by wisps of blonde hair falling out from beneath her brown velvet Chicago cuff hat. Her blue eyes, red around the edges, peered up at him from puffy eyelids without really seeing. Chills skipped up his spine, and he didn't think they came from the air's cold bite. "Come on, let's get you to the car," he urged her, thankful when Candace stepped forward to take Rachel's other arm and they set off together. Rachel barely acknowledged Candace, and he wondered if she even remembered her, so few were the times he had brought her home.

"I can't believe it, Jason. I just—I can't believe it," Rachel kept murmuring. "Just last week, we were making plans for our future, talking about John Jr. coming into the world, wondering how Meagan would feel about having a baby brother...."

"I know."

"He just finished painting the nursery, you know."

"I'm glad."

She frowned. "Tell me again what happened."

His throat knotted. "What? No, Rach, not here."

She slowed her steps to snag him by the coat sleeve. "I need to hear it again," she said, punctuating each word with determination.

"We'll talk later, but first, we need to get you out of the cold."

"Jason's right, honey," Mitch said, coming up behind them. "Let's go back to the house."

"But I don't understand how it happened. I need to understand."

"We've been over it," Arlene Roberts said as she joined them. Tanna came up beside her mother and held her hand as they walked. Like everyone else's, Mrs. Roberts's face bore evidence of having shed a river of tears.

"I don't care!" Rachel's voice conveyed traces of hysteria. She stopped in her tracks, forcing everyone else to do the same. "John was a good skier," she said. "He knew the slopes on Sanders Peak like the back of his hand. You said yourself you guys used to ski out there every spring." Her seascape-colored eyes shot holes of anguish straight through Jason—critical, faultfinding eyes.

A rancid taste collected at the back of his throat. "We did, Rach, and he was the best of the best, but it takes a champion skier to navigate Devil's Run. Come on, your car's just ahead."

Her feet remained anchored to the frozen ground. "Did you force him, Jason?"

"What?" The single word hissed through his teeth. "How could you even suggest such a thing?"

"Rachel, now is not the time for such—"

But Rachel covered her dad's words with her own. "Did you provoke him into taking Devil's Run? Witnesses heard you two arguing, Jay. Why would you be fighting on top of a mountain?"

"We weren't fight—"

"You've always been the risk taker, the gutsy, smug one, ever looking for a challenge. You pushed him to do it, didn't you?"

"What? No! What are you saying, Rachel? It was a stupid accident, that's all."

She stood her ground, her eyes wild now. "John isn't like you, Jay, never was. Why drag him to the top of Devil's Run if only a 'champion skier' can handle it? You of all people knew his capabilities—and his limitations."

Jason wanted to shake her but refrained, merely giving her a pointed stare instead. "I did not drag him anywhere, Rachel, and we've both navigated Devil's Run before. It's just…the conditions were extra bad that day. I told him not to try it. You have to believe me."

"Then why, Jason? Just tell me why he'd take the chance! Why?" she wailed, thumping him hard in the chest. Shock pulsed through his veins as he grabbed her fist in midair to prevent another assault. Everyone gasped, and Candace took a full step back, looking bewildered. Blast if he wasn't dumbfounded himself. Where did she get off blaming him for the accident? Didn't she realize his heart ached as much as hers over John's death?

Mitch stepped forward and put his arm around his daughter. "Witnesses say John went down of his own accord, honey, and the police ruled his death accidental. No one forced him down that slope."

Now she threw her father an accusatory glare. "How do you know that, Dad? Were you there?"

Mitch frowned. "Well—of course not."

As if that should have settled it, Rachel pulled away and marched up the snowy walkway, albeit with stumbling steps. In robotic fashion, everyone else followed, shaking their heads in dismay. Taken aback by her insinuations, Jason fell in at the tail of the procession. "She blames me," he muttered.

"She's completely rude," Candace said, taking his gloved hand in hers with a gentle squeeze.

"No, she's just not thinking straight."

"I don't see how you can defend her. She just hauled off and hit you square in the chest."

He cared very much for Candace, but she sometimes annoyed him with her snap assessments. "She just lost her husband, Candace."

Mitch reached the car ahead of Rachel and opened the front door for her. "Where's Meaggie?" she suddenly asked, almost as an afterthought, turning full around to scan the cemetery.

"Aunt Emily took her back to the house," her mother said, climbing into the back with Tanna.

"Oh."

Before lowering herself into the car, she glanced about, then focused on Jason. "He was a good skier, Jason."

Jason nodded his head in agreement. "Yes, he was, Rachel. No question about that."

"As good as you?" she questioned with a cynical hint.

"Yes. As good as me," he lied.

Seeming pacified, she bent her awkward, pregnant body and eased into the seat. Mitch closed the door behind her and went around to his own side, nodding at Jason's parents, Tom and Donna Evans, and the rest of his family before climbing into the driver's side and starting the engine.

When the car disappeared from view, Jason murmured again, "She blames me."

"It will pass," said Tom, removing his keys from his coat pocket. "Give her time."

As they approached his dad's late-model Chevrolet, Jason asked, "What about you, Dad? Do you think I'm to blame?"

"Son, please, let's not talk about this anymore."

"Well, do you?"

"Get in the car," his dad ordered in a tone Jason hadn't heard since his youth. Even though he was a grown man, he felt compelled to obey. Candace climbed in ahead of him, and they all rode back to the house in icy silence.

Chapter 1

Ten months later

"M ommy, will you play with me?" Meagan asked
for at least the dozenth time.

Rachel scanned the kitchen, overwhelmed
by the sight of empty juice bottles, a spilled box of baby
cereal, a pan of lukewarm potato soup, and a pile of several weeks' worth of mail. A quick glance at the clock on
the wall told her it was already 8:05 p.m. Her pounding
head and jangling nerves were additional reminders of her
upside-down life, and Rachel shot Meagan a weary look.
"Mommy can't play just now, honey. It's already past your
bedtime, and I still have to get you and your brother in the
bathtub." She wiped her damp brow with the back of her
hand. It had been an unusually warm day for September,
and the heat and humidity still lingered in the house, despite the open windows. In fact, the entire summer had
been the hottest and driest Rachel could remember.

"I don't want a bath."

"I know, but you played hard today. A bath will feel
good."

"Uh-uh. Baths stink," Meagan whined.

Rachel had a good comeback on the tip of her tongue,
but she kept it to herself.

"Can you read me a book?"

"Not this minute, no." Suddenly, it occurred to her that things were too quiet in the living room, where she'd left John Jr. Setting down her dishcloth, she headed toward the other room and found an assortment of magazines scattered about, their pages ripped out and thrown helter-skelter. Johnny looked up and grinned, his mouth jammed full with something. She ran across the room, knelt down beside him, and pried open his jaws, using her index finger to fish out a glob of wet paper. "Oh, Johnny-Boy, you little stinker, you'd better not have swallowed any of this."

"If he did, it'll come out in his diaper," Meagan stated.

In spite of herself, Rachel laughed, something she'd rarely done since becoming a single parent. In fact, more often than not, she laid her exhausted self in bed each night and cried into her pillow, counting all the ways she'd failed at her mothering job that day, wishing John were there to ease the load.

She whisked Johnny up and headed for the stairs, deciding to leave the kitchen mess alone for now. "Come on, Meaggie. It's bath time." She lifted the latch on the gate and allowed Meagan to pass ahead of her, patting her on the back to urge her up the stairs.

"Noooooo," came another expected whine.

Mustering up a bright voice, she said, "Remember, Grandma and Grandpa Evans are picking you up in the morning to take you to the circus! You'll see elephants, tigers, horses… and I bet you'll even see some clowns. Won't that be fun?"

"Is Johnny goin', too?"

"Nope. Tomorrow is strictly a Meagan day."

"Yay!" she squealed, her mood instantly improved.

Later, with the children tucked in bed, the kitchen cleaned, and the house put back into a semi-ordered fashion, Rachel collapsed into her overstuffed sofa and heaved a mountainous sigh. Her chest felt heavy, a sensation she'd come to expect.

Be still, and know that I am God.

"I know, Lord," she whispered, breathing deeply. "But it's hard. Sometimes, I don't feel Your presence. I will never understand why You took John."

Be still....

She leaned down and pulled John's Bible from a stack of books beneath the coffee table, guiltily wiping off a fine layer of dust. "Lord, I've been so busy, I haven't even opened Your Word for weeks. What kind of a Christian am I, anyway? Shoot, what kind of a *parent* am I? I can't even find time in a day to read Meagan a book."

Be still....

"I'm trying."

She opened the leather book, noting many highlighted verses interspersed throughout the slightly worn pages. John had been an avid reader, putting her to shame. She knew God more with her head than her heart, but John had known Him with both. She missed his wisdom, his courage, and his strength. Most days, it felt like she was floundering without her other half. If only she'd had the chance to say good-bye—then, maybe, she'd have fewer gnawing regrets. She gave her head a couple of fast shakes to blot out the memory.

I will never leave you nor forsake you, came the inner voice. It sounded good, but could she truly believe it?

Saturday morning dawned bright and full on the horizon, the skies a brilliant blue. The heady scent of roses wafted through her bedroom window. If John were still alive, he'd have headed out at daybreak and picked her a bouquet for the breakfast table. She smiled at the thought. Gentle, cool breezes played with the cotton curtains, causing shadows to dance jubilantly across the ceiling. She hauled her downy comforter up to her chin and turned her head to glance at the vacant pillow on the other side of the king-sized bed. *His* side always remained unruffled, no matter how much she tossed and turned in the night.

Two doors down, Johnny stirred, his yelps for attention growing by decibels. On cue, her breasts sent out an urgent message that it was feeding time. "I'm coming, Johnny Cakes," she called out, then sighed as she tossed back the blankets, donned her robe, and stepped into her slippers. She padded across the room, stopping briefly to touch the framed photo of John and her on their wedding day before continuing to the nursery, where her towheaded, nine-month-old baby was waiting in his Winnie-the-Pooh pajamas. Oh, how she thanked the Lord she still had her beloved children. Yes, they wore her to a frazzle, but they also kept her grounded.

When the doorbell rang at nine o'clock on the dot, Meagan sailed through the house in her pink, polka-dotted shorts and matching shirt, her blonde hair flying, and made a running leap into her grandpa's waiting arms, wrapping her legs around his middle. Tom Evans laughed heartily and planted a kiss on her cheek, and Donna smiled, tousling the child's head.

"Grandpa Evans!" Meagan squealed, reaching up to cup his cheeks with her hands. "You and Grandma are taking me to the circus!"

"No! Are you sure?" He feigned surprise. "I thought we were just going for a walk in the park."

"Uh-uh. Mommy says we're goin' to the circus. What's a circus, anyway?"

Tom laughed and began explaining what she should expect at the circus, while Donna took Johnny from Rachel's arms and moved to the bay window for a look at the gleaming sunshine.

While her father-in-law talked to Meagan, Rachel looked on, getting glimpses of John in his every gesture. Tom Evans's manner of speech, his pleasant face, his lean, medium build, the way he angled his head as he spoke, and even his rather bookish, industrious nature put her in mind of John.

She then thought of Jason, sort of the black sheep of the family, only in the sense that he was just the opposite with his tall, strongly built frame, cocoa-brown hair and eyes, and reckless, devil-may-care personality. And he was terribly likable to everyone—except Rachel, even though she, John, and Jason had been almost inseparable during their high school and college years. They had stuck together despite Jason's penchant for weekend parties and John's utter dislike of them; Jason had spent so much time socializing, it was a wonder he'd even graduated. But she and Jason had grown apart, especially after the accident, and she hadn't seen him since last Christmas—her own choice, of course.

Tom stepped forward to plant a light kiss on Rachel's cheek. "How are you doing these days, Rachel?"

"I'm all right," she said with a mechanical shrug and a wistful smile. She never felt like discussing her innermost feelings Tom narrowed his gaze as he set Meagan down. The child scooted over to her grandma, who smiled down at her, then looked up at Rachel and said, "Say, why don't you stop by the house tomorrow afternoon? You haven't been over for such a long time."

Visiting her in-laws' home was like walking into yesterday, and Rachel didn't know if she was ready to pass over the threshold again. The last few times had been too painful; she'd found herself glancing around the house and expecting John to come barreling out of one of the rooms. Silence followed as she bit down hard on her lip.

"Jason is coming home," Donna went on, bouncing Johnny as she moved away from the window. "He called yesterday, and I convinced him to come for dinner. He hasn't been home for a couple of months. I know he'd love to meet little Johnny. He asks about him every time he calls, and you know how much he loves and misses Meagan."

Just hearing Jason's name incited painful memories packed with guilt. For a time, Rachel had hated Jason, even blamed him for John's death. Now, she just resented him for reasons she couldn't define. In high school, the phrase "Three's a crowd" had never applied to them. Instead, "All for one, and one for all" had been their motto—until she and John had become a couple, that is. After that, the chemistry among the three of them had changed. Oh, she'd had warm feelings for both brothers, and she'd even dated Jason off and on, but John ultimately had won her heart in his final two years of college with his utter devotedness to her, his promise of a bright future, and his maturity and passionate faith.

"What do you say, Rachel?" Donna asked, turning her head to keep Johnny from pulling on one of her dangling, gold earrings.

"Yes, you should come," echoed Tom.

"I—I'm not sure. I think my parents are stopping over."

"Oh? I think they're coming straight from church to our place for lunch. They didn't mention that?" Donna asked, bobbing Johnny in her arms. The two families had always been close, having lived in neighboring towns and attended the same church for years. Then, when Rachel and John had gotten married, the bond had grown tighter still.

"Um, I guess they did, but I…I forgot." Panic raced through Rachel from head to toe. She didn't want to see Jason, couldn't picture him in a room without John there, too.

"Rachel." Donna touched Rachel's arm, her eyes moist. "We miss John more than you can imagine, but—we still have Jay. His birthday is Tuesday, remember? Won't you come and help us celebrate it like old times?"

Jason's birthday. She'd forgotten all about it. Yes, she did recall celebrating it as a family, just as they'd celebrated hers, John's, and every other family member's.

"I'm sorry; I just don't feel like celebrating anything or anyone."

"But he's your brother-in-law, sweetheart. Don't you want to see him? Remember how the three of you used to be so inseparable?"

"Mom, please," Rachel warned her. "It's all different now."

"Of course, I know that. But—"

"Leave it be, Donna," Tom said sternly. Meagan, growing as restless as a filly, tugged at her grandfather's pant leg. "I can understand why Rachel wouldn't want to see Jason. Too many memories, right, Rachel?" He reached up and touched her shoulder. "It's probably for the best—you two keeping your distance, at least for now."

She swallowed a tight knot and released a heavy breath. "Thanks."

Donna blinked. "Well, if that's how you feel…. But, at some point, I hope you'll reconsider." She shifted her fidgety body and frowned at her husband, then smiled down at Meagan and tweaked her nose. "Well, we should be getting to that circus, don't you think, pumpkin?"

"Yes!" Meagan jumped with unadulterated glee. *Oh, to be that innocent*, Rachel thought.

"We'll try not to be too late getting her home. How 'bout trying to get some rest when you put Johnny down?" Tom asked as Donna handed Johnny off to her. "You look plain tuckered out."

It sounded wonderful, but also completely unrealistic, considering the overflowing baskets of dirty clothes in the laundry room, the teetering pile of dishes in the kitchen sink, and the brimming wastebasket in every bathroom. *Whoever said "A woman's work is never done" must have been a single mom*, Rachel thought. Then, nodding with a forced smile, she saw the circus-goers to the door.

Chapter 2

September's azure skies were his canopy as Jason whizzed north on US-31 on his way to his parents' house. Unfortunately for the cluster of cows he spotted standing off in the middle of what should have been a grassy field, days of smoldering heat and a lack of rain had turned the rolling hillsides as brown as straw. He adjusted the radio dial from mellow rock to talk, then moved the AC knob up a notch. For some reason, he tilted the rearview mirror down to check his appearance. He wasn't a vain man, but even he wasn't blind to the new wrinkle in his forehead. Probably due to his years of squinting at the sun on the slopes. Candace said it lent to his ruggedly handsome appearance. Right.

Tuesday would be his thirtieth birthday, one reason he'd agreed to join his folks for Sunday dinner. He wasn't in the celebrating mood, but he'd decided to come for his mom's sake. She always had been big on birthdays, even going so far as to buy Rosie, the family mutt—some kind of terrier/poodle/spaniel mix—a bone when her special day came around.

Jason felt his cell phone vibrate in his pocket. Keeping his eyes on the road, he pulled it out, then glanced down at the number. "Hi, Candace," he said, looking back at the road.

"Hey! How's your drive going? Are you almost there?"

"A few more miles. What's up?"

"Does something have to be up for me to want to talk to the man I love?"

He gave an absent smile and silently berated himself for his lack of tact. "Are you on break?"

"Why do you answer all of my questions with questions?"

"Do I do that?" he teased.

"You just did it again."

He chuckled into the receiver. "It's hotter than blazes today."

"I wouldn't know. I've been stuck in this hospital since seven this morning. What time do you think you'll be getting home?"

"No idea. I'll stick around here for a while. I haven't seen my folks for several weeks. If I know my mom, she'll want to talk my ear off. I'll call you when I get home, if it's not too late."

"I wish I could've come along, especially since they're celebrating your birthday," Candace said in a pouty tone.

"I'm sorry you couldn't, hon." It was a partial truth. Frankly, he rarely brought her home because of the questions. "How serious are you two?" his mom always asked. "Are wedding bells in your future?" By not bringing Candace around, he could pretend their relationship hadn't escalated up the serious scale.

Yes, he'd purchased the ring. Candace had picked it out at one of the mall jewelry stores almost a year ago, and he'd gone back a few weeks later to buy it. But he hadn't given it to her. Instead, it lay in a velvet box in his underwear drawer. Just this morning, in fact, he'd shoved it way to the back so he wouldn't keep seeing it every time he fished out a pair of socks or boxers. He kept telling himself that the right moment hadn't come yet, but he couldn't help thinking there was more to it—John's accident putting the kibosh on his spirits, for one thing. In the meantime, Candace grew rightfully restless.

They talked until she had to return to her nursing station. Then, Jason stuffed the phone back into his pocket and started reading the familiar roadside signs: "Ella's Bed and Breakfast, 2 Miles Ahead!" "Little Bear Lake Restaurant (across from the high school)" "Fish Bait (1/2 mile)" "Spring Valley Ski Lodge, Next Right!"

In its usual fashion, his gut clenched. It happened every time he entered his northern Michigan hometown of Fairmount, the memories still so fresh and painful. To reach his parents' home, he had to pass through the main section of town. Turning at the appropriate corner, he passed candle and fudge shops, an antiques store, and several novelty shops, all indications of a flourishing tourist town. The second of three traffic lights glowed red, so he slowed to a stop and watched several folks cross in front of his black Jeep Cherokee, some holding packages, some leading leashed dogs, some carrying kids. All told, Fairmount's summer season hadn't quite reached its end, even though Labor Day had come and gone and the leaves had started turning from green to various shades of gold and red.

The Evanses' house never changed—brick front, pale yellow siding, and a roof that could use new shingles. As a builder, Jason always noticed when a house needed spiffing up, and his parents' place was no exception. At least the yard looked like something out of *Better Homes and Gardens*, thanks to his mom's green thumb and his dad's sprinkling well, which made for the plushest grass on the block.

A blue sedan sat in the drive, shaded by sprawling oaks. It looked like the Robertses had come for dinner. He hadn't seen them since the funeral. He thought about Rachel, and how he wouldn't mind seeing her and his niece, plus meeting his new nephew, but he doubted she'd show. Since she'd spewed those accusatory words at him in the cemetery, he hadn't heard a word from her—and he had never mustered up the courage to call and set things straight. But then, why should he have to be the one to make the first move?

Forgive, even as I have forgiven you came the Spirit's gentle nudge. Jason gripped the steering wheel hard before shutting off the engine.

God, what am I even doing here?

The front door opened, and his mom stepped onto the porch. She looked thinner than the last time he'd seen her, and a wave of guilt washed over him for not coming around more.

God, she's been through a lot.

He put on a wide smile before opening his door, climbing out, and going to greet her.

The meal tasted delicious—roast chicken, mashed potatoes and gravy, salad, rolls, and green beans. Since Candace hated to cook, and since she and Jason had especially hectic work schedules, they usually grabbed takeout, but partaking of his mom's feast made him long for more frequent home-cooked meals. He hoped Candace would acquire some kitchen skills before they married. He could grill a good steak, but he couldn't fry an egg to save his life.

Dinner conversation moved from one topic to the next, covering everything from Mitch Roberts's used-car dealership and Arlene's high school English classes to his dad's accounting job, then on to Tanna, Rachel's sister. Younger than Rachel by more than a dozen years, Tanna had been one of those "surprise" babies.

"What grade are you in now, Tanna?" Jason asked her.

"Tenth," she answered. She dabbed at her chin with her napkin, then set it down beside her mostly empty plate. "I go to Fairmount High now."

"Man, that doesn't seem possible," Jason said. "Weren't you just this tall"—he held out his hand, palm-down, about three feet off the ground—"just yesterday?"

Tanna blushed and giggled, and, for the span of a second, he saw Rachel—lithe, with ivory skin, robin's-egg-blue eyes, and honey-blonde hair.

"She just made the varsity cheerleading squad," Jason's mom announced.

"Taking after your sister, are you?" Jason said. He remembered stealing a glance at Rachel on the sidelines in her short cheerleading skirt, before catching a pass from the quarterback at the fifty-yard line. Looking back, he probably could have made more catches if she hadn't presented the distraction. He gave his head a little shake and asked Tanna how this year's football team was shaping up, which proved good fodder for another ten minutes of non-stop talk while the women cleared the dinner dishes and then delivered thick slices of chocolate birthday cake and steaming cups of coffee.

Afterward, everyone moved into the living room. Since Tanna had arranged to go to the movies with some friends, she left at the first beep of a horn in the driveway, but not before collecting a couple of bills from her father and then waving to everyone on her way out the door.

"Such a sweet girl," Jason's mom remarked to Arlene. "She reminds me so much of Rachel at that age." Since when had his mom become a mind reader? "Speaking of which, Tom and I tried to convince her to come over today."

Arlene tucked a few wisps of her shoulder-length, salt-and-pepper hair behind her ear and frowned. "I did the same thing this morning, but she declined, saying she needed to keep Johnny on his nap schedule." She shook her head. "She struggles to stay above water, that girl, but she does a fine job in spite of it. Mitch and I want to help her as much as we can, but she's independent enough to want to make do on her own. We're proud of her for that, but we still worry."

"As do we," said Jason's mom, her narrow shoulders slumping. She was normally stalwart and steady, but Jason thought she looked far older today than her fifty-seven years. He glanced at his dad and thought the same thing about him. Since John's passing, his dad had treated him differently—not in a way he could totally put his finger on, just different. When he might have enfolded him in a bear hug a year ago, today and on his previous visits, he had given him no more than a hasty squeeze or a pat on the shoulder. Jason felt the gnawing suspicion that his dad might hold him responsible in some way for his brother's death.

"How's that little nephew of mine doing?" Jason asked, sitting at the edge of an overstuffed chair, knees spread, hands clasped between them.

"Oh my, he's a little live wire," Arlene said. "I swear he was born with a little engine inside him. We all had better stand back when he starts walking, because he's liable to mow us down."

The grandparents all chuckled, and suddenly Jason felt cheated. He wanted to meet his brother's son. Not only that, but he missed his little sugar plum fairy, Meagan. He wondered if she'd even remember the nickname he'd tagged her with when she was just a baby. The notion that she might not triggered some heartfelt sorrow.

As the women swapped stories about Johnny's teething woes and Meagan's preschool class, the men listened for a while, then began a conversation of their own.

"How's your construction business faring, son?" Mitch asked Jason. *Ironic he should inquire ahead of my own dad*, Jason thought.

"I can't complain. Business is good, despite our sluggish economy. 'Course, things always slow down in the winter months." That's when he and John would take off for the mountains. Not this year, though. The fact was, he couldn't be sure he'd ever ski again, as much as he loved the sport.

His dad cleared his throat. There was an almost visible chill in the air from his reaction to the mention of winter.

Mitch looked at his wife. "Arlene, you about ready to go?"

"Yes." She brushed her hands together and stood up. "I'll just get my purse."

At the door, the five adults said their farewells, Mitch and Arlene hugging Jason and wishing him a happy birthday. "It was so nice to see you again, Jason," Arlene said. "Don't be a stranger."

Jason laughed. "I won't. I promise."

She touched his arm and leaned forward to whisper, "Maybe you should just go see them. I know Meaggie would love it if you did."

He nodded. "I think I might consider it."

He stayed another hour, sitting with his parents at the kitchen table, sipping coffee, and chatting about nothing, unless September's heat wave counted as a worthy topic. His mom forced him to down one more piece of cake, even though he'd protested he was no longer hungry. Rosie, who'd spent the afternoon in the fenced-in backyard, now dutifully sat at Jason's feet, waiting for a morsel of cake to magically fall to the floor. When his mom wasn't looking, he slipped her some crumbs.

"I'm going to go see Meagan and John Jr. on my way home," he announced.

His dad's face went several shades grayer. "That's not a good idea, son."

"Why not? Arlene suggested it herself. I have a right to meet John's son."

"He's right," his mom said.

Never one to send his wife a scolding look, his dad angled her one now. "Donna, I know what I'm talking about. Seeing Jason will only upset Rachel."

"Why, Dad?"

"Because, you—" He stopped himself and paused.

"What?"

"Rachel's not—she's been through enough already. If she doesn't want to see you, you should respect her enough to stay away."

"Tom, for goodness' sake," his mom said.

Jason put his hands on the table and pushed back his chair. Standing, he moved his gaze from one to the other. "She doesn't want to see me because she blames me. That's the bottom line, isn't it? Do you think I'm to blame, too? You never have been straight with me whenever I've asked."

A tight gasp escaped his mom's throat. His dad sat and stared, his mouth agape. "Tom," Donna whispered. "Tell your son that you don't blame him."

Silence filled a five-second gap. "He can't, Mom, because he'd be lying."

"Now, listen here, son," Tom said.

"What do you want from me, Dad?" Jason felt his anger rise higher than a gushing hot spring. He swallowed, feeling the tension slide down his throat and drop like a rock into his chest. Tears hid behind his eyes. "The police questioned me, and I told them how it all went down. Do you have something to ask me? Because, if you do, I'd like to hear it."

"Stop it, both of you," his mom said, sorrow seeping out from her tone, moistness brimming in both eyes.

"I'm sorry, Dad." Jason's voice went soft. "Sorry I took John skiing that day, sorry he took Devil's Run, sorry he didn't have the experience to handle the icy conditions. Does it make you feel any better that I begged him not to do it? I stood there at the top of the slope and pleaded with him not to do it, but he refused to listen. He went anyway, Dad." He thumped his chest. "How do you think that makes me feel?"

His dad's chin quivered. "There was something different about that night, though, wasn't there?" he said in a shaky tone.

Jason had no idea what his dad was insinuating, so he shook his head. "I'm not having this conversation." He moved around the table and bent to kiss his mom's cheek. It was wet, and he hated himself for making it so. "Thanks for the birthday dinner, Mom. It was great."

"I love you, son."

"I love you, Mom. Dad."

Like a poker stick, Tom Evans sat, refusing even to say good-bye.

Rachel felt relieved—she'd finally succeeded in getting both kids down for their naps. After church, she'd fed them, read to Meagan with Johnny on her lap, and later set Meagan up in her room with her dolls and some favorite toys so she could accomplish a few jobs around the house, albeit with Johnny on her hip and Meagan calling frequently for her attention. "Mommy, this broke." "Mommy, I can't do this." "Mommy, come see!" With every appeal, her voice grew crankier, and Rachel's patience grew shorter. By the time both children had been tucked in, she felt jittery and crabby.

Lord, I need strength to do this job—divine strength.

Rest. The word rang like a crystal bell.

"I can't rest," she murmured. The living room lay in shambles, with toys scattered across the floor, several pairs of sandals and shoes stacked up at the door, clothes draped over the sofa, and children's books tossed about. In the sink, a week's worth of soiled dishes were waiting to be washed, but first she had to find the time to put away the clean ones.

Rest? She barely knew the meaning of the word. Yet, her mind and body ached from exhaustion.

With the strength of a jellyfish, she pushed a couple of dolls off the sofa and fell into its cloudlike softness. She would close her eyes for five minutes. That's all she needed—just five uninterrupted minutes.

He knew she was home because she'd parked her minivan outside the garage. The garage door was open, and anyone driving past could have seen that the space needed a good cleaning. Rachel probably had no idea what to do with half of John's stuff. In fact, it looked like pretty much everything Rachel owned was stored in that two-car space. It irked him when people did that—used their garages for something other than their cars. He pulled up behind her van and cut the engine, allowing his arms to sag over the steering wheel while he gazed about.

The property had fallen into disrepair with its untrimmed bushes, weedy flower garden, and long, spindly grass. John had been a regular neat freak, especially when it came to his lawn. He'd be rolling over in his grave about now if he saw the condition of his yard. Of the two brothers, he'd been the meticulous one, spending the better share of his growing-up years teaching Jason how to hang up his clothes and make his bed. Now, his very house showed signs of neglect. Why hadn't Rachel hired someone to do the work? Jason knew she'd received a hefty insurance settlement, one that allowed her to pay off her debts and stay home with the kids, at least for a couple of years. Moreover, why hadn't either set of parents stepped in to help? But, then, he recalled Arlene's comment about Rachel wanting to make do on her own. A sort of morose spirit rose up in him. What had become of Rachel? Whatever kind of desperate state she'd fallen into, he determined in that moment to drag her out of it. He shoved his keys in his pocket and climbed out.

"God, give me wisdom," he prayed on his way up the walk.

❦

Some kind of ringing hauled Rachel out of her somnolent state. The alarm clock? She reached out to shut it off, but her hand fell into space. Opening her eyes, she tried to get her bearings, giving her head a little shake to get the fuzzies out, then recognizing the sound as the doorbell. For heaven's sake! Someone had come to visit her? She glanced about her messy house, then looked at the clock, which registered 3:15. Were the kids still asleep? Running her fingers through her blonde, shoulder-length hair, she straightened her wrinkled shorts and spaghetti-stained shirtfront and shuffled to the door, kicking the rumpled area rug out of the way in order to open it. Half expecting to greet her mom and dad, she stood in frozen shock when she locked eyeballs with Jason Evans, instead.

"Rachel," he said, stepping past her without invitation and making fast work of surveying the cluttered living room.

"Jason." He turned to look at her. "What are you doing here?"

"I came to see Meagan and John Jr. and to ask why half of your house is stored in the garage."

"They're sleeping, and the garage is none of your business." She still held the doorknob, squeezed it, actually, until she remembered her spaghetti stains. She released the knob and quickly hugged herself, hoping to cover them.

"It is my business, my dear sister-in-law. John would want me to make it my business."

She felt her brow furrow into several lines. "I had a flood. Satisfied?"

"A flood? We haven't had any rain."

She sighed, annoyed by his unexpected arrival. "A washing machine flood, all right? My laundry tub overflowed because a sock fell in there on washday and plugged the drain. To make matters worse, I sort of...well, left the faucet running full blast when I ran upstairs to answer the phone."

"Oh." His dark, sculpted eyebrows shot up. "Not good."

She ignored that. "I had to carry a bunch of stuff upstairs from the basement and put it in the garage to dry out."

"Well, that was a big job, Rach. Your garage is jammed."

"I'll have you know I'm not helpless," she spat.

"Has the basement dried?"

"Yes, but I haven't had time to move everything back down there."

"I'll do it."

"Beg your pardon? You'll do no such thing. You'll visit my kids and leave. As a matter of fact, I'll go wake them now." She shoved past him, but he grabbed hold of her arm and twisted her full around.

"First look at me, Rachel Evans. Here." He gestured with two fingers pointed dead center at his eyes.

He used to have the ability to rock her senses, and some of that sensation suddenly reawakened. So, rather than look him square-on, she settled for a spot just above his head. "How long are you going to hate me?" he asked in a hoarse whisper.

She sniffed and looked down at her bare toes. "I don't hate you. At least, not anymore."

"So, you did, but now you don't?" His voice held a blend of relief and amusement. "I feel so much better."

She stepped back and finally rewarded him with half a glance. His chocolate-fudge-brown eyes assessed her, toppling her nerves, and she hastened to look away, focusing on the awful condition of her house, with litter everywhere. "Just why did you pick today to suddenly show up? I—I would have cleaned up if I'd known—"

"I was visiting my parents. Yours were there, as well… and Tanna."

"Yeah, I know—your birthday. Hope it was happy." Her tone must have come off sounding caustic.

"It's not till Tuesday."

"I know that."

He shook his head. "Anyway, don't worry about your house." He lifted her chin a notch and bent his head forward. "How about I treat you and the kids to McDonald's later?"

"What? No, I—I already have supper planned."

"Oh, really?" He sniffed the air. "What are we having?"

She sucked in a breath and let it out her nostrils. "*We* are not having anything, Jason Evans, because you won't be here. Excuse me while I check on my kids." Once again, she stepped past him, and, this time, he didn't try to stop her.

Chapter 3

*A*t *least she still has some spunk in her,* Jason thought as he stood at the foot of the stairs awaiting a glimpse of Meagan and John Jr., vowing never again to let so much time pass between visits. Life was just too short and precious to waste. Besides, John would have wanted him to be present in his kids' lives, regardless of what Rachel had to say on the matter. Not only that, but her house was in shambles and she needed help. If she wouldn't accept it from her parents or in-laws, then she'd accept it from him, because—well, he wouldn't give her a choice.

He turned and looked at the living room. Toys, children's books, blankets, a sippy cup, throw pillows, and a laundry basket full of unfolded clothes were just a few of the items strewn about. He figured she'd been sleeping when he'd arrived, if her disheveled appearance and puffy eyes were any indication. And why shouldn't she have been? The girl had run herself into the ground trying to play the part of both mommy and daddy, plus maintain a household while dealing with the loss of a mate.

"Lord, she needs help," Jason muttered under his breath as he bent to pick up a doll and then laid it on a nearby chair. Not that he had a wellspring of time on his hands, particularly since he lived a good fifty miles south of Fairmount, in a little town called Harrietta, a few miles outside of Cadillac. It wasn't as if he could just drop over any old time.

"Uncle Jay!" Meagan's squeal of delight had the power to spin him around in less than a second. She ran down the steps as fast as her four-year-old body would let her and leaped through the air from the third step into his waiting arms. He laughed and spun her around as her arms, wrapped tightly around his neck, nearly shut off his ability to swallow. "Where were you?" she shrieked.

He laughed some more. "If you mean, 'Where have you been?' well, I've been busy with my job, and…life." He glanced over Meagan's head and looked straight into Rachel's eyes. "But I'm back now, and that's what counts."

Rachel dropped her gaze to the baby in her arms, her cheek resting on his downy head as he snuggled into her shoulder. The little tyke looked none too eager to meet his uncle.

Jason stepped closer. "Who's this?"

"That's John-John, silly," Meagan answered.

"So, this is the famous little guy." Meagan wasn't about to jump down, so he shifted her in his arms to free up a hand to touch the boy's rosy cheek. Rachel's breath caught, and she held it, making him want to ask why she was so skittish. "You look like your mommy," he whispered to Johnny.

Finally, the workings of a smile popped out on Rachel's delicate face. "Everyone says my kids are more Roberts than Evans, although I've compared his pictures to some of John's baby photos and I see some similarities."

Meaning nothing by it, he reached up and tugged a wisp of Rachel's blonde hair, smiling. "They're both little blondies, like you."

She gave a taut jerk of her head and stepped back, as if his slight touch equated to a scorching flame.

"What?"

"Nothing." She swiveled quickly and headed for the kitchen. For a second, he debated whether to follow but then went with his gut.

The kitchen was in worse shape than the living room, with dirty dishes stacked a mile high in the sink and the table cluttered with mail, magazines, and newspaper ads. In the center of it all was a drooping plant that looked as if it hadn't had a drink of water since spring. Under Johnny's high chair was a smattering of cheerios. "I could bring Rosie over here to clean that up," he jested, pointing at the floor.

Rachel gave a cheerless smile. "Very funny." Hoisting Johnny on her hip, she removed the tray and buckled the baby into his seat. "I usually don't have time to do a decent cleaning until the kids go to bed."

"I see." By the looks of things, they hadn't gone to bed in a week.

Rachel walked to the cupboard and took out a jar of baby food. On cue, Johnny started banging on the tray and jabbering.

Meagan had grown heavy in his arms, so he set her down and whispered, "How about playing with your toys for a few minutes so I can talk to your mommy?"

In answer, her pert little chin went down and her lower lip shot out. Quickly, he nudged her into the living room and out of her mother's earshot. "Listen, Meaggie," he said, getting down on one knee and snagging a golden lock between his thumb and forefinger. "Uncle Jason is going to spend some time with you in a bit, but I need to help your mommy with a few things first. Is that all right? Why don't you go pick out a book you'd like me to read to you, or maybe find a movie we can watch later?"

That perked her up. "You mean, like *Cinderella* or something?"

Not exactly his number one choice. "Absolutely. But you'll have to wait till I get done helping your mom."

Her oatmeal-colored eyebrows arched. "What you goin' to do?"

He heaved a long sigh. *Yes, what?* And where to begin was the next question. "Well, she carried a bunch of stuff into the garage that I'm going to take back to the basement for her."

"From when we had that lake downstairs and Mommy cried?"

"She cried, did she?"

"She cries a lot," Meagan said with a shrug. Like a sucker punch, the straightforward comment smacked Jason square in the chest.

He fingered the buttons on the front of Meagan's shirt. "You could help, you know, by picking up all your toys. Your mom would appreciate that a lot."

She looked thoughtful. "Okay, but first I'll get some books." She scampered off, making him wonder if she'd digested any of what he'd said.

Sighing again, he headed back to the kitchen and found Rachel feeding Johnny what looked like peas, judging by the green gook all over his chin and bib.

"Does he like that stuff?"

Rachel cast him a listless glance. "He'll eat it if it's the only thing available."

The only thing available? "Do you need me to make a grocery run for you?"

He heard her breathy intake of air, saw her shoulders go down in a slump. She scraped the bottom of the jar with a spoon and gave Johnny one final green bite. "I don't *need* you to do anything, Jason. Actually, I'd prefer it if you left."

"I just got here."

She let out a long breath, then snagged the Cheerios box from the table and tossed a pile of morsels on Johnny's tray before standing up to face him. Blowing a strand of hair off her face, she asked, "What do you want, Jason?"

He took a step toward her and weighed his words carefully. One wrongly chosen word, and she would send him packing. "I want to spend time with my niece and nephew. I stayed away for a while because I knew how angry you were with me—although I haven't figured out exactly why. But it's been ten months, Rach, and I need to see John's kids. Shoot, they need to see me. Also, I'd like to lend a hand around here. Don't tell me you don't need it, either. You do. I realized it the second I parked my car. The yard's a disaster."

She pursed her lips in a straight line but refrained from speaking, so he went on, treading lightly.

"I know you don't want to see me, and I can respect that, but don't deny me my niece and nephew, Rachel. They need me as much as I need them."

She moved to the sink and started rinsing dishes in silence. He walked up next to her, putting his back to the sink and folding his arms, his large frame dwarfing her small one. "Tell me what it is that makes you so angry with me."

"I don't feel like talking about it," she said flatly.

"Are you mad because I'm the one who lived?"

"Oh, stop it," she spat, bending to open the dishwasher.

"Or maybe you wish we'd gone together?"

"I said stop it," she hissed. In fast succession, she loaded plates, cups, and saucers in the dishwasher rack, hardly caring how she arranged them.

He sniffed and swallowed. "I can't turn back the clock, Rachel. You don't know how much I wish I could—or how many times I've replayed that day in my head, wondering what I could have said or done differently to keep him from taking Devil's Run."

Her teeth had a firm hold on her lower lip as a tear slid down her cheek. If he didn't think she'd bolt on him, he would have dabbed at it. "We've always been close, Rachel—you, John, and me. I know he's gone, but can't you and I at least be friends?"

"I—I don't know," she stammered, swiping the stray tear with the back of her hand. "And that's the plain truth."

"What do you want me to do?"

"Nothing. Absolutely nothing."

Rachel couldn't believe how the day was dragging on. Would the man ever leave? First, he'd made fast work of the garage, hauling items back to the basement and placing everything in its rightful place under her supervision. Then, he'd swept out the garage and moved her car back inside. Next, he'd set to changing lightbulbs, fixing a loose door hinge, replacing the batteries in all the smoke detectors, and finally mowing the lawn, with Meagan sitting on his lap and helping to drive the lawn tractor. Normally, Rachel hired someone for that job, but the sixteen-year-old who'd done it all summer had quit when school had started again, so it'd been a good two weeks since the lawn had been mowed. She made a mental note to look in the classifieds for someone willing to take on the task through the end of fall. By seven thirty, she and Meagan were hungry, but at the risk of having to invite Jason to stay, she delayed fixing anything. It wasn't that she didn't appreciate his hard work; she just didn't like feeling indebted—or encouraging his sense of obligation to her.

Seeing him for the first time in ten months had shaken her topsy-turvy world at a dangerous tilt, reminding her of long ignored issues—namely, issues that went back further than John's death, things Jason knew good and well she harbored. Oh, why couldn't he have left them alone?

She sat at her office desk, sorting through a wad of unopened mail. Johnny sat nearby, playing with blocks. Several minutes later, Jason sauntered in, all sweat and grime, and wearing a buttery smile. His dark, almost black, hair was a mess, and his matching deep-set eyes assessed her. Meagan clung to his pant leg like a wet noodle.

"I see you've had a chance to do a little cleaning."

Her housekeeping habits were none of his concern, and she resented his observation. "I couldn't very well sit idle while you sweated away, could I?"

His smile widened. She took care not to return the expression, going back to her mail, instead. "I do appreciate all you've done, Jason, but you can leave whenever. You're probably tired."

"Not till we've eaten. Come on; let me make a hamburger run."

"No need," she said, even as her stomach growled audibly.

"Yeah!" Meagan cheered, jumping up and down. "I want a kid's meal with chicken nuggets! Can I have a root beer?"

"Of course," Jason said, laughing. "You want to ride with me, sugar plum?"

"Yes!" Meagan squealed, jumping up and down like a grasshopper on caffeine.

"Do you have a child seat in your car?" Rachel asked, despising herself for relenting.

"I'll take your car."

Argh! Begrudgingly, she told him her order, then opened the desk drawer to get some cash, but he disappeared before giving her a chance to hand it over. "The keys are—," she called out.

"Got 'em!" he yelled back.

Once they'd finished dinner, Jason lingered for a while. When the kids had been put down for the night, he and Rachel sat on the sofa and watched a mindless TV sitcom, one that had them both laughing, despite her wish to remain reserved in his presence. The truth was, there were few things better than a satisfied stomach and a good laugh, and she'd been without both for a long time.

At the show's conclusion, they both stood up, she as if propelled by an explosive force, he in a leisurely fashion, unfolding his long, burly body and stretching both arms toward the ceiling, his supple muscles creating a distraction. With a hard swallow, she squared her shoulders. "Thanks for coming over, Jason. I appreciate all you did, and…well, it's been a while since I ate a good, old-fashioned, juicy cheeseburger."

"My pleasure," he said.

She walked him to the door and smiled, trying to make it look as genuine as possible. "I know Meagan loved seeing you."

"I plan to come back, you know. How's next weekend look?"

"I have plans," she shot out.

He arched a dark eyebrow. "Okay, then, but I promised Meaggie I'd watch some princess movie with her, and she needs to know I keep my word, so I do plan to return."

"Great. The next time you come visit your folks, I'll send her over with the movie. You can watch it there."

He angled his head and gave her that sizing-up look. "You're not still mad at me for the way I surprised you today, are you?"

"No, I'm not mad."

He leaned forward with a glint in his eyes. "Slightly annoyed?"

A hollow chuckle pushed out. "Well, after all, you didn't have an invitation."

"Would I have gotten one if I'd waited?"

"Point taken. Good-bye, Jason," she said, opening the door and stepping aside.

Thankfully, he didn't press her; he just grinned and tugged a strand of her hair as he walked past. "I'll see you, Rachel. And I do mean that in the literal sense."

He whistled a popular tune on his way to the car.

"Got a hot date tonight, boss? A little bird told me it was your birthday."

Jason loaded the last of his tools into the back of his pickup truck and looked across the yard at his foreman, Todd Carter. The rest of the crew had already cut out for the day. An overcast sky threatened rain.

"A little bird, huh? I suppose her name was Diane Leverance." Rarely did his office assistant forget anyone's birthday or anniversary.

"She told me today when I stopped in the office. Meant to wish you a happy birthday. 'Fraid I forgot."

"No biggie. Pretty much celebrated it this past Sunday anyway, up at my folks' house. Then, last night, Candace treated me to a steak at Harvey's Place. She's working the late shift at the hospital tonight."

Todd gave an absent nod. "So, you're spending your birthday alone, in other words."

"Birthdays have never been a big deal to me." *Especially not this year's*, he thought. Matter of fact, he planned to stop at Buff's Burritos on his way back to the condo. A big, spicy burrito would suit him just fine. After that, he'd jump on his bicycle and do his usual fifteen-mile trek on the paved path that wound around the lake.

"Same here. I'd just as soon forget about them altogether, and I probably would if it weren't for Carlene, who celebrates everything, including the dog's birthday!"

The two exchanged a chuckle. Todd removed his tool belt and threw it onto the front seat of his truck, then propped his arm over the door and surveyed the massive two-story, brick waterfront home they'd spent the last several months erecting, now complete as far as the outside went, save for landscaping the yard and pouring the driveway. "House has shaped up nicely," he commented. "Did I tell you this is Carlene's dream home? I tell her, 'Dream on, my dear. No paltry carpenter like me is gonna be buildin' something like this anytime soon.'" He combed four fingers through his hair. "I tell you, Wilcox spared no expense on this place."

Jason leaned against his truck and looked at the mansion-like structure. "Funny, I drove Candace past it last week, and she promptly insisted I build her the same house. Frankly, I wouldn't want the headache of owning this monster. Think of the upkeep on an eight-thousand-square-foot home."

"No kidding!" Todd said, crawling into his truck and cranking the engine. "Wilcox isn't what you'd call young, either. What is he, anyway? Seventy-something? Don't know what he'd want with a big ol' house like this when he could very well kiss the dust tomorrow."

They talked for a few more minutes before Todd waved good-bye and drove off. Jason slid onto the dusty cloth seat of his old Ford pickup, the vehicle he'd reserved only for work, turned the key in the ignition, and sat in the driveway, staring at the house, one hand resting on the steering wheel.

"What profit is it to a man if he gains the whole world, and loses his own soul?"

Not for the first time, the passage of Scripture skipped through his mind. So many of his clients looked for peace and contentment in material possessions. Why else would they fork out the dough for such extravagant houses? Not that he was complaining; every contract represented more capital for pouring back into the business. But he'd learned that a padded wallet does not generate happiness. Sure, he understood folks' thinking; he'd even once been of the same mind-set. *The more money, the bigger the party!* Throughout college and even after graduation, he'd been all about earning lots of money. But not anymore. Lately, since making a recommitment to Christ just after John's death, he wanted to be a good steward of his income, live simply and sensibly, make smart investments, and then prayerfully give the rest to worthy causes that advanced the kingdom.

Unfortunately, Candace did not share his heart for missions. No, she wanted the big house with all the bells and whistles, the fancy cars, the exotic vacations, and the stylish, name-brand clothing. He wasn't even sure where she stood in terms of her faith these days.

Perhaps that's why he was dragging his feet and had yet to put that ring on her finger.

Chapter 4

The last Sunday in September finally promised rain as storm clouds gathered—dark, gloomy, and restive. Rachel moved about the house in mechanical fashion, nerves taut, energy low, mood morose, matching the weather. She hated feeling sad, for it affected her ability to parent, which only dragged down her spirits even more.

The phone blared at eight thirty, just as she was sitting down to breast-feed Johnny one more time before church. She sighed and got up to answer it, crossing in front of Meagan, who sat on the couch watching cartoons, thumb in her mouth, a doll tucked under her arm.

"Hi, Mom," Rachel said into the receiver after checking the caller ID.

"Just thought I'd see how you're doing this morning, honey," Arlene Roberts said, her voice chipper. "Wanted to invite you and the kids over for lunch today. You feeling up to it?"

"Oh, I…I appreciate the offer, Mom, I really do, but I think we'll stay home today, if you don't mind."

"You spent last Sunday alone," her mother reminded her.

"Well, not entirely. Jason stopped over to see us."

"He did? You never mentioned that. Did you enjoy your visit with him?"

"He did a lot of things around the house," she replied, evading the question.

"Really? Oh, I'm so glad to hear that. You know your dad would be happy to—"

"I know, Mom. You guys have been more than generous with your time, taking the kids off my hands when I need a break, bringing over meals or inviting us to your place, even helping me sort through John's stuff. Truly, I know I can call on either of you when I need help around here. It's just...I don't like to be a burden."

"You're never a burden, honey," her mother assured her. "The thing is, well, Dad and I worry about you. We want to do whatever we can to lighten your load."

"Well, don't worry anymore, okay? We're managing fine," she fibbed.

A long pause and a heavy sigh carried over the line. "We'll look for you at church, then," her mother said.

After their good-byes, Rachel put the phone back in its cradle at the same time that Johnny let out an ear-shattering yell. Meagan switched up the TV's volume until the sound echoed off the walls.

"Meagan, turn that down," Rachel ordered as she picked up her howling son.

"I can't hear it good," she wailed back. "Tell Johnny to be quiet."

"I said, turn that down," she repeated.

Rather than obey, Meagan threw down the remote and ran to the stairs.

"Your clothes are lying on your bed," Rachel called after her, knowing very well she'd need assistance putting them on.

Plopping into a chair, she retrieved the remote and hit the off button, then situated Johnny in her lap so he could suckle.

"Oh, Lord, I'm too frazzled to go to church," she whispered. "I can't do this. I just can't do this."

"*I can do all things through Christ who strengthens me*" came the gentle reminder.

A silent tear slipped down her cheek.

Rachel tugged continually at Jason's thoughts. Since seeing her a week ago, he'd dredged up a lot of memories, recalling the early days when she used to play with John and him for hours on end. Because their parents had been close friends, the three had grown up together, shooting hoops and playing tag, hide-and-seek, hopscotch, and the occasional game of "Mother, May I?" to appease Rachel. Being together had been natural back then. In fact, often, they'd simply sat on the back steps and bantered back and forth about school, sports, and mutual friends. Rachel had been a sister in the truest sense, and either boy would have laid down his life for her—that is, until she and John had fallen in love, forcing Jason to take a giant step back. Oh, he and Rachel had remained friends after that, but the deep affection he'd held for her had ceased to exist, unless he counted their never-discussed, completely impromptu kiss just before she'd married John. He remembered it vividly, of course, and he had a feeling she did, as well. In fact, he didn't doubt it played into her angry feelings toward him and her desire to place blame, misdirected as it was.

He'd spent most of Saturday at the Wilcox homesite, determined to meet deadlines. He expected township inspectors next week, so, as was his custom, he made his rounds, reassessing the electrical wiring and plumbing—and enjoying the solitude.

Candace met him at church for the eleven o'clock service. They lived about the same distance from the church, yet in opposite directions, and so they usually met there and then left Candace's car in the parking lot while they went out for brunch afterward. Jason didn't mind restaurant food, but he would have enjoyed an occasional home-cooked meal, even if it meant making a joint effort of it. The trouble was, neither of them knew enough about cooking to whip up anything appealing. Not that he couldn't learn, he supposed. He just didn't have the gumption, and neither did Candace. He often wondered what life would be like for them if they got married. She talked about wanting a spectacular house. Would it include a gourmet kitchen? If so, for what purpose?

After brunch at Rawlings Family Restaurant in Cadillac, they headed for Jason's condo for an afternoon of lazing around. They drove both cars so that he wouldn't have to take her back to the church come evening.

When they entered his place, Candace kicked off her high-heeled pumps and walked barefoot to the sliding glass door to look outside. "Too bad it's raining," she mused aloud, "or we could have gone for a walk today. There won't be many more of these nice fall days. Look how the trees are starting to change colors already."

Jason tossed his keys on the sideboard table by the door and hung his lightweight jacket in the coat closet. Candace hadn't removed hers yet. "It is late September, hon," he reminded her.

Rather than join her at the window, he walked to the fridge to grab a soft drink. "Want anything?" he asked as he bent over to scan the mostly bare compartments and shelves. Briefly, he wondered if Rachel's fridge had a better supply, then scoffed at his wandering thoughts.

"No, thanks."

He flipped the tab on the can and took several swigs of the cold drink before walking into the living room, frowning at its unkempt state and wondering if Candace noticed or even cared.

His bi-level, two-bedroom, two-bath condo was nothing spectacular, but it was comfortable and decorated to fit his taste, with a leather sofa and matching chair, several chunky end tables, a couple of paintings by a local artist, a thick throw for those nights when he felt like stretching out in front of his wide-screen plasma TV, several bronze lamps, and a shelf full of books: novels, a few philosophy texts, several classics, and three different translations of the Bible.

The lower level included a recreation room, a laundry area, and plumbing for an additional bath, which he doubted he'd ever need. He and Candace had pretty much decided they would sell his place once they got married and build a bigger home. Of course, the notion had come more from her than him. She seemed to think that since he owned Evans Construction Company, building his own place would cost next to nothing. Wrong.

Candace pivoted her tall, slender body to face him, her black shoulder-length locks curving around her neck, her hands stuffed into her jacket pockets. "Can you come home with me next weekend, Jason? And don't dare tell me you can't, or I'll be very disappointed. Mom's birthday is October sixth, and I know it would mean a lot to her if you came."

He took another big swallow of cola. "Next weekend?" He didn't enjoy the long drive to her parents' home in the Chicago suburbs, but it had been a couple of months since he'd accompanied her there. "I'll try, but I can't promise. Deadlines are looming at the Wilcox house. I spent all day yesterday there."

"Jason, you have a whole crew working for you. Don't tell me you can't afford to take off one Saturday," she whined, reminding him of a pouty child. He opened his mouth to protest, but she went on. "You always come up with some excuse or another not to go with me." As pretty as she was, God had blessed her even more with the uncanny ability to guilt him into almost anything.

"Well, then, I'd better not try to come up with one," he teased.

To that, she responded by flinging herself at him in a full embrace. "So, you'll come? I'm excited! Wait till I call Mom. She'll want to fix something special, of course." She kissed him square on the mouth, and he found himself returning the brief kiss.

"Tell her not to go to any trouble," he said.

"Are you kidding? She'll treat you like royalty."

That's what bothered him. Lately, he'd been questioning his level of commitment to Candace. Going home with her wasn't something he took lightly, particularly since her parents would read more into his visit than he wanted. Even now, he questioned the wisdom in going. He peeled her hands from around his neck. "Want some dessert?"

"Hmm, what kind of dessert are we talking about?" she asked in a flirtatious tone, standing on tiptoe to kiss his cheek.

He grinned. "Not the sort you have in mind. I picked up a pumpkin pie at the market yesterday. It looked good."

She took off her coat and tossed it on the sofa, then followed him to the kitchen. "Why didn't you pick up something chocolate, instead? I'm not wild about pumpkin. Did you forget?"

He couldn't keep up with her likes and dislikes. He opened the freezer. "There's some ice cream in here, and… let's see…." He started searching the refrigerator shelves. "I think I have some chocolate syrup somewhere…."

"Oh, don't bother," she said. "I'm trying to lose a couple pounds, anyway."

He stood up straight and shut the freezer door. She didn't need to lose an ounce. If anything, adding a few pounds to her model-thin frame would give her a healthier glow. "Well, then, I guess I'll forgo dessert if you don't—"

"No, no, go ahead. I'll just watch you eat."

He didn't want to eat in front of her, but the pie looked good, so he cut himself a slice, set it on a plate, got himself a fork, and sat down at the table.

She pulled out a chair, sat down across from him with clasped fingers, and did as promised. Watched. "It's good. You should have some," he urged her, washing down his hurried bites with the rest of his cola.

"No, thanks," she said, beaming. She had a perfect smile, thanks to braces in junior high. She brushed several wisps of stray, shiny, dark hair away from her green eyes.

He finished off the pie in record time, scraping up the last of it with his fork, all the while knowing she watched in amusement. "What?" he finally asked, mindlessly swiping a stray crumb from his chin with the back of his hand.

"Just thinking, that's all."

"Uh-oh. We're in trouble now," he joshed. "What are you thinking about?" A signal flashed across his brain, warning him that he shouldn't have asked.

She showed him a dreamy-eyed gaze. "Oh, what it'll be like sharing life with you, waking up together, seeing each other off to work every morning, coming home after a long day and finding the other waiting…. Won't that be amazing, Jason?"

The statement caught him off guard. She didn't have a ring on her finger, yet she presumed they were going to wed. And why wouldn't she? It wasn't as if they hadn't discussed it, and she had to know that he'd already purchased the ring. A twist of his gut made him fear that his downed piece of pie would come back up.

"Won't it, Jason?" she pressed, the tiniest frown passing over her expression.

"Uh, sure." He pushed back in his chair and walked to the fridge for another cola, remembering the days when he would have reached for something stronger. Right now, he almost wished for it but knew better. Jason's personality did not mix well with alcohol, and since dedicating his life to the Lord, he'd discovered his desires for strong drink had lessened almost without his knowing it. Of course, he'd traded one addiction for another—alcohol for caffeine.

Rather than sit back down where he'd be forced to look into Candace's scrutinizing eyes, he walked to the sink, leaning the back of his brawny frame against the counter and crossing his legs at the ankles.

"When, Jason?" came the direct question. "When are we going to make it official?" Candace stood up and came over to him, wrapping her arms around his middle and snuggling close. Almost out of duty, he set down his drink to enfold her in his arms. "I love you, you know," she whispered.

He rested his chin on her brunette head. "I know," he said. *Coward.* What was wrong with him? He couldn't even whisper words of love to her anymore. *Lord, give me wisdom,* he prayed silently. *Tell me what to say. Help me know what to feel. I'm at a loss.* "I've been praying about us, Candace—our relationship."

She craned her neck and looked up at him. "What do you mean by that?"

Her reaction stunned him. "Well, haven't you?"

"Uh, of course, but…are you breaking up with me?"

Candace never had been one to mince words. A good quality in most, but, sheesh! He would have liked a little warning once in a while. Was he breaking up with her? "No! I'm just saying I think I need some time, that's all."

A pained expression shot across her suddenly ashen face. "Isn't that what you've had for the past year? Time? Haven't I been more than patient?" He couldn't fault her there. "How much more time do you need? Most couples come to some sort of conclusion about the direction their relationship is taking after two years of dating."

With his arms still loosely wrapped around her frame and his hands clasped at her lower back, he felt his stomach knot like a rawhide bone. "I hear what you're saying, Candace, I do. But, listen—remember when I recommitted my life to Christ not long after John's accident? I told you I'd been doing a lot of reading and studying God's Word, generally looking for true purpose." Her head bobbed up and down, her eyes probing yet wary. "Remember how I told you about that one night, when I dropped down on my knees and asked God to take control, to basically take all of me? Well, since then, things have changed in my heart and life. I look at everything in a different light now. Things that once held value to me, like having the best car, the best house—earthly possessions—they've moved down on my ladder of priorities. I really want my life to count for God, and I need to know that you share my convictions.

"This morning, Pastor Ray talked about having a sold-out life for Christ and what that means. Yielding our all to Him, saying, 'Everything I have is Yours, Lord. Take my life and do with it what You will.' Did that sermon touch you like it did me?" He prayed it had.

Candace turned her gaze away, her brow knit in a deep frown. "I think I found my mind wandering a bit. Sorry. Sometimes, Ray's sermons are a little too emotionally charged for my liking. I don't think God means for us to give people the very clothes off our backs. We'd all be walking around penniless if that were the case."

"Huh? That's not what Pastor Ray said, Candace. He was talking about surrender, giving God our all—telling Him that everything we have is His—and then living a life of obedience. That's where true peace and joy come into play. Sometimes, it means giving materially, but it mostly means realizing that God owns it all."

Her scowl only deepened, an expression made more ominous by the sudden flash of lightning outside the window, followed by a thunderous boom overhead. "Whoa!" she said with a jolt. "I think I might go home if you don't mind. I hate driving through bad storms, and it feels like one's coming. Besides, I think I need a nap before I start a new week."

He tipped her chin up with his finger, wondering if he'd pushed too far with his spiritualizing. "You can take a nap here, if you want. You only just got here."

"I know, sweetie. I'm sorry. I didn't realize this storm would move in so fast."

"Well, maybe you should stay and wait it out."

"I'd just as soon go home." She stepped out of the circle of his arms. "We'll talk more later, okay?" Funny how she'd been all about settling matters of their future until he'd started talking about Pastor Ray's message. It made him wonder, even bugged him, why she'd committed herself to him long before he'd squared things with God. Considering his former, rather untamed lifestyle, barhopping and living the high life, that didn't say much for her spiritual state, even though she never failed to attend Faith Fellowship Church with him on Sunday mornings. Even before committing his life to the Lord, Jason had always attended one church or another; it had seemed important and right, whether he was truly living for God or not. Besides, old habits took their sweet time dying. He'd gone to church since infancy. Unfortunately, he couldn't say the same thing about Candace. She seemed to go because he expected her to.

She put her jacket back on and slipped into her pumps. At the door, she merely blew him a kiss. "Call me tomorrow, okay?" she said.

"I promise."

She gave a desultory smile before closing the door behind her.

Jason stood in the kitchen entryway, staring at the front door. He half expected it to open, until a glance out the front window at a shiny, red Toyota pulling out of the driveway confirmed that Candace had left.

He expelled a heavy sigh and headed for his bathroom, where he kept his biking shorts. But what was he thinking? He couldn't take his usual bike ride in a drenching rain, much less a thunderstorm. He pivoted and walked to the sofa instead, prepared to watch some golf.

Call Rachel. The notion hit him as he plopped down on the sofa. Huh? He glanced at the cordless phone, lying on the coffee table. Rachel had made it clear that she had no interest in seeing or talking to him anytime soon. He decided to wait a bit longer before contacting her again, and he propped up his feet and grabbed the TV remote.

Call Rachel. The impression was more insistent. Still, he resisted picking up the phone, opting to wait and see if the inclination passed.

Chapter 5

Rachel spent the day in self-absorption, accomplishing the essentials but moving about the house as if her shoes had lead weights in them. Even taking care of her kids seemed an insurmountable task on this rainy, dreary day, and so, when her funk hadn't lifted by mid-afternoon, she called her mom to see if she might be willing to keep the kids for the night. All she wanted to do was curl up in a ball and hibernate.

"Absolutely," her mother said at her request. "We love taking them, but, honey, why don't you come and stay, as well? A change of scenery would do you good. Dad and I can watch the kids; you can just relax."

The offer sounded tempting, but Rachel knew that Johnny's persistent cries and Meagan's boundless energy would still grate on her nerves. What she needed was a twenty-four-hour escape from single parenting.

"I just need a little time to myself, if you don't mind."

"Are you all right?"

"I'm fine." Falling apart better described her current state. "Don't worry about me."

"You could always call one of your friends to come keep you company. I bet Allie Ferguson would love to come by for a visit."

"Mom, I don't need your advice."

"Oh. Well, of course, you don't."

"Sorry, I don't mean to be short with you. I'm just so…exhausted." When her mother didn't readily respond, Rachel sighed. "I need you to be strong for me right now, okay?"

"Honey, I'm trying to, but you're scaring me. I just have to say that."

Rachel forced a little bounce into her words. "Well, stop worrying. I told you, I just need a little time, like twenty-four hours, and I'll be good as new."

"I understand that," Arlene said after a little pause. "I don't have to work tomorrow, so it's really perfect for me to keep the kids overnight. I'll be right over. How's that?"

"Great. Thanks, Mom. You're a gem."

Within the hour, her mother came by to pick up the kids, scooping up little Johnny and taking Meagan by the hand. Rachel followed them out to the car with the diaper bag and Meagan's little "Going to Grandma's" suitcase. She hugged them and kissed their soft cheeks, buckled them in place, and then stood in the rain, waving and watching, until they disappeared around the bend. After that, she scuffled back into the house, but the sudden quiet didn't afford her the immediate relief she sought. Instead, it produced an intense heaviness, like the sensation of being wrapped in a wool blanket on a warm night, prickly and oppressed.

Oh, for a strong hand—someone purposeful and level-headed. Yes, she had her loving parents, but they tended to coddle her and try to fix everything, and, when they failed, they grew fretful, weighing down even more her already weary shoulders. Her in-laws were great, but they had lost their son. How could she look to them for courage when they needed it about as much as she did? This was true of her mother-in-law, in particular. Her father-in-law possessed an uncanny strength, but with it came a certain firmness that made Rachel leery. He loved her, yes, but from afar, always expressing deep regard for her well-being but never quite knowing the right words to say. Even her best friend, Allie, had no clue how to help. When it came down to it, no one did.

Lately, she worried about everything: her children, her inability to parent, her confusion about the future, her lack of energy. Why, even her milk production had slowed, increasing her feelings of inadequacy and forcing her to start using formula, which wasn't all bad, just another disappointment. And then, there was the matter of her morose spirit, which produced the disquieting notion that haunted her in the middle of each sleepless night—the thought that her children might be better off without her.

The phone rang at nine thirty, rousing her from the place on the couch where she'd planted herself several hours before. Immediately, she worried that something terrible had happened. What kind of mother was she not to have called to check on her children?

She snagged the phone after it rang a second time. "Mom? Are the kids all right?"

"Rachel?" She recognized the voice instantly—calm, quiet, temperate. Ever so briefly, her shoulders sagged with relief before agitation set in. She couldn't think of anyone she wanted to talk to less than Jason Evans. Forcing out a greeting seemed as if it would take the same amount of energy required to push a wheelbarrow full of rocks up a steep incline.

"Are you there?"

She breathed a sigh. "Yes."

"What's going on? Is everything okay?"

"Everything's fine. What do you want?"

"Hello to you, too. Did I wake you up or something? You sound groggy."

Glancing across the room, she noticed that the television was on, but the sound was off. She had no recollection of pressing the mute button. "I…I was just resting."

"Long day?" he asked.

Another sigh leaked out. "I guess."

"So, the kids are at your mom's, I presume?"

She could have kicked her own behind for not checking the caller ID before picking up the phone. "Yeah. I needed a little break."

"That seems reasonable. It must be hard playing the parts of both parents."

"Jason, what do you want?" she repeated.

The pause on the other end unnerved her. "I want to help, Rach. I think John would want it. He'd even expect it."

She folded her lower lip between her teeth and applied pressure as he continued. "This has been hard on me, too, Rachel. I lost my only brother and my best friend, and, some days, my heart feels like it's been stomped on by a herd of hippos. But I put one foot in front of the other and keep on going. It's been tough returning home, facing reality, but I'm back, Rachel, and I'm availing myself to you. I mean it. I want to do what I can."

"You mean you want to do penance. You feel guilty for John's death, you pity our plight, and stepping in on John's behalf will appease that." When had she become so snide and stonyhearted?

She heard his long intake of breath, sensed him holding it till his face went red. "You can say and think what you want; that's your right, but it doesn't change anything for me. I saw issues around your house that need tending, and I have the expertise to take care of them."

"I don't—"

"And you can hold your arguments, young lady. I've already made up my mind."

"You're a stubborn coot," she muttered.

His chuckle was low and throaty. "Always have been."

She stared across the room at the fireplace screen, which was covered with fingerprints, and thought about her next words. "I hate being a widow." A tear slid down her face and her throat clogged. "Sometimes, I can't take it. I'm lonely, Jason. I'm lost, heartbroken, mad as all get-out, and downright sick of life!"

"You're not alone, Rachel; you're never alone. God is sitting there with you right now."

God. The name seemed somehow foreign to her, breeding mountains of guilt in her soul. And since when had her brother-in-law taken up preaching? Had Jason Evans, the die-hard party boy, found the Lord? Her cynical attitude bit through her core. *Lord, I've drifted away from Your presence. Please forgive me*, she prayed silently, then said, "Listen to you. If I didn't know better, I'd say you found the Lord."

"And you'd be right. I got acquainted with Him not long after John's accident."

"Really?" She stretched her legs out in front of her, fanning her toes and making a mental note to remove the chipping nail polish. "Is this a ploy to pacify your conscience, Jason, or are you sincere?" Could she have been any more snide?

A tiny pause on the other end had her nearly apologizing, but not quite. "It's the real deal, Rach," he said, his voice quiet yet firm. "I reached a point where life got a little too crazy, and I had to step back and evaluate my goals. I came to find out that my priorities needed a good shuffling. Losing my brother…well, that started to put things into perspective. Instead of crawling out of bed to crack open a beer these days, I'm cracking open God's Word. I'm changed, Rach. I've traded in the old me."

She wondered why she found it hard to believe him. "How come you didn't mention it when you came over last Sunday?"

"I guess I hoped maybe you'd sense something different about me without my bringing it up."

She scrunched her eyes shut to push back her annoying tears. She had nothing to say in response because she had no desire to continue the conversation.

"What about you, Rachel? Are you keeping that Bible dusted off?"

"I'm very tired, Jason. Thank you for calling, but I just don't feel like talking right now."

"Then when?"

She relieved an itchy spot on her forehead with a swipe of her fingernails and sighed into the receiver. "I have no idea. I just…I don't feel like talking. Matter of fact, I don't feel like much of anything these days."

"What do you mean by that?"

"Oh, leave me alone, would you?"

"Rachel." His voice sounded all gentle and caressing. Blast him!

"I'm going to bed now. With a little luck, maybe I won't wake up."

She hadn't meant it, of course, not one bit of it, and yet the stupid sentence trailed off her lips, anyway. Naturally, there'd be repercussions.

"Rachel!" The pliant tone was gone.

"I didn't mean it like that." She hadn't—had she?

"Well, then, why'd you say it?"

Yes, why? "I have no idea. It was just a slip of the tongue, okay?"

"A bad one. Now, you've got me worried."

"Oh, for crying out loud, Jason, you're turning into a pest, you know that?"

"Have you talked to anyone…about your feelings?" he asked, passing over her remark.

"As in a grief counselor, you mean? Not that it's any of your business, but, yes, I have. I'm in a support group at church." Of course, she wouldn't mention that she'd missed the last few sessions. Even though her friends and parents all readily offered at different times to watch the kids so that she could attend the weekly meetings, she'd begun to find them tedious and had started making excuses for not going.

"That's good. I have, too."

Briefly, she wondered what he'd learned at his meetings and whether they'd helped him cope, but she chose not to inquire, drawing her knees up to her chin now and hugging them. "Good for you. Look, I've got to go, okay?"

"Mind if I call you again?"

"Yes, I do, actually. I'd rather you left me alone."

"Sorry, I'm gonna continue making a pest of myself."

"Please don't."

"Rachel, I—"

"Good night, Jason." She put the receiver in its cradle, and when the phone rang a couple of seconds later, she ignored it.

Just after eleven that night, Jason found himself on Rachel's front porch, pressing the doorbell and pacing with impatience. When she didn't answer, he put his hand on the doorknob and turned, finding it unlocked. *Crazy lady doesn't even lock her front door!* He entered through the well-lit living room. The couch looked rumpled and was stacked with pillows, a balled-up blanket, and a wrinkled magazine. He wasn't the best housekeeper, himself, but he knew Rachel. Before John's passing, she'd been a regular neatnik.

Like a spy on reconnaissance, he skulked across the room, into the kitchen, back out through the formal dining room, and then down the hallway, past a powder room and a spare bedroom, its door open to a bunch of boxes, stacks of unfolded clothing, toys, books, and other things he couldn't even name. *This must be the catchall room*, he figured. John would have had a fit. He'd liked order, not chaos. This was Chaos with a capital C. Another light glowed at the end of the hallway, but the house remained as quiet as a morgue.

"Rachel?" he called, tuning his ears for the slightest sound.

Nothing.

Any other time, he wouldn't have fretted, but in view of the way she'd sounded earlier, he didn't like the feel of things. Turning, he headed around the corner and up the stairs, tripping over a stuffed animal and then kicking it. If she'd gone to bed, why had she left half the lights on? He climbed the stairs two at a time, huffing when he reached the top. A hasty glance in Meagan's room revealed no Rachel, so he moved down the hall. Just then, a door swung open, and Rachel emerged, wet hair dripping, long robe dragging on the floor, bare toes peeking out. One look at him, and she released an earsplitting, spine-tingling, roof-raising scream.

He grabbed her to him, muffling the sound with his shoulder. "Rachel, it's me," he said soothingly into her ear. "Shh. You'll wake up the whole town." She fought him wildly with both arms, flailing her fists until he grabbed hold and secured them tightly between his hands. When she settled down, he eased his grip on her wrists, but she broke free and unleashed her anger by giving him a good pound on the chest.

"Don't you ever do that to me again, Jason Evans!" she yelled. "You scared me to death!"

"Well, don't leave your front door unlocked, woman! Don't you know how dangerous that is? I don't care if you live in a nice, quiet neighborhood; you should have your door locked at all times, even during the day. No telling who could come walking in. There're a lot of weirdos out there."

"Yeah, I see what you mean," she remarked, looking him up and down with disdain before giving him a stinging slap on the arm and stepping away. "What in the world are you doing here at this time of night, anyway?"

"I didn't like your tone on the phone. You sounded stressed. And when you made that comment about wishing you wouldn't wake up in the morning, it got me all worked up. I've spent the better part of the last hour worrying about you—and breaking the speed limit because of it, I'll have you know."

She shrugged and headed toward the stairs. He followed like a wounded pup. "I have no idea why I said that," she said with a slight toss of her head. "It was stupid."

"Yeah, it was."

At the foot of the stairs, she bent to straighten a pair of shoes, as if that would fix everything else. Then she padded down the hall to the kitchen.

"I understand your feeling desperate, Rachel," he said, still following her, "but don't say rash things unless you want people to knock down your door. Stuff like that tends to make a person a little crazy." He leaned his body in the doorframe, every nerve alert as he watched her open the fridge and take out a bottle of grape juice. Relief surged through his veins. He couldn't live another minute if something happened to her. "You will get through this, you know."

"What makes you the expert?" She opened a cupboard door and took out a drinking glass. "Care for some juice?"

"No, thanks." Her back to him, she unscrewed the lid and poured, then took a couple of good swallows before slowly swiveling her body to look at him. Her robe had seen better days, but it at least did a decent job of covering those parts he had no business looking at.

"I'm no expert, Rachel, but I know how it feels to lose someone you love. We're in this boat together, remember?"

She studied the rim of her glass, running her finger along it but saying nothing. Her golden hair, still wet from her shower, hung in a muddled mess around her oval face.

Suddenly, a notion came to him. "I have an idea," he announced. "Go get dressed."

"What?" She lowered her glass a fraction and threw him a perturbed glance.

"Just do it, okay?" He stepped forward to take her glass and set it on the counter. Then, he slowly pivoted her so that she faced the door and gave her a little push.

"But, I don't— It's late. I need to get to bed, and, besides, my hair is wet."

"So, what's the big deal? It's not like you'll be seeing anybody tonight, and you don't have to get up early, do you?"

"Not—exactly, but I just— What if I don't feel like going anywhere? Jason, what kind of scheme are you cooking up? I'm not much in the mood for doing anything."

"Don't be an old poop. This will be good for you, I promise. Now, hurry up before the clock strikes midnight and I turn into a pesky ogre."

"Pssh. Who said we had to wait till midnight for that?" she muttered as she shuffled toward the stairs. He grinned with satisfaction.

Chapter 6

Five minutes later, Rachel was seated comfortably next to Jason in his Jeep. They backed out of her drive and headed west as a calming, gentle breeze blew in through the partially open windows, brushing her cheeks and ruffling her damp locks. The streets were quiet, save for some light traffic and a few folks out walking dogs. With the exception of several well-lit gas stations, every establishment they passed was dark: drugstores, office supply stores, a furniture and mattress store, and several other small businesses.

They rode in silence until they came to the intersection at Lakeshore Drive and U.S. 15, where Jason made a right turn onto Lakeshore. "Are we going to the beach?" Rachel asked.

He smiled, his eyes trained on the road. "You gotta admit, it's the perfect night for it, and I haven't been down here in ages."

They followed the Lake Michigan coastline, which led to the state park. Along the way, they passed restaurants, bars, novelty shops, and ice cream parlors, all hot spots at the peak of tourist season but now much quieter with the passing of Labor Day.

Just past a playground area, Jason found a parking space facing the lake, pulled into it, and cut the engine. The clouds had parted to reveal a starlit night, unusually mild for mid-September. "Come on, let's walk," he said, opening his door and getting out before she had a chance to respond.

She didn't feel like walking, but the very pleasantness of the night pulled at her, so she found herself climbing out of the car.

Side by side, they set off down the paved walkway, neither speaking at first, just taking in the sounds of a few passing cars, a couple of dogs disturbing the peace, a door slamming, a distant foghorn blaring. "Nice, huh?" Jason said after a few minutes.

"It is," she admitted, folding her arms across her chest. She felt his eyes fall on her. "You're not cold, are you?"

"No, it's—it's a beautiful night. I'm glad you brought me."

"I knew it'd be good for you to get out of that house. I have a strong suspicion you don't get out much, young lady."

A tiny laugh escaped her lips. "Church and the grocery store. Those are our major destination points." She laughed again, and Jason's chuckle blended with hers.

They padded through a mound of sand that had blown onto the sidewalk. The full moon's reflection glistened on the nearly motionless lake. A late-night jogger approached, nodded, and continued on his way, and Jason brushed against her as he sidestepped to make room on the path.

"How's your business doing?" she decided to ask, realizing that everything so far had been about her, and that she'd selfishly allowed it instead of inquiring about his life.

For the next several minutes, he talked about his thriving company, his current projects, his hardworking crew, and even his condo, which she'd never seen, since he'd lived elsewhere the last time she and John had driven down for a visit more than two years ago. She asked about the development where he lived, the church he attended, and whether he had a good circle of friends. He filled her in, saying he liked his condo fine, loved his church and pastors, and had made a number of friends but had little time for socializing.

He managed to draw her into the conversation, as well, asking her about her church, her family, and some friends from the old gang they used to hang out with. He had the tact not to bring up his brother's name. Of course, she didn't hang much with the "old gang," as he put it. Losing John had put a damper on her former friendships, as many of the married couples usually found it awkward to invite her anywhere. She had several faithful girlfriends, though, who insisted on keeping her as busy as possible, namely Allie Ferguson.

"So, tell me about this woman you're dating. Candace, is it? Are you in love with her?" She glanced up and saw his Adam's apple bob like a fisherman's cork. Okay, so the questions had poured out with little forethought. They'd come to the end of the sidewalk, and now, nothing but beach stretched out before them. Hardly pausing, Rachel stepped out of her sandals, bent to pick them up, and proceeded through the shifting, sugary sand, knocking gently against Jason without meaning to, her damp locks falling around her cheeks. The starry sky reflected off the water as undercurrents swept miniature waves upon the shore. In the distance, a lighthouse flickered signals to incoming barges and small crafts, the pier on which it sat stretching out over the clear horizon like a pointy finger. A low, dull foghorn sent out its booming blast, skittering across the lake and creating ghostly echoes of warning.

Following suit, Jason stepped out of his shoes and edged closer to the water. "Hey, it's not that bad. Stick your toes in."

Feeling adventurous, she did so, amazed at how warm the water felt to her toes. "You're right; it's nice."

She glanced across the Big Lake's wide expanse at the dimly lit horizon. He must have noticed it, for he asked, "Remember how I used to say you could see Wisconsin from here if you looked hard enough?"

So, he planned to evade her question about Candace, did he? "Yeah, and I believed you." He gave a hearty chuckle that rumbled through the air. Again, their sides bumped lightly. "I must have been in sixth or seventh grade. You and John were always feeding me some line or another, probably laughing behind my back when I swallowed it, too."

"No. Us?"

She giggled at the memory, finding the feeling euphoric if not refreshing.

Wading back out of the water, she resumed walking through the dry, shifting sands. He followed, matching her steps. Their hands accidentally touched, so she quickly clasped hers behind her back, her sandals dangling by their straps from her fingers.

"You didn't answer my earlier question…about Candace. That is her name, isn't it? Are you guys serious?"

"Yeah, her name's Candace. Um, I guess we are…serious, that is."

When he didn't elaborate, she glanced up at his well-defined profile—straight nose, square jaw, and thick brows and lashes shading his deep brown eyes.

So different from John, she thought, *and yet still handsome in his own right*. John was classically striking with his neat-as-a-pin appearance, and he possessed a narrower, slightly shorter physique than Jason, with lighter hair and skin tone. Jason, on the other hand, had chocolate-colored hair and a tawny complexion, the result of hours spent in the sun. In addition to his rugged appeal, his distinctive air of self-confidence had set him apart from John, and people had often mistaken the boys for friends rather than brothers.

Rachel tried to lay aside all those observances and concentrate on the present.

"You guess? Why so cagey about the whole thing?"

He turned his gaze on her, but she couldn't make out his downward expression because of the shadow across his face. "Cagey?"

"You know—guarded, evasive. Haven't you been seeing her for a couple years? It seems by now you should be talking marriage."

She stepped in a hole a child had apparently dug while building a sand castle and started to go down, but he caught her with a strong hand, as if he'd been waiting for her to trip. "She'd like to think we are," he answered without missing a beat, dropping his hand back to his side again.

"So, you're dragging your feet, then?"

He chuckled and nudged her playfully. "You think you're pretty smart, don't you?"

For the first time, it occurred to her she'd begun to relax, even enjoy their banter.

"I'm pretty intuitive, but then, most women are."

"Yeah. Uncanny."

"So, what's the problem?" she prodded. How had she come from not wanting to talk at all to suddenly wanting the full scoop on his relationship with his girlfriend?

He released a light groan. "I just want to be sure God's the one directing us, that's all. If He's not, then I don't feel comfortable moving forward with marriage—or the relationship, for that matter. When I bring that up to her, though, she about has a coronary and thinks I'm breaking up with her right then."

She took a moment to digest that revelation. "You sure have changed, Jason Evans. There was a time when God didn't play a very big part in your life. In fact, you used to poke fun at John's faith."

He kicked up some sand, making it fly several feet. "I regret that now something terrible."

She smiled in spite of the memory. "I'm sure he forgives you."

"I apologized for my stupidity one time when we were out on the slopes—not that last time, but...." The sentence hung suspended between them. "John and I always got along great. Well, most of the time. We had our spats, like most brothers do."

"He thought the world of you."

"The feeling was mutual."

They came to a fence that marked the end of the public park and decided to turn around. The moonlight shimmered even more brightly on the lake as they made their way back in the direction of Jason's Jeep, letting the silence swallow up their thoughts again for at least the next three or four minutes as they plodded along.

On the sidewalk again, they slipped back into their footwear. "So, does Candace share your newfound faith?" Rachel asked, unwilling to drop the subject.

"Uh, yeah. She's just not as committed, I guess you'd say."

"You don't have to be at the same level spiritually. I always felt like John lived on a different plane from me, so mature and levelheaded, not to mention knowledgeable about Scripture. Everybody grows at an individual pace, you know. You should be patient with her, wait for her to catch up."

She felt his eyes fall on her. "You think?"

She smiled. "Sure. And you should put a ring on her finger soon. Otherwise, she might disappear, and then you'll be left with regrets."

They continued along, his feet kicking up more mounds of sand. "Can't have regrets," he mumbled through an obvious grin.

As they drove, Rachel leaned back in her seat and relaxed, allowing the Jeep's engine to rock her into a sort of dreamlike state. "That was nice, Jason. Thanks for the walk. And the talk," she added. "You were right; I needed it."

He glanced at her, but she kept her eyes trained on the winding road that led to her house. "You're welcome. Promise me something, will you?"

"Maybe. What did you have in mind?"

"Don't give up. The journey is hard, scary, and painful, but with God's help, you can do it. I hate to think about you quitting on me."

She closed her eyes and let the words hang there for a while. "I'll see what I can do," she quipped.

Moments later, Jason pulled into her driveway, shoved the gearshift into park, and cut the engine.

"Thanks again, Jason. I can see myself in."

"I'm sure you can, but stay put," he instructed her, stuffing his keys into his pocket and jumping out. She watched him run around to her side and open the door. When he reached out a hand, she hesitated, then took it, finding it warm but as coarse as sandpaper. John's had never felt like that, even though he'd built fences, planted gardens, and laid decorative brick at their house. His was a desk job, with weekends as his only times for household chores and yard work. For no particular reason, a shiver raced up her spine. As soon as she jumped to the ground, she started up the sidewalk ahead of Jason, somewhat flummoxed when he didn't just get back in his Jeep and drive away.

"This place is a mess, isn't it?" she muttered, groping for something to say as soon as they stepped inside her cool, quiet house. What had happened to that relaxed frame of mind she'd talked herself into on their drive back? Goodness, the Jeep's drone had nearly put her to sleep, and now, here she was, as jittery as a caged cat. She stepped over a stuffed toy, thinking she ought to pick it up, but why bother at this hour?

Jason came up behind her, rattling her nerves even more.

"There's plenty of time for catching up on your cleaning tomorrow. I've kept you up too late, so head for bed, kiddo."

Kiddo? Who was she, his little charge? She scratched her head and stared at him. Despite her annoyance, she couldn't hold back her wide-mouthed yawn.

Warm hands at her shoulders pivoted her body, pointing her in the direction of the stairs. "Go on, now. I'll see to things down here."

"What?" She gave her head a fast shake. "I—I should see if there're any phone messages. I left my cell upstairs, and Mom might have called. The kids could have—"

"I'll check. Answering machine's in the kitchen, right?"

"Yeah. Um…." He left her standing there and disappeared around the corner. She felt her forehead pull into a frown, her body tense. She wasn't quite sure what to think of this presumptive and solicitous attitude he'd adopted.

"No messages," he called, reappearing in an instant, his assuming frame taking up too much space in her living room.

They locked eyes for five measured seconds. "You want your pillow?" he casually asked, nodding toward the sofa.

"Huh? No, I—mine's upstairs. That one came from Meaggie's room."

"Good. I'll use that one, then."

The words stunned her. "Pardon?"

"All I need's a pillow, and I'll sleep like a baby." He gave her a wave of dismissal. "Go on, now. I'll turn stuff off and lock up."

"You cannot stay here, Jason Evans." His boyish grin had her shaking her head at him. "Somebody might—"

"What? Think ill of you because there's a Jeep in your driveway? Come on, Rach. It's no biggie. It's late. You gave me a bit of a scare earlier with the way you sounded on the phone, and I wouldn't be comfortable leaving you in the house alone. That's it, nothing more. Now, off to bed with you."

"Pfff," she blew through her pursed lips, hands at her hips, feet planted firmly, while she watched him breeze past her to shut off the lights.

"You don't mind if I leave that light on in the bathroom, do you? I'll need to see to get down there later." His casual tone made her feel like plastering him another good one in the center of his cement-hard chest. She let out another loud, labored breath.

He actually laughed. "Spit and sputter all you want, young lady. I'm not leaving till tomorrow, when I'm sure you're okay."

"I'm fine."

Ignoring her, he locked the front door, then double-checked it with a good yank. "I know the other doors are locked, 'cause I checked those before we left for the beach." He leaped over the back of the sofa with agility, pillow in hand, landing squarely on the other side. "This blanket will serve me fine," he added from his prone position. "Good night, Rachel."

"Jason, this isn't necessary."

"Yeah, it is. Now, leave me, woman, so I can get some sleep."

"Stop calling me woman," she protested. "This isn't the dark ages, Jason Allen."

"Humph. I haven't heard 'Jason Allen' since…well, since I threw a baseball through Mrs. Snively's front window when I was a kid and Mom gave me the business for trying to deny it."

Rachel ignored his comment, sighed again, and then marched across the room, taking every precaution not to glance at him on her way to the stairs.

When she was halfway up, he called, "G'night, Rachel."

She paused for an instant, and the tiniest, minutest smile tickled the edges of her lips before she resumed climbing. "Good night, Jason."

Chapter 7

J ason, where are you?" Candace asked as soon as Jason answered his vibrating cell phone.

"Good morning to you, too, sunshine," he replied sarcastically. "I'm on my way to work. What's up?"

"Nothing's up; I just wanted to hear your voice. I called your office, but Diane said you hadn't called in yet. You're late. You weren't answering your phone last night or this morning."

Why did he feel like he was getting the third degree? "I forgot to turn it on till a few minutes ago. Sorry. As for my being late, I'm the boss, remember? I'm allowed the privilege of setting my own schedule."

It was a crisp, sunny day, and, until now, Jason had been enjoying the picturesque drive along M-37 South, passing through the several small towns on his way to the Wilcox building site, just east of Cadillac. "I left a message on your home phone last night," she went on to say. "Why didn't you return my call?"

He didn't relish the idea of telling her where he'd spent the night, even if there was nothing to hide. "Sorry, hon, I—I didn't think to call you."

"You mean, you weren't thinking about me?"

He should have seen that one coming. "I...I didn't listen to your message."

"Why not?"

When he should have been grasping for excuses, his thoughts wandered to Rachel, instead—how she'd looked when he'd left that morning, refreshed and livelier, her hair falling around her face in soft swirls, a touch of makeup giving her cheeks a healthy glow, jeans and a bright-colored shirt showing off her curvy yet slim figure. *She'll be fine*, he'd assured himself as he'd downed a cup of coffee and a slice of toast in her kitchen and talked to her about what she planned to do with her day. He'd been relieved when she'd said she intended to dig into her housework with a vengeance and then retrieve her kids from her parents' house and take them to the park.

He'd prayed with her right there at the table, her small hand squeezed between his two big ones, albeit somewhat awkwardly since he still didn't have the whole praying aloud thing mastered. Still, it had seemed to bring her a measure of comfort, and she'd thanked him for his concern, promising to be more diligent in her Bible reading and personal prayer time.

He'd then glanced at his watch and, seeing it was already past nine, pushed back from the table and loaded his dishes in the dishwasher. She'd followed him to the door. "Thanks for coming," she'd said, clutching the door with both hands and leaning her slender frame against it. "I mean it. You really did help bring me out of my doldrums last night, and I appreciate it, even if I did a bad job expressing it. I don't even mind that you slept on my couch."

He'd chuckled and quipped, "What are brothers for?" Then, without forethought, he'd bent to plant a quick kiss on her cheek. *Her soft cheek*, he reflected.

"Well, I guess it doesn't matter," Candace was saying, breaking into his thoughts. "We can talk tonight—about yesterday, I mean. I didn't like the thought of driving home in that storm, so I left in a rush and with our conversation sort of hanging."

While he'd been with Rachel, Jason had shamefully put any thoughts of Candace on the back burner. "Yeah, we should probably continue that conversation."

"Well, I wanted you to know I have been praying—about our relationship, that is, and I just had a strong feeling last night that everything is going to be all right."

"Oh." He hated to be such a cad, but had she meant that, or had she said it merely to impress him? She'd never mentioned having much of a prayer life. "I feel the same—that everything will work out as God sees fit, and in His perfect time."

She giggled. "I think now's a pretty perfect time, don't you?"

He also hated it when she pushed him. He knew she wanted to set a wedding date, but did she have to keep pressing the issue? He ran his fingers through his hair. Doing so reminded him of his two-o'clock appointment for a much-needed haircut.

She must have sensed his hesitation, for she quickly changed tones. "Are you heading to that Wilcox house?"

"Yeah. I should put in a call to Diane and let her know my whereabouts."

"Which are?"

"What?"

"Your whereabouts. Exactly where are you right now?"

"Um, on M-37, heading south."

"What are you doing on M-37? That's nowhere near your condo."

He sucked in a breath and braced himself for her reaction. "I went to Fairmount last night."

"Oh!" That put her in a state of silence for all of five seconds. "You never mentioned anything yesterday about going to see your parents."

He braced himself even more. "That's because I didn't actually drive up there to see them. I…I went to see my sister-in-law."

"Your sister-in-law? As in, Rachel?"

"That would be the one."

"What in the world? You haven't seen her in months, have you?"

"I saw her briefly last weekend. I met my nephew for the first time. He's the cutest little guy. And Meagan, wow! She's shot up like a weed. It was good seeing them. Anyway, I just had the urge to head up there—sort of a spur-of-the-moment decision."

"Well." He heard her sharp intake of breath. "That's fine, I suppose, but why would you be coming back at this hour?"

He had little recourse but to state the truth. "Rachel's not doing very well right now…psychologically."

"Psychologically? You mean, she's having some sort of mental breakdown?"

"No, nothing like that. She's just overwhelmed and consumed with loneliness. I was sort of worried about her, so I spent the night on her couch."

"Her couch? Well, that's interesting. You wouldn't spend the night on *my* couch, Jason."

He laughed. "She's my sister-in-law, Candace."

"Yes, she is, isn't she? And a pretty one, at that."

"What are you getting at? You're not jealous, are you?"

"Of course, I'm jealous! What did you expect? Before you made this 'recommitment to God,' as you call it, you and I used to spend many a night together. Remember, Jason?"

He couldn't believe the turn in topics. "Candace, I just told you I slept on her couch. Absolutely nothing happened! And, yes, you and I used to be intimate, but, as I've told you before—and hoped you agreed—a sexual relationship outside of marriage is just not what God intends for His children."

"All the more reason to make it legal between us, Jason."

She had a definite point. *God, forgive me—again—for not always using my head in the past.* Sex outside of marriage had far-reaching consequences, one of which tied two individuals together for life in every emotional sense. Should he make it legal, despite his ever-growing doubts? Shoot, he couldn't even be sure anymore that he completely loved her. And yet, there remained that physical tie between them, that sense of emotional attachment and, well, obligation.

He groaned inwardly. "I'd rather not talk about this on the phone, Candace."

A pause followed, and he was certain he heard a giant sigh. "Fine. I'll see you tonight, right?"

"Sure. I'll take you out to dinner. How's six?"

"I'll be waiting."

Ever since Jason's visit, Rachel had felt a little extra fervor for tending to her children and their needs. Why, she'd even started tackling the guest bedroom, which had somehow become more like a giant closet over the past months. Staying busy worked wonders with her mind and body, and, of course, her children always kept things interesting: Johnny with his rascally antics, like hauling all of her plastic storage containers out of the lower cupboard in the kitchen, and Meagan with her continual, almost obsessive desire to follow her around, reciting the alphabet over and over and demonstrating how high she could count.

At Jason's advice, Rachel had begun picking up her Bible more regularly, especially when the kids were asleep, and seeking God's presence. Her grief counselor had told her to choose a verse a week, post it on her mirror or any place visible, and commit it to memory. This week's verse was 1 Thessalonians 5:18: *"In everything give thanks; for this is the will of God in Christ Jesus for you."* Today, she'd repeated it aloud while scrubbing the toilets, and, after she'd flushed the last one, she'd actually caught herself smiling.

As a matter of fact, she'd begun making an effort to smile more often. Jason had told her to try getting her focus off herself and to enjoy her children more—play games with them, read to them, delight more in their presence. For the first time since John's death, she'd begun to feel herself crawling out of her deep, murky pit—slowly, to be sure, and only inch by inch, but climbing nonetheless.

All this, thanks to her brother-in-law. She dared not think too much about last Sunday night, when he'd come upon her fresh out of the shower and dressed in her shabby robe, lest it lead her into reminiscent, if not dangerous, territory. Still, she couldn't help but be thankful for the unexpected visit, for it had indeed worked a miracle on her morose mood and set her feet on a forward-moving path.

And Jason Evans had found the Lord. Talk about another miracle! Whereas John had been the passionate one when it came to strong faith and Christian principles, Jason's passions had long lain in partying, booze, sports, and trucks, his fast-paced lifestyle feeding his very lifeblood—and attracting untamed, somewhat shameless women. It made Rachel wonder how Candace had come to lasso him in, considering how he used to play the field with such flair and finesse.

John had always said that his brother would come around. After all, he'd been raised in a Bible-believing home by a mother who spent long hours on her knees. But Rachel had been cynical, always countering John's hopes by saying, "Jason lives for Jason. I can't imagine what would ever change that."

Now, here she was, eating her own words. It had taken her husband's death to bring Jason's thinking around, and a tiny piece of her resented him for that, until she gave herself a mental scolding.

"Mommy, are we going to Grandma's pretty soon?" Meagan made a running dash into the kitchen and slid onto the area rug as if it were home plate, interrupting Rachel's thoughts like a sudden burst of thunder on a clear summer's day.

"Soon, honey, and Mommy would prefer it if you didn't run through the house like that." She reached down to give the girl a quick hug.

"Your hands are wet," Meagan complained, pulling away from her. She made a beeline for the refrigerator and opened the door.

"I've been cleaning," she said, wringing out a dishcloth and laying it over the sink. "Oh, please, close the refrigerator door, Meaggie. We're going to Grandma's for lunch, and I don't want you ruining your appetite."

"But I want a snack," Meagan whined. "My tummy's making growly noises."

"Close the door, please," Rachel said again.

The door closed with a thump, and Meagan's featherlight hair bounced as she folded her arms and put her chin to her chest, her lower lip extending far past her upper.

Rachel wiped her hands on a towel and pivoted. "Growly noises, huh?"

The girl's head bobbed. "And it hurts a little bit."

Rachel felt herself caving. "Well, how about one little cookie, then? I baked a batch while you and Johnny were napping."

Meagan's head shot up and her eyes widened till the whites were visible all around the pupils. "You baked cookies? I didn't know you could bake cookies."

Her breath caught. Had it really been that long since she'd performed the simple domestic pleasure? Meagan did a fancy twirl. "Hooray for cookies!" she cheered, greedily snatching one from the platter Rachel held out and taking an enthusiastic bite. "Too bad John-John can't have none. He's too little."

"Any. Can't have *any*," Rachel corrected her. "And you're right. He's not nearly as grown up as you. Speaking of which, did you pick up your toys, like Mommy asked you to?"

"O'course I did," Meagan said between chews.

Just as Rachel was turning to unravel a piece of paper toweling to wipe away the smudge of chocolate on Meagan's chin, the phone rang.

"I'll get it!" Meagan screeched, stepping up on tiptoe and snatching the phone.

"Hello?" she said, still munching. Rachel winced, hoping whoever was on the other end could understand her child's muddled greeting.

Her stomach did a strange little flip when Meagan squealed, "Uncle Jay!"

They talked for a few minutes, Meagan giggling every few seconds, apparently finding her uncle's words entertaining. "Mommy baked cookies," she announced. "Uh-huh.... Yeah.... When are you gonna come see us again?... Okay.... Yeah, she's standin' by me.... Aw-right. Bye."

With hardly a moment to gather her composure, Rachel cleared her throat and took the receiver. "Hello?"

"Hi, Rach. Just calling to check on you. How are things?"

"Everything is fine, thanks," she said, quelling her silly nerves. This was her brother-in-law, for crying out loud. Forget that his voice sounded like velvet. "How are you?"

"Great. Getting ready to head down to Candace's parents' house for the weekend. It's her mom's birthday."

"Oh. Well." She swallowed a stony lump. "Have a wonderful time." How utterly ridiculous for her to experience a pang of jealousy!

"They live in a small town south of Chicago. The leaves are starting to turn, so it should be a pretty drive."

"Absolutely. The leaves are actually starting to fall up here. I'll be raking soon."

"Need help with that?"

"No," she answered in haste. "We can manage fine. My dad promised to lend a hand, and I can always hire some of the teens from church, if need be."

"You shouldn't have to hire anybody. I'll try to come up one of these days."

"Don't bother, really. We're fine."

"Rachel, I promised to lend a hand, remember? And besides, I still have some Cinderella sort of movie to watch with Meaggie."

"And I told her she could watch it with you at Grandma Evans's house the next time you visit them."

An awkward pause ensued. "We'll see." More silence. "How's the little man doing?"

"He's napping right now, but...well, I should go wake him so he'll go to bed at his usual time tonight. Thanks for calling, though, Jase. It was thoughtful of you."

"You're welcome. You sure you're doing okay?"

"I'm doing better, thanks." And the sooner she hung up, the better off she'd be. "You have a safe trip."

"We will. And you call me if you need anything. You have my cell number, right?"

"You wrote it on my calendar, remember?"

"Yeah, just making sure. I'm praying for you and the kids."

"Thanks, I appreciate that."

After another minute of small talk, Rachel placed the phone back in its cradle and refocused on the here and now. Meagan had skipped away, singing some little ditty at the top of her lungs and waking Johnny, who was whimpering. Rachel shook off the foolish notion that her brother-in-law faintly attracted her as she hit the light switch by the door, walked out of her spotless kitchen, and headed upstairs to check on the "little man."

Jason hadn't really felt like taking time off to visit Candace's family, what with his looming deadlines at the Wilcox house, but he'd avoided the trip one time too many, and doing so again would probably make him unpopular with the Peterson family. Still, going there never failed to put him on edge, and this particular visit was no exception, as subtle hints about their impending engagement dropped like flies all weekend.

"Remember Jenny Morris?" Candace's mother, Muriel, asked at the dinner table on Saturday night. "She's getting married this fall. Isn't that lovely?"

"I heard that. She texted me," Candace replied, wiping her pert little chin with her napkin and taking care to tangle her foot around Jason's ankle while she talked. "Apparently, she's found herself a lawyer."

"Mmm-hmm, and a successful one, too. Claire tells me he owns a yacht," Muriel said.

"Purchased by her old man was what I heard," Gene, Candace's father, interjected in his habitually gruff tone, whether that was intentional or not. "An early wedding present. Humph. Craig Morris has enough dough to fill the Grand Canyon. I saw him in the cigar room at the club yesterday, and the arrogant so-and-so couldn't stop bragging about his latest investments." Gene shoved a forkful of mashed potatoes into his mouth before continuing. "If you ask me, the girl's marrying for money. Not that there's anything wrong with that, mind you." He tossed his wife a coy look and chuckled low. "After all, that's what your mother did."

"Oh, Daddy."

"Gene, for heaven's sake," Muriel scoffed, patting her powdered forehead with the back of her hand. "Don't be so rude."

The conversation continued, though the topic didn't stray from Candace's many friends who were about to either get married, have children, or get divorced and then remarry. Jason couldn't help but wonder if it wasn't all a ploy to awaken him to the fact that while most of Candace's friends had made it to the altar at least once and were already working on families, Candace had yet to get to square one: fitting a flashy diamond on her left ring finger.

Seeming oblivious to the women's agenda, Gene, a successful investment banker, tried engaging Jason in a business discussion to which he had little to contribute. Meanwhile, Candace's older brother, Ralph, a serious-minded accountant, and his pretty young wife, Loraine, were in their own little world, busy trying to keep their two-year-old daughter, Rosette, entertained at the table.

Amid the banter, Jason glanced around the Peterson home and thought about how little his parents had in common with the Petersons, and how very uncomfortable he felt in the presence of Candace's parents.

Lord, I've changed. Or, rather, You've changed me. Show me where I belong.

"You were rather quiet this weekend," Candace muttered on Sunday during the drive back home. "Can't you be a little more talkative?" They'd been riding along in silence for the last twenty miles. Jason had found it blissful, actually.

"I'm sorry," he murmured. "I guess I didn't find the conversations all that stimulating."

He glanced at her in time to see her china-doll face wrinkle at the forehead and her arms fold in a pouty, indignant manner. "And you couldn't have tried to make them more interesting? You might have talked with my brother; the two of you hardly know each other."

"Your brother and his wife seemed pretty preoccupied with your niece, and I didn't see him attempting to make conversation with me."

Candace unfolded her arms and clasped her hands in her lap. "Rosette is adorable, isn't she?" she asked, her voice brighter. Apparently, she didn't want to address the subject of her standoffish brother.

"Yeah, she's a cutie."

"I hope to have a daughter someday. A son would be nice, too, of course. Do you have a preference?"

"What?" Jason wriggled in his seat and pulled his collar away from his neck.

"I'm talking about having children. Would you rather have a son or daughter first? We've never actually discussed that."

"Candace, I—sheesh, do we have to talk about kids just now?" He lowered the window a crack.

"Don't put the window down. It's so chilly today, not to mention cloudy and dreary."

After putting the window up again, he pressed his back against the seat, stretched out his legs as far as space would allow, and cracked the knuckles of each hand in turn while holding the steering wheel with the other.

As if to ease the tension she'd stirred, Candace said, "Mom loved that painting we gave her. I think she'll put it over her sofa, even though Daddy will object. Mom's trying to make some subtle changes from traditional to more contemporary, but Daddy's so stubborn. You have to go slow with him."

No kidding. "She seemed to like it fine," Jason said. Frankly, he'd had little to do with the selection or purchase of the modern painting, other than to throw in a couple hundred bucks to help pay for it—so they could say it came from both of them, Candace had insisted.

"You didn't like it, did you?"

He sent her a hasty smile before setting his eyes back on the steadily moving traffic up ahead. "The main thing was that your mom liked it."

She reached across the seat and grabbed his right hand, pulling it to her lap. He granted her another look. She really looked lovely; there was no denying it. He squeezed her dainty fingers, and she gave him a gleaming, straight-toothed smile. "We were meant for each other, you know."

What could he say to that? When she'd come to ski school the winter they'd started dating—later confessing she'd enrolled in his class solely for the tutelage of the handsome instructor—he'd fallen quickly for her. Besides her undeniable beauty, he'd admired her spunk, her friendly personality, her cute, dimpled chin, and her head of seductive, dark hair that spiraled around her slender shoulders like a waterfall.

But that was then, and this was now. Somehow, things had changed—slowly, yes, but irreversibly. It had begun, really, with John's death, which had sobered him significantly, and then his decision to live with purpose and put his out-of-whack priorities in proper order: Christ first, family/

Candace second, work third, and so on. He'd hoped she'd follow suit—pursue his same passions, at least show more interest in matters of the Lord. But she hadn't, except to attend church with him and feign interest in spiritual growth.

At one time, he would have pulled her as close as possible and kissed her silly, even while driving. His eyes would have wandered to her shapely legs and soft, rounded hips as they molded perfectly into the black leather seat of his Jeep Cherokee.

But not today.

No; today, his thoughts wandered to his condo, his to-do list for the week, and his conversation with Rachel a few days ago. Was he insane? When he should have been thinking about the woman beside him, the one for whom he'd purchased a diamond ring one year ago, he was concerned instead with a petite blonde some hundred or so miles north, one with a cherubic oval face and two adorable children.

She was his brother's wife, for Pete's sake!

God, what is happening to me?

"He who has ears to hear, let him hear!"

The familiar statement from the Gospels got his attention.

I'm listening, God.

"If you love Me, keep My commandments."

Lord, what are You trying to tell me?

He waited for a jarring epiphany, yet nothing but contemplative silence followed. That, and the sound of his Jeep tires hitting the seam in the asphalt with a *blip-blip* sound every five seconds.

Chapter 8

Late summer turned to autumn, and with it came a rush of vibrant colors—oranges, reds, and golds. Some leaves clung as if with their final breaths to their life-giving branches; others relented by drifting to the ground in blankets of brownish hues. Brisk air dictated that schoolchildren bundle up in wool jackets and scarves while waiting for buses at dawn, their chirpy voices carrying on the hollow breezes. Jeans and slacks took the place of shorts, while shoes replaced open-toed sandals. Air conditioners and underground sprinklers ceased to operate when fall rains lambasted Fairmount, as if making up for lost time. Rivers threatened to flood as water levels rose to all-time highs, utterly mocking the arid summer that had just come and gone.

Rachel worked in the yard when the weather and her kids' nap schedules permitted, which wasn't often enough, considering the rate at which the fallen leaves accumulated. If John were alive, he'd have a fit; he was always one to use the leaf blower every night after work, all season long, and to rake every ounce of debris from the shrubs, as well, right down to the roots. Unfortunately, Rachel had never shared his passion for maintaining an immaculate yard.

Friends and family members came over to help, but, no matter how many bags accumulated at the curbside, every new morning brought another field of crisp, freshly fallen

leaves to rake. To top matters off, it seemed that the draping, hundred-year-old oak at the end of the driveway would
wait stubbornly until the last minute to shed its orange-
brown hue.

The never-ending task was a delight to Meagan alone,
who loved bundling up from head to toe, running around
the yard, and diving into the neatly raked piles of damp
leaves. Once, even Rachel tossed aside her inhibitions
and dove in with her, undoing all her hard work but earning yelps of pleasure from both Meagan and Johnny, who
watched from his baby swing.

On a Saturday in late October, Rachel had just put a
sleepy-eyed Johnny down for his nap when the doorbell
rang. Thankfully, the gong didn't deter him from closing
his eyes.

"Somebody's here!" Meagan shouted from her room.
Seconds later, Rachel heard her bound down the stairs like
an excited pup.

"Check who it is before you open the door!" she called
down to her, stepping out into the hall and quietly shutting
the nursery door behind her. Ever since Jason had ordered
her to keep the house locked up tight, she'd complied, for
the most part.

She hadn't talked to him since just before he and Candace had set off to visit her parents some weeks ago, so it
came as a jolting surprise to hear Meagan screech, "Uncle Jay, you came! Are we gonna watch *Cinderella* today?
What took you so long to come back?"

"Hey, there, my little sugar plum fairy! How are you doing?" came the familiar low, mellow voice. Rachel peeked
over the banister just as Jason bent to sweep up his niece
in his arms and swing her around. He was dressed in a
leather bomber jacket and fitted jeans, his dark hair tousled,

as usual, and she couldn't help but stare a moment longer than necessary.

"Good," Meagan said, cupping his chiseled cheeks with both hands and giving him a once-over when he stopped twirling. "I almost forgot what you looked like."

This provoked a round of good-hearted laughter that did strange things to Rachel. On the one hand, it touched her that he was making the effort to connect with his niece and nephew, for they certainly needed and deserved his attention. On the other hand, it upset her that he'd shown up unannounced. If he'd come expecting a warm welcome, he wouldn't be getting it from her. Why, she looked a sight in her stained T-shirt and torn jeans, and her straggly hair, dirty fingernails, and pallid cheeks devoid of any makeup did little to help her appearance. What was with him dropping by with no warning?

She cleared her throat, and at the sound, he glanced up to watch her descend the stairs. A smile sprouted on his fine-looking face, and she noticed that the hint of a dark beard had started to grow. "Hi, Rach. Hope you don't mind my dropping over."

"You have a habit of doing that, don't you?" She shoved her hands into her pockets.

His boyish grin threw her for a small loop. "I stopped over to see Mom and Dad and decided to swing by here." He glanced about the house, as if to assess what needed to be done.

"Well, I'm glad to hear you visited them. I know they appreciated it. You should have called, though. I could have brought the kids over to their place." She swept a hand through her mussed hair.

His Adam's apple bobbed with a deep swallow. "Mom mentioned your yard being full of leaves."

"Why'd she tell you that? I'm managing just fine."

"So my dad tried to tell me. And I could see right off how very much you have things…uh, under control." This he said with a wry smile while jostling Meagan. "Have you been helping your mommy rake?" he asked, tweaking her nose.

"Yep!" she exclaimed cheerily, wrapping her arms more tightly about his neck. "She's got a big blower that makes the leaves go all over the place. She can't work it very good, though." She wrinkled her nose. "Then she gets the rake and makes a big pile, and I jump in! After that, Mommy rakes it back up, and we put all the leaves in big paper bags. John-John can't help, though, 'cause he's too little. He just watches and laughs. Mommy says, wait till he starts walkin', 'cause then we're gonna be in big trouble."

That produced a good round of laughter from Jason. "Is that right? He's a busy boy, eh?"

"Mommy says he's busier than a honeybee in a handbag, whatever that means."

Jason rested his chin atop Meagan's blonde head and grinned at Rachel. "It means he's a live one."

If he expected a smile in return, he could just stand there and wait for it. She'd intended to work on the yard after putting Johnny down for his nap. What was she supposed to do now, offer him a chair?

He set Meagan down and brushed his hands together. "Well, what are we waiting for, ladies?"

"Pardon?" Rachel asked, blinking at him.

Granting her a blank stare in return, he said, "Get your coats on; it's brisk out there."

"Wh—?"

"You might want some gloves, too."

"Are we gonna play outside?" Meagan squealed.

Jason leaned down and tapped her head. "We, my dear, are going to work our little tails off. Are you up for it?"

"You mean rake the yard?"

Her small shoulders started to slump, but Jason was having none of it. "That's what I mean, but don't worry; there's going to be some play involved. Now, go put your coat on, okay?"

Like a bear cub full of vim and vigor, she raced up the stairs and disappeared around the corner, singing another of her ditties, until Rachel issued her a warning not to wake Johnny. That baby slept through storms and fireworks, though, so she probably needn't have worried. She turned to cast Jason a wary look.

"What?" he asked.

"Nothing."

"Are you upset with me?"

She pursed her lips and blinked again. "You should have called first. Look at me."

His innocent grin unnerved her. "You're cute."

"Oh, stop it." Warmth crept up her neck. She swiveled on her heel. "If it wasn't for Meaggie, I'd tell you to leave. I don't need your help."

"Ouch! You are mad at me."

Saying nothing, she opened the hall closet and took her shabby work coat off a hanger.

"House looks nice," Jason said, gazing about.

"Thanks," she muttered, pushing her arms through the sleeves and then fastening the buttons. She turned to look at him and had to crane her neck, noting that he'd always been a couple of inches taller than John. She then admonished herself for making the comparison. "I've been doing slightly better at keeping up and, well, keeping the focus more on the kids than on me." She wouldn't tell him she'd made the extra effort largely because of him.

"That's great, Rachel." He gave her arm a gentle squeeze, the warmth of his grasp penetrating her sleeve. Thankfully, Meagan raced down the stairs at the precise moment she drew away.

"I'm ready!" Meagan declared, even though she wasn't—her coat was only half on, with her mittens sticking out of the pockets. Rachel stooped to finish dressing her, all the while sensing Jason's watchful gaze as she zipped her up, tied her hood securely, and worked her thumbs and fingers into each mitten.

Outside, the sky was overcast, the air biting. Next door, Ivy Bronson's Pomeranian, Buffy, pounced against the chain-link fence and barked. Ivy, a widow in her seventies, would normally step out on her front porch and ask if Meagan wanted to play with her pooch. But Rachel had seen her pull out of her driveway about half an hour ago, probably bound for the corner market.

Jason chuckled. "Vicious dog your neighbor has. Bet she keeps the street safe."

"*She*'s a boy, Uncle Jay," Meagan corrected him. "And he only barks at strangers. He doesn't know you yet."

Rachel retrieved two rakes from the side of the house, where she'd put them three days ago, then entered the garage to get the electric leaf blower. Jason shuffled behind her. "The leaf bags are stacked over there," she stated, pointing to a shelf on the wall.

"Got 'em. Anything else?" he asked.

"Nope." She didn't know why her mood had turned sour, but she had a feeling Jason's presence played a part.

⚘

Well, this was interesting. Not only had Rachel given him the cold shoulder since he'd shown up on her doorstep, but she'd also made a point to avoid conversing with him, pretty much speaking only to answer a question or to say something to Meagan. He didn't let it bother him, though. He figured she had good reason for being annoyed, seeing as he had arrived without an invitation. Again. He made a mental note to call her ahead of time in the future, since she apparently didn't appreciate surprises of this nature. Funny how she'd remarked on her appearance, as if it mattered how she looked in his presence. Of course, she would look good with a bag over her head. Rachel Evans just had what it took to turn a man's eye.

Not that he was looking.

"Watch me, Uncle Jay!" The nonstop chatterbox made a running leap for the leaves he'd just blown into a nice pile.

He grinned and stepped aside, setting down his leaf bag. "Whoa! Good dive! Ever think of training for the Olympics?"

The girl emerged, looking like some sort of prehistoric swamp rat. Leaves clung to nearly every inch of her body, from her woolen cap to the bottoms of her pant legs. "What's the Lim Picks?" she asked with tilted head and wrinkled nose.

Rachel met his eyes and burst out laughing. The sound made his pulse quicken, though he didn't let on; he just joined in, bending over to pick up Meagan and hoist her over his shoulder, then giving her head a playful knuckle rub. "The Olympics, goofy brain."

Meagan started thumping on his back. "You're the goofy brain."

"Well, you're a—a fuddle-head," he countered.

"You're a cock-a-doodle-doo," she shrieked with glee.

Rachel's laughter rose to the heights. "You two are silly."

Wind rustled the leaves around, and a crow swept down to snatch up a twig in its beak and carry it off. "Oh, yeah?"

he asked, giving Meagan a good-natured spank. "Then you're a monkey's mother."

Gleeful laughter tumbled out of Meagan as he held her by her legs and twirled her several times. "And you're a baby's—butt," she spouted, hesitating slightly on the last word.

"Meagan Joy!" Rachel covered her mouth with a gloved hand. "Don't say that word."

"Why not?" She braced her hands on Jason's back and lifted her head. "Grandpa Roberts says it. He tol' Grandma his butt hurt from watchin' so much football, and she tol' him the pain would go away if he'd get off it and start raking."

Rachel joined him in another round of laughter. "My goodness! I'm going to have to remind Grandpa Roberts about your little ears," she said as her smiling eyes met Jason's and tugged on his heartstrings. *For pity's sake, Jason. This is Rachel.*

Jason adjusted his grip so that he held Meagan by her ankles. "It's getting late, stinker-toes, and we still have leaves to bag." Dangling her from behind, he twirled her again, as she squealed with delight, and finally lowered her to the ground.

And so it went—spurts of laughter and good-natured teasing intermingled with work, mostly on Jason's part, especially after Rachel went inside to check on Johnny. She reappeared ten minutes later with the little guy, a bundled ball of energy in a stroller. The sight of the two of them, and of Meagan running around the yard, did another number on his emotions, and he had to give himself a stern reminder that this was his brother's family, not his.

As he raked the leaves and bagged them, he thought about the discussion he'd had with his dad before coming to Rachel's today. They'd been standing on the porch at his parents' house, talking about her. "She seems to be doing pretty well, considering what she's been through," his dad had said. "Right now, I think it's best you let Rachel be, son. Drive on back to Harrietta. I'm sure your girlfriend—what's her name? Carla or Catherine—"

"Candace," he'd supplied, unafraid to let his annoyance show in his tone.

"That's right. Candace. I'm sure she's waiting for a call from you. Do you have plans with her tonight?"

Jason had huffed an impatient sigh. "She's working, but that's beside the point. Why would you suggest I leave Rachel be, especially when she clearly needs help?"

"Of course, she needs help," his dad had agreed, irritation lining his voice. "Just not from you."

"Not from me?" It'd been hard to keep his voice down. "Why do you keep saying things like that, Dad? She's as much a part of me as she is you."

His dad had pulled at a string on his coat sleeve, yanking until the thread started to unravel. "I...I know a few things, that's all."

"What is that supposed to mean?" Jason had hissed through gritted teeth. "What 'things' are you talking about?"

His dad had straightened his shoulders, blown out a loud breath, and looked away, never one to face a topic head-on. "I'd rather not discuss it now."

"Of course. Now's not a good time, is it?" Oh, he could have said so much more. Like how he had always lived in John's shadow—*perfect* John, *smart* John, the son who never failed to earn his dad's approval. When would it be Jason's turn to make his dad proud? Probably never, considering how he'd somehow wound up being the one to blame for John's death. At least, that's how it seemed, if the vibes he got from his dad were any indication.

Instead of responding with a caustic remark, he'd bitten down hard on his lip, and thankfully so, since his mom had opened the door and come outside at that precise moment. She'd given him one more hug and asked when he planned to return.

Chapter 9

D ear Lord, when is he going to leave?" Rachel mumbled while running a bath for both kids, the rushing water drowning out her words. The bathroom clock registered 8:22, well past both kids' bedtimes. Across the hall in Meagan's room, Jason's long, muscular body was spread out on the floor, belly down, as he helped Meagan build a tall tower with stackable cubes. If Rachel leaned back far enough, she could see his legs from the calves down. Johnny was delighted by his uncle's sprawl, for it provided him a fun hill to climb up and over, his wild giggles making even Rachel smile as she held her hand under the faucet to test the water temperature. It wasn't that she didn't appreciate the attention he paid her kids—they were his niece and nephew, after all—but his presence put her on edge. She'd forgotten how alluring and utterly charming he could be, something she had managed to ignore since marrying John.

And ambitious, and bold, and generous, and friendly, and driven. Goodness!

He'd accomplished so much for them today. In addition to the yard work, he'd taken her car to a nearby shop for an oil change, not to mention a wash, and then, with Meagan his constant shadow, he'd gone to the hardware store for supplies to fix a drippy faucet and a faulty wall socket. When Rachel had protested, saying she could just as easily call in a repairman, he'd winked and said, "I *am* the repairman."

In between bursts of work, Rachel had made grilled cheese sandwiches and tomato soup, a completely non-fussy, kid-friendly supper, yet Jason had called it the best meal he'd had in months.

"Come on," she'd said, skeptical. "I'm sure Candace is a great cook. She probably spoils you rotten with all sorts of gourmet dishes."

"Oh, we eat gourmet, all right," he'd said with a laugh. "Gourmet takeout from Francine's Deli, Morgan's Steak House, and the Harbor Inn, a fancy little place down on Lake Mitchell. There're more. Would you like me to list all of our favorite restaurants?"

She'd laughed. "Okay, so you eat out a lot."

"How's exclusively sound?"

"Good," she'd joshed. "Mighty fine, actually."

"Candace doesn't cook," he'd said with a chortle. "Problem is, neither do I. That makes us quite a pair, wouldn't you say?"

She'd shrugged. "Nothing wrong with eating out, as long as you can afford to, I guess."

He'd taken another big bite of his sandwich, from which melted cheese had started oozing out the side, and winked across the table at her. "Nothing like a home-cooked meal, if you ask me. I could order this very thing at Francine's, and I'd bet my last nickel it wouldn't taste half as good as what I'm eating right here in Rachel Evans's kitchen."

After the kids had been bathed and tucked in, nighttime prayers complete, Jason still made no move to leave. Instead, he plopped onto the cushy sofa in the living room and propped his stockinged feet on the coffee table, the surface of which was marred from Meagan's banging toys on it as a toddler and, now, from Johnny's fingerprints, as he liked to hold on to the table while maneuvering around it.

Rachel settled into the big chair next to the sofa. "You said Candace is working tonight?" she asked.

Jason didn't respond but folded his arms across his chest and closed his eyes. *Don't you dare go to sleep, Jason Evans*, her mind screamed. "Shouldn't you be calling her or something?"

With eyes still shut, he replied dully, "She'll call my cell if she wants to talk."

"You make her call you?"

"It's a two-way street. I call her; she calls me."

"Oh. Well, I guess it would be that way, since you're practically engaged."

He opened one eye a slit and peered at her. Rather than replying, though, he closed it again and adjusted himself in the sofa as if settling in for a long nap.

"Don't think you're going to spend another night on my sofa, Jason Allen."

He grinned. "Hadn't thought about it, but it's not a bad idea."

"It's a terrible idea. As a matter of fact, you should be going now. It's…." She gave an exaggerated yawn. "It's getting late."

Jason knew she was right, but his totally spent body kept him temporarily glued to the comfy sofa. With his eyes shut, he thought about the satisfying events of the day, from raking Rachel's yard to playing with the kids, from running errands to making some much-needed repairs around the house. And then, there was the lively supper they'd enjoyed and the fun of helping bathe the kids and tuck them in.

What could be better? Despite Rachel's anxious sighing in the chair nearby, he just couldn't bring himself to go home quite yet. Something about this room, this house—this woman—made leaving the hardest chore of the day.

At last, he opened his eyes and stared at the ceiling. "Your kids are great, Rachel. You're doing a terrific job with them."

"Thanks. We're getting by okay, I guess."

"How 'bout I come back next weekend to do some more raking?"

"How 'bout not?" She sounded adamant. "I'm calling a yard service tomorrow to finish the job. You have enough on your mind without having to concern yourself with my housework."

He noted her protruding chin and folded arms. Such a proud show of determination! His chest heaved with some deep emotion when it occurred to him how impressed his brother would be by her grit.

"You can call a yard service, if you like, but it won't keep me from coming back. I still need to watch that blasted *Cinderella* with Meaggie. Let's plan a movie night, complete with popcorn, one of these weekends."

"Let's not."

He couldn't help the chuckle that rolled out. "You are too much, Rachel Kay. You try with all your might to be all independent and stubborn, but I know it can't be easy. Sheesh, just getting those two kids bathed and ready for bed tonight was a chore. I can't imagine you doing it every night by yourself. I admire you for the way you're holding yourself and your family together. All I'm offering is a little help now and then. Is that so hard to accept?"

She unfolded her arms and fiddled with the cuff of her plaid shirtsleeve. The urge to reach across and wipe at the smudge of dirt on the tip of her nose was strong, but he restrained himself. Chin down, she whispered in a hoarse voice, "Rachel Kay? When have you ever used my middle name?"

"Since you started calling me Jason Allen, I guess."

"Let's make a pact to quit it."

He grinned. "Fine. I never liked my middle name, anyway."

"Me, neither." He could see she didn't want to smile, but a tiny smirk spread across her lips.

"Now, about that movie night—"

"I don't think you should keep coming around," she stated, her gaze still slanted downward.

He shot her a stare, but she didn't look up. "And why is that?"

"Because, it's—it's just not a good idea, that's why."

Jason sighed. "That's exactly what my dad said today. What's the problem? All I'm trying to do is keep this family united."

A look of confusion washed over her face. "I don't know why your dad would...." She left the sentence dangling in midair.

"Nor do I, Rachel. Unless...." He left his words hanging, as well.

Her brow crinkled, and she finally met his eyes with an expression of dread. "Unless what?"

"Unless you told him about...." He tilted his face to study her. "You know."

The blood seemed to drain from her face as her spine went stick-straight. "What? No! Of course not. I would never...."

Funny how they'd never talked about that long-ago kiss, and yet, without as much as a mention of the word, the memory of the event stood out like a two-ton elephant in a twelve-foot-square room.

Silence fell on them, and Jason looked at the ceiling, Rachel at her hands, as if the awkwardness would pass if they waited long enough.

After a minute or two, Jason finally spoke. "That's it, isn't it, Rachel? You still think about it."

"I don't think about it at all."

"Liar. You must think about it, or you wouldn't have known what I was talking about." More silence followed his observation. "Rachel, we didn't do anything wrong."

"What?" she exclaimed. "Of course, we did. I was engaged to your brother, for crying out loud."

He chuckled at the recollection of the kiss. "Which is a long way from being married to him."

Her face went from pale to beet-red. "No, it's not. Being engaged is a serious matter. You shouldn't have kissed me."

"You kissed me back."

"Stop it."

In one fluid move, he slid his feet off the coffee table, sat up, and propped his elbows on his knees, studying her with his eyes. "Listen to me, Rach," he said in a softer tone. "You're hanging on to something you should have let go of a long time ago. That kiss was innocent."

"Stop. I don't want to talk about it."

"You can't even say the word, can you? *Kiss*. Say it."

Like a child, she poked her fingers in her ears and started to hum, which provoked a few amused chuckles from him. On impulse, he stood and walked over to her, pulling her up by her wrists.

"What are you doing?" she asked, trying to wriggle out of his hold.

He kept laughing. "Trying to make you look at me, silly."

His persistence made the fight go out of her, and his laughter died down to nothing. His hands slowly moved up her arms and stopped midway to her shoulders. He studied her downcast face, wishing he could earn back her trust. Carefully, and with utmost respect, he put a hand to the back of her neck. "Come here," he said, folding her gently, slowly, into his arms, her small frame tense and trembling, at first, but finally coming to relax in his embrace as a shaky little sob broke loose from her chest.

God, help me, she is so beautiful.

"It—it shouldn't have happened," she whimpered, the warmth of her breath tickling his neck.

He chuckled softly. "Stop torturing yourself, Rach. It was just a kiss, nothing more."

Wet eyes looked up at him. "It meant something, Jason, and don't say it didn't."

He pulled her close again and rested his chin on her head, smiling to himself. "Okay, it meant something—probably a lot more than either of us wanted to admit at the time."

"I—I feel so ashamed!" she wailed.

"Shh." Her soft, wispy hair tickled his nose, and he smoothed it down with one hand. "That was a long time ago, honey. Good grief, I can't believe you've let it bother you all this time."

She let loose a shuddering sob, as if she'd been mortally wounded. "It was only a week before my wedding, Jason Allen! What was I thinking?"

"I thought we made a pact not to use middle names."

"Never mind that," she said with a sniff, then rubbed her nose on his shirtfront. The innocence in that single act made his heart melt like lava. "What were we thinking, Jason?"

"Ha!" He squeezed her closer. "I know what I was thinking." For the first time in a long while, he let his mind fully consider that memorable day. "I wanted you to reconsider marrying my brother. I got my comeuppance when you slapped my face, though, remember?" She gave a tiny, hopeless nod against his chin, and he gave a halfhearted chortle. "As if I was prepared to marry you, myself, even if you had changed your mind about marrying John. Sheesh. That was my brother, Rach. I wouldn't have hurt him for the world."

She gave another deep sniff. "We never would have done that. Besides, I loved John with all my heart. I truly did, Jay."

"Of course, you did, honey. I never doubted it. You guys had a great marriage."

A wave of silence swallowed them up for the next few moments, and he gently rocked her. Finally, he spoke. "That kiss…it was just something that happened unexpectedly. We were talking old times, you and me, swapping stories about how John and I used to fight over you in junior high. We joked, we laughed, we talked about how we'd always be friends, even after you and John got married. And then, I don't know…I just…went for it, sort of a last-ditch effort on my part." He smoothed her hair down again, becoming more aware of their close proximity, and cautioned himself. He wiped a tear from her cheek with his thumb. "Man, did you get mad at me. I saw fire in those pretty blue eyes after I kissed you."

"Well, it was a shameful thing we did."

"Terrible," he agreed in a facetious tone. Another moment passed. "You can rest assured that I never mentioned it to anyone. I always treated it like it was our little secret."

Lightning-like tension ripped through her body. He saw it start at her toes and felt it move upward. Hoping to ease it, he said with lightness, "Sure was a nice kiss, though—sitting in the loft of your grandpa's barn. I never did forget it, you know."

She pulled back and cast him a look of rebuke, then gave him a playful whack. He laughed and embraced her again. Her hands, which had been wrapped loosely around his middle, now tightened just a hair, awaking a need in him he hadn't felt in some time. Her face moved slightly, almost invitingly, upward, and the temptation to drop another kiss on her mouth was almost beyond resisting.

But then, Candace's face slipped into a dark corner of his mind, and he dutifully set Rachel back. "I should probably get going," he said with a gravelly voice, his brow damp with sweat. He gave it a quick wipe with the back of his hand.

Rachel took a giant leap backwards, as if just coming awake from a long nap and feeling guilty for having allowed herself the indulgence. "Yes—yes, you should be going." She brushed her hands on her form-fitting jeans.

Close one, he thought. Strange how he hadn't considered the consequences of kissing her those many years ago, but, now that she was free, kissing her again seemed implicitly wrong—not because she was his sister-in-law, but because matters with Candace remained unsettled, and it wouldn't be fair to her.

God had captured his heart and given him a conscience! "I'll call you soon," he said, turning to leave.

"You don't need to, Jay. We'll be fine."

He took his coat out of the closet and slipped it on, hearing his keys rattle in the pocket. He smiled down at her and tweaked her nose. "I have no doubt you will, but I'm still going to call."

"I wish you wouldn't. In fact, it's best you don't. I think we need to put some distance between us."

God, I want to kiss her. "You're a stubborn woman, you know that?"

She lifted one shoulder and tilted her head at him, making her dangly, silver earrings dance in a splash of light. "Bye, Jay."

He opened the door, then turned in the bracing night air to give her one last probing look. "Not 'Bye'; good night. And don't forget to go to church in the morning."

She sighed. "I won't. Now, go. And tell Candace I said hello."

Chapter 10

Jason left several voice mails for Rachel, sent a few e-mails, and even texted her, but all he received in response was one e-mail that said:

> We are doing fine, Jay. Don't worry about us. Thanks for your concern and all your help around the house and yard. I really do appreciate it.
>
> Rachel

It was all he could do to keep from jumping into his Jeep and driving the fifty miles to her house to see what gave. He knew she wasn't sick, because he'd talked to his mom twice in the past week and she'd mentioned going to Rachel's last Wednesday to watch the kids while Rachel ran errands and had lunch with a friend. He'd been happy to hear she was getting out, especially socializing with friends, and the fact that he was being blatantly ignored rankled him plenty.

"You've been awfully quiet today." His office assistant, Diane Leverance, reeled in his wandering thoughts, plunking a stack of mail bound by a rubber band beside several blueprints spread out on his desk.

"Have I? Guess my mind's in a million different places." Interlacing his fingers, he extended his arms, inverted his hands to crack his knuckles, and looked up at her. In her mid-forties, Diane was married and had two grown children. Her efficient ways and outgoing personality had long made her an asset to his company. Unfortunately for him, God had wired her with a special radar to detect when things weren't quite right, and she usually made a point to investigate when her intuition told her something was amiss.

Diane crossed her arms, shifted the weight of her big-boned frame to one side, and studied him hard, arching a penciled eyebrow. "Is it that Wilcox project? Harold can be a nag, I've found."

"No kidding."

"You have to know how to handle him."

Jason chuckled. "You got his number right off, didn't you, Di? First time he came in here, you treated him like he was the King of Siam, and ever since then, he's been eating out of your pretty little palm. It's downright nauseating."

"I tell ya, you've got to find out what makes people tick, then see to it you keep their tickers well greased. With Harold, you just have to keep assuring him he's the boss, then go about your business."

"He is the boss, Diane. It's his house."

"Well, of course, it is, but you don't let him bully you into believing he knows how to run things."

"I don't."

She screwed her lips into a thoughtful pinch. "No, you don't." Uncrossing her arms, she leaned forward and steepled her fingers. "All right, then, what's got you so tied up in knots? And don't tell me it's just the stresses of work, because you've always had to deal with deadlines, grumpy inspectors, incompetent workers, late shipments, no-show subcontractors, and…well, need I go on?" She narrowed her brown eyes to little slits and lowered her chin. "Are you trying to figure out that perfect moment for popping the question to Candace?" she asked in a near whisper. "Because, if that's it, well, listen. I can give you a wealth of ideas."

He raised a hand to halt her in her tracks. "I don't doubt you for a minute, Di, but that's—a long way off. I'm not sure—I don't know."

"Ah." She folded her arms again. "Having doubts, are we?"

He picked up a pencil and started tapping the eraser end on his desk, wondering if he ought to seek her counsel or just keep his mouth shut. To date, he hadn't breathed a word to anyone—except for Candace, herself, that Sunday in his condo. Ever since, their relationship had been on shakier ground. As if sensing his dilemma, Diane pulled a nearby chair closer and plopped into it.

"All right, out with it, boss."

For the next several minutes, Jason confessed his mounting qualms about Candace, his concern over her apparent absence of true faith, and his utter lack of passion and zeal for the relationship. One thing he left out was any hint that his sister-in-law might somehow play into the scenario.

Diane had always been a good listener, and today was no exception. She leaned forward as he talked, kept her eyes focused intently on him, and nodded or shook her head empathetically where appropriate. When he finished, she pressed her back against the chair, crossed her legs and arms simultaneously, and lifted her chin. "Seems to me you've come to a crossroads, Jay, and it's time you made a decision about your future with Candace. One thing is certain: you can't leave her hanging much longer. It's not fair to her."

That statement stung but also rang true. He set to tapping his pencil again, staring for mind-numbing seconds at the drawings under his nose and the bound stack of unopened mail. "You're right, I know; it just isn't easy. It's not that I don't care for her. We've been through a lot together, including the loss of my brother. She was right there for me."

Diane nodded, compassion in her countenance. Her gaze lifted to the window behind him. "Well, speaking of Candace, here she comes now. She's looking gorgeous as ever."

Jason dropped his pencil and swiveled in his chair. Yep. And she was dressed to the nines, looking ready for a night on the town. He couldn't help the frown that played around his mouth. After all the time they'd dated, she'd certainly earned the right to show up at his place of business unexpectedly. So, why did it irritate him to see her prancing up the walk now in her fitted, black pea coat, skinny pants, and high-heeled boots, the fringed ends of her fuchsia scarf flying in the breeze?

Probably because that fluttery feeling he used to get when he saw her had been replaced with a sense of dread. He had to figure out a way to end it with her. And soon.

✂

Rachel kicked the drift of sand with her booted toes, glad she'd bundled herself in her down jacket to ward off the harsh winds. Her nose stung, but she rejoiced in the simple pleasure of experiencing the pang. Just weeks ago, she'd been almost devoid of feeling, not much caring if she lived or died, but, lately, she'd sensed a rekindled awareness tickling at her core that reminded her of the preciousness of life. She had two healthy children who needed her and cherished memories of a mostly blissful marriage.

Of course, there'd been bumps in the road—what couple didn't have those times? But most of their journey together had been sweet, save for those last few weeks of protracted silence that had followed that dreadfully heated argument. Oh, it pained her now to think about those days leading up to John's departure for Colorado, but, for reasons she couldn't quite grasp, she'd decided to force herself to deal with them. It seemed she had to get past them to heal.

"Lord, my faith is so fragile," she confessed, her voice swallowed up by the hammering waves. "I need the strength of Your loving arms. Please, carry me."

"Have you not known? Have you not heard? The everlasting God, the Lord, the Creator of the ends of the earth, neither faints nor is weary. His understanding is unsearchable. He gives power to the weak, and to those who have no might He increases strength." Words she'd read from Isaiah just the other night came back to bathe and cleanse her anxious mind as she trudged the sandy beach. The sun was beginning to set on the horizon, its reflection shimmering on the water like a ripe red apple.

"You're hanging on to something you should have let go of a long time ago," Jason had told her. *Easy for him to say,* she thought, kicking a piece of driftwood. He didn't know about the argument she and John had had before the two brothers had set off on their ski trip—unless John had told him. How could she let go when she carried such shame? The secret memory of the kiss she'd shared with her husband's brother must have saddened God; she knew it had saddened John when she'd stupidly confessed it. Oh, she hadn't said something like she'd carried a torch for him, because she truly hadn't. Still, she had owned up to that kiss in a moment of thoughtlessness, of cruelty.

Just after Halloween, John dragged out their age-old argument over money, warning her not to overspend at Christmas. As usual, she defended her right to indulge her friends and family with gifts. The debate escalated when he started picking apart her spending habits, saying she made too many frivolous purchases—jewelry, pairs of shoes to add to her ever-growing collection, dresses she wouldn't be able to wear until she'd lost her "baby fat," one more pink outfit for Meagan, and so much stuff for their unborn son that they had barely enough room to store it all. His biting words still haunted her, particularly the remark about her baby fat and the unspoken implication that her bulging belly made her less than attractive in his eyes.

From there, the argument exploded. Rachel asked how he could justify his skiing trip to the Rockies with Jason if finances were as tight as he implied they were. "I've been saving for that all year, and you know it. Unlike you, I save for my purchases," he fired out at her.

After that, things turned nastier still, with words flying every which way, angry and accusing, baseless and ugly. Rachel impulsively and groundlessly accused him of finding his secretary, Ashley Forkner, prettier than she. Rather than tell his overly emotional pregnant wife how wrong she was, he chose to spit out that she might have been better off marrying Jason. "He loved you, too, you know!" he sneered.

The declaration jolted Rachel into a moment of stunned silence, until she sassily announced that Jason had kissed her exactly one week before their wedding. As soon as the words tumbled out and she saw the way his face dropped, she wanted to take them back. "I'm sorry, John," she backpedaled. "I didn't mean—I shouldn't have—" But any attempt to explain herself went unheard.

The color of his face went from red to white, and his response shook her to her toes. "I knew it, Rachel," he said, his voice sounding oddly dull and dead. "You've always loved my brother."

"What? That's ridiculous!" Panic surged through her veins as he brushed past her on his way to the door, and she followed on his heels, weak in the knees from his

accusation. *"John, that kiss—it was foolish...childish,"* she *stammered, fighting back her useless tears while he opened the closet door and reached resolutely for his coat. "You were the one I loved. You always have been."*

His glower sent shivers up her spine. "Where are you going?"

"Out. I need to think."

"About what?"

He paused with his hand on the doorknob, his back to her, but then he turned the knob and quietly walked out.

And that had been the extent of things. They'd never resolved the issue; they'd just avoided speaking about it at all costs, treated each other somewhat civilly, and said their good-byes with a brief kiss before he and Jason had left for the airport. Rachel had felt desperate to right things between them yet had been stubborn enough to think it was his duty to make the first move. How tangled and tattered things had been during those final days of his life—and how utterly helpless she still felt about all of it.

This memory only cemented in her mind the absolute necessity of keeping Jason at a distance, no matter how close he'd come to kissing her the last time she'd seen him, or how much she'd inwardly longed for it. Goodness gracious, she had no business entertaining thoughts of her brother-in-law, nor would she encourage his continued visits. For that reason, she'd all but ignored his attempts to contact her. She hoped he'd soon get the hint that spending time together wasn't only foolhardy; it was plain wrong!

Glancing at her watch, she discovered that the time had come and gone when she'd promised her mother-in-law she'd return. Donna was so generous about volunteering to watch the kids, but she still suffered a good deal from the pain of losing her son and didn't have quite the stamina necessary to take care of them for long periods. What Rachel had intended to be a simple trip to the grocery store had turned into a long walk on the beach when the sandy shores had called to her as she'd driven past the park.

With resolve, she stepped up her pace and made her way back to her van as an indefinable sense of divine peace came to rest upon her soul.

"All I need is You, God. You alone. Please give me strength as I sort through these unsettling memories," she prayed.

Rest in Me, My child. My grace is sufficient.

Chapter 11

It irked Jason profusely to find himself seated in the middle of a concert hall that night, listening to the city orchestra, when he would have preferred to be at home, snacking on take-out and reading, surfing the Internet, or watching a mindless movie—or sitting at Rachel's house, taking in the delightful sounds of Meagan's squeals and Johnny's babble while he conversed with their mother. But that particular notion quickly fell away when Candace grabbed his hand possessively.

"Aren't you glad I surprised you with concert tickets?" she whispered during a concerto, leaning into him and batting her pretty lashes. The signature, floral scent of her perfume created sickening waves in his gut.

"Yeah," he muttered. He pasted a smile on his face and tried to appear completely taken in by the swelling tempos and complex harmonies, yet all they produced in him was an unnervingly restless spirit.

Lord God, I've got to tell her, he privately confessed somewhere midway through the third or fourth movement of some classical, seriously boring, unbelievably long opus.

After the concert, they drove back to his office, where Candace had left her car. From there, he followed her to her apartment, all the while praying for direction, hoping that somehow during the course of the evening, a door would open and present him with an opportunity to end their

121

long-standing relationship—without a mountain of harsh words spoken between them or a flood of hurt feelings. He figured he might as well wish for the moon.

"Okay, so you hated the symphony," Candace said the second they entered her apartment, whirling around and producing a pouty frown. "Don't think I didn't notice you squirming in your seat." She cast off her coat and flung open the closet door, grabbing a hanger and slipping her coat onto it. "Good grief! You yawned so loud that the guy in front of us turned around and gave you a dirty look." Not offering to hang up his coat, she shut the door and turned to face him. He tossed his coat on the back of the nearest chair.

"I'm sorry, Candace. I truly appreciated the gesture. It's just that I—"

"What?" She looked at him with those crystalline eyes.

Lord, give me strength. "I'd have preferred to just relax after the long week."

"For heaven's sake, going to the symphony is supposed to relax you."

Yeah, except when you're wound tighter than a spool of thread.

Her expression turned soft as she reached up and slid her hands behind his neck, running all ten manicured fingernails through his hair. A skittish feeling swelled around his chest, but he hid the emotion. "Oh, I get it," she whispered, a sly smile finding its way to her plump lips. "You'd have preferred that we snuggle up on the couch, maybe watch a romantic movie, and, who knows, perhaps even wind up doing something more interesting than going to that old symphony." She stood on tiptoe, closed her eyes, and waited for a kiss.

He sighed, took her by the wrists, and lowered her arms. "Candace, we need to talk."

In an instant, her countenance melted into a pool of worry, but she quickly recovered. "All right, but how about I make us some coffee first? Shall I turn on some music?" He could tell by the counterfeit buoyancy in her tone that she wanted to postpone any kind of serious discussion.

"No thanks on both counts." He took her by the hand. "Let's sit."

In an almost robotic manner, she followed him to the sofa. They made themselves as comfortable as possible, she curling her legs beneath her slim body and folding her hands in her lap, he sitting forward, knees spread, elbows resting atop them. "Go ahead," she said with forced lightness in her tone.

He prayed silently for courage. "Remember when we started talking a while back, and then you left early because of that storm? We were discussing Ray's sermon and that whole topic of surrendering our all to Christ."

"Well, of course, I remember. You started getting all preachy on me." She giggled, but he failed to see any humor. She immediately sobered and laid a hand on his arm. "Jason, I know where this is going."

He raised his head and gave her a penetrating look. "You do?"

"We belong together. You know that, don't you?" This she said with determined vigor, almost desperation. "What is it you want from me, Jason? Do you want me to learn to cook? I can do better; I know it."

He could hardly believe it. "This isn't about food, Candace."

"Jason, I'll do anything, really. I love you. I'll stop nagging you to set a wedding date. I know I've pushed on that issue. I can be patient; no worries." She squeezed his arm. "If it's about my poor Bible reading habits, I can improve there, too." He hated that it had come to this. "We can do more things that interest you, like watching football, going to sporting events...I know I talk you into things you're not wild about. Let's face it; I'm spoiled. You can blame my dad for that." Her words tumbled out in rapid succession to the point where he took pity on her. "We could go hiking in the spring, start working out together, go skiing this winter...now, that's something I do enjoy."

Instant ire raised the hairs on his arms. Hadn't he told her he'd given up skiing, at least for the time being? The fact was, he couldn't stomach the notion of stepping into a pair of skis. Her insensitivity astounded him, even rendered him temporarily speechless, particularly when she didn't attempt to right it. "I know I'm not terribly religious, Jason," she hurried to say, "but I'm working on that. And have I ever once complained about going to church with you?"

"Candace." He couldn't let this slip by without a comment. "Knowing God personally is not a religion; it's a relationship. And I wouldn't want you to seek God on my account. It has to come from an inward desire to know Him better." He let out a tired sigh and shook his head. "I think you and I...well, we've come to an impasse."

Her mouth fell open in a disbelieving stare. "What are—? Don't you dare tell me you're breaking up with me."

"I'm sorry, Candace; really sorry. We've had great times, wonderful times."

Her eyes, damp in the corners, drilled holes of guilt through his heart. "We've had more than that, Jason," she murmured, her tone frigid.

Her allusion to their physical connection produced a river of sorrow in him. "I know, and I regret that. I should have honored and cherished you more." He felt himself running out of words but grasped for more when he saw her jaw twitch as the tears started falling. "You are a wonderful person, Candace," he said hurriedly. "Someday, God will point you to the right man if you—"

Without so much as a second's warning, she turned and dealt him a hard, stinging slap in the face. "How dare you?" she hissed.

"Wh—?" He rubbed his cheek, stunned by her impulsive act.

Her tears streamed faster, harder. "We slept together, Jason!" she wailed. "You told me you loved me, even talked marriage, and now, suddenly, you end our relationship and suggest I start looking for another man?"

"No, no, I didn't suggest that—Candace, listen. This isn't just a rash decision on my part. We've been struggling for months to hold things together, and you know it. More and more, I've sensed our differences. Please forgive me, but I just can't go on living this lie. It's not fair to you."

She got up from the sofa and glared down at him. "I gave you my everything, and I do mean everything."

He understood her hurt and wrath. He, too, rose, taking care to step around her to avoid another lashing. "I'm sorry, Candace," he muttered, walking across the room to pick up his coat. At the door, he paused and turned, saddened by the way she stood there hugging herself, cheeks wet, eyes puffy. "I hope…I hope things go well for you." She turned her back to him, so he quietly left.

Outside, the arctic air assaulted his senses, but he still walked with a certain kind of optimism. Yes, he regretted hurting Candace and lamented over the sins for which God had forgiven him, but he couldn't dispute the sense of relief this breakup brought forth.

Nor could he stop thinking about the future and its myriad possibilities. Oh, the possibilities! He seized his keys from his coat pocket, tossed them up in the air, and then hastily snatched them back with a deft move. He was even tempted to whistle, and he might have, if it weren't for the sting of that slap on his jaw.

Rachel hummed the tune of a new chorus she'd learned in church the previous Sunday while she vacuumed up a mountain of cracker crumbs under Johnny's high chair, keeping one eye on her task and another on Johnny. He occupied himself by hauling out measuring cups, rubber spatulas, and wooden spoons from a low kitchen drawer. Darn! They'd all have to go in the dishwasher—again. At eleven months of age, he'd already taken a few steps on his own and was showing hints of a mischievous streak, getting into everything imaginable and claiming it all as his. Heaven forbid should his four-year-old sister come along and pick up one of his toys or books, or, worse, declare that her own playthings—Barbie dolls, stuffed animals, puzzles, and tea sets—were off-limits to him. Fortunately, her attending preschool three mornings a week now gave Rachel some reprieve from settling squabbles between the two siblings.

Satisfied with the job, she hit the switch on the electric sweeper and started winding up the chord when the phone rang. "Ho!" Johnny instantly squealed, his eyes round as he looked at the phone.

Rachel smiled at his attempt to mimic her greeting and went to check the caller ID. It was her mother-in-law. "Hi, Mom," she spoke into the receiver.

"Hi, Rachel. I've been telling Tom I want that caller ID feature, but you know your father-in-law, Mr. Tightwad himself. He won't even invest in a cell phone, for goodness' sake.

We live in the dark ages, don't we? Anyway, we're doing all right for the most part. I keep thinking about…well, you know, the anniversary. How are you holding up, honey?"

Rachel's heart tripped at the mention of the dreaded remembrance of John's passing. It was all she could think about lately, and she knew it had to be paramount on everyone else's mind, as well. She briefly wondered how Jason was handling it and then pushed down a swell of shame for having ignored his recent phone calls. All of those momentous "firsts" had been hard to grapple with—Christmas, New Year's Eve, Valentine's Day, John's birthday, their wedding anniversary, and, now, that one-year mark two days after Thanksgiving.

"Oh, I'm hanging in there—with the help of my friends and family," Rachel answered. "My girlfriends have been calling a lot, and, as you know since you watched the kids, I went out for lunch with Sarah Michaels last week. She was so thoughtful to ambush me." They shared a little chuckle before she went on. "Of course, the kids give me strength to keep putting one foot in front of the other, and that support group at church is helping me cope."

"Oh, I'm glad to hear you're still going to that," Donna said.

"We've been reading through the Psalms this month, and it's been a great encouragement. You and Dad should be going to that group. A good number of people there are around your age." That was one of the reasons Rachel had skipped some sessions at the onset. Not many people lost their spouses at twenty-nine, and, in the beginning, she'd felt out of place rather than comforted. But, thanks to Jason's subtle urging, she'd resumed attending. She had since come to realize that grief knows no age barriers, and that those who grieve can relate to one another on many levels.

"We have the Lord to help us through our sadness," Donna said. "Besides, Tom would never bare his soul to a bunch of people. Heavens, I can't even get him to join a small group at church."

"You could go without him," Rachel offered. "I could pick you up sometime."

"Oh, I wouldn't want to go without him."

No, she wouldn't, Rachel mused. Donna and Tom did everything together, he depending on her to provide the meals, she relying on him to drive her to the grocery store. Donna had a driver's license but simply preferred to have her husband transport her everywhere. In fact, Rachel wasn't sure she'd ever filled the gas tank herself.

Sometimes, she was amazed by how close her parents were to Tom and Donna when she considered how outgoing, independent, and sociable they were compared to her in-laws. Of course, their long-standing friendship, plus the fact that they shared grandchildren, strengthened their bond.

"Changing the subject," Donna said, "would you mind bringing a salad to Thanksgiving dinner?"

Oh. Rachel had wanted to do away with Thanksgiving this year and had secretly hoped everyone else would feel the same way. But how did one go about giving up a family tradition such as that even for one year? "Sure, I'll be glad to," she replied, putting on a chipper tone.

"Your parents are coming, of course, and Jason will be here. Last year, he went to Candace's parents', but we have him all to ourselves this year."

"So, Candace is coming with him?"

"Oh, no. They've parted ways. I guess I thought he might have told you."

A surge of adrenaline blasted through her veins, but she maintained a calm tone. "No, I actually haven't talked to him in a while."

"Oh. Well, he mentioned something about trying to call you the other night, so I thought perhaps you'd talked. Anyway, yes, they've ended the relationship; rather, he ended it, thankfully. I never have felt right about that girl. Oh, I think she's a fine person, don't get me wrong; just not suited for Jay. I didn't tell him that, of course, since it's just a hunch on my part, and he really didn't bring her around enough for us to get that well acquainted."

"I vaguely remember her from the funeral," Rachel put in.

"Personally, I think he's holding out for someone else," Donna went on. "And I have no doubt the Lord will provide that certain someone at just the right time." She rambled on a while longer, but Rachel hardly heard a word. She was trying to digest the news of Jason's breakup with Candace.

Their conversation turned to an entirely different subject—the recent price increases in produce, of all things—and they hung up shortly afterward. Almost immediately, the phone rang again. This time, it was Allie Ferguson, her closest girlfriend since high school. They attended the same church, Harvest Community, and occasionally got together for play dates with their children, who were close in age. Allie was a teacher and often entertained Rachel with stories about her third graders. She was animated, generous, caring, funny, and encouraging, all rolled into one. Not only that, but she faithfully called Rachel at least once or twice a week to check on her. Sometimes, Rachel needed a simple distraction, or a shoulder to cry on—and, every so often, a little pep talk. Allie was good for all of the above.

"Hey, Rachel! How are you?" she asked in her usual, chirpy voice. "You busy right now?"

Rachel walked to the kitchen table and sat down in a chair chosen for its clear view of the living room, where

Johnny had moved after abandoning the utensil drawer. She could have stood, of course, but her legs had grown weary from a long morning of chasing him down every hall and around each corner.

"Hey, you! I think this is the first I've sat all morning. I tell you, John-John is turning into a little tiger, constantly on the prowl. Lately, he gets into everything." She glanced at her watch. "I have to bundle him up in exactly ten minutes and go pick up Meaggie from preschool. After that, it's lunch and naptime. Thank goodness. What are you doing calling me from school?"

"Oh, I'm on break and probably should be grading papers, but I'm not in the mood. I thought I'd call you instead and tell you what one of my students said first thing this morning."

"Oh, goodie! I love these stories. Tell me, tell me!"

"Well, Richie Cochran walked up to my desk all proud and tickled to tell me his dad got a new Chevy, and I said, 'That's cool, Richie. What kind of Chevy is it?' and he got all confused in the face and said, 'Hmm, I'm—I'm not sure. I think it's a Ford.'"

Rachel burst out laughing. "Oh, my goodness. *'Out of the mouth of babes....'*"

"And then, oh, my word, I did the stupidest thing yesterday."

"What?"

"You won't believe it. It's almost embarrassing to admit, but, hey, I can't resist making you laugh."

"Good, I need it."

"Well, I went to the drive-up window at the bank yesterday after work, filled out my deposit slip, signed a check, and stuffed it in the canister. Then I waited for, like, forever. Three cars pulled up behind me in the meantime, so I shrugged at the guy directly behind me, as if to say, 'Sorry for the clerk's incompetence,' but then this little buzzer rang in my ear and the lady said, 'Ma'am, are you just about ready out there?' Rachel, I forgot to push the send button!"

"Oh, no." Laughter rolled out of her like it hadn't done in weeks, perhaps months. "You are crazy, girl. You make me laugh."

"So, I quick pushed the button, waited a minute more, grabbed my stuff from the canister, and sped out of there. But, then, guess what I did," she screeched into the receiver.

"Oh, I can't imagine. What else?"

"I got so flustered that I rolled my front wheel up onto a curb. I know the people waiting in line behind me must have thought I was high on something. But the worst is yet to come. I got halfway home and saw that I'd thrown the canister on the seat next to me!"

This had Rachel rolling, heaving, and holding her stomach to catch her breath.

"And I haven't returned it to the bank yet!" Allie tacked on. "Will you do it for me?"

"No!" Rachel managed between giggles, still holding her stomach. "I mean, can you just imagine that guy behind you? What he was thinking when he *finally* drove up to the window and discovered you'd taken the canister with you?" Another round of laughter rolled out, and then Allie joined in on the other end.

By the time the two hung up, every care had slipped away—at least for the time being.

On the way to Meagan's preschool, Rachel couldn't get the smile off her face just thinking about Allie's stories—that, and the unrelenting mental reminder that Jason and Candace were no longer dating.

Chapter 12

T hanksgiving Day ended up being a nice day for a drive, with sunny skies and dry roads. Only a smattering of white remained from last week's snowfall, the first of the season. Jason couldn't help but wonder what today would bring, having gone about three weeks without talking to Rachel. Curious to see how the family dynamics would have changed without John there, he was concerned for his mom and worried about having another confrontation with his dad. He shifted in his seat, stared straight ahead, and watched the oncoming cars whiz by, one hand on the steering wheel, the other tapping a jumpy left knee.

Okay, admit it. You're as nervous as a rabbit in a fox's lair. He decided to veer his mind in another direction, and thoughts of Candace immediately surfaced. In some ways, he missed her, but only because he'd grown accustomed to their patterns and routines. They'd meet two or three times a week for lunch or supper, hang out on the weekends when neither of them had to work, and attend church on Sundays and have brunch at a restaurant before spending Sunday afternoon at his condo or her apartment, where they'd watch movies or sports, take walks, or swim laps in the indoor pool at his neighborhood's clubhouse. Their habits had become comfortably familiar to him, and, sadly, Candace had become somewhat of a convenient companion to him rather than a sweet treasure. He felt guilty at the realization but was also relieved to be out from under the weight of a relationship gone stale. He hoped and prayed Candace would somehow learn to forgive him and find healing.

When he pulled into the driveway at his parents' house, he saw his dad standing on the front stoop, as if awaiting his arrival. It was sunny, but not particularly warm, and yet the man wore nothing more than a sweater over his shirt. He had to be freezing. Jason cut the engine and hopped out of his Jeep. "Hi, Dad. Mom make you step outside to smoke?" he joked by way of a greeting.

The man put a half smile on his face and nodded, glancing over Jason's shoulder. "How long you gonna keep that vehicle?"

"My Jeep? A while still. Just got 'er a couple of years ago."

"She drive nice?"

"Okay. She's not what you'd call a family car, but she suits me fine."

His dad pulled on his longish chin to peruse the black, late-model Jeep Cherokee. "No, no. It wouldn't be a family car, and now that you and that Catherine woman—"

"Candace."

"Whatever. Now that you two have ended things, guess you won't be worrying about raising a family for a long time. Unless you already started datin' somebody else."

"No! Sheesh, Dad. Where's Mom?"

He sniffed. "In the kitchen, I s'pose."

Jason glanced back at the driveway. His Jeep was the only vehicle in sight. "I see Mitch and Arlene aren't here yet." He also noted the absence of Rachel's van, but he refrained from asking about her for fear of really getting the third degree. The thought occurred to him that she might have decided to forgo Thanksgiving, given how it almost coincided with the first anniversary of John's death. He wouldn't have blamed her, considering he'd been tempted to do that very thing. Why couldn't they have combined Christmas and Thanksgiving this year, somewhere in between both days?

"Why don't you get yourself a decent truck?" his dad asked him, not letting go of the car topic.

"I have one. Think my next car will be an SUV, but I'm getting ahead of myself. Need to keep this thing around for another year or so."

For some reason, his dad hadn't opened the door yet, so they stood on the porch like two old geezers, shooting the breeze and shivering. "I had me a good truck when you boys were little. Used it a lot for hauling. It was a Chevy, 'member that? Wouldn't get me anything but a Chevy."

No, there're a lot of habits and old notions you'd never break. "Sure, I remember that truck. John and I used to ride in the back as often as you'd let us. Blue, wasn't it?"

"Yeah, and she was a beaut. Yessir, a Chevy's the best truck on the road."

Jason thought about pointing out how reliable his Jeep was. *Don't start anything,* he cautioned himself. He decided to switch topics.

"When I pulled in, I noticed you could use a new roof. You want me to reshingle it this spring?"

"I been thinkin' about that. I planned to check out the yellow pages."

"Why don't you let me take care of it? I can make the calls, get you the best deal—probably even at cost. I have some good connections."

His dad made a sniffing noise, stuck his chin out, and stuffed his hands into his pant pockets. "Don't put yourself out. You have a company to run."

"It's no trouble, Dad. It's what I do. I'll handle it for you."

"I'll handle it myself." His tone sounded almost as obstinate as his retort.

Jason's spine stiffened with ire, matching his dad's stubbornness. "Okay, fine. Have it your way. Far be it from me to offer my help. I probably wouldn't do it to suit you, anyway."

At precisely the moment his dad opened his mouth, the door also opened.

"Jason, honey, when did you get here?" his mom asked, mouth and eyes equally round. She wiped her hands on her stained apron and swept four fingers through her short, dyed brown hair. "Goodness, I never even heard you drive up." She looked from one to the other, her forehead etched with worry lines, then quickly snagged Jason by the coat sleeve as if sensing the tension and pulled him toward her. "For goodness' sake, get yourselves inside this instant. It's freezing out here."

He gave his dad a penetrating look, but the man refused to acknowledge it; he just slipped past his wife and into the house in a swift, wordless move. Jason shook off a chill and bent to kiss his mom on the cheek and whisper a greeting, hating that the day had started on a sour note for which he was somehow responsible.

"Sometimes, I think he'd have preferred to bury me, instead," Jason said moments later in the kitchen, hands folded over his chest as he watched his mom make final preparations, scurrying from the stove to the sink and back to the stove again. His dad had retreated to the living room to turn on the television. Music from the Macy's Thanksgiving Day Parade resonated from the room.

With dropped jaw, his mom turned and propped two thin hands on her narrow hips, shooting Jason a disdainful look. "Jason Evans, don't you ever utter such a ridiculous thing again, do you hear me? Your dad loves you more than you know."

"But John was always his favorite."

"Why would you say such a thing?" She picked up a gravy-laden wooden spoon and resumed stirring. The kitchen was filled with the most delectable smells, and his stomach grumbled, eager to partake of the meal. "Your dad came to all your sporting events. You've always made him proud."

Skipping over her reassurances, he moved away from the doorframe and came to stand next to her, his back to the counter, legs crossed at the ankles. "He never asks about my work," he muttered under his breath, though loud enough to reach her ears. "John had a desk job in a big sales firm, big office—big windows overlooking the big city. Me? I sit in a dirty chair behind a cluttered, marred-up desk in a little Podunk town. I think Dad sees me as less successful than John. He doesn't even know I run a multimillion-dollar business. John got the nice, big, two-story house, the landscaped yard, the wife, and the two kids. In Dad's eyes, I'm probably still floundering." He hated using his mom as a sounding board, but sometimes his frustration mounted almost to the boiling point.

"No, Jay, he doesn't see you like that." She drew her shoulders back and exhaled deeply. "It's your perception of things."

"I just offered to reshingle your roof this spring. Why wouldn't he accept?"

"He's proud."

"Other things around this house could use some sprucing up, and I could take care of them for you, too, but he's so blamed stubborn."

She winced and gave her head a single shake. "Don't I know it. Your dad loves you, honey, rest assured of that, but he's been having an awful time lately. I think it's that, you know, the one-year mark is only two days away."

"Mom." His voice gentled. "Don't you think I know that? I was there, remember? I relive it in my head every single day."

He could see the tears building in the corners of her eyes, and he hated to have caused them. He put a hand on her shoulder, and she ceased her activity, turned to face him, and placed a palm to his cheek. Those worry lines returned to her aging yet pretty face. "He carries something, but I'm not quite sure what."

"What do you mean?"

"I can't explain it, really, but it's as if he hauls around a burden that he won't lay down. I wish he could learn to give his hurt to the Lord…the way you have."

Her words sent a rush of regret through his blood—regret for allowing his dad to generate in him such anger and defensiveness. *Yes, indeed. The way I have.*

Lord, please take away these feelings of distrust and confusion and mend my relationship with Dad before it's too late.

Rachel and the kids arrived at the same time as her parents and sister. Meagan rushed across the room to leap into her grandpa Evans's arms, failing to notice Jason standing off to one side. *Just as well*, he told himself. He needed to gather his bearings after getting his first glimpse of Rachel in over three weeks, anyway. So, he hovered in the shadows, enjoying his obscurity. Man, she looked good—cheeks flushed, blonde hair curved around her oval face and spread unevenly across her shoulders, wisps of it catching on her red wool coat as she handed off a salad to Jason's mom, then gave her a hasty hug. The room was aflutter with excitement and friendly greetings. Tanna, carrying a bundled Johnny on her hip, bent to pet Rosie, the Evanses' overexcited terrier, and Arlene and Mitch Roberts talked as they removed their coats and hung them on hangers in the entryway closet, their covered dishes having been placed on the nearby sideboard.

Finally deciding to make his presence known, Jason moved away from the fireplace in the adjoining room and the overstuffed chair he'd been standing behind and caught Rachel's eye. It was not his imagination, the glimmer of pleasure he saw in that single glance they exchanged. Yes, he saw it all right, even though she quickly adopted her casual manner.

"Hi, Jay. How are you?" she asked.

"Very good, thanks." He stepped forward and gave her a light squeeze—quick, friendly, and reserved. It took great effort, but he managed to turn his attention back to everyone else. Hugs all around seemed to be the order for the next several moments, Meagan leaving the circle of her grandpa's arms to rush into Jason's, little Johnny squirming to get out of his heavy winter gear, and Tanna happily helping him. When Rachel finished unbuttoning her coat and slipped out of it, Jason's dad stepped forward to take it from her. She thanked him and, in the process of handing it off, shot Jason another hurried glance, this one accompanied by a timid smile.

She looked like a million bucks in her fitted jeans, coral-colored cable-knit sweater, and floral neck scarf; her glossy, mauve lips looked sweet enough to kiss. *Lord, help me; I can't take my eyes off her.* No sooner had the thought struck him than his dad shut the closet door with a sort of pronouncement, prompting Jason to look at him.

When he met his dad's eyes, he saw a savage fire in their depths.

"Grandma, pass the rolls." Meagan's chipper voice interrupted the flow of the dinner conversation.

"Please," Rachel inserted, giving her daughter a look that propelled her to sit up straighter.

"Please."

The rolls were passed without incident as Johnny banged incessantly on his tray, seeking everyone's attention, and Rachel attempted to quiet him with another spoonful of mashed potatoes, which he promptly spit out. For at least the dozenth time, Jason caught her eye and smiled, making Rachel's heart react with strange little pitter-patters. She could have screamed at herself for letting his presence affect her so. She'd thought for sure ignoring the majority of his phone calls, e-mails, and text messages would have cured her of these unwelcome emotions, but no. As a matter of fact, all she could think about was that "almost kiss" some three weeks ago.

Her parents and in-laws kept up their constant prattle, covering everything from the recurring cancer of an elderly lady up the street to last Saturday's church potluck, from the knock in Tom's car engine to, of all things, her dad's dental appointment last week and the discovery that he'd need a tooth implant. Glancing around the table, she noticed that almost everyone had finished eating, so she started to clear the table.

"You don't need to do that, dear," Donna said, blotting at her chin with a napkin and then pushing back her chair.

"It's no bother, really. You and my mom prepared most of the meal, so cleaning up is the least I can do. Tanna, could you watch Johnny?"

"You bet!" the teen said, grinning. "It beats rinsing dishes any day."

"I'll help clean up," Jason offered as he scooted back in his chair and stood.

"You?" Donna asked with a smirk. "When was the last time you carried anything to the kitchen sink?"

"Come on, Mom. I'm a decent housekeeper," he protested. "Well, okay, if you don't mind dust and clutter."

"Hmm. Yes, I've seen your condo," Donna said.

She and Rachel's mother tittered and resumed their discussion. Thanks to their countless years of friendship, they never wanted for topics of conversation. The men took up the subject of college football and exchanged speculations about the upcoming face-off between the Detroit Lions and the Green Bay Packers.

In the kitchen, Jason and Rachel worked side by side, he handing off plates to her, she rinsing and then stacking them in the dishwasher. "So, good job of ignoring all my voice mails these last few weeks, young lady. What was up with that?"

She scratched the tip of her nose, then wiped it dry with the back of her hand, avoiding his gaze, even though she felt his eyes fall to her face, where, she was certain, a blush had blossomed. "I told you that we needed to keep a good distance between us. I was doing my part to make that happen."

"Ah, yes, I remember you saying that." He scraped food remains into the wastebasket and handed her another plate. Rosie sauntered in, toenails tapping the tile floor, tail wagging, doubtless hoping for a handout. "You're my sister-in-law, Rach, so we're bound to run into each other. It's not a crime, you know." He leaned too close to her ear. "Are you still beating yourself up over that long-ago kiss?"

"Don't bring that up," she hissed through clenched teeth, suddenly feeling the beginnings of a headache.

A blessed moment of quiet passed between them, albeit short-lived. "Candace and I broke up." The plainspoken disclosure caught her off guard. He handed her a couple of water glasses, and she placed them in the top rack. Then, after dropping a piece of leftover turkey into Rosie's drooling mouth, he passed her one last plate.

"Your mom told me. I was sorry to hear it. Are you— all right with it?" She finished situating the plate and stood up straight, allowing herself a glimpse of him. He slanted his face and arched one thick brow, his cocoa eyes catching her gaze and holding it captive. After a moment, his lips curved into a furtive grin and he cut loose a slight sigh. "Actually, yeah, I'm good." A nod followed. "Really good."

Just then, Meagan bounded into the kitchen. "Uncle Jay! I just had a really, really, really good idea!"

Her towheaded child wrapped her arms around his middle and planted her feet on top of his shoes, balancing like a ballerina. He put his hands on her shoulders and looked down, grinning. "You do? And just what is this brilliant scheme of yours?"

Her luminous, blue eyes gazed up and twinkled with purpose. "That you can come over to my house after a while and watch *Cinderella*!"

Chapter 13

Of course, Rachel had tried coming up with a number of reasons why watching *Cinderella* that night wouldn't work. First try: "Uncle Jay probably needs to get up early for work tomorrow." *Wrong*, he'd told her. He'd given his crew the weekend off. Next attempt: Meaggie had to get to bed at a decent time. *Fine.* They could make that happen as long as they started the movie before six o'clock. Third try: Uncle Jay would probably get bored. *Another negative.* How could spending time with his adorable niece possibly be boring?

With all of her arguments defeated, Rachel had relented.

Now, hours later, they were seated on the sofa at Rachel's, Johnny snoring in her arms, a light blanket thrown over his pudgy body, Meagan tucked between Rachel and him, dressed in pajamas, fully intent on the animated movie. Out the corner of one eye, Jason glimpsed Rachel—couldn't help himself—and warmed at the notion that they resembled a little family. But then, he reminded himself of the utter foolishness of such musings. Rachel was his sister-in-law, and he would do best to keep that fact straight in his head—and his heart.

While the ugly stepsisters ranted their evil taunts at Cinderella, Jason stared blankly at the widescreen TV above the fireplace, his mind reliving the day's events—watching football with the men after dessert while the women played

Scrabble in the dining room and Meagan bounced from one end of the house to the other, Johnny squealing with delight at his ability to pull himself up and stand on his own, snagging the attention of his grandfathers between football plays. Jason had kept one eye on the next room, where Rachel had been seated at the card table with her back to him, and the other eye on the "big game."

Any other time, he would have been enthralled to watch the rival teams compete, but thoughts of John had been so close to the surface, and last Thanksgiving felt like yesterday. He'd noticed the lack of any mention of John during dinner and figured the others either didn't want to deal with the pain or hoped not to upset Rachel. Frankly, he'd been just as happy to let the subject rest. He could only imagine his dad's accusing eyes shooting arrows at him. No, it was best left alone.

Rachel had begun her leave-taking around five o'clock, and Meagan had spoken on Jason's behalf, announcing that he was coming home with them to watch *Cinderella*. The women and Mitch had been unfazed by the news, even enthusiastic, but his dad's face had frozen in a blank stare.

"That's wonderful," Arlene had said.

"Yes, enjoy the movie," his mom had chimed in.

"You see to it he stays awake, Meaggie," Mitch had added, touching Meagan's nose and grinning up at Jason.

"He will!" Meagan had giggled, hugging Jason's leg like she would a porch post. "'Cause he never saw it before."

After putting on his coat, helping Johnny and Meagan into theirs, and rounding up the diaper bag and Rachel's salad bowl, Jason had scooped Meagan into his arms and gone to hug his mom good-bye with a promise to call her soon. She'd tugged them close and kissed Meagan on the cheek. "You have a nice time at Rachel's tonight," she'd whispered in his ear. "It'll be good for you two to spend some time relaxing. Maybe you can even talk about...you know."

"John?" he'd returned in a hushed tone. She couldn't even say his name. "Maybe." He'd glanced past her at his dad, who hadn't budged from his place in the arched entryway to the family room, where he'd stood with his arms crossed stiffly. "See you, Dad."

He'd given a straight-lipped nod, one that had made his jaw muscle flick. Then, as if it had required all his effort to move, he'd stepped forward and extended a hand. "Well, we'll see you next time, then," had been his curt words.

Fine way to send me off, Jason had thought. *Lord, what did I do to make him resent me so?*

Later, while Rachel and Meagan had been making popcorn in the kitchen before the movie, Jason had overheard a quiet discussion between mother and daughter. "Do you like Uncle Jay?"

"Of course, I do. He's my brother-in-law."

"What's a bruvver-in-law?"

"It's the brother of one's spouse—er, husband. He is your daddy's brother, which makes him my brother-in-law."

"You don't got a h-hubsband," Meagan had said, stumbling over the word. "Daddy's in heaven."

"That's true. But Uncle Jay is still my brother-in-law; he always will be."

"I wish he could live with us."

"What? Meaggie, where do you come up with these ideas?"

He'd grinned to himself and quietly stepped away from the door unnoticed, tempted to hear how the conversation played out yet not wanting to embarrass Rachel with his eavesdropping. He'd wanted to get a drink of water but decided it could wait, so he'd gone back to making minor repairs around the house—oiling a squeaky door hinge, checking the furnace filter, and replacing a lightbulb on the front porch, whistling while he worked. Puttering had always been one of his loves, so finding a few things to do while Rachel worked in the kitchen had provided him a great deal of satisfaction. And, as he'd tinkered, he'd made an interesting observation: the house looked thoroughly clean and organized. It would seem Rachel Evans had turned a corner on her grief.

When the movie ended and the closing credits began, Meagan's mouth went as round as the moon as she yawned. "Well...?" she asked sleepily. "Did you like it?"

Jason brought his chin to the top of her head and met Rachel's gaze. In her arms, Johnny slept, unmoving. "It was the best movie I've ever seen," he said, kissing Meagan's downy head without taking his eyes off Rachel. He gave her a lazy smile, and she returned only a trace of one, then slid forward on the couch.

"Well, it's bedtime, kiddo," she said in a near whisper, "and your uncle has a long drive home."

"Aww, why can't he stay?" Meagan whined.

Jason noticed a blush forming on her cheeks. "Because...he can't." She stood up, cradling Johnny in one arm, and held out the other for Meagan to take her hand. But the girl remained glued to Jason's side. Rachel frowned and heaved a sigh of frustration. "Give your uncle a night-night hug."

"I want Uncle Jay to tuck me in."

Without hesitation, he rose, his knees cracking in the process, and extended his arms. "Come on, little Cinderella. Time for beddy-bye."

Ten minutes later, with the kids tucked in, Jason slumped into the plush sofa again, this time extending his arms over the back and propping sock-clad feet on the coffee table.

Rachel stood there, shoulders squared, looking resolute. "Jay, it's about time you went home."

"I thought we'd talk. You don't mind, do you?"

She swallowed hard and put her hands on her hips. "Yes."

He laughed. "Oh, come on. Sit." He patted the spot beside him. "I promise not to bite."

A tremor touched her pretty lips. "I'm not one bit worried that you will."

"Good, then it shouldn't hurt for you to sit for a few minutes. Take a load off."

"Isn't that what we've been doing for the last hour and a half?"

"Yeah, with a talkative four-year old who felt it her duty to inform me of every upcoming scene."

Now she succumbed to a smile. "She's only seen that movie about ninety-seven times."

"I figured." On impulse, he reached up and snagged her by the wrist, easily pulling her down next to him.

"Jason!"

"Relax, would you? Let's have a brother-sister talk—with no mention of the you-know-what."

And that's exactly what they did for at least the next hour, he telling her about his church, job, friends, and the grief group he attended, she talking about her church, the one he'd attended growing up, and her own group of friends, one named Allie in particular, and her goofy story about some comedy of errors at a bank drive-up window. They laughed a lot, and Rachel relaxed to the point of curling her legs up under her body and reclining against the back of the sofa with a knitted blanket over her lap.

"It feels good, doesn't it?" he said, leaning back and looking up at the ceiling. "Just sitting here talking, laughing, not caring if there's a lull."

"Yeah," she confessed.

He clasped his hands at his belt buckle and angled his head at her. "See? No biting."

"You're silly."

Another chuckle passed between them, but then a melancholy frown flitted across her features. "It's been a whole year, Jay"—her voice went soft as a kitten's—"and yet it feels like yesterday."

"I've been thinking the same thing all day." *Lord, I'm glad she mentioned it.*

"How could an entire year have slipped by already? We'll soon be celebrating John Jr.'s first birthday."

"I'm coming to his party, invited or not."

This time, she tilted her head at him and revealed a tiny grin. "There'll be no party crashing. You'll get an invitation."

Another reflective, sixty-second lull passed. "Does it feel like things are getting better for you—I mean, less painful?"

She considered his question with creased brow and narrowed eyes, opening her mouth, then closing it again. She reached up and scratched her forehead, disturbing a lovely little blonde lock. He took the opportunity to check out her perfect nose and lips while he was at it. "Little by little, I suppose," she finally said. "Some days, I'm downright good, but then I feel almost guilty for it, like I should be spending every minute grieving, and if I quit, then I'm not honoring his memory like I should be."

"That's not the way John would want you to feel."

"I know."

"Those are natural feelings you're having. It becomes a journey of two steps forward, one step back, rather than three steps back and one forward. God's mercies are new every morning. He gives us just what we need for each day."

"I'm finding that to be true." She kept her gaze trained on him, her face only a foot or so from his. "You sure got smart over this last year." This she said with a hint of playful sarcasm, but then her expression turned thoughtful. "And dedicated—and unswerving in your faith. It's quite remarkable to watch, especially when I consider what a hellion you were in high school and college."

"Loss will do that to a person—bring him to his knees or have him shaking his fist at God." He harrumphed. "I preferred the former, you know? Looking back, I'm sure I gave my parents some giant headaches. 'Star Football Player Goes on Drunken Binge, Destroys Mailboxes on Johnson Avenue.' 'Member that newspaper headline? To this day, I don't know how I kept my spot on the team. I should have gotten more than a two-week suspension from school. 'Course, I got myself into some, um…situations in college, too, but those are better left unmentioned. All I'll say is this"—he cleared his throat and let out a light chuckle—"God's grace and mercy extend far beyond our worthiness."

"Beautifully said."

He took a deep, hard swallow. "I don't think John ever gave our dad a second of grief. I'd have given anything to be more like him, but he was a hard one to compete against. I never measured up to him."

With gaping mouth, Rachel stared at him, back straight and shoulders taut. "Are you kidding? John always looked up to you, even though you were younger. He admired you for your grit and carefree spirit. He used to say, 'My brother is a pain in the hind end right now, but you watch; he'll get his act together one day and be the most passionate of all of us about his faith.' I'm the one who used to say, 'Yeah, right, that'll be the day that pigs fly.'" She gave him a playful pat on the arm. "No, I'm just kidding."

He gave a short-lived grin. "Thanks. I think."

She settled back again, their shoulders barely touching as they stared at the ceiling. "Your dad's proud of you, Jay; he just doesn't do a good job of showing it. He never gets very emotional, you know."

"No? I see emotions in him all the time, and they're called anger and disappointment. John got all the grades and the honors, even landed the suit-'n-tie job."

"You were the star athlete," she quickly countered. "And you own a very successful construction company."

"He was class president for four years—levelheaded, intelligent, and highly respected. Shoot, he went all the way to state with the college debate team. He could've run for president today and been elected."

"You were popular and got all the attention, especially from the girls."

"Ha! But he landed the one girl that really mattered, didn't he?" He bumped against her playfully. In one fluid move, she slid out of reach and glanced at her watch. He might have stepped over the line with that one.

"I should probably go, huh?" Hesitating for all of three seconds, he put his hands on his knees with purpose, intending to stand. But then, something impelled him to give her one last thorough look. If she hadn't returned it, he might have ignored the urge to kiss her, stupid and impractical and poorly timed as it was, but he couldn't resist, and so he decided to go for it—that old, carefree spirit John had envied rearing its monstrous head.

In jagged stops and starts, he lowered his face to be level with hers, pausing just shy of her lips, thinking and then not thinking, waiting for her to come to her senses by ducking away from him, knowing that if she didn't, it'd be too late for both of them. Ever so slowly, he tipped her chin upward, finding it most hard to ignore the thudding of his chest. *Lord, God, help me; keep me from doing this.* But if he thought the Lord was about to burst through the front door and throw him to the floor, he was an idiot through and through.

At first, his mouth touched hers like a fine brush to its palette, gently flicking and skimming, almost like a whisper. Jason dared not move for fear of spooking her, so he kept his arms at his sides. But then, something happened. She made the first attempt to adjust her seating, turning to face him more squarely. He took the move as an invitation to deepen the kiss, and his lips swept over hers with fervor, like a passionate artist first putting brush to canvas. For long moments, they kissed, tasted, pressed, devoured, his arms gradually gathering her to him, his hands tenderly kneading the hollows of her back, tracing over her shoulder blades, exploring the sweet indentations of her spine. He knew that the moment she retreated, he would respect her by stopping, but she astounded him by wrapping her arms around his back and locking her hands.

Jesus, I love her. I love her! he exclaimed in the depths of his soul, extending the kiss all the more, willing it to go on forever.

I make all things beautiful in My time.

The inner voice spoke precious truth into his spirit, but with it came a silent yet unmistakable nudge to end the kiss.

Oh, he wanted to ignore that still, small tapping at his conscience, but he knew that if he did, he'd almost certainly face regrets. He'd been down that road and learned some valued lessons. Gently, he pulled away, and they stared at each other for what felt like hours, both of them taking in short, exhilarating breaths.

"Well, now." In rather slow motion, Rachel stood, her brow furrowed in confusion, her mouth, puffy from the pressure of his kisses, slightly agape. "That was—um—a little inappropriate, don't you think?"

Rachel's erratic pulse set her in a state of momentary panic. She ran a hand through her hair, then put it to her throat and swallowed. *Dear God, forgive me. I didn't mean to let that happen.* "You need to go," she stated simply.

Jason slowly rose, his steady, assuring gaze impaling her like an arrow to the heart. *What have I done? My brother-in-law just kissed me, and, oh, God, I kissed him back.* Her brain went into immediate tumult, and she spun her body around while trying to get her bearings. *Coat. Jason's coat. I must get it and then push him out the door.*

As if reading her thoughts, he clutched her by the arm and stopped her midway to the closet. "Settle down, would you, Rach? We did nothing inappropriate—maybe a little premature, but not inappropriate." His hand was locked loosely around her forearm and seemed to sear the skin beneath her sweater sleeve, and his voice, soothing enough to calm a skittish cat, nearly made her cave. Yet she recovered in an instant and withdrew, looking down at the floor. "Just go. Now. Your coat's in the closet."

"I know, and I'm going. But, listen—I want you to know, I'm starting to feel—"

"Don't!" she pleaded. "You feel nothing, you hear me? Nothing." She said this with such fierce conviction that she barely recognized her own voice.

He gave a light chuckle and touched her cheek. She took a giant step back and wrapped herself in a tight hug, biting down on her lip and blinking back the sudden urge to cry.

"Aw, Rachel, don't do that. I'm sorry if I've—no, I'm not sorry. Sheesh, I wanted to kiss you—and I think you wanted it, too. And now you're having this inner battle about thoughts you don't particularly enjoy entertaining." He dared to come close again, then bent down to her level, his piercing, dark eyes searching her face. "Am I right?"

"I am not entertaining any thoughts about you, Jason Evans, nor will I. Now, please go."

"If it makes any difference, I'm scared, too, Rach. But I'm not about to let it keep me from pursuing what I think is right. What if the Lord is telling us to consider this—this—"

"He's not!" she exclaimed with certainty. "He would never do that. You're my brother-in-law."

"Yes, so that makes me the enemy?"

"It makes you…untouchable."

"Does it? Think about it. We've always been great friends. This is just taking our friendship to the next level."

"John would hate that!" One stray tear found a path down her cheek. He reached up and brushed it away with his thumb.

"John's not here, honey, and I think he'd be glad to know I was taking care of you."

"I don't need you feeling sorry for me…or feeling responsible."

"I don't," he whispered in haste. "I feel a lot more than that."

She bit hard on her lower lip, hoping the pain would distract her from this sudden surge of emotions. More tears threatened, but she chased them back, raising her chin now to look him square-on. "You—can't. It would be wrong because, well, because he knew."

This tiny declaration had him squinting down at her and giving his head a mild shake of confusion. "What are you talking about? Knew what?"

She swallowed down what felt like a jagged rock. "I told him about the kiss—our kiss—before you left on your ski trip."

"You what?" he whispered in a disbelieving tone. "Why would you do that? He didn't need to know."

"We had a fight about money—a big fight."

"He told me that much, that you'd had a fight."

"And during our arguing I blurted out how we'd kissed. It was awful of me, I know." She covered her face and dropped her chin to her chest. "I told him that you and I had at one time…felt things for each other."

"What? But we—that was way before, Rachel. I mean, yeah, John and I both had crushes on you all through school, but once you settled on John, that sealed it for me— except for that stupid kiss in the barn." He let a mild curse slip off his tongue, and she looked at him. He winced and looked away, his eyes coming to rest on something across the room. "I wish you hadn't told him. Man."

"I was pregnant and irrational," she cried. "And he made some thoughtless remark about my being fat or something, I don't know. It hurt, and I just wanted to lash out, so I did—in the worst way."

At that admission, his brows flickered a little. "I thought you made a very radiant pregnant lady."

"Pssh. On the best of days, maybe."

His slight smile faded as he grew thoughtful. "That day—out on the slopes—he made a rash remark, and it made me so stinking mad."

A chill shot down her spine as she searched his eyes. "What did he say? Tell me, Jay."

"He had the gall to accuse me of trying to steal you away from him, claiming that I'd always loved you." He creased his brow and looked close to tears himself. "It all makes sense now. I nearly slugged him in the gut for making that ridiculous accusation, Rach, but if you had told him we kissed just before his wedding day...well, he probably thought—I'm not sure—that you weren't fully committed to the marriage in the beginning, maybe, or that you hadn't even taken your wedding vows seriously." His gaze dropped. "The guy had to be hurting."

Unstoppable tears started flowing, and she let them come. "I'm such a fool. If only—"

He touched her elbow. "Shh. Don't punish yourself over something you can't do anything about. It's done. If anything, it's my fault. I should have forced him off that mountain and made him come back to the lodge with me so we could talk it out. Maybe I could have gotten him to tell me what had him so hell-bent on thinking you and I still harbored feelings for each other." He shook his head. "Not that he would've listened. Shoot, he wasn't even thinking straight that day. When we got to the top of Devil's Run and realized how bad the conditions were, I wanted to take the lift back down, but he wouldn't listen. He got it in his head to challenge me, and I wouldn't accept the challenge."

"And so you argued about it." Tears clogged her throat. "Witnesses overheard you quarrelling. Down deep, Jay, you knew you'd win that challenge."

"I didn't feel like competing against him. For crying out loud, all we ever did our entire lives was compete, and I got tired of it. That was not the day for sibling rivalry. His anger freaked me out, and I didn't get it at the time. He never told me you made that confession. Man, why didn't I dig deeper for answers?" He fisted one hand and frowned so deeply that his eyes nearly disappeared in the crinkles. "If only he'd told me. I could have assured him that kiss was all my selfish doing, that in no way did you initiate it. It might have stopped him from going down that icy slope in a fit of anger, as if he had something to prove to me."

She couldn't let him take full responsibility. Several jagged sighs slipped out. "It takes two willing parties to kiss, Jay. Looking back, I don't know why I let you do it, but I did. And afterward, I felt ashamed and embarrassed. But I also knew I still loved John with all my heart." She looked at him, yearning for answers. "Does that make sense?"

He tilted his head to the side, studying her face, and gave a slow nod. The fact that he made no further move to touch her didn't escape her notice. "Yeah. It satisfied a curiosity in both of us. We had to know before you married John that you were doing the right thing. And you were."

Her thoughts tangled into a firm knot, one she couldn't loosen or sort through. But she did know one thing. "So...." She closed her eyes and raked her fingers through her hair, then looked at him with newfound resolve. "That is why we cannot entertain any further notions of kissing or going any deeper with our feelings. It is simply not an option, Jay. Not for me, anyway. To do so would be to dishonor my husband's memory."

"Is that so?" The clock on the wall struck eleven gongs. "I'll respect you for that—for now, anyway. I think we both have some things to ponder and pray about."

"Bye, Jay."

He stared at her for all of ten seconds, and she could hear the slow intake and release of each breath. "I'll see you at Johnny's birthday party—how's that?" he said.

"I suppose we'll have to see each other on occasion."

He touched the tip of her nose and chuckled low in his throat. "We can't avoid each other entirely, Rachel."

Just before he turned to head for his car, he murmured, "Kiss the kids for me."

Chapter 14

On Sunday morning, Rachel sat in a pew near the back of Harvest Community Church's sanctuary and tried to focus as Pastor Eddie Turnwall delivered his message. Distractions were more demanding, though, so rather than try to memorize the major sermon points, she allowed her eyes to drop to the open Bible in her lap, and she read the first verse her eyes settled on, Psalm 139:17: *"How precious also are Your thoughts to me, O God. How great is the sum of them! If I should count them, they would be more in number than the sand; when I awake, I am still with You."*

The words breathed truth into the very fibers of her soul, sending a river of comfort straight to her heart. Still, she couldn't shake the stream of despair that ran alongside it. *Why did I tell John, Lord?* she berated herself for the hundredth time since talking to Jason on Thanksgiving. *Will I ever be able to forgive myself?* Fresh twinges of guilt trickled through her veins. Sniffing, she opened her purse and fished for a tissue.

"Are you all right, hon?" whispered her friend, Laura King, who was seated next to her. Rachel usually sat with her parents or in-laws, but she'd been running late this morning, and so, after taking Meagan to Sunday school and Johnny to the nursery, she'd snuck in at the back of the sanctuary, where Laura had snagged her before she sat down. Having just gone through a bitter divorce, Laura was alone, too, and dealing with her own set of problems. In the past several months, the newfound friendship between the two women had been good for both of them.

Rachel smiled and nodded. "I'm good."

Of course, saying it and meaning it were altogether different. She blew her nose and dabbed at the corners of her eyes, wanting desperately to keep her eye shadow, liner, and mascara intact.

"Jesus provides abundant life," Pastor Eddie said from the front, catching her attention. "Abundance, you ask? Are we talking health and wealth, pastor? No, no, we're talking abundance of the Spirit. He wants us living beyond mediocrity. That's not to say we won't encounter trials and hardships along the way, but *in* them we can experience the peace, rest, and joy of Christ. That is abundance, my friends."

Rachel took hold of his words and mentally filed them deep within her heart, planning to pull them out later for further contemplation. Could she find peace and rest in the shadow of an unresolved conflict? Additional questions haunted her: Had John carried his pain and anger to the grave? Had he been picturing her with Jason as his skis had hit that steep slope of death and he'd lost control, slamming into a tree?

She looked down at her Bible again and read an earlier passage from the same psalm:

Where can I go from Your Spirit? Or where can I flee from Your presence? If I ascend into heaven, You are there; if I make my bed in hell, behold, You are there. If I take the wings of the morning, and dwell in the uttermost parts of the sea, even there Your hand shall lead me, and Your right hand shall hold me. If I say, "Surely the darkness shall fall on

me," even the night shall be light about me; indeed,
the darkness shall not hide me from You, but the
night shines as the day; the darkness and the light
are both alike to You.

Those words, along with the bits and pieces she gathered from Pastor Eddie's sermon, filled the empty places
of her heart, at least for the moment. Now, if she could just
find a way to make them last.

That Thursday, exactly one week after Thanksgiving,
Rachel took up the task of cleaning and organizing drawers
and closets, a job she'd put off for well over a year. With
Meagan at preschool and Johnny spending the day with
Tanna, who had the day off from school, it provided her the
opportunity to concentrate on her chore.

After John's death, she'd taken several items of his
clothing to the nearest charity organization, but there still
remained a good share of his things—stuff she simply
couldn't part with yet, like his everyday shoes, a rack of
his favorite ties, and the cozy robe she still slipped on at
night if she needed to feel his nearness. And then, there
was that large plastic tub of his keepsakes. She had never
taken it down from the high shelf where it was stored, in
part because it was too cumbersome, but also because lifting the lid might very well wreak emotional havoc. So, she
left the box alone and straightened the lower closet shelves,
disposed of some of her old jeans and shirts, and sorted
through her large collection of shoes.

From there, she moved on to her drawers of socks, summer shirts and shorts, and sweaters. She kept two garbage
bags at the ready: one for anything with holes or stains, to
be thrown away, and the other for items in decent condition, to be donated to charity.

When she finished her chore and was tying the bags,
the doorbell chimed. She went to the window to look down

at the driveway and spotted her father-in-law's car. Rarely did her in-laws drop in unannounced. Donna, in particular, considered it improper.

She skipped down the stairs, surprised to discover only Tom standing on her doorstep. "Dad? Well, gee whiz! To what do I owe this honor? Come in, come in," she said, holding the door open with one arm and giving him a quick hug with the other.

He wore an awkward expression as he glanced around the foyer. "Don't mean to barge in on you, but I was in the neighborhood. I had coffee with several of my cronies at that River House restaurant."

"Yes, I know the place. John and I went there on occasion. You didn't have to work today?"

"Naw, I took the day off. Got a lot of vacation to use up before year's end."

She brushed several blonde hairs out of her eyes and thought about her awful appearance—her stained T-shirt and holey, worn jeans. "Would you care to sit down?" She gestured toward the living room.

"No, I— Are Meagan and Johnny here? Just thought I'd stop by to see them."

"No, sorry. Meaggie's at preschool, and Johnny's at my parents' place. Tanna's watching him."

"Ah." He gave a slow nod and inhaled. "I smell Lemon Pledge. Have you been cleaning?"

"Yep! I've been organizing closets, sorting through drawers, straightening shelves…."

"Sounds like a lot of work."

"You sure you don't want to sit?"

"No, I'm heading over to the lumber store. My son pointed out a few things around the house that need fixing, so I'm getting at it. Kid's got an eagle eye when it comes to houses. 'Course, Donna's plain overjoyed."

"You should just have Jay do it for you. He thrives on that sort of thing."

"I can take care of my own house." His tone carried a stubborn tautness. "I heard he's been doing some odd jobs around your house. That's...good." Outside, the wind picked up, drowning out the classical piano CD she had set at low volume. Tom looked at the front window. "You heard from him since Thanksgiving?"

"Jason? No, why?"

He waved a hand. "Oh, nothing. Just wondered, is all." He looked down, assessing her with his gray green eyes. "You seem like you're doing better these days."

"Do I? I still have lots of hard times, but it's nice when people tell me they've seen subtle changes. It's hard to believe it's been an entire year since—the accident. How are you and Mom holding up?"

"Us? Oh, good. Fine."

Of course, he never came clean with his true feelings. "I've been memorizing Scriptures—especially verses from Psalms," she said. "The support group I attend at church has been a big encouragement to me, too. I was telling Mom a few days ago that you guys ought to come with me sometime. It'd be good for you."

"Pfff, that's not really my scene. I'm findin' my own way to work through this thing."

"With the Lord's help, I hope."

He looked at his shoes, then scratched his head before giving her a sideways glance. "I s'pose I got some issues— about the accident an' all."

Her stomach soured in an instant. "Like what?"

He gave another wave of dismissal. "Aw, it's not worth talking about."

"No, really. You can tell me." So seldom did Tom Evans speak about that day that it seemed imperative she draw out whatever she could about how he thought or felt, despite her slight apprehension to know the truth.

He pushed up his left coat sleeve to look at his watch. "I better get going. Donna will wonder what's become of me."

"Okay," she said, placing a hand on his arm, "but tell me something first. Do you blame Jason for the accident? I said things at the cemetery I had no right saying, remember?" His head bobbed slowly. "Shock overruled my common sense, and I lashed out at him. Why didn't you stand up for your son that day?"

He pulled his arm away and turned toward the door. "This isn't the time for talking about it."

"Of course, it is. There's nobody else around. If you carry blame in your heart, at least you can tell me why. Sometimes, it just helps to get your feelings out in the open."

With his back to her, he put his hand to the doorknob but didn't turn it; he just stood there staring at his hand. "They argued," he murmured.

"I know that. Brothers tend to. Did he ever tell you what they argued about?"

"No, and I don't want to know!" he shot back in a gruffer tone than he'd ever used with her. "Sorry," he said, immediately turning to look at her with regret in his shiny eyes.

"It's all right."

He pinched the bridge of his nose and huffed. "It's just—whatever they were fighting about precipitated the accident. Jay could have prevented it."

"How could he have prevented it? John acted of his own free will when he set off down Devil's Run."

Her father-in-law took several labored breaths and looked at the low-burning fire she'd started that morning. "I don't like to think about that hill."

"Nor do I," she whispered.

"Then, let's not discuss it further. I'll—I'll talk to you later, all right?"

"Dad." She touched his arm again and breathed a prayer for strength. "Jay feels like he can't measure up to your standards...that he's always lived in John's shadow."

"What? That's ridiculous. Why would he think that?"

"Well, have you ever driven down to Harrietta to check out his office or seen the houses he's built? Have you ever swung through some of the neighborhoods he's developed? He told me he put a bid on a new housing development just ten miles from here, and they accepted the deal a week before Thanksgiving. Did you know that?"

Tom's chest swelled, and he arched an eyebrow. "Really? That's somethin', huh?"

"You ought to tell him you're proud of him."

"Pfff, he knows that," Tom grumbled. "Why are you so concerned, anyway?"

The sense that her father-in-law harbored the tiniest bit of resentment toward her made her stomach lurch. "He's my brother-in-law, and I care about him."

"Humph. You know, there was a time when I thought you and Jason were better suited for each other than you and John."

She rocked backward, nearly losing her balance. "I loved John very much," she said firmly, emphasizing every word. *Is he actually calling our marriage and my love for John into question?*

He backpedaled. "Oh, 'course, I know that now. I just wondered, you know, if you ever wished you had married, well—"

"What? No! Gracious, no!"

He let out a slow sigh and shifted his weight. "Well, I was just a little curious."

"Dad, for goodness' sake! I can't believe you'd even hint at such a thing. John was the love of my life."

He looked down at her and bit his lower lip. Then, with a manufactured grin, he said, "Oh, I know that. Good grief, I hope I haven't upset you, honey. That wasn't my intention. Sorry if I have."

"It's all right—it's fine." Now, she was the one not wanting to express her true feelings. But how could she have shared them, given the simmering anger his subtle accusation had provoked? She might say something she'd regret.

"Well, I'll be going now."

This time, she made no effort to stop him.

You idiot! What are you trying to prove?

John adjusted his goggles and ski cap and grinned a smile that lacked warmth. "Challenging you to a race, brother."

"On Devil's Run? You must be crazy. Come on, let's take Steeple Run instead."

"What? You scared I'll beat you for a change?"

"Don't be stupid. It's not safe—not today. Look, it's starting to sleet. Come on, John, quit playing."

"You think I'm playing?" John yelled. "This is not playing, bro."

"What's been eating at you?"

Ski poles stuck firmly at his sides, John hollered against the biting, stinging wind and icy sheets of sleet. "You've always wanted her, haven't you?"

"What?" Jason stepped closer, his gut tumbling and his brain whirling with sickening disbelief. "What are you talking about?"

"I guess I always knew it, but I kept pushing the notion aside—until now. You'll never marry that Candace woman. She's not really what you're looking for in a wife."

"John, you're making no sense. What are you suggesting, anyway?"

"You know very well what I'm suggesting. I've seen it in your eyes. You've wanted Rachel since ninth grade, and now you think you can steal her right out from under me!"

"What in the—? I liked her back in school, sure. Those were the days you and I battled back and forth over who would finally win her. And it was you she wanted, remember? You're the one she married. She loves you, John!" This he screamed as if to someone at the top of the next mountain peak, wanting to make it good and clear. He figured it was better than punching John in the gut for his foolish words. He'd known something was gnawing at him ever since they'd left for the airport. John had spoken no more than a few sentences during the flight, and Jason had finally gotten out of him that he and Rachel had not parted on good terms. A lovers' spat, Jason figured. It would iron itself out by the time John was home again.

"Don't think I don't know, Jason!"

"Don't know what? You're making about as much sense as a drunken buzzard!"

"Meet me at the bottom, lunkhead—if you're man enough, that is. Or does the Run scare you today?"

Jason was unsettled by the enigmatic, accusatory challenge in those eyes. *"What the—?"* His head whirled with confusion, and then, suddenly, John shoved off and out of visibility down the steep ravine. Wind and sleet cut Jason's exposed cheeks like shards of glass as he searched for his form in the blinding whiteness.

"John!" he yelled, planting his poles to give himself a thrust into the obscurity. *"John, hold up!"* He hoped he

166 • Sharlene MacLaren

could catch up to him before he lost control and veered off the trail.

But he was wrong. Dead wrong.

When Jason spotted him, he skidded to a stop. There was blood everywhere, crimson-red against a blanket of white, and then a body—John's—bleeding from his face and head, his neck bent abnormally, his eyes open yet not seeing. Several yards away stood the ancient tree he must have hit. His skis were splintered, and the trunk was splayed with snow.

"Help! Help!" Jason screamed to the blurred skies.

Cold and wet, he dropped to his knees beside John's motionless body and shivered uncontrollably. It wasn't long before he heard the drone of snowmobiles. The ski patrol had arrived. They'd get him airlifted. In a couple of days, they'd be laughing at his foolhardiness, and they'd get this whole misunderstanding about Rachel and him squared away.

But that wasn't to be, either.

Jason awoke in a pool of sweat and a mass of rumpled sheets. His blanket had been tossed to the floor, and his pillow was at the foot of the bed. The clock on the bedside stand registered 5:45. He hauled himself up, swung his heavy legs over the edge of the bed, and put his feet on the floor. Bending over with exhaustion, he buried his head in his hands, waiting to catch his breath and willing his pulse to slow. After several minutes, he mustered the strength to stand and stagger to the bathroom to prepare for another day on the job.

Chapter 15

The month of December ushered in more snow than Fairmount had seen in the past two winters combined. A major snowstorm, now classified as a blizzard, had shut down virtually every school within a seventy-five-mile radius, forced motorists off the roads, and even closed down some area businesses. Local and state police asked citizens to stay in their homes to allow the road crews to do their jobs. The trouble was, the snow kept coming down, and the plows were soon forced to abandon their work.

Rachel had been busy and managed to miss the weather reports, so she wasn't prepared for the storm when it hit. As payback for her ignorance, she was running low on diapers, baby food, and milk, not to mention the prescription refill for Johnny's asthma medication she needed to pick up.

At four o'clock in the afternoon, Rachel got a call from Ivy, her next-door neighbor. "You and the kids come over here," the elderly widow insisted when she heard about her predicament. "I have a pot of stew cooking on the stove and plenty of milk and supplies."

Rachel gratefully accepted the invitation. When Meagan and Johnny had been bundled up, Rachel put on her coat and boots, and they trudged through the knee-deep snow to Ivy's house. Rachel walked in front of Meagan to carve out a path, Johnny clinging tightly to her neck and squealing with delight at the fast-falling snow. On Ivy's front porch,

167

they stomped their feet on the mat before walking into the warmth of her house.

While the wind bellowed and the snow fell outside, Meagan played with Buffy, tossing a ball for him to retrieve, and Johnny explored uncharted territory. Two bookshelves, a magazine rack, and a basket of fake fruit were a few of the items he found the most fascinating. As the children played, Ivy and Rachel engaged in a game of Scrabble near the fireplace, Rachel's still-frozen toes propped up on the raised hearth, seeking warmth. She jumped up every so often to send Johnny in a different direction, trying to keep him away from Buffy. The last thing she wanted was for him to have an asthma attack.

Yet, in the next hour, she thought she detected a slight wheezing in his breath and decided that she couldn't put off picking up his medication much longer, even if it was just a precaution. So, around six o'clock, she turned to Ivy and said, "Do you think you could watch the kids for about half an hour while I make a quick run to the pharmacy? Johnny usually takes his asthma medication around this time, and I need to pick up his refill."

The woman furrowed her age-wrinkled brow and stared at Rachel as if she'd just grown a second nose. "Sweetie, you can't go anywhere in this weather. I mean, I'd be happy to watch your children, but I just don't think— Are you sure you don't have any extra medication at home?"

"No, I used the last of it yesterday. I'm going to have to go out, but I'll be fine, and I'll be quick."

"Goodness, gracious. Don't be quick on my account, dear. Take it slow and easy if you really must go. What about your driveway? You could get stuck."

"The guy who's contracted to plow for me came by about twenty minutes ago; I heard him in the driveway. It should be relatively clear." She rose and looked down into

Ivy's fretful eyes. "Don't worry, Ivy. I'll be back in no time at all."

Rachel made it to the pharmacy without a hitch, her tires skidding only a few times, and she vowed never to take the luxury of the drive-through window for granted again. But going home was a different story. The trip, which should have matched the five-minute drive to the store, had already taken fifteen, and now Rachel was beginning to wonder if she'd gone too far. The heavily falling snow had turned into a whiteout, confounding her perception and making her think that she'd missed the turn to her neighborhood. She negotiated the steering wheel with care, traveling at a breakneck speed of fifteen miles per hour, which only added to her anxiousness to get home.

Finally, she spotted the familiar bend in the road just before her neighborhood entrance. Sighing with relief, she flipped on her turn signal and slowed ever so carefully, pumping the brake. Just as she began to turn the wheel, a great thud from behind jerked her forward and caused her minivan to veer over to the shoulder and off the road. Thankfully, a nice, tall snowbank stopped her vehicle from straying any further.

"Lord Jesus," she muttered shakily when she heard her engine sputter and opened her eyes to get her bearings. A moment later, someone knocked on her window. "You all right, ma'am?"

She turned, dazed, to see a man about her father's age peering in through her window. She did a mental body check, surprised that she felt no pain from the impact, and gave a slow nod. The windshield wipers hadn't ceased their back-and-forth motion, but now they clunked loudly against the snow clumping on the window.

"Sorry I didn't see your turn signal in time," he shouted, his breath fogging up the window for a moment.

She gave another dull nod.

"You sure you're all right?"

"Yes, I'm fine." She fumbled in the dark for her purse, then pulled out her cell phone.

"I just called 9-1-1. The police should be here soon. It was my fault, ma'am; you don't have to worry."

She stopped fumbling. "It was—an accident," she returned, wanting to get out and survey the damage to her minivan but opting to wait till the police arrived.

"I'll just—go back to my car, then." He thumbed at his vehicle behind him, and she mouthed an okay.

When he walked away, Rachel tried to restart her minivan, but the blamed engine wouldn't work. So, she sat there and shivered for what must have been a good six or seven minutes. Finally, flashing red lights announced the arrival of help. Not for the first time, she berated herself for failing to anticipate the storm and needing to go out in the middle of the worst of it. Surely, the cops would give her a good tongue-lashing for venturing out.

In a moment, a state trooper tapped on her window. She fished in the glove box for her registration and insurance papers, then lowered her window a few inches and handed them over, along with her driver's license. When she met his eyes, she wondered where she'd seen him before. "You all right, ma'am?" he asked, taking the papers from her.

"Yes, thank you," she answered. "A little shaky, but otherwise fine."

He studied her license, then looked up with a smile. "Rachel?"

"Larry?" That was it! Larry Rossini. He and his mother had moved up the street from the Evanses' house right before eighth grade, and he'd hung out with John and Jason throughout high school. He'd often come over when she and her parents had been visiting the Evanses, and the four kids had shot baskets in the driveway, played crazy eights at the picnic table, or sat on the back stoop and talk about nothing in particular. More times than not, all three boys had vied for Rachel's attention, trying to make her giggle at their antics or hoping to impress her with their athletic prowess. She recalled seeing Larry at John's funeral and remembered that she hadn't thanked him for coming. Now didn't seem like the right time to do that, however.

"Very good seeing you—well, not under such circumstances, mind you—but, you know," he said.

"I'd forgotten you were a cop," she told him, passing over his remark and putting on a smile, even as she felt desperation to get back to Ivy's house and anger at this snowbank holding her captive.

"Yep, going on seven years now." The nasty wind and blowing snow prevented them from carrying on much of a conversation, and she found herself wanting to raise her window to block out the elements.

Larry moved toward the front of her minivan and surveyed the damage, then walked to the back, checking out every side before sauntering back to her window. "Looks like we're going to need a tow truck. Your front fender seems to have suffered the most damage; looks like you hit a strong pole beneath this snowbank.

"A pole?" Rising up in her seat, Rachel was able to spot the sign sticking out of the snow where it met the hood of her van. "Oh, I hit that 'No Littering' sign—go figure."

Larry leaned toward her window and pierced her with his brownish-black eyes. Under that snow-covered hat, she knew, lay a thick layer of black hair. It came back to her now. His Mexican-born mother had married an Italian chef—they'd met at some international cooking institute, if she remembered correctly, and had had a whirlwind love affair. Funny how Larry's background, plus his given name of Luigi, which he'd never wanted to be referred to as, started coming back to her in small segments. "Are you sure you're all right? I can have an ambulance here in no time."

"No, no, I'm fine; just a little shaken up, is all. Really."

He nodded at the front of her car. "Did your engine die?"

Rachel turned the key again but with no results. She gave him a helpless glance.

"No worries," he told her. "After we get this whole matter squared away, I'll drive you home. Any particular reason you decided to come out on a night like this?"

She gave him a sheepish smile. "I needed to pick up my son's asthma medication."

He grinned back. "And you couldn't have done that before the storm? You shouldn't have watched all those daytime soaps today."

"Very funny. As if I have time for—"

"I'm kidding, I'm kidding." He laughed playfully. "Gosh, these things happen all the time, folks not turning on the TV and missing any severe-weather warnings."

She harrumphed. "I sound like a hermit, don't I?"

"Not at all. I'm sure you have your hands full raising two little ones. It is two, right?"

"Yes, but it feels more like four sometimes, when they're at opposite ends of the house."

Larry threw back his head for another snort until the fellow in the other car gave a tiny tap of the car horn. "I'll be right there, sir!" he hollered with a wave of his hand. "Argh, some people," he murmured to Rachel.

"Listen. I think I have all the information I need from you at this time. What say you go back and sit in my cruiser—front seat—and get yourself warmed up? We'll get you home again in short order." She found his demeanor friendly and pleasant, if not downright reassuring. He studied her a moment longer as a layer of snow collected on the rim of his cap, then straightened and opened her door. "Should be a pretty clear-cut case. We'll be on our way before you know it."

She climbed out of the van, feeling foolish for having worn slippers instead of her boots, which had been wet with snow after the trek back from Ivy's. "Holy cow!" Larry said, looking down at her feet. "You really were unprepared for this storm."

She gave him another sheepish grin. "I know. I'd worn my boots to the neighbor's, and they were soaking wet, and I figured I wouldn't need to walk outside since I was just going through the drive-through at the pharmacy."

He took her firmly yet gently by the arm and led her to his vehicle. "I'm sorry for bringing you out in this, Larry."

He chuckled. "It's my job, Rachel, and any chance I get to save a beautiful damsel in distress just makes my job all the more pleasant. Looks like I found one tonight."

As he'd predicted, it was a clear-cut settlement. The fellow who had rammed her acknowledged his responsibility, insurance information was exchanged, and stories from both sides were shared and recorded. Soon, the man set off in his oversized SUV, which hadn't suffered so much as a scratch.

Larry and Rachel waited until the tow truck arrived from the local auto body where John had always taken their vehicles for service. Meanwhile, Rachel thought to call Ivy and let her know what had happened. Finally, it was time to go home and get Johnny his medication.

"You still live on Westfield Lane?" Larry asked, maneuvering his cruiser with finesse over the snow-covered road.

"Yes, but my kids are at the neighbor's house, so you can drop me there."

She couldn't help staring at the gizmos and gadgets on the dashboard—flashing signals, buttons and switches, and a two-way radio, on which an operator sent out constant updates in codes Rachel couldn't decipher. Between spurts of conversation, Larry picked up the receiver and reported his whereabouts.

"How are your kids, by the way? And you?" he was kind enough to ask.

"We're holding up as well as can be expected. Thanks for asking." Rachel felt she didn't know Larry well enough to reveal anything deeper than surface-level details. "I wonder what the exact damages were to my van." It seemed important to change the subject.

"I don't think it'll cost you too much. Your engine probably just flooded, or maybe a cable or belt snapped from impact. The fact that your airbag didn't deploy tells me the damages were minimal. You got a big deductible?"

"I—I don't even know. Isn't that awful? Those were things John—"

"No, that's not unusual. Shoot, before my divorce, my wife took full charge of the bank accounts—foolish mistake on my part, looking back. Come to find out she'd been spending money we didn't have, accrued debts I'm still paying off as part of the divorce settlement."

"That's a sour pill to swallow."

"You're not kidding."

"Well, rest assured, John didn't leave me with any debts. If anything, he was a tightwad with a capital T." She chortled, wanting to keep things between them light. "Do you have any children?"

"One, which proved to be another sucker punch to the gut."

"How so?" He turned his cruiser onto Westfield Lane. "Ivy's house is the fourth on the right," she added, pointing.

When he pulled into the driveway, he shifted the gear-shift into park and kept the engine running, placing his hands at the top of the steering wheel and staring straight ahead. "I thought the boy was mine for the first two years of his life. But just after his second birthday, my ex and I had a huge fight, and she confessed to affairs I'd known nothing about. I found out she'd conceived Haydn while I was attending a strategic training course in D.C. Of course, I demanded paternity tests, and the rest is history."

Rachel gasped. "Oh, how awful for you."

"Yeah, apparently the two of them had some sort of history before I even met her, but that's all water under the bridge. Little Haydn is almost six now and doing well living with his dad and stepmom over in the Detroit area, his dad having earned full custody of him a few years back."

Her heart broke for him. "So, you never get to see him? Haydn, I mean?"

He shook his head. "Naw. Broke my heart at first, but once I met the real father and determined he'd turned his life around and truly wanted a relationship with the son he never knew he had, well, I couldn't deny him, and neither could the judge. Fact is, Haydn's better off where he is—in a good, stable home with people who attend church real regular and seem to have high morals. The ex, now, she's another story. Last thing I heard, she was down in Florida, living it up with some rich old geezer."

"Hmm. Seems to me you're better off without her."

"No joke."

Dancing shadows behind the curtains in the picture window made Rachel imagine Meagan bouncing around Ivy's living room, perhaps to some of the woman's favorite polka music. She was impatient to go inside, but it seemed like Larry needed to talk, and she supposed that after what he'd done for her, the least she could do was listen for a few more minutes. Out the corner of her eye, she saw his gaze upon her. It lingered off and on for a few seconds. "You see much of Jason? Man, we used to have good times, the four of us." He faced forward again.

"Not very often, no." In fact, it'd been a full ten or so days since she'd heard from him, and she felt guilty missing him.

"What's he doing now?"

"He owns a construction company down in Harrietta, over by Cadillac. He does very well."

"Is that so? Cripes, he was a wild dude back in the day." Larry laughed and slapped the wheel.

She couldn't hold back her own spurt of laughter, sedate as it was and mixed with a strange sense of nostalgia. "He could be a troublemaker, for sure."

"Remember that time he and a bunch of other guys stuck quarters in the machines at Winslow's Car Wash in the middle of the night and then managed to rig them so they'd run continuously?"

Rachel smiled. "The village water department had to shut off the water."

"Yeah. They had Ryan Warsaw with them. Remember him? He looked like he had the brain of a peapod, but that kid was a genius. I'm sure he's the one who figured out how to do it; the rest just egged him on, Jay at the front of the line, I'm sure."

They talked and joked for a couple more minutes, reminiscing about old times and dragging up a few more stories. Finally, she turned to him and said, "Well, thank you very much, Larry. I appreciated the ride, but I'd better go inside. I need to give my son his medication."

She reached for her car handle, but he stopped her. "It won't unlock on its own." He grinned and raised his eyebrows. "You're trapped."

"Oh."

"Don't look so worried, Rachel. I'm only kidding." He bit down on his lower lip, his face mere inches away, his breath skimming her cheeks. "Before you go in, I was just…uh, wondering…if you'd like to go out with me some-time—when the weather clears, of course."

Shock seemed to siphon the blood from her head, and Rachel felt almost dizzy. "I…uh…."

Larry's eyes widened with a startled look. "It wouldn't have to be a date. If you didn't want it to be, I mean. I was just thinking…you know…we could maybe meet for coffee or something. Nothing serious."

Her hand went to her throat. *A date?* Since John's death, no man—with the exception of Jason—had approached her in any way but casually, and she knew exactly why. She had closed herself off from men, and with good reason. The very notion of dating again provoked a wave of angst within her.

"I—well, thank you for asking, but—"

"No, that's fine. It's too early; I should have been more sensitive. Here, let me help you to the house."

He went for his door, but she stopped him with a hand on his arm. He paused and turned. "I'd love to," she heard herself say. "Have coffee with you, that is."

Chapter 16

P hone's for you," Diane announced from her cubicle in Evans Construction Company. "Says his name is Larry Rossini."

"Larry Rossini," Jason muttered under his breath as he tried to clear the cobwebs in his head and place the name. "Larry Rossini?" he repeated aloud. If it was the same Larry Rossini he'd grown up with, he hadn't seen him since John's funeral, and even then, their interaction had been limited to a brief hello.

"That's what he says."

He dug for his phone under a mountain of paperwork, finally laying a hand on it and bringing it to his ear.

"Jay Evans, here. Is this who I think it is?" Larry had been one of those rare finds who had enough in common with the two brothers to be fast friends with both. They'd pretty much lost contact after high school, as he and John had gone their ways and Larry had enrolled at the police academy.

A familiar deep chuckle came from the other end. "Hey, Jay! Larry Rossini. How you been?"

"Luigi!" Jason bellowed into the receiver, knowing full well his friend had never liked his given name. "Not bad. You sound pretty decent."

"I can't complain, all things considered."

They exchanged a few laughs, along with some personal details; Jason got him caught up on his mundane life,

178

and Larry spoke briefly about his divorce and the ensuing custody battle over a boy he'd discovered all too late wasn't even his own. Jason felt bad for the guy and told him so. From there, they discussed Larry's job as a state trooper, his parents and his family, and even the weather, which had been a hot topic ever since the last whopping storm had dumped sixteen inches of snow on northern Michigan in less than forty-eight hours. Shoot, they were still digging out from it.

It was nice to hear Larry's voice, but after several minutes of hearing him ramble on, Jason needed to get to the bottom of what had prompted his call. "Hey, what can I do for you, man? And don't tell me you want me to build you a house. I'm what you'd call buried up to my eyebrows in contractual agreements right now." He tapped his pencil on his desk calendar. *How is it December 11 already?* he wondered. He hadn't bought a single Christmas present, and the mere thought of fighting the crowds to do it made him cranky. Last year, he'd let Candace do the bulk of his Christmas shopping. Oh, the convenience of a girlfriend!

"Nope. Don't need a house. Actually, I've just been thinking about you lately and finally decided to give you a buzz. I heard through the grapevine you've been running a successful business and keeping out of trouble. I just had to see if it was really true."

"Ha! It's true, all right," Jason said, laughing. "The 'keeping out of trouble' part, anyway. Truth be told, I got my life squared away with God just after my brother's accident."

"Oh! Well, wow!"

He noticed that Larry's expression of surprise did not give way to a word of commendation or congratulations, not that he would have expected it to. He'd long thought of Larry Rossini as a die-hard partier. Shoot, he'd been one, himself. There was nothing wrong with it, he supposed, it was just no longer the life he chose. That didn't mean he wouldn't welcome the opportunity to catch up with the guy over lunch, for old times' sake.

"So, what grapevine do you follow these days, anyway?"

"Ha! I ran into your sister-in-law the other night, and she got me caught up."

"My sis—oh!" His heart spun a little cartwheel. "That so? Where'd you happen to see her?"

"Poor thing had a little fender bender. I took care of—"

"What? No one called me." Jason tossed his pencil down and dropped his feet to the floor as he sat up straight. "Is she all right? Were the kids with her? Is everyone okay?"

"Whoa, take it easy, man! Everyone's fine. She was alone and on her way back from the pharmacy on the worst night of that storm. Her kids were at the neighbor's."

Jason took a few deep breaths and commanded himself to stay calm. "What happened, anyway?"

"Oh, some guy hit her from behind and pushed her into a snowbank. I got called to the scene, so I took good care of her, wound up driving her home afterward. Man, it was good seeing her again—brought back a lot of memories. You got a cute niece and nephew there."

He'd driven her home? He'd met her kids? Across the room, Diane peeked out from her cubicle, then ducked back inside.

He lowered his voice and rubbed his forehead. "Well, I—I'm glad you responded to the call. Thanks for taking care of things."

"Hey, it was my pleasure. Like I told Rachel, if ever I get the chance to assist a beautiful damsel in distress, it makes my job worthwhile. We had a great talk. In fact, I'm taking her out for coffee tomorrow night."

"You—really? Tomorrow night, huh?" A prickly sensation of heat had him pulling at his collar.

"Yeah. I was thinking, you know, that it might be too soon to ask her, but I took the plunge and went for it."

"And she accepted."

"Yep." A silent pause filled the next five seconds. "Well, anyway, like I said, I've been thinking about you since I saw Rachel, so I thought I'd check up on you. Didn't I hear something a while back about you being engaged or something?"

"You may have, but that particular grapevine failed you. I guess Rachel didn't mention that I'd broken up with Candace?"

"Nope, 'fraid not. I got the feeling she doesn't see you very often. You, John, and I used to have some good times back in the day, 'member that? Rachel and I were talking about some of the wild stuff you used to do."

Jason forced a chuckle. "I sewed a few wild oats. I hope she mentioned how I've mellowed."

They talked for a few more minutes, Jason doing his best to remain calm and cordial. When the conversation finally winded down, they made an empty promise to meet up sometime and then said their farewells. If the Lord had been looking for an example of brotherly love in that moment, He surely would not have cited Jason Evans.

As soon as Jason hung up the phone, he pushed back in his chair, the legs scraping against the floor, stood up, and grabbed his coat.

"Where're you going?" Diane asked.

"Out for a bit."

"Is everything all right?"

"Yeah, all's ducky," he answered, throwing the door open wide and stepping out into the frigid air.

"What were you thinking, Rachel?"

"Johnny needed his medicine, Jason."

"And you couldn't have waited?"

"Would you rather I had waited and he'd ended up in the emergency room with an asthma attack?"

"You should have picked up his prescription before the storm."

"I didn't know a storm was coming."

"You must have been the only one in Michigan, then. It's winter, Rachel. You have to be prepared at all times."

"I'm not a Boy Scout," she said, trying to make light of the moment. She remembered the motto from when John and Jason had been Scouts.

"Be serious, Rachel. What if something had happened to you?"

She could admit it—she'd been secretly elated to see Jason's number show up on the caller ID. But his berating her decision to go out on the worst night possible put a damper on her joy. If anything, it irritated her to the heavens. He was not her guardian, and she was not his charge. She thought she'd made that clear on Thanksgiving night. *Thanksgiving night.* The night he'd kissed her. Passionately. And the night she'd told him they must never pursue a deeper relationship, lest they dishonor John's memory.

"Well, nothing happened to me. I'm fine; my van is fine, now that it's had a few minor repairs; and the kids are great. Everything's great," she said in spurts. Yes, she'd used sarcasm to get her point across, but at the moment, he deserved it.

"And what is this about you going on a date with Larry Rossini?"

Now she was put out—not only with him, but also with Larry. What had possessed him to call Jason, anyway? Had there been some hidden agenda on his mind, a need to check out how things stood between Jason and her? All she'd done was agree to have coffee with the man. "Gracious, news does travel fast, doesn't it?"

"It's that old grapevine, you know."

"Why are you so ticked?"

"I'm not," he blurted out, almost cutting her off. "But you could have called and told me about the accident. Why'd I have to hear it from someone outside the family? And another thing—isn't it a little early for you to be seeing other men?"

Ah, there it was. "That's a personal decision, different for every individual."

"Ah, so it's all right to see other men, just not your brother-in-law. Have you forgotten about our kiss?"

The mere mention of that event sent a shiver down her back. She took a calming breath and swallowed, measuring her next words with care. "And have you forgotten why we won't be doing that again?" When he didn't answer, she wondered for a moment if they'd lost their connection, but then she heard him quietly clear his throat. "All right, I'm sorry you had to hear about the accident from an 'outside source.' I'll be sure to inform you right away the next time someone rear-ends me—or I land in the hospital. I'm just kidding," she added with a giggle. She couldn't help it; Jason made her feel strange things, things better pushed to a back burner and stuffed under a lid or even laughed off with a pathetic joke.

"Where're you two meeting for coffee, anyway?" he asked, disregarding her silly remark.

"He's picking me up."

"Ah, so it is a date, then."

"No, it's coffee. There's a difference."

"Larry Rossini is not your type. Never has been."

"Well, thank you for that."

"In junior high, he got into a fistfight that earned him a weeklong suspension."

"Is that so? Did you spend the week in suspension with him?"

"Very funny."

"Well, regardless of what happened in his past, he's a state trooper now."

"A divorced one. Did he tell you that?"

"Of course."

"Oh."

"Jason, go back to work, would you? I'll see you on Christmas Day."

"No, you'll see me on December eighteenth—Johnny's party, remember? You can't uninvite me," he quickly put in.

She sighed and bit back a nagging smile. "All right, then, next week."

"If not before."

"Next week will suffice, Jay."

A noise like the low growl of a dog came across the line. "Don't go having too much fun tomorrow night. Luigi Rossini is Mexican-Italian."

She pinched the bridge of her nose and looked at her bare feet. The low-lying winter sun shone through the front window, casting a beam of light across her wood floor and revealing a layer of disregarded dust. One corner of the living room had been cleared more than a week ago to make space for a Christmas tree, but she'd dragged her feet in putting one up. It just sounded like too much work. "Huh? What is that supposed to mean, Mexican-Italian?"

"I have no idea. I'm just sayin'."

She couldn't help her sudden spill of laughter. "Oh, Jay, you are such a goof. Good-bye."

Still giggling to herself, she hung up the phone quietly and walked upstairs to check on Johnny.

On Friday night, she had a very pleasant evening with Larry Rossini. They shared lighthearted laughs at a cozy little corner booth in Rex's Diner while they chomped on juicy hamburgers and fries and sipped cola. Okay, so it ended up being a little more than "just coffee," but it was fun and relaxing. One thing was certain, though—after Larry walked her to the door and they said good night, Rachel realized she had no interest whatsoever in taking her relationship with Larry Rossini one step beyond friendship. He was nice enough, no longer the junior-high thug Jay made him out to be, but he'd been right. It was too soon for her to date again.

Or maybe it was just that Larry Rossini didn't turn her crank in quite the way Jay Evans did.

Allie Ferguson called the next morning and insisted on taking her to lunch, and Rachel regretfully turned her down. "I just left the kids with a sitter last night," she explained. "I can't desert them again today."

"What about dropping them off at your parents' or in-laws'?" Allie suggested. "Going to Grandma's house is never considered desertion."

"My mom has another commitment today, and Donna had them Wednesday night, when I went to grief group at church. I can't keep taking advantage of them."

"Well, shoot, something has to give. We need to get in some Christmas shopping together."

Ah, Christmas shopping. Last year, she'd failed to finish it after John's accident, and this year hadn't been much better—what a difference from her holiday shopping habits of earlier years. With Johnny's first birthday party only five days away, Rachel had no idea how or when she'd find the time to buy Christmas gifts for the kids, plus her parents, in-laws, and Tanna, not to mention Jay. They'd always exchanged gifts with him, with the exception of last year, and she supposed she would continue the tradition.

And then, there was the matter of that empty space in the corner, and their Christmas tree still sitting in some lot, waiting to be picked. There was simply too much to think about!

No sooner had she hung up the phone than it rang again. Thinking Allie had come up with another suggestion as to where to send the kids while they had lunch and shopped, she failed to check the caller ID before answering.

"Did Luigi behave himself last night?" said the familiar mellow voice. In an instant, her senses came alive, and she had to sit down to collect herself.

"He was very much a gentleman."

"So, where did you grab this cup of coffee?"

"Rex's Diner."

"That's not a coffee spot."

She couldn't get the smile off her face. "Was there something you needed, Jay?"

"I'm at my parents' house, and I was wondering if I could pop over to see my kids."

His kids? The presumptuous remark, which might have been met with indignation, instead gave her a brilliant idea. "You can babysit them, if you want. My friend Allie just called to invite me out for lunch and shopping, and I had to decline for lack of a sitter."

"Is that so? Well, you have one now."

Jason arrived fifteen minutes ahead of Allie, the infamous teacher with all the funny stories. He liked her on the spot for her quick wit, her pleasant smile, her obvious affection for Rachel, and her contagious enthusiasm. As soon as she walked through the door, Meagan leaped off his lap and ran to greet her, squealing with delight and engaging her in a chase throughout the first floor.

He'd be crazy to say he hadn't given Rachel a quick once-over when he'd come inside. Her blonde hair hung loosely, framing her beautiful face, with a bounce that indicated a fresh cut. She wore slim jeans and a pale-yellow fitted turtleneck sweater, its cling accentuating her soft curves, and she looked the picture of perfection, right down to her tan high-heeled boots. It'd taken every morsel of strength not to draw her into his arms, especially with those freshly glossed lips looking hungry for a kiss. But it was her hesitant smile and careful demeanor that kept him from it.

Lately, he'd been learning to surrender his irrefutable love for Rachel to God and asking Him to fill his heart with the love of Christ, instead. Yet, every time he prayed "Lord, I don't want to love her against Your wishes, so please take away these feelings if they're not from You," it seemed he loved her more, and so his garden of tender passions continued to grow, nurtured by the sense of peace the Lord returned to him.

Chapter 17

Where's your Christmas tree?" Jason asked Meagan as soon as the door closed behind Rachel and Allie. He'd noticed a box of ornaments and a tree stand in the corner between the fireplace and the front window but no sign of a tree.

"We don't have one," Meagan replied, putting on a glum face. "Mommy says she doesn't have time or gun-shun."

"No gumption, huh? What about you? Do you have gumption?"

With hands clasped at the top of her head, she did a couple of ballerina twirls, then paused to look at him, bright-eyed. "I don't know. Is gun-shun fun?"

He snatched up Johnny from his wobbly standing position at the coffee table and jostled him up and down. The little boy giggled with delight. "Oh, yeah, gumption's fun," he replied. "Tell me where your mommy keeps your coats and stuff. We have a Christmas tree to buy."

After bundling up the kids, a chore unto itself, he found Rachel's van keys hanging in their usual spot, got the kids buckled in their car seats, and set off for the nearest tree lot. Luckily, he found one not a mile away. A church group was selling trees in the parking lot. The pickings were slim, but the three of them managed to find a suitable fir tree with long, thin, soft needles, perfect for hanging ornaments because they wouldn't prick fingers. Getting it home would be another story, though, as he hadn't found any rope in Rachel's garage. With Johnny riding on his hip, it had been difficult to do a thorough search. So, after a little bit of pleading and playing the helpless uncle, he prompted one of the men selling trees to offer to follow him home in his pickup truck, tree in tow.

Setting up the tree was a cinch, as John had purchased the best kind of tree stand. All Jason had to do was trim the trunk at the base, then set the tree in place, make a few adjustments with a foot hoist to straighten it, tighten down a few clamps, and there she stood, as regal as a queen, reaching up toward the nine-foot ceiling.

He had no idea how Rachel would want the tree to look, but since she had no "gun-shun," as Meagan had put it, he figured however they decided to decorate it—with Meagan in charge, of course—would be fine. Rachel could make adjustments later if she wasn't happy with the result. The lights went on first. Several strands had burned out, but Jason didn't feel like bundling up the kids again and heading to the store to buy more. So, he made do with the few strings that did work.

Soon, the tree was sparsely lit and adorned with a multitude of strategically placed ornaments, most of them arranged in strange clusters among the lowest branches. Decorating wasn't his thing—it never had been—but doing it with Meagan while Johnny watched, draped in garland and playing with several plastic ornaments Jason had placed around him, made the task nothing short of enchanting. When they were finished, they stood back to admire their work, which, when inspected at close range, resembled the worst Charlie Brown tree Jason had ever set eyes on.

After cleaning up, Jason took a sleepy-eyed Johnny up to the nursery for a diaper change and an afternoon nap. The baby put up a regular fuss about having to settle down, but Meagan assured Jason that he "fussed like a trapped cat" every single day—probably an expression she'd borrowed from her mother. So, after giving the boy a friendly pat on the forehead, they walked out and quietly shut the door. After a minute, Johnny piped down, so they padded downstairs and headed for the kitchen to tackle another chore he'd never attempted before: baking Christmas cookies.

Meagan squealed with delight as he told her one silly knock-knock joke after another while rolling out cookie dough on the countertop to make various designs with the cutters he'd found stashed in a drawer. Hopefully, Rachel wouldn't mind that he'd scrounged through every cabinet before finally locating them or that he'd used up the frozen dough he'd found at the bottom of her freezer. He knew how to roll out dough only by calling up memories of his mom performing the task decades ago. Somehow, though, she'd made it look much easier than it really was, and more than once he was tempted to call and ask her to come over. But he decided against it. This was his and Meagan's day. Together, they would master the art of baking Christmas cookies.

"We're makin' a mess, aren't we, Uncle Jay?" Meagan said, wiping floury hands on her shirt.

"That's half the fun!" Jason looked at the floor, his own shirt, the countertop, and the wall. All he saw was flour.

"Is Mommy goin' to be mad?"

"Nah. We'll have it all cleaned up long before she gets home," he assured her, glancing at the clock on the wall and praying he was right. The oven timer buzzed, indicating that the first batch of cookies had finished baking. Wiping his flour-covered hands on his blue jeans and then grabbing a potholder, he slid the tray out of the oven. "Stand back and enjoy these golden specimens. Get a whiff of that glorious, magnificent scent, my dear."

"Can we eat one?"

"Well, what are they for, if not to eat? Let's allow them to cool for a few minutes. And we'll have just one, or we'll spoil our appetites before we get to the frosted ones."

The phone rang as he was setting the tray on the cooling rack. He threw off the oven mitt and pointed a finger at the gleeful Meagan. "Do not move, my fair maiden."

"Well, for goodness' sake, Jason, how are you?" He recognized the voice of Arlene Roberts, Rachel's mom. "I surely didn't expect to hear your voice, but I'm happy nonetheless. Are you visiting for the day?"

"Actually, I drove up to see my folks, then called Rachel to see if I could drop in and see the kids. She did me one better and offered to let me babysit while she and her friend Allie had lunch and went shopping. Your granddaughter has been keeping me pretty busy."

Arlene laughed. "She has enough energy to power a few lightbulbs, don't you think? What have you been doing?"

"Are you sure you want to know?"

She laughed. "More so now than ever."

He told her about their tree decorating adventure and the mountain of flour he stood in. "I'd offer to come help you, but I'm afraid I have plans," she said. "And, might I just add, 'Thank You, Lord'?" He joined in her laughter. "Well, don't let me keep you from your domestic chores. Just tell Rachel I called, would you? Nothing important; just checking up on her. I'm so happy to hear she's out with Allie for the day. Thank you for helping make that happen, Jay. You've been such a great friend to Rachel over the years, but especially now, and I just want you to know how much Mitch and I appreciate it. You're helping to fill a void in the kids' lives, as well, and we are so grateful."

He hadn't expected the compliment, but he was glad to take it. Nice to know there was someone in the family who thought his friendship with Rachel was a good thing. To keep the peace today, he hadn't mentioned anything to his dad about going to see Rachel and the kids. He'd merely bid his parents good-bye and said he'd see them next week at Johnny's first birthday party.

Rachel and Allie chatted nonstop on the way back from the mall after a successful afternoon of shopping, as evidenced by the bags they'd stashed in the trunk of Allie's Toyota Corolla. Rachel had made most of the purchases: a few toys for her children, a sweater and a bottle of nice perfume for her mother and Donna, new wallets and leather belts for her dad and Tom, a mall gift card and a necklace and earring set for Tanna, and, for Jason, a pair of leather gloves and a wool scarf. She'd debated whether to buy him a gift at all but somehow sensed that John would want her to. Whether Jason chose to reciprocate mattered little.

"You're sure you don't need anything else?" Allie asked Rachel as they drove along. "Wrapping paper? Tape? Ribbon? Christmas bags? An ice cream sundae?"

Rachel laughed. "I have plenty of wrapping supplies on hand, and I need a sundae right now about as much as I need a toothache. I'm still full from that slice of pie you talked me into today, and then that big hunk of fudge from the candy store. What are you trying to do to me?"

"Put a little meat on your bones. You don't eat near enough."

"I eat plenty," she countered. "But my two little personal trainers keep me burning calories faster than I can take them in."

"I hear you there. I spend my days chasing other people's kids, then come home and chase my own."

Drifts from the big snowfall still lined the city streets and clogged the intersections, but Allie maneuvered her car like a pro. "I'm glad you invited me, Al," Rachel said. "Thanks for helping me decide what to buy everyone. I hadn't felt up to shopping this year, but you actually made it lots of fun."

"What am I here for, my dear, if not to enhance your shopping experience?" Allie giggled. "It's nice that Jason volunteered his services so you and I could spend time together—and wonderful for your kids, his being involved in their lives. He seems like a great guy."

"He's...a good guy."

She felt Allie's eyes on her. "And handsome as heck. John was good-looking, too, of course," she quickly added. "For being brothers, though, you'd think they would have looked more alike."

"Tanna and I don't really look alike."

"Well, that's true. You're blonde, and she's got that beautiful, long brown hair. How often does Jason stop by?"

"As often as he can, I guess. He made himself scarce for almost eight months after the accident, but a little while ago, he started coming around again. He wants to connect with Meagan and Johnny more, and I think he's got it in his head that we're his charges. He's been doing odd jobs around the house and just seeing what he can do to make life easier for us."

"That's awesome. I wouldn't mind a handyman as fine-looking as he hanging around my house. I'd be manufacturing jobs left and right."

"I bet Rick would love that."

"Are you kidding? Anything to shorten his honey-do list."

They laughed, and Rachel changed the subject. "So, what do you and Rick have planned for the rest of the day?"

"Nothing special. We'll probably watch a movie after we put the kids to bed. What about you? You think Jason will hang around?"

"Jason? I have no idea."

Again, Allie's eyes wandered back and forth between the road ahead and Rachel.

"I don't think I just imagined something special in the way he looked at you, Rach."

She quirked her brows at her friend. "I don't know what you mean," she fibbed.

"Oh, pooh. Of course, you do. He's got something going on for you, sweetie. Are you going to tell me about it or leave me to my imagination?"

Drat! She hadn't wanted their conversation to come to this, but knowing Allie as she did, she realized there'd be no relief until she came clean. "Well, he has voiced some sort of feelings for me."

"Some *sort* of feelings? As in, more than brotherly?"

"I suppose, but it's ridiculous."

"Why do you say that?"

Rather than look at Allie, she turned to look out the window. "Because he's my brother-in-law, and the whole notion sounds preposterous."

"Not to me, it doesn't. Hey, in Old Testament times, widows married their husbands' brothers to carry on the family name. It happened all the time."

"Well, thank goodness we're living in the twenty-first century. How would you like to marry Rick's brother?"

"Ugh. Thank goodness he's taken," Allie said, snorting with a burst of laughter as she made the turn onto Westfield Lane.

Just the sight of Jason's Jeep in her driveway filled Rachel with a flutter of excitement. It also made her curious to know what he could possibly have done to keep her children occupied all day. Had he succeeded in putting Johnny down for his nap? Had he changed his diaper? Had he remembered about his bottle in the refrigerator and the jar of sweet potatoes on the kitchen counter? And what about Meagan? Had he thought to give her a proper snack? Oh, she wished now she'd have spent more time giving him directions. What kind of mother was she to leave her children with a man who knew next to nothing about taking care of children? Moreover, what kind of a disaster should she expect to walk in on after being gone for so many hours? She began to brace herself for the worst.

"Well, I'll be," Allie said as she pulled into the driveway. "Is that a mirage I'm looking at or an actual Christmas tree?"

Rachel lurched forward in her seat and stared at the front window. He'd actually gone out and found a tree to decorate? She tried to imagine even John taking that chore upon himself. Mouth agape, she scratched her temple and tried to speak.

"My stars in glory, girl, that man's a keeper."

Rachel rolled her eyes, thanked Allie again, and carried her purchases to the front porch. "Mommy! Mommy! Come see all that we did!" Meagan exclaimed when Rachel walked through the door.

The first thing Rachel noted was the tantalizing aroma floating out from the kitchen. Yes, she'd had a slice of pie and a piece of fudge that day, but the lingering smell of fresh-baked cookies never failed to tempt her. Her eyes met Jason's, then roved down to his rolled-up shirtsleeves, which revealed muscular forearms she had no business studying. But his shirt and arms alike bore sprinkles of flour and smudges of cookie dough, and the sight made her heart take an unexpected leap. Quickly, she crouched down to Meagan's level. "You'll have to tell me all about it, beginning with the Christmas tree."

For the next several minutes, Meagan talked nonstop, describing how the three of them had driven up the street and found the prettiest, straightest tree in all of Fairmount, and how Uncle Jay had made it stand as tall as a soldier. She then informed Rachel that she really needed to buy more lights, but she could wait till next year, because Uncle Jay said so. Next, she told how, after putting Johnny down for his nap, she and her uncle had found some cookie dough in the freezer and baked two batches of cookies using the special roller and the cookie cutters with the fun Christmas shapes. The best part, she said, was the frosting, which Uncle Jay had made with the little hand beater.

Rachel tried to hide her surprise. "You made frosting?" she asked, looking at Jason.

"Well, after I found the recipe online and then hunted down all the ingredients, including the food coloring. Hope you don't mind that I went through every one of your drawers looking for stuff."

"Not at all."

"It's a good thing you didn't come home half an hour ago, or the sight might have sent you into shock." When he gave her a slow, crooked grin, her heart jumped. *Sweet Lord*, she prayed, *is it possible I'm falling in love? Guard my heart, Father.*

Precious child, you must trust Me. As long as you give Me all of your heart, you can be certain I will keep it safe, came the whispered assurance.

Chapter 18

Most people Rachel knew had thrown elaborate parties for their babies' first birthdays. They'd ordered multitiered cakes, spent oodles of money on decorations, and invited friends and relatives from far and wide. Rachel had done the same for Meagan, but she had decided some time ago, considering John's absence, to keep Johnny's celebration a low-key affair for immediate family only. There would be many more birthdays and plenty of opportunities for big parties—just not this year. Besides, what did Johnny know or care about a birthday bash as long as he had his mommy, sister, grandparents, Aunt Tanna, and Uncle Jay—and his cake—close at hand?

As it turned out, he wasn't all that excited about the presents, but the colorfully wrapped boxes and festive bags with tufts of tissue paper sticking out of them surely caught his attention. He sat on the floor and giggled with delight at the sights and sounds of crackling paper and ribbons that came apart with the slightest tug, and everyone agreed that even had they stuffed the packages with newspaper, he still would have been as happy as a clam in the sand.

Rachel took great care not to pay Jason any special heed, and it appeared he had decided to do the same to her, exchanging only an occasional glance with her while sipping punch, eating cake and ice cream, or contributing to various conversations, most of which revolved around the children. Rachel couldn't help but watch him, though, when, after

Johnny had opened all his gifts, Jason tossed him and then Meagan into the air, spinning them around like tops until the roomful of adult onlookers felt dizzy, themselves. His hearty laughter and the giggles of her children mingled like fine music. Tanna joined in the fun, picking up whoever was waiting for Jay's attention, twirling and dancing as she sang some popular tune from the radio. In those moments, Rachel thought so much about John, wishing he were there to share in the joviality, wondering if he would have tossed the children playfully instead of Jay but reaching the conclusion that both brothers probably would have.

She could be sure of one thing: Jason loved her children, and, whether or not things ever worked out between them, he would surely insist on maintaining a relationship with Meagan and Johnny.

And she could never stand in his way and sustain a clear conscience.

Jason never had been a fan of crowds or malls, so holiday shopping ranked low on his list of favorite things to do. But, with Christmas just three days away, he had little choice but to join the thousands of other last-minute shoppers, the majority of which seemed to be men.

Armed with a list of ideas he'd compiled, with Diane's help, he made the rounds through the Traverse City Mall, beginning at the toy store for items for Meagan and Johnny, then going into several department stores in search of watches and perfume for Arlene, Tanna, and his mom, then the sporting goods store for new putters and golf balls for his dad and Mitch. Buying for Rachel was the toughest, as he wanted to get her something special and unique without going overboard or appearing too forward. Arms full, he stopped to gaze in the window of Parks Jewelers and saw a pair of earrings he thought she'd like. Yes, they were more expensive than what he'd just purchased for the other women in his life, including his own mom, but then Rachel had suffered the greatest loss. He told himself she deserved a little spoiling.

"May I help you, sir?" asked an attractive, middle-aged woman when he walked through the door.

"Yes, uh…I guess I'd like a closer look at those earrings you have on display."

Her eyes brightened. "Oh, the ones with the diamonds set in the small hearts? Aren't those pretty? Several men have asked to see them today, but, so far, no one's bought them. They're right here." She reached inside a glass case and carefully brought out the earrings, laying them on a piece of black velvet. The lights overhead made them shimmer and sparkle from every angle. Even with his limited knowledge about jewelry, Jason could tell that these had rare value. He bit his lower lip to keep from asking the price.

As if reading his mind, the saleswoman stated it, and he nearly dropped his jaw to his knees. "That's a bit much."

"Oh, but they're twenty-five percent off today," she said.

He perked up at that news. "Really?" He quickly calculated the sale price in his head.

As if reading his mind again, the saleswoman grabbed a nearby calculator and figured the total, including tax, and gave him a second to digest it. "Can I wrap these for you?"

Lord, what am I doing? Will she even accept the earrings? It suddenly occurred to him to purchase something else for her, as well—a new Bible, a candle, or some expensive lotion—and put the earrings away for a later time. On impulse, he said, "I'll take them, but could you wrap them in generic paper? They aren't necessary a Christmas gift."

She winked. "Foil and a pretty ribbon will do the trick."

On his way to the car, he hummed a familiar Christmas carol, trying to get beyond his disbelief at what he'd bought for Rachel. He'd never bought Candace anything quite as fine as those earrings, unless he counted the engagement ring he'd never put on her finger. The silly thing still sat in a box in his underwear drawer. He told himself that one of these days, he'd try to sell it online. Until then, though, he'd tuck the new earrings in the drawer next to the ring and then wait for the perfect opportunity to present them to her.

Lord, please let there be a perfect opportunity, he prayed.

"Mommy, how long till Christmas?"

"Not long now, sweetie." Rachel knelt at Meagan's bedside, having just completed their nighttime prayer. In the other room, Johnny slept soundly, while downstairs, the TV droned with some sitcom and embers crackled in the fireplace. As usual, Meagan was using every stalling tactic in the book to keep her mother kneeling at her side.

"Is it tomorrow?"

"No, darling, not tomorrow. It's two days after tomorrow."

"Is Daddy going to be watching us?"

Rarely did Meagan mention John anymore. Generally, if he came up in conversation, it was at Rachel's prompting. She so wanted to keep Meagan's memories fresh but knew with certainty how quickly they would fade. "I'm sure he will be, honey. He'll be smiling down on us and telling us not to be sad."

Meagan fingered the edge of her blanket thoughtfully. "Does he still love us?"

"Of course. He will never stop loving us. And we'll never stop loving him, either." She tenderly touched Meagan's nose with her index finger.

"Why did he have to leave us?" she asked, eyes squinting as she studied the ceiling.

Rachel felt like her heart was being squeezed. "I don't know, darling. There are many things in life we don't understand. What we do know is that God loves us and wants us to trust Him." Funny how just a couple of months ago, she might not have been able to give that response. Indeed, the Lord had been working to heal her wounded spirit.

"Is Daddy going to celebrate Christmas with Jesus?" Meagan asked in tender innocence.

"I'm sure he will. After all, it marks the day that Jesus was born. It would seem to me that all of heaven will celebrate."

"I love God," Meagan announced, her eyes round with sincerity.

"I know, honey. Me, too."

"I love Uncle Jason, too," she added as an afterthought, as if he and Jesus somehow belonged on the same plane.

Rachel stood and put her fingertips to Meagan's cheek. "You do, huh? Well, lucky for you, he loves you right back."

"I know. He tol' me."

Rachel's heart warmed to overflowing, and she got a little misty-eyed about the way Jay insisted on seeing her kids and providing a father figure for them, something even their grandfathers couldn't quite pull off. Why, just thinking about the cookie-baking episode and how he'd so selflessly given of his time that day made her feel all mushy inside. He hadn't hung around long afterward—after all, he'd come not to see her but to see the kids, as it should have been. So, why was it that she looked forward with eagerness to Christmas Day, when she knew he'd be at Tom and Donna's place? She berated herself for her seesaw emotions.

"I bet he's gonna buy me a present."

"You think so?" It would surprise her if he didn't.

"What did we buy Uncle Jay for Christmas?"

"We bought him a nice pair of leather gloves and a wool scarf."

She pondered that for a moment. "I thought just ladies weared scarves."

"No, men can wear them, too, especially on very cold days."

"Oh."

She leaned over to plant one last kiss on Meagan's cheek. "Sweet dreams, dearest. Go to sleep now."

Rachel sat at the kitchen table and read her Bible for about half an hour, sipping hot tea and nibbling on a Christmas cookie Jason had decorated. When she began to feel fatigued, she climbed the stairs to her room and suddenly found herself fighting off a wave of loneliness.

God, please fill this heart of empty longing. I don't want to love or need Jason; I just want my soul filled up with thoughts of You. Sometimes, I worry about my allegiance to John, Lord. Please keep John's memory fresh and alive in my heart, she prayed.

Do not fret, My child. I have everything under control. As I've said before, you must entrust your heart to Me. All at once, the words she'd just read from Philippians washed over her spirit:

Rejoice in the Lord always. Again I will say, rejoice! Let your gentleness be known to all men. The Lord is at hand. Be anxious for nothing, but in everything by prayer and supplication, with thanksgiving, let your requests be made known to God; and the peace of God, which surpasses all understanding, will guard your hearts and minds through Christ Jesus.

After washing her face, brushing her teeth, and running a comb through her hair, she walked to her closet to hang up her clothes. Not for the first time that day, she gazed up at the box of John's mementos, still sitting on its high shelf. She didn't feel prepared to look through it yet, but she decided she could at least bring it down. So, she nabbed a nearby stool, hoisted herself up, and lifted the heavy box from its resting place, surprised at how long she'd put off carrying out that one simple chore. She set the box down with a gentle thud on the floor beside her shoe rack, flipped off the closet light, and padded off to bed.

On Christmas morning, Rachel awoke in her old bedroom. She and the kids had spent the night at her folks' house after eating a leisurely supper, attending the five o'clock Christmas Eve church service, and coming home to have their own family celebration and gift exchange. They had opened gifts on Christmas Eve for as long as she could remember, a tradition that had begun when her parents had gotten married and spent Christmas mornings at their parents' homes, alternating between both sets each year.

Outside her window, large snowflakes fell steadily, piling powdery pillows on the already thick mounds that had collected. The distant sounds of Meagan's excited chatter and little Johnny's shrieks of joy prompted her to pull back her feathery comforter and sit up in bed. Goodness gracious! What time was it? And how had she come to sleep right through her own children's waking? Craning her neck to see the clock on the dresser, she was shocked to discover it was already 9:15. Quick as a cat's wink, she leaped out of bed and made for the shower down the hall.

"Mom, how could you have let me sleep so long?" she later asked at the table while sipping on a cup of hot tea in the cozy new robe her parents had given her the night before. Tanna lay sprawled on the floor, allowing Meagan and Johnny to climb all over her.

"Honey, you obviously needed it. I mean, when was the last time you actually slept in?"

"Maybe in high school?" Rachel said with a giggle.

"My point, exactly. You and the kids ought to spend the night more often just so you can catch up on sleep from time to time."

"Yeah, you should," Tanna chimed in. "It's fun waking up to these little goobers."

"I'll second that," her father said, coming into the kitchen to refill his coffee cup, yesterday's newspaper folded under his arm.

"Don't tempt me with such an offer, you guys. I'm liable to take you up on it."

"Well, you should. Single parenting is one of the hardest jobs in the world," her mother said, pushing her chair back and rising to gather up what few dishes remained on the table. Rachel stood up to help her. "You sit back down, young lady. This is Christmas, and I intend to spend the morning spoiling you."

Ah, she thought as she eased herself back into her seat, I *could get used to this*.

At noon, they left for the Evanses' home, Rachel's parents toting all the gifts and food items in their own car, Tanna riding with the kids and her. No sooner did she start her van than Johnny fell asleep, thumb in mouth, the other hand clinging to his favorite blanket. Rounding the turn to her in-laws' home, she spotted Jason's black Jeep. On cue, her heart skipped a beat.

As if he'd been watching for them, Jason came bounding down the porch steps as soon as the two cars pulled into the drive. "Merry Christmas, everyone!" he shouted as they all started climbing out of the vehicles. Clad in blue jeans and a collarless grey pullover sweater with three buttons down the front, he looked the picture of masculinity, his broad shoulders nearly bursting out of the cotton fabric of his shirt. His dark hair looked recently trimmed, despite the few stubborn strands falling over his forehead and shielding one thick eyebrow.

"Merry Christmas!" Rachel called in return, feeling oddly shy. *He is my brother-in-law, nothing more*, she reminded herself as she opened the rear door, where Johnny slept on, oblivious.

"Mind if I get him?" Jason asked in a low voice.

"Be my guest," she said.

Their sides brushed as he slipped past her to release Johnny from his car seat.

"I'll get Meaggie," offered Tanna.

"Hey, Tanna! Merry Christmas!" Jason said.

"Merry Christmas to you, too!"

"Uncle Jay, it's Christmas!" Meagan bellowed as Tanna hefted her out of her seat.

"It is? I wonder if Santa brought you anything?"

"He did! I saw him at the mall, and he promised he would."

And so it went, everyone shouting greetings and carrying in children, dishes, packages, and diaper bags. As Rachel walked across the threshold and into the warmth of her in-laws' home, Jason turned and met her eyes for the first time, her sleeping son in his arms, and in their dark depths, she saw something like a promise.

⁂

As usual, Jason had to force his eyes to settle on someone or something other than Rachel, lest people grow suspicious of his mounting feelings for her. Man, he could feast his eyes on her all day if he didn't think folks would notice.

Her soft, blonde hair fell in waves around her slender neck, and he wanted to take a handful and give it a playful tug—anything to get her attention.

But she skillfully avoided looking his way most of the afternoon, tending to her children instead. She helped them at the dinner table; later, while they opened their gifts, she insisted that Meagan stop to thank each person for her present despite her impatience to move on to the next package. He found it enchanting to watch how she mothered them. One thing Rachel had was grit, and the more he knew her, the more it showed.

He'd been watching his dad throughout the day. While he'd put on a smile most of the time and engaged in conversation, even echoing Mitch's appreciative expression for the new putters Jason had given them, he still showed a reserved side that put Jason somewhat on edge. He longed to know what went on inside his head and why he was never able to reach his dad's core. The suspicion that his dad blamed him for John's death haunted him continually, and Christmas Day was no exception. Some days, he wanted to shake the man, but today wouldn't do.

"I like the gloves and scarf a lot," Jason whispered in Rachel's ear. He'd finally caught her standing alone in the living room poring over some family photos on the fireplace mantel, and he had the courage to sneak up behind her. She gave a little jolt. "Didn't mean to scare you," he added.

"That's okay." She turned and gave him a tentative smile. "I'm glad you like them. I didn't know if…you know."

"They're perfect. The gloves fit me—like a glove."

She giggled. "You're silly. Oh, and I love the lotion and candle—and the beautiful Bible. You bought more for me than you should have."

She would really think that if she knew what was in the back of his sock drawer!

"Thanks for what you wrote in the Bible, too."

It had taken him more time to figure out what to write on the dedication page of that Bible than it had to make all his Christmas purchases. He'd finally written something as simple as: "May the words in this book be a light to your path. Love, Jay." It was the "Love, Jay" part he'd pondered for minutes on end, wondering how she'd construe it. He took the word seriously and actually had wanted to write, "I love you. Jay." Of course, he'd ended up taking the safe, common-sense route.

"You're welcome." Her eyes went back to the photos, and he found himself moving closer to catch her scent. He allowed himself to study the photos he hadn't perused in several months—some shots of John and him as young boys, several of them with their parents, and others of the family after Rachel had joined it. The most recent picture of the whole family had been taken last Thanksgiving, just two days before their fateful trip. Rachel was big with baby, and Meagan clung to her daddy's leg. Jason noticed that John's arm was not around Rachel, as it usually was in photos of them, and he wondered if the rift between them had been to blame. It sobered him to realize he'd inadvertently played a role in that argument.

"I don't like that picture," Rachel said of the very photo he'd been studying. "I wish Mom would take it down."

"It was the last one of all of us, honey," he said, touching her elbow, the endearment slipping out almost automatically. "Besides, Mom wouldn't understand your asking her to do that. Someday you'll come to appreciate the photo."

"I hope so." She swallowed and shook her head. "There should be one of John and me with both the kids."

His heart ached for her. "I know." It was all he could think to say. The wounds were still so fresh.

"Sometimes it feels like only yesterday," she said, absently fingering the edge of her sweater sleeve.

"I know what you mean."

"I hate that I can't always bring his face into view in my head. Sometimes I actually have to look at his picture before it comes to me."

"That's normal. I have to do the same."

He reached an arm up and drew her close. Blessedly, she didn't object; rather, she leaned into his strength. "You need to think about all the positive, good things you guys shared, you know that? And stop dwelling on those last few days."

"I know you're right, but it's hard. My mind keeps going back to our argument."

"John wouldn't want that, honey. I guarantee he's not giving it any thought. You two had a great marriage, Rach—a strong, loving, rock-solid marriage. Let your heart and mind dwell on that."

She raised her face so that their eyes met, their breaths mingled. Had they not been discussing her marriage, the moment might have been considered intimate. "You're right, of course."

They ceased talking and turned to look out the window, his arm still around her, their backs to the entryway. Snowflakes fell like giant petals, floating, drifting downward, lending tranquil comfort to the moment.

"Rachel, you know I want to be more to you than just a friend," Jason ventured to say. Now wasn't the time, of course, but out it came, anyway. To his great surprise, she didn't jump away as from a feral fox.

"And you know that cannot be, Jay," she said calmly. "We've been over this already."

He brought his chin to rest atop her head. "Do you know you're on my mind around the clock?"

"Well, you'll have to chase me back out, then."

"Impossible."

"Start dating again."

"Also out of the question." He kept his chin on her head, nearly eating up her delicious scent. She breathed out, long and slow. "You're not planning to see Luigi again, are you?"

"I don't know."

"That wasn't the answer I wanted to hear, Rach. If you're going to see him, you may as well see me."

"Maybe I don't want to," she said stiffly, then gave a playful chuckle. The tiniest hint of flirtation floated through the air.

In the living room, coverage of a football game blared on the TV. Meagan's shrill screams filled the house as she played chase with Tanna. Jason assumed that the moms were still yakking in the kitchen, if the clatter of pots and pans and the occasional outburst of female laughter were any indication. He was so glad his mom had a friend in Arlene Roberts, as she had a true gift for loving people and helping them forget about their woes. As for the men, the last he knew, his dad had enticed Mitch to check out his new snowblower.

Finding Rachel impossible to resist, he took her by the shoulders and pivoted her to face him, capturing her almond-shaped blue eyes with his. "I don't believe that," he whispered. "I kissed you, remember? And you kissed me back."

"Don't remind me." She pressed her rosy lips together in a stubborn pout, making him want to laugh.

"You're worried what people will think, aren't you?"

She shrugged. "Not especially."

He bent closer. "Fibber."

"Oh, stop it."

"What happens between us in the future is strictly between you, me, and God, Rach. No one else."

"Yes, but what if—?"

"What's between you and God?" Jason's dad stood in the doorway, his face twisted with palpable anger, his arms folded tightly across his chest.

Rachel leaped back, startled, and Jason would have been lying to say the intrusion hadn't caught him off guard, too. He dropped his hands to his sides like a boy caught trying to sneak a cookie before supper and tried to think of a proper response.

"Well?" his dad roared. "What have you got to say for yourselves? And, so help me, I want the truth!"

Chapter 19

Dad, calm down, would you? I don't know what you think is happening, but Rachel and I were having a private discussion."

"There'll be no private anythings going on in my home, do you hear?"

The women came rushing into the room, as did Mitch, Tanna, and even Meagan. Johnny's whereabouts should have been of greater concern to Rachel, but, right now, preserving her dignity seemed paramount.

The insinuation behind his remark sickened her, and she felt beads of sweat pop out on her forehead like dewdrops on a windowpane.

"Absolutely nothing is going on, Dad," Jason said through gritted teeth, his face about as red as a beet.

"You kids can't fool me," Tom said, seething. "Don't you have a conscience? Your brother hasn't been dead much longer than a year, and already you're trying to steal his wife."

Gasps arose all around the room. "Tom!" Donna spat with a shudder.

"That's insane," Jay said, his body shaking. "It's a little hard to steal a dead man's wife."

"Why, you...." Tom started coming at Jason, but Rachel's dad stepped between them.

"Stop it, both of you," he said, firmly yet not loudly. "You need to calm down."

Donna started whimpering. "This is Christmas. I—I wanted us to—have a good day." Rachel's mom quickly stepped up and wrapped a comforting arm around her, even as her eyes slanted with worry.

"Mom." Jason pinched the bridge of his nose and breathed loudly "I'm so sorry, but there are obviously things Dad needs to get off his chest. Maybe you should go in the other room."

Pulling back her narrow shoulders, she set her gaze on Tom. "I'm not going anywhere. If something needs saying, then say it, Thomas Evans. But I won't have harsh words spoken here." She looked back at Jason to add, "Not from either of you." It was about the sternest Rachel had ever seen Donna with her husband and son.

"Tanna, please take Meagan out of the room," Rachel's mom said quietly. Rachel felt like a fool for not having been the one to suggest it.

Tom looked at Donna, his mouth set in a straight line. "Your son has some explaining to do, Mother."

"What are you talking about?" Jason asked, his brow furrowed with confusion. "You come barging in on Rachel and me while we're having a conversation, demand to know what we're talking about, make insinuating remarks that we're being less than decent in your house, accuse me of stealing my brother's wife, and then you want me to do the explaining? I think you have this backwards."

Tom squinted with displeasure as his eyes roved from Jason to Rachel, and his pointed glare made a shiver run the length of her body. That's when the realization hit that her father-in-law resented her as much as he did his living son. She felt the urge to retch but held herself together by biting down on her lip and taking several bitter-tasting swallows.

"You betrayed your brother," Tom said, his tone low and piercingly cold.

It seemed like even the walls let out a gasp. "How did I do that?" Jason asked, his tenor surprisingly controlled.

"John told me everything."

Jason shook his head. "I'm not following you. I have no idea what kind of misconceptions John filled your head with, Dad, but I can tell you one thing—there was nothing, absolutely nothing, going on between Rachel and me. There never was."

Tom's jaw jutted out and his chest swelled. "So, you deny kissing his wife?"

"Thomas Evans, that's enough of this nonsense. Stop it this instant," Donna said before wilting into a nearby chair.

"Listen, Tom. This has gone far enough," Rachel's dad said. Mitch Roberts never had been one for confrontations, but Rachel swore he looked near to busting through his skin. She just couldn't tell with whom he was angriest: Tom, Jason, or, worse, her.

"Ask him to deny it, Mother."

Slowly, Donna turned to look at Jason. "Mom, I did not kiss John's wife."

Rachel struggled to find something to say in his defense but instead prayed, *Dear God, please mend these hurts.*

Donna's face showed mild skepticism.

"Sheesh, I can't believe we're even having this conversation!" Jason blurted out. He turned to Rachel and cast her a sorrowful look. "I'm sorry, Rachel," he said in a softer voice, then gazed about the room. "The truth is, I kissed Rachel a week or so before she married John—before she was his wife. There, it's out in the open. Are you happy, Dad? Yes, we kissed, but that marked the end of our flirtation. She loved John, and she made it very clear to me that night with a cold slap to the face." He looked at his feet, then back at Rachel. "I resent that you dragged that out of me, Dad. It was private information." This he said with eyes focused solely on her.

"That may be, son, but that little bit of 'private information'"—he made quotation marks in the air with his index and middle fingers—"led to John's death. John was distraught when he left for Colorado. He was convinced his own brother had been deceiving him."

"Well, he was wrong, then."

"And you were arguing on the mountain."

"Yep. John was acting his old, bullheaded self."

By now, tears were streaming down Rachel's cheeks, but nobody seemed to notice, caught up as they were in the sordid saga. "Would you two just stop it?" she finally spoke up. "I'm in the room, you know."

"Rachel," Jay whispered.

"Just stop." She raised a shaky hand. "If anyone's to blame here, I am, all right?" She looked Tom in the eyes. "I didn't need to tell my husband about that kiss, but, God help me, John and I were fighting, and I thought I had to find a way to lash out at him, so it slipped off my tongue. Do I regret it? Of course, I do. Is there any way I can change history? Oh, God, I wish I could!" she wailed. "That kiss—it haunted me. I felt guilty for years. A part of me just wanted to put the whole thing to rest. Unfortunately, it backfired."

"It's all right, honey," her mom assured her, leaving Donna's side to comfort her daughter. "It's over. Done."

"Yes, it certainly is," Donna said, coming to join them. "I don't want to hear another word about it. Shame on you, Tom Evans, for even bringing it up."

Rachel looked at her father-in-law through blurry eyes. "They were standing next to each other in my living room, all cozy and sweet-like," he muttered.

"Oh, for crying out loud, so what?" Donna almost exploded. "They are adults and don't need babysitting. For what it's worth, Tom, this is my living room, too. And another thing—don't you think it's time you stopped placing the blame for John's death on Jay? You've lost one son already. Don't tell me you want to lose them both."

At her poignant remark, Tom put on a sheepish expression. But if anyone expected an apology, Rachel was betting they wouldn't get one tonight.

Suddenly, a racket from the other room had all gazes turned in the same direction.

Rachel's heart stopped when she recognized the scream as Johnny's and realized it was no ordinary scream.

When they got to the hospital, the emergency room was aflutter with doctors, nurses, and technicians, all busy with their own cases and seemingly oblivious to the wails of the latest arrival.

Jason stood at the nurses' station, waving his arms demonstratively. Rachel hoped he would get someone to help them, but the woman seated at the desk merely nodded her head and pointed at a chair in the waiting area.

"She said to be patient," Jason said upon returning. "An X-ray technician will be along shortly."

"Well, can't they at least give us a room?" Tom said, pausing in his pacing. "I'll go ask."

"No point, Dad. They've already said every bed is full. Besides, if his arm is broken, as the doctor who checked him suspected, then he's better off sitting bundled up tight to Rachel's side so his arm won't move. We can sit as easily here as in some cramped room."

Her father-in-law went mum after that, apparently seeing the logic in Jason's words. Rachel sat on a straight-backed chair with her pounding head against the wall, both moms on either side of her whispering soothing words to Johnny and trying their best to keep him entertained. Rachel suspected it wasn't so much from pain that her baby fussed and cried as from the utter confinement forced upon him. She was thankful that her dad had taken Tanna and Meagan back to her parents' house to await a call with the prognosis. The last thing she needed was a whining four-year-old asking when they could go home. *What a way to spend the remainder of Christmas Day*, she mused.

A fresh tear rolled down her cheek. Drat! She thought she'd finally gotten them under control.

"Honey, don't worry," her mother whispered. "Everything will work out just fine. We've prayed and asked the Lord to take control here, and so now it's up to us to trust."

"I do trust Him," she moaned, "but that doesn't wash away my guilt for being so neglectful. I knew he wasn't in the room with us, but I never should have assumed he was safe."

"None of us knew that door was open, sweetheart," Donna said. "We all should have been watching."

"He's my responsibility," Rachel argued between sobs.

"You had no way of knowing, Rach," Jason offered from the chair where he'd planted himself. He sat with his hands clasped on his knees and both heels bouncing up and down. Tom had disappeared down a long corridor, probably in search of a restroom or vending machine. "In the back of my mind, I thought Tanna was watching him."

"And Tanna thought someone else had taken him upstairs to the crib," Donna said.

"It was just an accident, one of those things that sometimes happen, and no one's to blame," Jason said.

"I'm a terrible mother," Rachel muttered, choking back more tears.

"No, don't say that," her mom chided her.

"Mrs. Evans?" The entire ER waiting room hushed momentarily as Rachel and Donna both raised their heads.

"Yes?" Rachel replied.

The nurse gave her a polite, practiced smile. "You may bring your baby back now."

Jason stood, prepared to accompany her, but she stopped him. "I want our moms to come with me."

He nodded and sat down again.

"Where'd everybody go?" Jason's dad asked, plopping into a chair two seats down from him and draping his coat across the chair between them.

"Somebody came for Johnny. Rachel wanted Mom and Arlene to go with her."

"Ah, understandable."

They sat in awkward silence. All around them, folks waited for assistance with coughs, cut fingers, and other matters Jason didn't care to think about. He prayed for Johnny's safety and thanked the Lord that nothing more serious had resulted from his tumble down the stairs. Besides his misshapen arm, he didn't appear to have suffered any other injuries, save for a couple of minor scratches and a slight bruise in the temple area. Poor Rachel had been beside herself if not hysterical when they'd discovered Johnny at the bottom of the stairs, screaming to shake the rafters—a sure sign he was okay, Jason had immediately ruled. She blamed herself, of course, which he regretted. Accidents simply happened, especially where active toddlers were concerned.

Out of the corner of his eye, Jason could see his dad two chairs over, looking down and twiddling his thumbs. He was still seething at his dad's accusation, but he knew it was the biblical thing to do to make amends before putting his head to the pillow that evening.

"Dad—"

"Son, I—"

"I'll go first," Jason said.

"No, let me," his dad insisted.

He gave a slow nod and waited. Suddenly, his mind meandered back to the days of fishing out on Lake Michigan with his dad and John—back when life was so simple, so sparklingly perfect. Why did it have to take so many cruel twists and turns?

"About tonight—back at the house. I said some things, and, well, I'm sorry 'bout all of it."

Jason couldn't remember the last time he'd heard an apology come out of his dad's mouth. "It's all right. I said some things I regret, myself."

"I taught you boys how to ski, you know."

Of all the things he might have expected his dad to say next, that wasn't one of them.

"Please don't go blaming yourself now."

His dad shook his head. "None of this would've happened if I hadn't given you boys that first lesson. I'm as much to blame for the accident as anyone."

"Don't go there. The world is full of what ifs and shoulda, coulda, wouldas. It's not worth it. Let's just forget about tonight, okay?"

"You're a very good skier, you know," he went on. "The sooner you get back on the slopes, the better off you'll be. Kind of like that ol' horse saying."

He couldn't believe the turn they'd taken. *Thank You, Lord.* "Maybe next year."

They kept their faces down. "I was pretty good in my day, you remember that?" he mumbled. Jason glanced up and saw a half-grin.

"Yeah, I remember. You taught us well. I bet you'd still handle those slopes with ease. Why'd you quit?"

"Aw, the arthritis, you know, and that bum knee I had surgery on a couple years back. Anymore, I can't take the extreme cold."

"You used to say you didn't even notice it."

He chuckled. "Weren't those the days?"

They sat in silence again, each pondering his own thoughts.

"Sorry 'bout that big guilt trip I laid on you," his dad blurted out. "Deep down, I knew it wasn't your fault. I really did. I guess this whole thing with John Jr. puts stuff into perspective. If I hadn't been actin' so all-fired stupid, probably none of this would've happened."

"Who knows? Like I said to Rachel, accidents just happen. Sometimes, we just have no control over them. She's really carrying the blame right now, saying she should have been keeping a better eye on him."

"She didn't know the door to the basement was open."

"Try to tell her that."

"I will," he muttered. "Among other things."

The nurse called another patient's name, and an old fellow got up and hobbled to the back with her. It suddenly occurred to Jason how important family—especially his dad—was to him. "I love you, Dad," he said.

"Me too, son. Me, too." It wasn't "I love you back," but it would do. "She's a fine woman, that Rachel," he quietly added.

Jason's head shot up, and he saw a full-blown smile on his dad's face. "I'd have to agree," he said.

Several hours later, Jason carried a sleeping Johnny with a tiny plaster cast on his arm out to Rachel's car and carefully placed him in his car seat. "Can you manage the buckle?" she asked from behind. "Be careful with his arm. Here's his blanket."

With a few minor hitches, he secured him, tucked his blanket snugly under his chin, pleased with himself when the baby didn't so much as flutter an eyelid. "Done," he said, sliding the door closed. It was already warming up inside the van, thanks to Arlene, who had brought it around and had been idling there for several minutes with the heater blazing.

He took Rachel's arm and walked with her to the passenger side. "Merry Christmas, huh?"

She gave a slow, tired smile. "Some Christmas."

"Next year will be better."

She nodded. "Good night, Jay."

He stopped her with his hand when she went for the door handle. It was no time for small talk, what with the air so cold they could see their breaths. "I just have to say this, Rachel. I love you."

"Oh, Jason, I wish you wouldn't say—"

"Sorry, but it was coming out one way or the other. My dad and I talked in the waiting room, by the way. It was good."

"I'm happy for you, but you and I—it's not going to work, Jay. Please, just get that clear in your head."

He gave a half shake of his head and shrugged. "Not going to happen. I'll call you soon."

Her eyes rolled heavenward. "You're impossible, Jay."

He raised a hand in surrender. "Guilty." Then, he opened her door and leaned down to say good night to Arlene as Rachel climbed inside the van. He pushed the door closed and watched until they disappeared from view.

Chapter 20

The days that followed were busy ones for Rachel. Between visits to the doctor's office to keep a close watch on Johnny's arm and carting the kids along on trips to the grocery store, the post office, the bank, and her parents' house, there were no dull moments. The hardest thing of all was trying to keep John Jr. somewhat contained. Since learning to walk, all he'd wanted to do was explore every inch of the house, which is exactly what had gotten him into trouble at her in-laws' house on Christmas Day. If anything else happened to warrant a trip to the ER, she'd be getting calls from child protective services, for sure!

On the day after Christmas, Tom Evans had showed up on her doorstep under the pretense of checking on Johnny. However, before leaving, he'd offered a humble apology for his behavior on Christmas Day. "I don't blame you for anything," he'd said. "Never have, never will. Just want to make that good and clear. I think I must've misconstrued some things John said to me 'bout that kiss between you and Jason, and it wasn't my business to interfere, anyway, so I hope you'll forgive me for what I said yesterday."

"Don't worry about it, Dad. It's over and done with, and I'm putting it straight out of my head."

"I feel somewhat to blame for what happened to John Jr. If I hadn't been carryin' on so, folks would've had their eyes on his comings and goings."

"It's not your fault, Dad. I'm his mother, and I should have had my eyes out for him. But, aside from that, everything that happened at the house probably needed to be said so that you could put some worries to rest. I'm just sorry John unloaded on you before he left for Colorado. Then again, I guess he felt he needed to talk to someone, so he chose you. I still regret that he and I didn't settle things before he left. That's why the Bible says not to let the sun go down on your anger. Unsettled arguments live on and on."

He'd pulled at his chin and nodded. "I've been askin' God to forgive me for my bitter heart."

That had comforted her. "And He has."

On his way out, he'd paused at the door and turned. "As for what happens between you and Jason, well, that's you-all's business—I just want you to know that."

"I appreciate that, but nothing's going to happen, so you can relax."

"Both my sons are fine boys. I need to let my younger one know that more often."

She'd leaned forward and kissed him on the cheek. "Yes, you do." When he'd left, she'd watched him out her front window and thought she detected a lighter step to his gait.

Jason had called three days later, making simple conversation about his busy work schedule and asking about Johnny and Meagan for the first few minutes until she'd told him his dad had stopped by to see her. "He did? What'd he say?"

"He apologized," she'd answered. "And I accepted it."

"That's great. He's coming around, Rach. I don't see anything holding us back, do you?"

"Jason." *How can I make him understand I'm not ready to commit to a relationship?* she'd wondered. Yes, it did appear the doors of acceptance had started opening, but with that knowledge came a newfound fear. Perhaps *fear* was too mild a word. *Panic* seemed more fitting. Whatever feelings she had for Jason remained clouded over by grief and loss, and she would not give her heart to another man, Jason or anyone else, until she'd finished trudging through the valleys. The act of trying to sort through all those emotions put her in a real frenzy.

For years, even while she'd been married to John, she'd felt a special bond with Jason. After all, they'd been good friends since childhood. But that had been the extent of it. She'd fallen in love with John. Sure, folks had teased her, saying she ought to marry them both, considering how the three of them seemed to be attached at the hip. Yet it had been John's stubborn love, his relentless chase, and his driving passion to make her his bride that had finally won her over, heart and soul.

Oh, Jason had pursued her, too, but not with the same diligence, and not when he had a dozen other girls all vying for his attention. Besides, the chemistry between them had changed entirely once she'd given her heart to John. Still, she may have harbored an ounce of attraction to Jay, even after accepting John's proposal. For how else could she explain having allowed that foolish kiss?

But did she love Jason today in the way he claimed to love her? Before, she'd been able to lean on the pretext that people wouldn't approve—Tom, in particular. But now that he'd started backing down and apologized for intruding, her wall of protection had begun to crumble.

"I'll give you time, Rachel. Just tell me how much you need."

"Jason, I don't know how much time I need. In fact, it may be that no amount of time is enough for me to be ready to be in a relationship again."

"You were ready for Luigi."

"Would you stop? That was just a casual date."

"I thought you said that wasn't a date."

She'd rolled her eyes. "Oh, Jason. What am I going to do with you?"

"How about going out with me on New Year's Eve?"

"No."

"I'll take you to the same diner Luigi took you to."

"He would hate it if he knew you were calling him Luigi."

"I know."

"I can't, Jay. Don't ask me again, okay?" Silence had answered her on the other end. "I'm sorry, but it's the way it has to be for now."

"Well, I guess I can accept that, but only because 'for now' gives me hope that this is just temporary."

So, here it was, December 31, and Rachel found herself treading in a pool of regret for having no one with whom to spend New Year's Eve. There was simply no satisfying her. She could almost imagine John teasing her with the words, "Fickle woman!"

"Mommy!" Meagan bellowed with joy when Rachel entered the living room armed with dusting spray and cloth, followed by Johnny with a stuffed toy in hand. In less than a week, he'd learned to maneuver himself quite efficiently with one arm in a cast. "Watch me jump!" she announced, leaping from a chair onto the sofa. Johnny let out a whoop as he toddled past her. Before Rachel had a chance to protest, she jumped to another chair and then another.

"Meagan, get down. We don't jump on the furniture. You know better than that."

"Mommy, these are not furnitures," she insisted. "These are my boats and my island."

"Really?" Rachel paused, intrigued by her daughter's imagination.

"Yes!" Meagan spread both arms out. "This room is the ocean, and the mean sharks are trying to get me, so I have to jump really high from this flower boat to this striped boat. And that"—she pointed at the sofa—"is the island, where it's safe."

"I see. Well, why don't you just leap on back to that island and stay there?"

Meagan's eyes went round as the sun as she exclaimed, "'Cause I like to live dangerously! How else you gonna learn not to be scared of stuff?"

Suddenly stricken, she found herself sitting down in one of Meagan's "boats." How was it that a four-year-old could pack such a punch with so few words? Was that what she herself had been doing then? Staying put where life was safe? Never straying too far from shore, to places where she'd be expected to take risks and trust God with the unknown?

Around five thirty that afternoon, the doorbell sounded. Rachel had just popped in a movie for Meagan, set up a little TV tray for her with a sandwich, applesauce, and some chocolate milk, and put Johnny in his high chair with a few crackers and a sippy cup of juice. It wasn't the norm, but with its being New Year's Eve, she figured they would have a little party.

She looked out the window to see a police cruiser in her driveway. The sight unsettled her until she looked through the front window and then flung wide the door. "Larry! For goodness' sake, I wasn't expecting you."

A hangdog expression whisked across his face. "I know, I'm sorry. Am I interrupting something important?"

"No, no, of course not. Come in."

He stepped over the threshold and wiped his feet on the welcome mat. She closed the door behind him and felt a gust of icy air curl around her ankles. "Well, I was just on some routine calls in the neighborhood and thought I'd stop by to say hello," he said, removing his hat. "Everything going well for you?"

"Yes, thanks." It was nice of him to think of her, although she wouldn't have said she appreciated his dropping in unannounced. "Um...." She clasped her hands. "Happy New Year."

He smiled and nodded. "Same to you!"

Meagan was hanging over the back of the sofa, staring at them. "Are you that police guy who brought Mommy over to Mrs. Bronson's house?"

"Well, I certainly am. Good memory. You're Meagan, right? Do you remember my name?"

"No, but I remember your gun."

"Oh, well." He chuckled and glanced at Rachel. "Most kids do remember that."

"This is Mr. Rossini, Meagan. Can you say hi?"

"Hi," she said, still gawking. The Disney movie played on, unwatched.

Larry gave a hurried look around and spotted Johnny across the room. "Well, for cryin' out loud, what happened to that little guy?"

"He broked his arm at my grammy's house on Christmas night when he falled down the stairs," Meagan informed him.

"Aw, poor kid," Larry said.

"Mommy wasn't watching him."

Rachel would have loved to have some sort of magic button to turn Meagan on and off at the appropriate times. She looked at Larry and shook her head. "She's right, unfortunately."

"Hey, don't worry. My mom tells me I fell down a flight of stairs in my walker when I was about one. Stuff happens, you know? 'Course, my brother never fails to bring that up every so often, saying it's the reason my brain's slow."

He meant it as a joke, of course, so Rachel laughed.

He looked at Johnny. "He doesn't look like he's suffering too bad."

"No, he's doing fine. So, you said you were making some routine calls?" She hadn't invited him to sit down and decided to keep it that way for now.

He turned his hat in his hands and shifted his weight. "Yes—let's see, a domestic dispute a few streets over, a shoplifting incident at the Shop-N-Save, and a little fender bender over on Harvey Street."

"Ah, those fender benders," she said with a chuckle.

"Yeah, hope you haven't had any more run-ins with SUVs."

The phone rang, and, as usual, Meagan leaped at the chance to answer it. "Where's the phone?" she asked.

Rachel looked around. "It's not on the hook? Oh, I think I walked off with it. Check the kitchen, Meaggie. And be polite when you answer. Remember the rules!"

On the one hand, she was glad to see Meagan bound out of the room momentarily. On the other hand, one never quite knew what might pop out of her mouth. She prayed that the caller would be her mother.

"I shouldn't keep you, really," Larry said, shifting his weight again. "Like I said, I was just in the neighborhood, and...uh, decided to stop by. Um, I was wondering...would you maybe care to go out again sometime?"

❧

"Uncle Jay!" Meagan's excited greeting did its usual job of boosting his ego. "Are you coming to my house? We're watchin' a Disney movie tonight."

"Sounds fun. I might do that. Is your mommy available for me to talk to?"

"Uh-uh. She gots company."

"She does? Who is it?"

"Some police guy. Mr. Rosy, or something like that."

"Mr. Rosy." He let that piece of information sink in, and, as it did, his stomach soured. "You mean, Mr. Rossini?"

"I guess. He has a big gun on his belt. He bringed her home that night of the big snow and we went over to Mrs. Bronson's house and played games an' stuff. Mr. Rosy took Mommy on a date after that." She giggled. "He prolly likes her."

Why, that lowlife. "What's he doing there now?" He felt like a bum trying to finagle answers out of a four-year-old.

"I don't know. They're laughing and talking."

Inside, he seethed. She would turn down a date with him on New Year's Eve and accept one with Luigi Rossini? "Want me to tell Mommy you called?"

"No; could you please tell her I want to talk to her?"

"'Kay. Mommy!" she bellowed. He held the phone away from his ear.

"Hello, Jay," came Rachel's voice a few seconds later.

"Luigi's there? Let me talk to him."

"What? Absolutely not."

Of course, he had no idea what he'd say to a guy with a gun. He might politely ask him to leave his girl alone, but then, he had to remind himself he had no claim on her. Good grief! How could he possibly compete with someone like Luigi Rossini, a strapping, masculine cop? "What's he doing there on New Year's Eve? I suppose you're going to tell me you're planning to ring in the New Year with him."

"I—"

"And you find him attractive."

"I think he's very nice-looking, yes."

"Well, this is just great, Rachel. I go and bare my heart to you, and you turn around and rip it to shreds."

"Jason, if you could just hear yourself—"

"I just told Meagan I might come over and watch a Disney movie with her."

"And I already told you I had plans for New Year's Eve."

"No, you didn't mention plans. You simply turned me down."

"Jay, listen. I—you need to give me some space, all right?"

"So you can fill it up with Rossini?"

"Jay, I'm hanging up now. I will talk to you another day when you're a little calmer and less insane."

Argh! He could string Rossini up by the neck—if he could find a rope big enough to fit around it. If he recalled correctly, Rossini was no dwarf.

God, what's happening to me? I'm losing my mind over a woman!

Before he had the chance to put in another word, he heard a click on the other end. In all his born days, he could not dredge up a single memory of a woman ever hanging up on him.

Larry stayed another half hour or so before bidding Rachel good-bye, and when they parted, they did so strictly as friends, she making it clear she wasn't ready to date and he graciously accepting that fact. Now, if she could just convince another man she knew to cooperate in the same fashion. Clearly, she just did not know her own heart right now, only that it felt muddled.

As she got ready for bed that night after tucking her kids in, she prayed, "God, show me Your ways. If I am to love again, please give me peace and assurance that I am following Your plans and purposes for my family. Sometimes, I am so afraid of what the future holds."

"There is no fear in love; but perfect love casts out fear, because fear involves torment. But he who fears has not been made perfect in love."

She recognized the words from fourth chapter of 1 John, having read them that very morning during her quiet time.

Do you love Me, child?

Yes, Lord.

Then trust Me to reveal Myself to you and guide you down each winding path. Love Me first, and everything else will follow accordingly.

She switched on her radio and turned the knob to her favorite Christian music station. Words of hope rang out over the airwaves like cool, soothing liquid sliding down a parched throat. She flung herself onto the bed and indulged in a moment of rest and reflection. Staring up at the ceiling and then closing her eyes briefly, she allowed the music to permeate her soul. After a while, she rose and went to her closet to put on her pajamas. And that's when she saw it— John's box of mementos on the floor beside her shoe rack.

Was tonight the night to delve into it? "Happy New Year," she muttered to herself.

Bending down, she gripped one end of the box and dragged it out of the closet to the middle of her bedroom. The possibility of investigating its contents had long felt like intruding on John's very thoughts, for amid his personal items like watches, old photos, files, financial papers, college essays, and books were also his journals and diaries. An easy flick of the wrist and a light tugging motion would have the lid off in no time. Rachel took a deep breath to gather courage, then lifted it off with trembling hands and let her eyes slowly take in the sight—beginning with a silver-framed 5 × 7 photo from their wedding day lying right on top.

When eleven o'clock rolled around, Jason thought he might go crazy with worry over Rachel. Had she enjoyed spending the evening with Luigi the lowlife? He couldn't conceive that she had much in common with the former high school athlete-turned-cop. Actually, Larry Rossini wasn't a lowlife at all, but the fact that he had eyes for Rachel made him less than likable in Jason's eyes.

His memories of Larry were not necessarily those of a mild-mannered schoolboy. If anything, he'd been wild, but then, who was he to talk? He'd given his parents plenty of headaches in his day. As teens, Jason and John had always liked Larry and even spent a lot of time with him. He and John had exchanged wit and wisdom on the debate team and served jointly on student council; he and Jason had shared athletic equipment and played team sports together. Even so, their friendships had never gone much deeper than that. Larry's family was entirely different from theirs. Having been raised by a single mom who brought home her fair share of male friends, Larry would often complain about not wanting to go home at night, particularly when his mother's latest beau came calling. So, Jason's mom had made the living room couch available to him for as often as he needed it. Too bad Jason didn't have a little more of his mom's goodwill.

He was sprawled on his parents' sofa in his running shorts, chomping on Doritos and sipping cola, his bare legs outstretched across the coffee table, trying to avoid the wet ring formed on the glass surface by his tumbler. Were his mom awake, she would have had his hide. The TV remote lay idly in his hands, his fingers punching random numbers. It seemed that every show focused on the approaching midnight hour. Times Square revealed hundreds of thousands of celebrants, and non-network stations played old movies and sitcom reruns.

"You're still awake?" His mom's quiet voice interrupted his musings. Instinctively, his bare feet hit the floor. Amazing how the years had failed to slow his automatic response at being caught with his feet on the coffee table. She laughed. "For goodness' sake, Jay, I didn't mean to startle you." She moved into the room and plopped lazily into the chair across from him, drawing her well-worn housecoat snugly around her while balancing a toeless slipper on one foot, her graying brown hair mussed from lying down. He'd intended to go back to his place tonight, but after talking to Rachel earlier, he'd decided to stay at his parents and then call her first thing in the morning to find out how her date with Luigi had gone. Maybe he'd even go over there to ask her in person.

"I didn't expect you to be up and about. You come out here to watch the ball drop?"

She chuckled. "Hardly. That kind of thing doesn't interest me. Just came out to check on you and maybe get a drink of water. Want anything?"

He shook his head and leaned back against the sofa cushion, careful to keep his feet square on the floor. "Still checking up on me, are you?" He pointed the remote at the TV to flick it off. Moments with his mom were more meaningful than listening to some senseless monologue or ridiculous sitcom.

"Once a mom, always a mom. When I look at you, I don't always see a thirty-year-old man."

"Really?"

She smiled. "Sometimes, I see that little five-year-old skipping down the sidewalk on his first day of kindergarten, backpack almost too much to handle. And, sometimes, I see a junior high boy trying to find his identity, making mistakes along the way, falling, and brushing himself off before regaining his balance and going on his way." She looked at the low-burning flame in the gas fireplace. "And then, there are times when I see the grown man I'm just so proud of, I think my buttons will burst."

"Mom." He didn't know what else to say.

"Your dad feels the same, you know. He just has a harder time expressing it."

He paused before responding. "Speaking of Dad, why has he always been so hard on me? And don't tell me it's just my point of view. It's been obvious over the years."

She gave a heavy sigh. "Oh, I don't know. Maybe you're just a little too much like him—stubborn and usually right. I think"—she scratched her temple and seemed to weigh her words—"in some ways, he's jealous of you."

"What? Jealous of his own son?"

"Well, maybe I chose the wrong word. I do know this: your dad always regretted never earning a college degree. His parents were so poor, they couldn't rub two pennies together, and he never did raise enough on his own for tuition."

"What about student loans? Need-based scholarships?"

"You know what a miser your dad is. He never believed in debt—not even for college."

That much was true. While John and Jason had both held jobs to help with their books, tuition, and room and board, their dad had scraped the bottom of his savings account every year so they wouldn't have to take out loans. Jason wondered if he'd ever once thanked him for making that sacrifice.

"He always wanted the best for you boys. Maybe he tried living out his dreams through you, to a degree."

"He's done well in his job with the postal service. He should be proud of himself for his accomplishments."

"I've told him that many times, always thanked him for being a great provider."

"John always knew from the beginning what he wanted out of life. Dad liked that. I was too erratic, too impulsive. I can imagine how I drove Dad nuts. You, as well."

"You kept me on my knees," she said with a tiny spurt of laughter. "I never doubted for a minute that you would come around, though, and my prayer was always that God would keep you safe until that day. Thank the Lord He did." She paused, as if hesitating, then added, "And John was not a perfect son, honey."

"Pretty near perfect."

She glanced at her watch. "I thought you might have gone to Rachel's tonight." The abrupt change in topics indicated how very difficult it still was for her to talk about her deceased son. "You can't fool me, honey. I've seen the way you look at her."

"I'm still not convinced Dad approves."

"This has nothing to do with your dad's approval."

"I guess it doesn't matter one way or the other, anyway. She still sees me as just her brother-in-law."

"I think it goes deeper, honey, but she needs time. You need to respect that."

"She spent this evening with Larry Rossini."

"Larry Rossini? He's a policeman now, isn't he? I'm pleased to hear he's made something of his life. I just had no idea Rachel—"

"Me, neither. She's making me crazy, Mom."

"Now, don't go worrying yourself over some little innocent date with Larry Rossini. If God wants this relationship to happen between you two, it will come to fruition in its time."

He knew she was right. He pulled his big frame from the sofa and sauntered over to his mom. "Happy New Year,

Mom." He bent and kissed her warm cheek. "I'll see you in the morning. Thanks for tonight."

She patted the side of his face. "You sleep good, son," she said.

And for the span of a few seconds, he slipped back into that little boy skin as he padded off to his childhood bedroom.

Chapter 21

Bright sunlight peeked in through a slit in the blinds, creating an arc of colorful light that bounced across Rachel's bedroom ceiling. She forced her eyes open to its brilliance. They were crusted over from tears she'd freely shed in the night, and so opening them was difficult. She rubbed at the corners and noted the golden ray of light coming in from outside. Apparently, the snow had stopped, and now the sun's glow created perfect images of glistening diamonds on the windowsill. In those wee hours, she thanked the Lord for His love and faithfulness and for the promise of spring after a long and dreary winter season. It would come, just as surely as her wounded heart would heal.

Slowly, she turned her head to look at John's box of mementos, which now held no more mysteries. Strewn about were old yearbooks, faded letters, school papers, and notebooks containing facts and figures that he had memorized for his debate team tournaments. There were a couple of trophies, an old book of poems, some of which had been marked and underlined, and the brown, leather-bound Bible he'd received from his parents as a high school graduation present. He had used it from then until Rachel had bought him a new one several Christmases ago. She'd thumbed through the featherlight pages and read over passages he'd highlighted over time.

There were childhood photo albums, a small box of pictures he'd never organized, and several journals he'd kept over the years that she'd never before found the courage to read. Shifting under the covers, she swept a hand across the thin layer of paper she'd been holding on to when she'd finally drifted off to sleep. It was a love letter from her husband, one he'd never given to her. Perhaps he'd meant to wait till that perfect moment. She read it now for at least the dozenth time.

My love, words cannot possibly express how grateful I am that you chose me as your life partner. I am swept away with wonder every time I think of it. I was struck by something C. S. Lewis wrote in *The Four Loves* to describe love as a great risk. He said, in essence, that to love is to be vulnerable. If you love something—anything—your heart will be hurt and might even get broken. If you want to guard it and keep it in one piece, you can't give it to anyone, not even a pet. You must avoid filling it with any enjoyable activities and should instead lock it up in a safe, selfish place. But in that place—a coffin, an airless casket—it will change. It won't get broken, but it will become unbreakable, impregnable, beyond redemption. To love, you must be vulnerable. Being vulnerable with you is easy, as you are so thoughtful and careful not to hurt me. Yet, even if you were to take my heart and run it through a shredder, my life would still be richer for having loved you.

The moment I first laid eyes on you at Harvest Community Church, my little seven-year-old heart did a flip. Your golden tendrils seemed to stretch clear to the bottom of your back; your dancing blue eyes matched the summer sky. You see, even then, I knew a real beauty when I spotted one.

Unfortunately, my younger brother had designs on you, as well. But I let him have it in the kisser a time or two until he finally got the hint that you would one day be mine. We certainly had our moments all through school, didn't we? Your trying to decide whom to choose, Jason or me. Thank you for making me the victor! One day I hope my brother will forgive me. (Ha!)

The day you said "I do" was the day I realized my full purpose in life. God put us here to worship and honor Him, and marrying you made that easier for me to do. In you, I saw purity, honesty, and goodness. Your love and worship of the God who created and designed us to love each other made loving and honoring Him all the more natural. Thank you, my darling wife. I sometimes wonder what our children will be like. I hope they wear your smile and inherit your sweetness. God knows they'll be better off if He patterns them from your blueprint!

Sometimes I think you will outlive me, although I can never pinpoint why I have that notion. If you do, remember me with devotion, but don't waste time living in my memory, Rachel. Instead, live to make a divine difference in someone else's life. Give of yourself and perhaps even love again, if God so wills it. Now, this may sound strange to you, but I'd truly approve of you marrying my brother if he were available. (And why I wrote such an idiotic thing is beyond me! A twinge of jealousy just came over me.) The truth is, it is hard to imagine you with anyone else but Jay, probably because we spent so much time laughing, running, joking, playing, crying, and eating together. Remember the forts we built out behind Mr. Frandsen's property? And the dead snake we buried, followed by the pact we made to never walk over that grave as long as we lived? And do you remember that time I first kissed your cheek on our back porch and then ran into the house out of sheer embarrassment? What were we, twelve and ten?

We had no idea what it was to have a care back then, did we? Oh, I love the innocence of childhood play. If only we could turn back time. Or not. I think perhaps it's best to always live in the moments God gives us—with hearts of gratitude and joy.

Now the question: Why did I write this, and will I actually give it to you or put it to rest? I believe I'll ponder it for a while, maybe stick it in "my box."

I am forever yours, my love, no matter what the future holds.

John

Tears rolled down Rachel's cheeks as she carefully re-folded the paper along its original creases. John must have written it shortly after they'd married, for they obviously hadn't had Meagan yet. She was amazed by the irony—his haunting notion that he would leave this earth ahead of her; his declaration, albeit in jest, that he would approve of her falling in love again with no one but his own brother; his hint at future children. The funny thing was, most people did say that Meagan and Johnny favored her in looks and personalities.

The phone rang, and she picked it up before it sounded again, not wanting it to wake the children. Wiping at her tears, she willed strength into her voice.

"Hello?"

"How was your date with Luigi?"

Her heart leaped, and she reveled for a moment in the sound of Jason's voice before her pulse settled down again. "You couldn't say hello before asking?"

"Hello. How was your date?" He sounded snappish.

"Happy New Year, Mr. Crank." A wisp of a smile tickled the corners of her mouth. The clock registered 7:30. Had he been stewing all night? The very thought made her want to giggle. Should she put him out of his misery?

"Same to you. So, what did you two do, anyway? Did you get a babysitter? Did he give you a New Year's kiss? Don't even tell me he did, Rachel."

"Larry Rossini is a gentleman, Jay—a fine one, which is more than I can say for some men I know."

"He used to be a party-going crazy man."

"And you would know that because you were with him at these parties, correct?"

"I've changed. Has he?"

"I couldn't really say. We didn't talk that much."

"You didn't talk? Well, what did you do, then?"

"Um, let's see here—"

"Rachel, I'm going a little crazy with jealousy. I don't care how much of a gentleman you may think he is; he's still a man."

"Brothers-in-law are not usually crazy with jealousy, Jay."

"I wish you'd quit reminding me how we're related, Rachel Kay."

An unexpected giggle erupted, and it suddenly occurred to her that besides Allie, he was about the only other person she could name who truly made her laugh.

"All right, all right. If you must know, I didn't go out with Larry Rossini last night. He stayed for about half an hour, we had a nice visit, and then he left. End of story."

"Really? But I thought you said—"

"Meagan told you he was here, and you jumped to the conclusion that he was taking me out."

"Oh." A hush settled for a moment. "Well, why didn't you just say so? I could have come over, and then neither one of us would have been alone."

"I wasn't alone," she put in. "I have my kids, and that's all I need. Of course, they were in bed long before midnight."

"Well, then—"

"I didn't feel like celebrating, Jason. Instead, I went through a bunch of John's things, so, in a sense, I spent the evening with him. It was nice." This she said with all sincerity.

"What sort of things? Clothes? Books? Tools?"

"Old letters, notebooks, trophies, stuff from high school and college, some photographs."

"Sentimental stuff."

"You could call it that."

"Did you cry?"

"Of course."

"Aw, Rach, I wish I could have been there with you. I miss him, too. I wonder if you know how much."

Her bubbling giggle from a few seconds ago vanished with another emergent tear. "I know, Jay. He was your brother."

"But he was your husband."

"Yes, and a dear one."

Silence hovered like a hawk. "I guess that's it, then." His tone sounded suddenly resigned.

"What do you mean?"

"You're never going to let him go, are you? Every time you look at me, you'll think of him."

"Jason." How could she refute him?

"Whenever winters roll around, you'll think about the accident and look at me with accusing eyes."

"No, I won't. I don't—" His ~~words~~ stung to her toes, though, because there was something in them that rang true.

"No matter how hard I try to help you forget, you never will."

"Of course, I won't forget. And, Jason, it's not your job to make me. I've told you many times I'm not your charge. You can't fight my battles for me. That's a job for God and me together. And here's something else. You won't like it, but I'm going to say it, anyway."

"What?"

She gulped and fingered the down comforter, pulling it up to her chin. "Sometimes, I think you believe you love me because of the guilt you still hold inside. You feel that if you could just take care of the kids and me, then you'd somehow make up for John's death."

"You know, Rachel, you are normally a very bright and intelligent young woman, and I'll even go so far as to say you're right on most things. But on this, you completely missed your mark. I have no doubt whatsoever about my feelings for you. I won't express them again, though, until I think you want to hear them."

The peculiar cloud that hung between them thickened, threatening the fragile bond holding them together.

"Can I stop by to pick up Meagan today? I promised her last week that I'd set aside some time to come play with her, and I don't want to let her down. You could have her all ready to go so I wouldn't need to linger long at your place. I can drop her back home after an hour or so. I might take her to a park if you bundle her up good."

What exactly was he saying? That he didn't want to see her? "You don't have to do that, Jason. I mean, I can bring her over to your folks' house."

"No, I'll just stop by to get her, if you don't mind. What do you say I come by around eleven?"

An uncomfortable lump formed in her throat. "I'll make sure she's ready."

"I'm glad we talked, Rachel. At least I know better where I stand and what I have to do."

Blinking back more tears, she asked with croaky voice, "What do you mean, you know what you have to do?"

"I think it's clear. I have to let you go," he stated firmly. "You're right; I can't be responsible for healing your pain any more than you can fix mine. And who am I to stand in the way of God's divine work?" Why did it suddenly feel like her lungs had caught fire? "I'll do my best to honor your wishes and stay away. I'll still try to see the kids as much as I can, though—if that's okay. You can bring them over to my parents' house before I get there. I'll have Mom let you know when I'm coming. How does that sound?"

Horrid. "Fine."

"Okay, so I'll stop by around eleven for Meaggie. You'll have her bundled up, right?"

"Yes."

"Good, I'll see you then."

Why did he have to sound so calm about the whole thing? If she had it straight in her head, he was saying good-bye to her, in a sense. She felt sort of like an old coat he'd suddenly decided to discard. Oh, that brat!

He hung up the receiver without so much as a good-bye. She should have been relieved, shouldn't she? After all, hadn't she discouraged him from pursuing her? Hadn't she even rebuked him for declaring his love for her? Time. Space. That's what the two of them needed, she'd told him.

So, why was it that she felt backed up against a wall— alone, devastated, and more miserable than ever before?

For the next fifteen minutes, she allowed herself another good cry. Only this time, the tears fell for a different reason. *Oh, Father God, show me Your ways. Lead me in the path I should go. Erase the clouds of confusion that obliterate Your face, that keep me from hearing Your voice and receiving Your guidance.*

And in those quiet moments, before waking her children to begin another day, she let His love wash over her weary bones.

Jason had no choice but to back off. Until now, he'd been too accessible. Rachel wasn't ready to receive his love—might never be, in fact, and he finally stopped denying the truth. Hearing her talk about going through John's mementos made him realize afresh how deep her wounds still were—and why would he have expected it to be otherwise? He must have been kidding himself to think he could make her love him. She still had pictures of John all over the house. His coat still hung in the hall closet—he'd seen it a few weeks ago. Her heart was still too fragile to love again, and, even if she reached the point of giving it away again, it might not be to him. Hard as it was to admit, he had to face the facts. January 1 seemed as good a day as any to start the process of letting go.

I have to do it. I have no choice, he told himself. "Now, Lord, help me keep my word to myself, to Rachel, and to You," he muttered under his breath.

His dad padded out in his worn slippers, pajama pants, and T-shirt just as Jason stuffed his cell phone into his hip pocket. "Did I hear you talking to someone?" he asked.

"I was checking with Rachel to see if I could spend some time with Meagan today. Thought I'd take her sledding."

His dad nodded and poured himself a cup of coffee. "Rachel's not going?"

"Nope. This is strictly a Meagan morning. Besides, Johnny's arm—you know." No way would he be spilling the beans about his conversation with Rachel.

"Meaggie'll like that. She needs a man in her life."

"She's got you and Mitch, too."

"True, but you're the one with all the energy," his dad said, bringing his mug to his lips and looking over the rim at Jason. He took a sip and lowered it. "Take her to Ridgemont. That's a great hill. I used to take you boys there, remember?"

"You know I do." Memories of Ridgemont ran deep.

His dad grinned, took another sip of coffee and gazed out through the window over the sink. "You boys used to whoop and holler all the way down that hill. You'd stand up and try all kinds of daredevil tricks when you were only about five and seven. Your mom would've had my hide if she'd known I let you pull those stunts. That's when I knew I had to start teaching you the basics of skiing. Turned out you were both excellent, but you probably had more natural talent than John and me put together."

Was his dad actually praising him? Jason walked to the cabinet for a mug, poured himself a cup of black brew, and waited to see if the compliments would continue.

"Yep. As you know, your grandpap taught me. Back then, we didn't have access to the ski slopes we do today, just little hills, but it was enough to get the ski bug in my blood. Pap taught me to love the outdoors."

"So, that's where you get it from, except you're into fishing and hunting, too, and that's not me."

"Well, everybody's different, I s'pose." His face went into reflective mode. "I know I compared you and John. Never meant to, but your mom brought that to my attention the other day. I'm sorry for placing blame and showing favoritism."

"You already apologized, Dad. No need to go over it again."

"I know, I know, but I suspect there were times I thought you could've done a little better in school and such. You made a few choices out in the world your mom and I didn't approve of, and...I don't know. I just wanted the best for both you boys."

What he was trying to say was that John had been the more academic and better-behaved of the two but that he was sorry for comparing them. Jason would take it. He stepped closer and gave his dad a slight punch in the arm. "You and Mom did good by us, Dad. Your prayers paid off."

"Well, your mom spent more time on her knees than me. I just stood at the window and watched for your car, hoping you'd miss the mailbox on your way in."

"Oh, man! Sorry I brought you guys so much grief. Thank God for His protective grace."

His dad puffed out his whiskered cheeks and whistled. "You aren't kiddin'. He had to come up with an extra measure of it for you."

They chuckled, and, as they continued sipping their coffee, Jason said a silent prayer of thanks to God for restoring their relationship.

At eleven o'clock, Jason pulled up at Rachel's and saw the pathetic path she had shoveled down the driveway and along the sidewalk. His first thought was to ask why she hadn't used John's snowblower, but then he reminded himself that she wasn't his responsibility. She had to get by without his interference. Moreover, what she couldn't do on her own, she could hire somebody to do—if she could get past her stubbornness.

She answered the door after the first ring of the doorbell, Meagan right on her heels and jumping with glee at the sight of him. He kept his hands deep in his pockets to fight the temptation to pull the woman into his arms. "Uncle Jay, you came!" Meagan shouted as she wrapped his legs in a bear hug.

"Well, of course I came, sugar plum. I keep my promises." He tapped her on the nose, taking care to avoid any undue eye contact with Rachel. So far, so good. "You ready?"

"Yep! Look, I even gots my snow pants on. Mommy said to wait till you got here to put on my coat."

"That was wise." He kept his eyes trained on the child as she scampered into the dining room and grabbed her coat, which was draped over a chair. Across the room, Johnny stood, teetering, at the table, still not terribly sure-footed but doing well for a kid with a cast on his arm. "He's holding his own, I see."

"Oh, Johnny? Yes, he is," Rachel said with a practiced smile. "I can't let my eyes wander off him for a second, though, or something ends up toppling, either him or a piece of furniture."

They both laughed, albeit with a touch of discomfort. Clearly, their phone conversation earlier that morning had made some sort of an impact on her. He just wasn't quite sure what kind.

She stood in the doorway, and he couldn't imagine she wasn't freezing-cold. Still, she held her ground and didn't invite him in—not that he expected her to.

"I suppose you saw what a rotten job of shoveling I did," she suddenly blurted out.

"What? No, not at all. Well, I guess I did wonder why you didn't use the blower."

"It quit working."

"Oh." On the tip of his tongue was an offer to have a look at it when he returned Meagan, but he resisted. "You should probably take it to a repair shop. Ask your dad or mine to suggest someone reputable."

"I—I plan to do that. Thanks."

"Coming, Meaggie?" he asked, still avoiding eye contact at all costs. Oh, man, he hated this strained awkwardness.

"Yep!" Meagan came bounding into the room, oblivious to any disharmony between her mother and uncle. "Mommy, do my mittens."

Rachel quickly bent down to stuff a mitten onto each of Meagan's hands, then put a kiss on one of her rosy cheeks before zipping up her coat. "You have fun with Uncle Jay, and mind your manners, okay?"

"Does she have to?" Jason asked, his first attempt that day to make her laugh.

She forced a smile and gave her daughter a little push toward the door. "You guys have fun."

"Oh, we will! Won't we, Uncle Jay?"

Finally, he let his gaze rest on Rachel's oval face and her big, blue eyes, which looked damp in the corners.

"I'll have her back in no time."

She forced another smile and looked down. "Great. Did you…uh, want me to fix some soup or something for when you get back? Um…you could take it to go, if you'd like."

Soup to go? "Oh, no, don't bother, but thanks. I'll take Meaggie to her favorite restaurant after we finish sledding. I mean, if it's all right with you."

"Sledding?" Meagan let out a whoop.

Rachel nodded. "Well, okay. I'll see you when you get back, then."

"I'll just drop her off in the driveway. I'll give a little honk. How's that?"

"A honk. Oh."

He wished he had a hidden camera in his jacket lapel to catch her shocked expression. No doubt about it, he'd caught her off guard with his laissez-faire manner.

Good. She needed to realize he'd meant business when he'd promised her time and space. Apparently, she didn't need him, and he planned to give her plenty of time to reassure herself of that fact.

Chapter 22

In the days and weeks that followed, Rachel fell into a routine of sorts. After the holidays, Meagan's preschool resumed, and Rachel and three other mothers of children in Meagan's class set up a car pool. This eliminated the need to get Johnny all bundled up every time Meagan had to go to school. However, on the days when it was Rachel's turn to drive, it also meant carting five children, including Johnny, to school and back. More times than she could count, Rachel thanked God for the brilliant engineer who'd invented the minivan.

Sharing the responsibility of transportation with the other mothers also offered her the opportunity to stay at home some days, freeing her to complete a few household tasks while her daughter was in school and Johnny napped. And she had even more time to herself and for Johnny when Meagan started attending class four times a week instead of three. Her teacher, Mrs. Beasley, had identified her as a precocious, fast-learning, outgoing student, and she'd suggested the expanded schedule as a way to provide more stimulating opportunities. Already Meagan had begun associating letters and numbers, and the extra day allowed the teacher more time for individual support. At first, Rachel hadn't welcomed the idea, not wishing to push her daughter unnecessarily. But, when Allie Ferguson had encouraged her, claiming Meagan needed to be challenged, she'd gone along with it.

Another change came about when Allie and Rachel joined a women's Bible study at church. Feeling ready to branch out, Rachel had decided to leave the grief group, which met on the same night as the Bible study. Weeks ago, she hadn't been prepared to leave the grief group behind and launch into a study where most of the women were happily married, save for a few divorcées, older widows, and happy-to-be single ladies. But, since then, something had helped her turn the corner on her insecurities and fears. Maybe it was the realization that she'd made it through the year of "firsts" without John and survived. Regardless of the reason, it felt as if day by day, sometimes even moment by moment, she was gaining back a tiny portion of her identity, discovering afresh who she was apart from her husband and coming to believe that perhaps—just perhaps—she would make it through her second year of widowhood, as well.

The Bible study focused on living a Christ-centered life. It involved daily readings, which forced Rachel to be more disciplined about delving into God's Word routinely. As a result, she began to develop a closer walk with the Lord. She enjoyed making new friendships and reading her Bible, the one Jason had given her for Christmas. Life held so many uncertainties, but, lately, she'd been more aware than ever of God's faithful love and unfailing grace. Yes, she still battled loneliness, but she'd been learning some new methods to pull herself more quickly out of the depths of despair.

Though she shouldn't have expected it or even hoped for it, she'd been almost certain that Jason would have called her by now. But then, maybe he'd been waiting for her to make the first move. Things between them were shaky at best. On New Year's Day, when he'd told her he was ready to cool things for a while, he'd had a certain air of aloofness about him. Even now, she couldn't be sure how to interpret his rationale. Had he intended it to be a final good-bye, a "Never mind; I didn't mean it when I said I loved you"?

She couldn't bear the thought of not seeing him on a regular basis, even if that would contradict what she'd asked of him. But even Meagan had started noticing his absence, inquiring as to when he planned to come again— and asking if she could call him. Of course, Rachel had denied her request, fearing Jason might think the idea had been hers. Oh, the whole matter threw her into a state of perplexity. On the one hand, she wanted to see him, and on the other, she knew doing so might encourage the profound feelings of affection she refused to admit even existed. Besides, how could she allow her heart to entertain so deep a feeling when she'd already decided that doing so would dishonor her husband's memory?

Then came a Friday afternoon in early February. Rachel had just picked up Meagan and three other four-year-olds from preschool and made the rounds to their respective homes. Between them and Johnny, the car had been abuzz with childish chatter, giggles, and something close to mayhem. Now, the quietness of home was a welcome and pleasant relief, despite Meaggie's ongoing drivel and Johnny's constant whining. His lunch was over, and she had only to change his diaper and put him down for his nap.

"And then, Miss Beasley said that I could have a treat, 'cause I was the one who had the bestest writing," Meagan said, running into Rachel's back end when she bent to retrieve the baby's stuffed lion and toss it into the toy bin.

"*Mrs.* Beasley," Rachel corrected her gently. "She's married, remember? So, you had good handwriting today?"

"The bestest in the class."

"The best."

"I know."

"What else happened today?" she asked, trying to be attentive, even though she had dinner to plan, Bible study reading to finish, and vacuuming to do. She bent to pick up another toy.

"Nothing. Oh, 'cept Robert, that loud boy, made a face at me today. Miss—uh, *Mrs.* Beasley says it's because he likes me. Blech!" Meagan screwed up her mouth in a comical way, and Rachel couldn't help but laugh.

"Let's go upstairs so I can change dirty-diaper boy. You can keep talking." Rachel swept her son into her arms and headed for the stairs, Meagan scampering ahead of her.

"So, this Robert," Rachel said in the nursery while removing Johnny's diaper and wincing at the odor. "Besides liking you, as Mrs. Beasley says, what other reason might he have had for making a face at you?"

"I dunno. Maybe 'cause I did a little squiggly line with my crayon on his paper."

She glanced down at Meagan while wiping Johnny's bottom. "Meagan Joy, that wasn't nice. Why would you do that?"

"Well, he wouldn't share the paste, which Miss Beasley said he had to do. He's a meanie, Mother, so I accidentally made that purple line."

Mother? Rachel arched one eyebrow. "Accidentally, huh? Well, after this, you treat his property with respect. If you have a problem, talk to Mrs. Beasley. And what's with this 'Mother' stuff? You've never called me that before."

"That's what Merline Thompson calls her mommy. She always says, 'Mother lets me watch the Disney channel until eight o'clock every night' and 'Mother works for the dentist' and 'Mother makes me peanut butter and jelly sammiches whenever I want them,' and stuff like that. Merline wears very pretty dresses every day, Mother, and a diamond necklace that sparkles real nice all the way across the room."

"Oh, really?" Rachel stifled a snicker. "Well, I'm sure they're not real diamonds."

"Merline told me she took that necklace right out of her mother's jewelry box. Do you have a diamond necklace I could wear? Also, I want to wear a dress next time. Like maybe that red velvet one I weared on Christmas day? Can I, Mother?"

"We'll see."

"That way, Merline won't be the prettiest girl in school all the time."

"Oh, my goodness, Meaggie. You shouldn't be worried about such things at four years of age—or at any age, for that matter."

"Know how many months till I'm five?" Meagan asked, changing the subject. As usual, Rachel could barely keep up with the child's nonstop chatter.

"Well, let's see here," she said, securing a new diaper on Johnny as he kicked and flailed, waving his arms and nearly smacking her in the chin with his cast.

"February, March, April, May, June, July!" Meagan recited, using her fingers to count off the months. "That's"— she studied her hand—"one, two, three, four, five, six months!"

"Since when do you know the months of the year?" Rachel asked, pulling up the baby's pants and lifting him into her arms. How heavy he'd gotten! His cast didn't help matters, she supposed. Two more weeks, and the thing could come off, providing the X-rays indicated the arm had healed enough.

"Mrs. Beasley shows us that number thing every day what gots all the months on it and so today I just decided I was goin' to learn the months by my heart."

"Just like that?" Perhaps her daughter could be termed precocious after all.

"Yep, just like that!" She started reciting them in order in a singsong fashion while Rachel kissed Johnny on the cheek and laid him in his crib, covering him with his favorite blanket and then popping his pacifier into his mouth. Despite Meagan's racket, his eyes were heavy.

"Okay, nice job," Rachel whispered, putting a finger to her lips, "but now, we have to be quiet. Come on." She guided the chatterbox out of the room and closed the door behind them. "Time for lunch, then a nap for you, as well."

"Aww, when do I get to stop taking naps?" she asked with a groan.

"Oh, when you're about ten or so," Rachel teased, urging her toward the stairs.

"Huh?"

"Shh, come on."

Meagan talked all through lunch, taking intermittent slurps of chicken noodle soup and munching on her crackers, and Rachel would have missed the light tapping sound on the living room window if her daughter hadn't finally paused long enough to take a drink of milk.

Thinking a bird or a squirrel was responsible for the noise, she peeked around the corner and nearly fell over at the sight of Jason peering through the glass.

She rushed to the front door and threw it open wide. "What are you doing knocking on my window?"

He looked only a little sheepish and a whole lot handsome in his leather bomber jacket and the scarf and gloves she'd bought him for Christmas. His dark eyes made her dizzy, and she had to hang tightly to the door to maintain her balance and composure as he picked his way through the shrubbery on his way to the front step. A swath of dark hair fell across his forehead, and he swept it back before setting his gaze on her.

"Didn't want to ring the doorbell since I figured it might be naptime. Is it?" He looked over her shoulder, and his expression brightened as Meagan raced out from the kitchen, her footsteps pounding on the floor as she flew past Rachel and made a giant leap into Jason's arms, yipping like an overexuberant pup. How Rachel admired her daughter for her total lack of abandon when it came to seeing her uncle—the way she allowed her face to glimmer with excitement, her voice to peal with unadulterated glee, and her arms to hug his neck so tightly his face turned purplish from all the squeezing. Rachel stepped back to watch the mutual adoration with something close to envy, folding her arms for lack of anything else to do with them.

"Hi, muffin," he said, hardly paying Rachel any mind. He seemed to have a dozen different endearments for Meagan. "Oh, hi, Rach," he said, almost as an afterthought. "I tried to call first, but you didn't answer."

"My phone's been on the fritz; the telephone company's doing some line repairs. And I'm afraid my cell phone battery died. It's recharging as we speak."

"Ah. Well, that explains it, then. I guess you didn't check your e-mail, either. I sent you a message this morning."

"Oh, I'm way behind on my correspondence." Shoot! She was beginning to sound like a dunce. "Sorry."

"No problem." She noticed how Meagan refused to let go of his neck, her skinny legs wrapped tightly around his middle.

"Um, come in. Pardon my manners." He stepped inside and closed the door with his back. She could barely stop watching him.

"I've been over at my folks' house helping my dad with a few repairs. He took the day off when he found out I was coming. Work's been a little slow for me the past couple weeks. Winter, you know—hard to build in the snow."

"Yes, well, I suppose that's how it is in construction. So, what were you doing—at your parents' house, that is?"

"Just some minor things," he said, his eyes falling briefly on her before glancing around the room. Was it that hard for him to look at her? "Repairing a leaky faucet, fixing a drip in a pipe under the sink—Dad hates plumbing—figuring out why their TV's been cutting in and out, changing out some stained ceiling tiles in the basement, replacing some old wall plugs, and fixing Mom's clothes dryer. Stuff like that."

What can't he do? Rachel wondered, realizing that John probably would have hired someone for every one of those problems. "I'm glad to hear your dad's accepting your help."

"Ha! He's still a stubborn fool, but Mom recruited me, and Dad's been pretty good about it."

"So, things are...better."

He tipped his head slightly, and there went that shank of black hair again. Oh, she had to fight the urge to set it back in place. "I'd say we're making headway, Dad and me."

And what about you and me? Of course, she kept that nagging question to herself and shifted her weight from one stockinged foot to the other, wishing she could think of something brilliant to say.

His gaze moved to the stairs. "I suppose Johnny's sleeping."

She nodded and patted Meagan on the back. "And this one's next."

He gave a slight wince. "Would you mind if I took her for a quick walk or something first? I've missed the little rascal. Johnny, too, of course."

"Yes, yes! Please, Mommy?" *No "Mother" this time*, Rachel observed. She also noticed how Jason hadn't mentioned her among those he'd missed. Had he finally accepted her need for time and space? Maybe he'd given up the notion that he loved her. She had accused him of loving her out of a sense of guilt and duty. Perhaps he'd come to believe it himself, now that he'd been keeping his distance, neglecting even to phone her. The possibility did little to comfort her.

"I—I guess that would be fine," she finally acquiesced. The afternoon was sunny and mild for February.

"Yeah!" Meagan exclaimed, wriggling down. "I'll go get my coat." She raced off toward the mudroom.

In her daughter's absence, a feeling of awkwardness and insecurity came over Rachel. "You been all right?" Jason asked, his tone husky. He cleared his throat.

"Yes, very well." She wanted him to think of her as being fully independent now. "Actually, I dropped out of the grief group and joined a women's Bible study with Allie."

"Really?" He smiled. "I'm glad to hear it. You felt ready to leave the grief group, did you?"

"Yes," she said with conviction, even though her breath was shaky. "What about you? Are you still attending your group?"

"I haven't gone in a while, either. I'm—handling things pretty well."

"Oh, good."

They both tilted their heads at each other, she assessing his expression, looking for signs of emotional healing, and he looking like he might be doing the same thing. Nothing more was said, though, for Meagan came bounding back into the foyer armed with her winter gear.

"We'll just walk around the block a few times," he said when Meagan was ready to go. With that, he opened the door, letting in a gust of brisk air.

Rachel clasped her hands behind her, finding them clammy. He certainly had a way of rousing her to the point of nearly toppling. She'd loved John to the uttermost, but their love had been mostly uncomplicated, safe, and sometimes even lacking in emotion and—dare she say it?—romance. Jay had to go and make her heart thud against her chest in a most uncomfortable way, and she found herself resenting it. Why, she almost wanted to give him a little kick in the shins for affecting her in that way.

"Ready, sugar?" he asked Meagan, throwing out another endearment.

"Yep!" she said, sticking her mittened hand into his big gloved one. "Bye, Mommy. Yes, I'll watch my manners, so don't remind me again."

Rachel blinked twice, rendered speechless. Jason glanced at her and chuckled, giving his head a little shake before pivoting the child in the opposite direction. When Rachel went to close the door, the last thing she heard was Meagan reciting the months of the year in rapid succession.

Chapter 23

Although spending time with Meagan proved to be just what Jason needed to cure his grumpy mood, he couldn't push away the image of Rachel, especially that hint of surprise and perhaps even pleasure at seeing him. Had he detected a ray of affection that went beyond the sisterly kind? The way she'd stood there with her hands clasped behind her, looking almost shy and awkward, reminded him of the demeanor of a schoolgirl with a crush. She hadn't wanted any reassurances from him in the past, so he hadn't given her any today, even though he'd longed to tell her nothing had changed in the way he felt about her. But reality settled in as thoughts of John surfaced. Who was he kidding? When last they'd spoken, he'd told her he was letting her go. Perhaps the tension between them had been brought about by her fears that he meant to stir things up again. The woman drove him crazier than a lassoed loon. He loved and despised her simultaneously.

"Can you take me out in Grandpa Evans's fishing boat next summer?" Meagan asked as they trudged through a deep snowdrift on an unshoveled section of sidewalk. Residents were responsible for clearing the sidewalks in front of their homes, but some didn't adhere to the ordinance.

"Sure, pumpkin. Did he take you out last summer?"

"I don't 'zactly remember. I was still three, you know, but I'm going to be five on my next birthday, which is July twenty-second, and Mommy says that's getting to be growed up. Sometimes she says she wants to put a heavy brick on my head to keep me from growing taller. That's silly, huh?"

Jason chuckled, picturing it. "I guess mommies hate to think of their babies getting too big to hold and carry around."

"And boss," she quickly put in. "When I'm a mommy, I won't be a bossy one."

"Your mommy's not bossy, honey, and when you're a mommy someday, I bet anything you'll want to be just like her. How would it be if she gave you no boundaries?"

"Fun!"

He should have seen that coming. "No, it would mean she didn't love you very much—and you'd wind up pretty unhappy."

"Merline Thompson gets to watch the Disney Channel as much as she wants."

"Who's Merline Thompson?"

She went on to tell him about some little girl in her preschool class and all the privileges she apparently got— also about the beautiful ribbons she wore in her hair and something about a diamond necklace. Besides making him picture some spoiled little brat, it got him to thinking about the earrings he'd bought for Rachel but never given her.

"Back to my dad's boat," he said, reining in his thoughts. "I'll be happy to take you out in it this summer. But we'll have to be careful not to tip over if an alligator bumps into us."

She giggled. "Uncle Jay, you're funny." He wasn't feeling all that funny, but her saying so meant he made for a moderately good actor.

The house felt cozy and warm when they stepped inside after their walk. Rachel closed the door behind them, and Jason stood on the welcome mat and watched her unzip Meagan's coat and help her take off her boots. "Time for a nap now, stinker."

Meagan's eyes rolled upward and met his. "See what I mean, Uncle Jay?"

He cracked a grin and chortled, pulling off the child's hat and watching her blonde hair rise with static. "I think a nap sounds like a good idea about now. Don't think I didn't see you cover a couple of yawns out there."

A low fire crackled in the fireplace. Was it his imagination, or had Rachel put on a tougher exterior in the last half hour? Why, she didn't even question Meagan's remark or bat a single inquiring eyelash at him. He took her lack of response as a cue to say his good-byes. He bent to give Meagan a hug and kissed the top of her downy head. "I enjoyed our walk, little missy. You be good for your mommy."

"Can you stay for supper tonight?"

"What? No, sorry. I'm going back to Grandpa and Grandma Evans's house to help them with some jobs."

"But you can come back over when you're done," she whined. "'Sides, you didn't even see John-John, and he'll be mad when I tell him you were here."

That was a lame argument, for Johnny wouldn't mind missing him at all, and Rachel knew it as well as he did. He chanced a quick peek at her.

"You're welcome to come back later—I mean, if you want to," she said.

Well, this was something new—a half invitation. "I guess I could do that, but only if you're sure." This he said directly to Rachel and in a low, husky whisper, his throat having suddenly gone hoarse on him.

"If you don't mind eating something simple. All we're having is spaghetti, garlic toast, and applesauce."

He grinned, regaining his voice. "That's my kind of supper."

On the way down the driveway, he had to keep himself from skipping like a six-year-old.

He could barely concentrate on the remaining jobs his mom had listed for him to do that afternoon. Nor could he keep from whistling while he worked. Rachel had invited him to supper. Well, actually, it had been Meagan who'd extended the invitation, but at least Rachel hadn't retracted it.

"You're acting chipper," his dad said, looking over his newspaper from his seat at the kitchen table.

"Am I?"

"Was Meaggie excited to see you?"

"She sure was. I took her for a walk around the block. Didn't have much time for playing with her, though, since she had to take a nap."

"Too bad. I'm sure she put up a fuss about that."

"You know your granddaughter pretty well," Jason said as he tightened the last screw for the bracket of the new curtain rod his mom had purchased, for which she was out buying a new set of curtains right now. "That should about do it," Jason said, standing back to assess his work, then taking the pencil from behind his ear and checking off the final item on his to-do list. The clock above the pantry said 5:10. "I should probably load up my things."

"You don't want to stay for supper?"

He'd smelled his mom's beef stew on the stove all afternoon. "Tell Mom I'm sorry, but I'm going back to Rachel's house for supper—at Meagan's insistence."

"Well, that's fine, then." Not even an ounce of orneriness edged his tone.

Jay chanced a look at his dad to see if he could detect anything in his expression. "You're okay with my going over there?"

His dad lowered his paper and looked him straight-on. "If you'll recall, I apologized for interfering in your friendship with your sister-in-law. I was suspicious of something going on between you before the accident, and I was out of line. I still don't know the full extent of what transpired between you and your brother on that mountain, but I've decided I don't need or want to know."

"Dad, what happened on that mountain is no secret, really. Yeah, we argued, but it was all over something that didn't exist. Unfortunately, John went to his death thinking I still carried a torch for his wife, which isn't true."

His dad nodded, took a sip of what had to be a cool cup of coffee by now, set the mug back down, and then folded his newspaper. "That is unfortunate. The good news is, he's not given it a moment's thought since. And I plan to dismiss it from my mind, as well. I haven't been able to entirely, mind you, but I'm working at it."

Jason sighed, pulled back a chair, and plunked himself down. "I haven't either, Dad. Hardly a day goes by when I don't think about all the what-ifs. What if Rachel hadn't told John? What if they'd just settled the whole matter before we set off on that trip? What if John and I had talked about it on the plane? What if we hadn't taken that lift to Devil's Run?"

"What if you'd never kissed Rachel in the first place?"

Jason fiddled with the corner of a placemat. "Especially that."

Long moments of silence passed between them, making the minute ticks of the wall clock's second hand sound deafeningly loud. Finally, his dad made the first move and pushed back his chair, the legs of which squawked in protest against the worn tile floor. "Well, it doesn't matter, I suppose," he said, putting both palms flat on the table. "What does matter is that I keep my nose clean—and out of your business. At least, that's what your mother tells me." He smirked. "That woman sure can put me in my place when I need it.

She doesn't do it very often, but when she does, phew! You should've heard her Christmas night after we got home from the hospital. That whole matter with John Jr. never would've happened if I'd been minding my own business."

"Don't say that, Dad."

"No; I had everyone so riled up that no one, not even Rachel, gave a second's thought to what the baby might be doing. I have thanked the Lord so many times that nothing more serious happened to that child. I couldn't have forgiven myself. Ever." More seconds of contemplative silence followed before his dad stood. "Well, you best get yourself to Rachel's house before they eat without you." Jason stood, too, and they faced each other across the round table. His dad smiled. "Thanks for all you did around the house today. You do good work, son. Your mother and I will have to drive down to Harrietta one of these days and have a look at some of those houses you've built."

Well, now, where had that come from? "I'd like that. Afterward I'll take you to a nice restaurant on the lake."

The spaghetti dinner was about the best he'd ever had, though he couldn't say whether that was because of the savory marinara sauce, the crispy garlic toast, or just the company itself. All he knew was that they'd all laughed and enjoyed good conversation, almost like a real family. He would not allow his mind to dwell there, though, since just a month ago he'd told Rachel he intended to let her go, thereby giving her time and plenty of room to make her own way in life. In his mind, that decision had not changed. Still, it sure felt good to sit back and watch the kids interact, listen to Meagan's unending chatter, laugh at John Jr.'s antics, and exchange a bit of small talk with Rachel.

After dinner, they all chipped in to help clean up—everyone but Johnny, who kept up a constant order for "mo!"

garlic toast. They set up an assembly line of sorts, Meagan and Jason delivering dishes to Rachel, who rinsed them and then loaded them in the dishwasher. The whole process took less than five minutes to complete. After that, Rachel wiped the table, stove, and countertops, and then went to change Johnny's diaper.

Meagan and Jason went into the living room, where Meagan had already set up Chutes and Ladders and Candy Land, having talked her uncle into playing both. They sprawled out on the floor while Meagan spouted off the directions, and it was a good thing, as it'd been decades since he'd played either game. As Meagan made a pudgy-fingered turn with the spinner and landed on the six, moving her yellow piece six spaces, Rachel entered with a fresh-faced Johnny and sat down on the sofa to watch, tucking her bare feet beneath her slender body and releasing Johnny to head for a big truck he loved pushing around, with Jason as his primary target.

"Ah, you got me!" Jason yelped, rolling on the floor. The little guy giggled and repeated ramming into him. When Rachel finally laughed, the sound tugged mightily at his heart.

"Uncle Jay, it's your turn," Meagan said, raising her voice above the clamor. "Johnny, you go push your truck over there."

"Now, don't be bossy, Meaggie," Rachel said, still laughing.

The game continued, as did Johnny's crashing into him, Meagan's attempts to keep him on task, and Rachel's bubbling giggles. My, he could listen to that lighthearted sound all day and feast unblinking eyes on her for endless minutes. A year ago, he'd been aching from the loss of his brother, carrying the weight of grief everywhere he went, reliving each moment of that fateful day over and over again. Certainly, he'd never pictured himself one year later playing Chutes and Ladders with his niece or wrestling on the floor with his one-year-old old nephew, much less falling in love with their mother.

Rachel decided she could watch Jason interact with her kids for hours on end and not grow weary doing so. His unconditional love for them brought her great comfort. Not only that, but she plainly enjoyed watching Jason—the movement of his sculpted muscles beneath his cotton shirt; his thick crop of dark hair, which tapered neatly to his collar; and his arresting good looks and downright delicious appeal. She was startled to realize anew that he captivated her, brother-in-law or not!

Every so often, their eyes met, and she found her heart reacting in ways she hadn't allowed before—racing, quivering, stopping, and starting. Still, she'd told him many times over that a relationship between them couldn't work; it wouldn't be fair to John, particularly since he'd been suspicious of something between them before his death. How could she ever in good conscience permit herself to give her heart to another man, especially Jason? No matter how long and hard she tried, she couldn't wrap her mind around the idea. Besides, she still had lingering, unresolved questions in her mind regarding the accident, questions to which she had to find answers before she could move forward with her healing.

Soon, she would put Meagan and Johnny to bed. Perhaps, tonight, the Lord would give her courage to ask them.

Chapter 24

Jason knew he'd overstayed his welcome. There he sat on the sofa with Rachel, two feet separating them. The kids had been tucked in bed and prayed over, the TV showed a crime drama he was in no mood to watch, and she was fidgeting with her shirt hem, staring at the screen and probably wishing he'd leave.

"Well—," they said in unison.

Glancing at his watch and seeing it was 9:10, he pressed his hands to his knees in preparation to stand up. "I guess I should go."

"Jay."

"Yes?"

"About the accident."

His heart took a dive as a wave of irritation came over him. "What about it?"

"I was just…I don't know…thinking about it a while ago. I still have questions."

He tightened his grip on his knees. "Don't we all, Rach? Will you ever let it go?"

"Probably not. I mean, not as long as I have questions."

"Then you'll never find peace."

"You were there. I wasn't," she said, her tone defensive. "You've never told me…everything."

"What do you mean? I don't know what else I can tell you."

"I want more details." Her voice held resolve and a kind of grit, as if she'd been dwelling on the matter all night; as if her mind had been filled with gnawing questions, even as she'd smiled, laughed, and seemed to enjoy watching him play with her kids. Did she still blame him, even though she'd adamantly denied it?

He sighed, resigning himself to the thought that she would never be satisfied. "What do you want to know?"

She reached for the remote, turned off the TV, and shifted her body to face him. "Well, you said that you and John didn't talk on the plane, but did you talk before you went skiing—once you got to Colorado, I mean?"

He let his mind wander back to that day. It'd been a while since he'd visited that place, but now the memory came back afresh. He sucked in a cavernous breath, released his grip on his knees, and fell back against the soft cushion, slowly letting out the air. "We had lunch before we hit the slopes. That's where our discussion started, and it grew more heated as the day wore on."

"What happened, exactly? How did the conversation go? You've never told me."

He wondered about the wisdom of giving her the details now, but, doggone it, she asked for it, and maybe it would help to tie things up for her—at least partially. "This isn't going to bring John back, you know," he whispered.

She gave him a dumbfounded stare. "I know that."

He frowned with concern. "What I mean is, if you're looking for a pat answer as to why it happened, desperately searching for one last puzzle piece to solve the mystery, then I can't help you. I'm as mystified as you, Rachel."

She laced her fingers together and bent her head, studying them. "I'm well aware of that, but I would still like to know what you talked about."

"All right, then. He told me you had fought, but he didn't expound on the argument; he just said he'd left you in a fit of anger. I felt uncomfortable asking him for details because I thought for sure you two would settle it when he got home. But then, he asked me flat out if I still had romantic feelings for you. I was stunned. Mad, really. In fact, I freaked out on him."

Her lips parted, and she gripped the arm of the sofa with white knuckles. "What did you tell him?"

"The truth."

"Which was?" she pushed.

"Rachel, I never could have betrayed my brother's trust. I told him the truth. I carried no torch for you." He sniffed. "He didn't believe me, though. There we were, sitting in the hotel restaurant; I'm trying to enjoy my lunch, and he's accusing me of trying to steal you away from him."

"Did he really say that?"

"Not in so many words, but he definitely implied it. He asked me why I hadn't fought harder for you in those early days of our friendship." He sought her eyes now and found their blue depths glittering with interest. "My brother loved you, Rachel, more than you'll ever know."

She swallowed. "I have no doubt about that."

He felt a half grin pop out when a memory flashed unexpectedly into his thoughts. "Do you happen to remember my getting a black eye in high school?"

"Vaguely, I guess. Why?"

"You and I were seniors, and John was a sophomore at Michigan State. He'd come home for the weekend to see you and to watch my final game. You and he were in the stands together. Later that night, Mom and Dad were in bed; he'd returned home from a date with you, and he and I sat up watching reruns. We were goofing off, throwing popcorn at each other, talking about stupid stuff, and somehow during the course of our antics I blurted out that I still had a crush on you."

It looked as if her eyes might pop out of their sockets. "You did? I mean—you did? How'd he take it?"

"How do you think? That black eye, which I told everyone, my parents included, came from a tussle on the field with Curt Brower, really resulted from John's fist."

She gasped and covered her gaping mouth. "Oh, my goodness! You're kidding. Did you hit him back?"

"Not really. We rolled around a little bit, he threatened to kill me, and that about ended it. He packed a punch, let me tell you."

"Did Dad ever find out?"

"No way. Somehow, I knew saying I'd gotten in the way of Curt's elbow during the game would sit a lot better with my dad than telling him my brother slugged me."

At this, they shared a brief chuckle. He sobered first. "Don't think I wasn't tempted to flatten his nose, but what I did instead was accept the inevitable—that he had won you over, and I wasn't to interfere. Deep down, I knew retaliation could do irreparable damage to our relationship. Besides, Dad would have killed me if he'd learned we had a regular knockdown fight in the living room—and over John's girl. Shoot, I was already out of his good graces, and I didn't need another shenanigan to lower me even further in his eyes."

They shared a short-lived laugh before he continued. "If you want the truth, that was the turning point for John and me. After that, we seemed to rub each other the wrong way, no matter how much I tried to right the situation. I'd admitted having feelings for you, and he couldn't forget it.

"So, anyway, that fight came up at lunch. He asked if I remembered it, and I couldn't lie. And he said, 'So, you still want her, don't you?' I told him no, of course not; I was serious about Candace, for crying out loud. Of course, he told me I'd never marry her, and he was right about that. He never mentioned that you'd told him about our kissing in your grandpa's barn just days before your wedding. That must have been eating a terrible hole through his gut."

"I feel sad about that." Her misty eyes revealed deep, unsettled emotions. "What happened after that?"

"Not much. We both left the table angry and hit the mountain. I'll tell you, Rachel, I was seething inside. He wasn't himself, and it made me mad. I hadn't saved all that money for a trip with my brother so I could spend it fighting over his wife. In fact, I tried to convince him to call you and make things right, but he was acting plain stubborn and refused."

A little sob slipped past her throat, tempting him to reach for her hand, but he sat there as still as an ancient statue, deciding it was best to keep his distance. Going to her now would only weaken both their defenses. "He could be so stubborn, but then, so could I," she said. "Yes, I wanted to settle matters before he took off on that trip; I wanted to apologize profusely. But I also wanted him to ask forgiveness for calling me fat and unattractive."

"He didn't mean any of that stuff, Rach. He was so proud of you for carrying little John. Before our trip, when we were in the planning stages, and before you two had fought, he told me how excited he was about having a son and how much he loved you."

"He did?" Her misty eyes brightened like blue fluorescent lightbulbs. "Thanks for telling me, Jay."

They sat there for a time, wrapped in private thoughts. Jason stared at the ceiling with his legs stretched out before him, his hands clasped behind his head. Finally, he broke the silence. "If it's any consolation, I think he would have called you in a day or two. He never was happy staying mad. Even when we were kids, he was always the first to apologize and suggest making up after a fight. Looking back, I think he was angrier with himself than anybody else—furious, really—for letting it reach that point between the two of you. I wish he had told me he knew about the kiss. I could have made things right with him on that score, and he would have called you after that. I just needed one more day, Rach. That would have cinched it." He swallowed hard, surprised when wet tears filled the corners of his eyes and started to seep out. It'd been forever since he'd cried. "One more day," he muttered to the ceiling, wiping his eyes.

Rachel reached out and touched his arm, which he experienced as a sort of spark. "I know," she murmured. "What happened on the mountain, Jay? Tell me."

He rubbed his eyes, quickly regaining composure. "More of the same. He wouldn't let it go; kept pushing me, drilling me, questioning every event leading up to his marriage and everything after."

"What do you mean?"

"Well, for example, when you and I were juniors in high school and he was a freshman in college, he came home in October, and we all went on a canoe trip with the church youth group. Remember that?"

She nodded and looked away. "Gosh, I haven't thought about that in ages."

"Yeah, well, apparently, you and I had more fun together than you and John—at least, from his perspective. I don't remember too much about it, except that you and I both jumped in the water and swam to shore while he maneuvered the canoe to the dock on his own. He said we were flirting the entire day."

"We weren't!" she blurted out, then quieted with a panicked look. "Or were we?"

He chuckled. "Could've been, I guess. Shoot, how should I know? I was a sixteen-year-old kid with out-of-control hormones. No telling what I was doing that day. It just mystified me that John would bring it up in the midst of our argument. It told me one thing—he was grasping for proof."

She sighed and twisted her face into a tight little frown. "Well, you did kiss me before my wedding."

His defenses sprang up with a vengeance. "And you allowed it, my dear lady."

"I know. I don't deny that. It made me question things."

"I'm sorry. I shouldn't have put you in that position."

"No, it's fine. After I was married to him for several years, there was no doubt I'd made the right decision. I loved him with all my heart."

And you still do.

He thought that would be the end of it, but then she pushed for more. "Why exactly did he take Devil's Run?"

"Rach, I've told you before, I can't answer that question. It's something I ask myself all the time. I tried talking him out of it, believe me."

"I do, Jay, I do." Her voice softened, even as it cracked. "I've thought about it myself, and I think he must have been trying to prove himself to you—somehow show you he was the better man for having won me. Does that make sense? Obviously, my confession rocked his sense of security and self-esteem. That makes me feel so terrible."

"Well, it's over now, and there's nothing more to be said about it. I'm sorry it happened, Rachel—so, so sorry." More tears threatened to fall, so he swallowed them back as best he could. Good grief! He had to go before he started blubbering.

Again, he put his hands on his knees and prepared to stand. She touched his arm once more, and additional shock waves rocketed through his veins. "Thanks, Jay. I'm glad we talked. I will try to put it to rest now."

Try. Big word, he mused. She kept her hand on his arm. What was she doing to him? He stared at her slender fingers gently clenching, heard the intake and outtake of her uneven breaths. He decided to stand, and when he did, she shot up, as well, as if someone had lit a fire right under her little behind.

"You're welcome," he said with clogged throat while staring down at her, their bodies inches apart, her golden hair mussed in an attractive way. "I guess we both needed it. I didn't know it would affect me so much, though—you know, talking about it—but it was good."

"Yes," she whispered. "It's good to get those emotions out of you, especially if you've been burying them." Had he?

He should have backed away, but instead he kept his eyes trained on her delicate face. Instinctively, he lifted her chin with his index finger. Something like a jolt of current flashed between them. She challenged him with her azure eyes.

Lord, what game is she playing here?

Without any thought about the ramifications, he reached a hand behind her neck and drew her to him. Then, slowly, giving her an opportunity to retreat, he touched his lips to hers, gently, softly at first, then building in intensity and passion. She lifted earnest arms to encircle the broadest part of his back, which only prompted him to wrap her in a warm, protective embrace.

God, how I love this woman.

The kiss continued and could have gone on indefinitely, but he knew his limitations and was well aware of the pounding in his chest, not to mention his strong need of her. It went beyond reason, beyond anything he'd ever before experienced, far beyond any teenage fantasy he'd ever had, or even his previous feelings for Candace.

Lord, wash me anew and prepare me for the priceless gift of this lady, he prayed silently. Don't let me blow it with her. Give me the wisdom to make right choices and discern Your leading. I don't want to get ahead of You, God.

As quickly as the kiss had begun, it ended when he took a step back and dropped his hands to his sides. Obvious disappointment washed across her face, but he didn't care. He had a newfound agenda and he meant to follow it.

"I'd better go, Rach," he whispered huskily. He hadn't planned to kiss her, but he decided against trying to explain it. Better to leave her wanting more. He needed to know if there was a chance for them, so he would leave it to her to make the next move. After all, she'd been the one insisting they maintain their distance.

He walked to the closet and took his jacket, quickly slipping into it and throwing his scarf around his neck. Rachel followed him to the door, her arms dangling at her side, her face unsure. Good. He liked seeing her in that uneasy, fretful state. It meant the kiss had made an impact on her.

"Are you…um, coming back again? Meagan and Johnny love seeing you."

He tipped his chin down and fought back a grin. "Meagan and Johnny, huh?"

"Well, I—I enjoyed seeing you, too."

So, was that her way of inviting him back? "I don't know," he said with as much nonchalance as he could muster. "Probably not anytime soon. Work will be picking up again."

Her face noticeably dropped, and his heart leaped, but he maintained calm. "Rachel, you said yourself it wouldn't work between us, remember? Do you still believe that?"

She bit her lower lip, and her shoulders went up and down in a tiny, noncommittal shrug.

He touched the tip of her nose. "Well, until you can give me a more definitive answer, I can't come around. It wouldn't do either of us any good, much less the kids. I'll try to pop in to see them when they're at Mom and Dad's."

Her nod came off weak and unsure. Leaving was the toughest decision he'd made in a long while, but he had no qualms about doing it. Until she made a wholehearted commitment to love him without reservations, he would not kiss her again or go out of his way to see her.

She left him no alternative.

Chapter 25

Rachel flipped the calendar to February, albeit two weeks late. Short, cold, sunless days became sparser as the daylight lengthened and the temperatures climbed ever so gradually. Southern Michigan reported unseasonably warm temperatures and an early thaw, while temperatures in Fairmount hovered in the thirties but one day reached a mild forty-four degrees. The sun had showed itself a record three days in a row, lifting the spirits of northerners accustomed to winters lingering until late April. Of course, the mercury rising made ski resort operators unhappy, since their source of income depended on frigid readings and plenty of snowfall. Yes, they fired up the snowmakers when needed, but any true enthusiast would avow that the man-made stuff didn't compare to Mother Nature's yield.

Rachel filled her days with household chores, meal preparations, Bible study, running the children back and forth to preschool and elsewhere, and visiting her parents and in-laws. One night, Allie insisted on going out for dinner and a movie. Rachel objected at first, claiming she couldn't expect the grandparents to babysit every time the urge to venture out hit. So, Allie took it upon herself to arrange and pay for a babysitter, a teenage girl in the church youth group she often employed.

It was February 13—"Valentine's Day Eve," as Allie put it. Though she had plans with her husband on Valentine's

Day, she insisted on being Rachel's "date" on this particular Wednesday night. Rachel hadn't heard from Jason in more than two weeks. Afraid to ask Donna whether he'd called or visited, she'd simply learned to accept the apparent reality that he didn't plan to call her. She missed him, but swallowing her pride and taking the first step to let him know it felt awkward. Did he really expect her to do that? The notion tied her heart into a huge knot. Worse was the memory of that last, searing kiss.

John's kisses had always been nice, but she'd somehow grown accustomed to them over the years, just as she had gotten used to their stable, comfortable, somewhat lackluster marriage. Oh, there'd been no question of their mutual love, but when it came to romance, John was no Don Juan. It hadn't dampened things between them, though, since she'd come to accept the fact that she hadn't married Romeo.

With John, there'd been a level of coziness, honesty, and freedom, all worthy components of a happy marriage, but with Jay—well, the impassioned kisses they had shared unfortunately made her long for more. The memory of each one seemed imprinted on her heart, tempting and teasing her to consider loving again.

Had she committed her heart to John too early? Thinking back, she'd married so young, barely out of high school, and minus all the bells and whistles. She could scarcely believe her parents had allowed it, but when she recalled those days, she realized they'd almost expected it. In some ways, it had been like an arranged marriage, especially considering how close their two families had been. Her naïveté surely must have shown back then, and she was struck by how much she'd learned about her inner self over the past several months. She supposed that's what pain and loss did to a person—forced her to look within and face her true self.

Well, no matter. She determined to enjoy her night out with Allie, even if she never heard another word from Jason. Yet, even as she mustered her resolve, she couldn't shake off the gnawing worry that he might never call again.

Jason put on his workout clothes and running shoes after an evening spent at the computer in his home office, answering e-mails, balancing his checkbook, catching up on paperwork, and preparing invoices. As usual, he'd put these things off till the last possible minute, until he was no longer able to enter his office and see the clutter without getting a queasy feeling in his stomach. Now, with the necessary papers filed, his desk tidied, and his computer put to sleep, he was about to go for a moonlight run. He'd put in several long workdays in a row and figured running off his pent-up frustrations would do him good. It wasn't that things weren't going smoothly at work. No, his foreman, Todd Carter, needed little direction when it came to the job. He ordered materials, lined up subcontractors, and kept everyone on task so that they met their deadlines. Of course, he consulted Jay when needed, but he mostly just did his job, giving Jason the opportunity to field calls from the office, meet with clients and developers, and drive to the various sites to check on progress.

Truth be told, his frustrations were mostly from missing Rachel and the kids. Tomorrow was Valentine's Day, and here he was, stuck without a sweetheart. He couldn't count the number of times he'd thought about sending her flowers but stopped himself before picking up the phone to place the order. He could get the kids something, he realized, but that would necessitate including Rachel, too, something he wasn't prepared to do.

He layered on several sweatshirts, which made him think about the process of bundling up for a day on the ski slopes. Funny how his priorities had taken a drastic turn. Stranger still how disaster and tragedy could turn off the appeal of former passions.

He looked at his unmade, king-sized four-poster bed and cluttered room, where stuff was strewn about helter-skelter—everything from dirty dishes to soiled socks, tattered magazines to wrinkled shirts. Even his *NIV Study Bible* lay open on top of his disheveled comforter.

"I need a wife," he murmured as he kicked a shoe out of the way. Immediately, his mind drifted to Rachel, as it had done a thousand times before.

Would she ever call? Maybe he should call her—just a friendly call, of course, nothing serious. He could say that his main purpose for calling was to inquire after the kids. With every passing day, his patience grew thinner, like mountain air. Still, something inside him told him to ride it out, take each day as it came, and place his total trust in the Lord. In his nightly ritual of Bible reading, he'd come across a Scripture passage in Isaiah that kept echoing in his mind: "*Forget the former things; do not dwell on the past. See, I am doing a new thing! Now it springs up; do you not see it? I am making a way in the desert and streams in the wasteland.*" Somehow, he knew God had his and Rachel's best interests in mind. Now, if only he could let go and let God have full control.

With a sigh, he flipped off his bedroom light and made for the stairs, glancing over the railing at his unkempt living room below. He bounded down the stairs but nearly lost his footing when the doorbell rang as he hit the bottom step. Nobody rang his doorbell these days! His heavy work schedule and deliberate withdrawal from the social scene since becoming a Christian had cut down on the formerly high number of people who used to convene at his condo following a long day on the slopes. Many were the weekends the old crowd had gathered there, drinking themselves into a stupor and then stretching out on vacant pieces of furniture or open spaces on the floor until Jason kicked them awake and chased them out the door in the morning. He grimaced at the memory, realizing he didn't miss a thing about those days.

At the door, he peeked out the peephole, then opened it wide. "Dad? What on earth? Is everything all right? It's eight thirty, and you hate driving after dark. What are you doing here? Where's Mom?"

His dad slanted him a grin. "Can't a man visit his own son? Everything's fine, including your mom. Are you going to invite me in or make me stand out here in the cold?"

Jason cast a glance at his dad's blue Chevy parked in a visitor's space out front, then quickly stepped aside. "Come in, come in." Jason quickly shut the door to keep out as much cold air as possible, then rushed ahead of his dad to push some newspapers and an issue of *TV Guide* off a chair. "Here, have a seat."

Before sitting, his dad looked Jason up and down. "You're all decked out in workout clothes. I'm not interrupting your plans, am I?"

"No, no, it's fine." Jason slipped out of the extra sweatshirts he'd put on and plunked down in a chair, immediately jumping back up when he felt the remote control beneath him. He tossed it onto a side table and lowered himself again as his dad sat, too. For a second or two, they just stared at each other in awkward silence.

Then, his dad glanced around. "Looks like you could use a maid."

Jason couldn't have agreed more, although a wife would have been more to his liking. He wouldn't expect her to do all the housework, of course, but it would be nice to have someone to help get him organized. He thought about those days when Rachel barely kept her house livable and how he'd helped to get her back on track. How was it that he'd advised her on the basics of keeping a clean house but couldn't keep his own place in decent shape to save his life?

"Wouldn't hurt to hire a pretty one while you're at it."

Jason laughed. "I can't believe you said that. Anyway, what brings you here? Can I get you something to drink? A soda? Some juice? Water?" He started to get up.

"No, nothing, but thanks. Just sit down. Please." He did some more exploring with his eyes. "Been a long time since your mother and I came to visit. She'd have come with me, but she's fighting a cold."

"Sorry to hear that. You could have waited till the weekend. Don't you have to go to work in the morning?"

"I do. Durn post office never closes in the middle of the week unless it's a holiday. Too bad Valentine's Day doesn't count."

"Speaking of, did you get Mom a card?"

"Sure did. 'Course, she reminded me," he said with a chuckle. "I should probably take her out to supper tomorrow night."

"You should. That would be nice."

His dad glanced at the Bible lying on the coffee table. "I'm glad to see you're reading the Good Book. You've sure changed a lot, son. I'm—proud of you." The words came hard, Jason could tell. How many times had he rehearsed them in the car, he wondered? It didn't matter. His heart flip-flopped.

"Thanks. I'm proud of you, too."

"You are?" His eyes showed surprise. "I'm humbled to hear that."

"You've done really well for yourself, Dad. Mom's grateful, and so am I. You always provided for our family and even picked up the tab for a college education for John and me. That was a huge sacrifice."

His dad waved his hand. "Wasn't that much. In-state tuition, you know."

He studied his dad's furrowed brow. "Well, I doubt you came here to talk about college tuition."

"You're right about that," his dad said with a chuckle. "I've come to…make a confession."

"A confession? Really? About what?"

With a toss of the head, he combed four fingers through his thinning, gray hair and breathed deeply. "I made a lot of mistakes raising you two boys, and I'm not proud of them. Your mother says I best make some things right with you if I want to keep you around. I decided tonight was as good a time as ever to drive over here and tell you that."

Jason smiled and folded his hands between his knees, then bent his head to study his sneakers. "I thought we sort of talked about this already—you know, back in the ER on Christmas night."

"I know, but I just wanted to reinforce a few things."

"All right."

"I was hard on you, drove you more than I should have, probably even expected more from you than I did from John. Your mother says you're too much like me, that I've always tried to live my life through you, somethin' like that." He screwed up his face and swallowed, making his Adam's apple bob. "We both got a stubborn streak, you and me, but I gotta say, you've mellowed out. Wish I could say the same for myself."

Jason grinned. "You're not so bad."

"That's a stretch." Now they both laughed. "But, seriously, Jay, I'd like to start over with you—if you'd consider it. I said some things regarding the accident, and I just want you to know, for the record, that I don't hold you responsible."

Jason swallowed the thick lump in his throat. "I know you don't, and I like the idea of starting fresh."

"You do? Good. That's great. What would you think if your mother and I came down here Saturday morning to check out some of those houses you've built?"

"Fantastic! I've been waiting for you to set a date."

A sly, somewhat crooked grin tipped one corner of his mouth. "We could bring Rachel and the kids. Want me to invite them?" Now, this was a surprise.

"Um, I don't think that would be such a great idea."

"No? Are you two on the outs?"

"I don't know what we are right now, Dad. I'm waiting for Rachel to tell me."

Chapter 26

When the month of March rolled into view, Rachel flipped the calendar on time for a change. Something about the start of a new month gave her a sense of exhilaration, sort of like launching into a new chapter of a good book or having the chance to start fresh on an old project. Even though snow still stood like mountain peaks in parking lots, having been dropped there by city plows, and the temperatures struggled to get above the mid-thirties, the sun shone today like a crystalline ball, sparkling through dusty windows and glancing off salt-encrusted cars.

The promise of spring hovered in the air, but so did the reminder of that age-old chore loved and loathed by most women: spring cleaning. In Rachel's kitchen alone, the cupboards and drawers were in need of a good scrubbing, the sink, stovetop, and oven needed to be scoured and polished, and the refrigerator required a ruthless purge of expired items. So, with newfound energy, she dived into the job. Later, she hoped to move on to the rest of the house, depending on how much time her kids allowed her. Thankfully, Meagan had been invited to a friend's house for the afternoon, and Rachel's mom had offered to pick up Johnny for an outing. Rachel rarely turned down these kinds of offers, as they afforded her some much-needed time to herself.

Sunshine filtered through the open blinds and warmed the wood floor beneath her stockinged feet, making her pause to thank the Lord for His protective warmth. And, while she stood there giving thanks, she couldn't help but think how far she'd come since losing her beloved husband. Oh, she still had far to go—some days she still ached from longing and utter misery—but more frequent were the days she walked with a lighter step, enjoyed her children to a greater degree, smiled more often, and drew joy from the simple things of life—taking walks with the kids on brisk afternoons, watching cartoons with Meaggie while Johnny napped, or merely cooking dinner for the three of them.

Along with the glistening sunshine, something else boosted her spirits that day—Jason had called! Of course, he'd asked to speak to Meagan right off, but when she'd told him she was at a friend's house, he'd lingered on the line for twenty minutes, asking what she'd been doing lately, inquiring about Johnny, and wanting to know how Meagan was faring in preschool. She told him that Johnny's arm had healed and how, since the cast had been removed, she worried like a mother hen over her chick that he'd break it again, what with his fearlessness on the stairs and his constant need to climb on the furniture. Jason had laughed, and the sound still rang in her memory. "You have to let him be a boy, Rach. What can I say? Boys climb, and they're usually fearless about it." She'd tried to picture Jason as a baby and had been shocked and a little annoyed that she'd imagined Jason's toddling body before John's. Yet, somehow, she knew without ever asking Donna that of her two sons, Jason had been the more adventurous, carefree risk taker, while John had been the ever-guarded, plodding, vigilant observer. Their opposing personalities made for a fine combination when the two worked together but proved disastrous when any kind of competitive spirit rose up. The accident probably wouldn't have happened if John had just swallowed his pride and said, "Look, I don't want to argue. You're the better skier here. I'll take your advice and not risk it."

But, no. He'd decided to try taking on the part of risk taker. Skill and finesse are hard to fake, however, and, as a result, he'd met his tragic end.

"My dad came to see me a couple of weeks ago," he said, interrupting her thoughts. Good. She didn't like dwelling on John's final moments.

"He did? Did Mom come, too?"

"Nope, he came alone. He showed up on my doorstep around eight thirty on a Wednesday night."

"It must have been urgent. Was everything okay? I mean, your dad hates driving after dark."

"Were you hiding in the bushes or something? Those were my exact words. Guess he felt that what he had to say couldn't wait another day, so he surprised me by showing up. He said much of the same stuff he'd said in the ER on Christmas night, but apparently, he wanted to clarify a few things. It was all good." She heard him pause for a quick breath. "Then he and Mom came back that Saturday, and I showed them around my office and then took them out to some of my sites before treating them to dinner at a nice lakeside restaurant."

"Oh, Jay, that's so nice." She felt almost jealous to have been left out. "You guys must have had a great time. I wish—" But she cut short her sentence, not knowing quite how to end it. She couldn't very well admit her disappointment at not being invited.

"You wish what?"

"What? Oh, I wish that—well, I haven't seen your office since John and I—"

"Wait. Are you saying you would have liked to come along with Mom and Dad?"

"Um...."

"Gosh, I'm sorry. We could have invited you. I guess we just weren't thinking."

Well, now, that certainly made her feel special. They hadn't even thought about her? "No, it's okay. I was probably busy, anyway," she hemmed, trying to remember that particular Saturday.

"Well, I mean, you haven't called," he said.

"Pardon me? I haven't called?" she squeaked. "You're the one who hasn't called."

"Uh, Rachel, correct me if I'm wrong, but didn't you at one time tell me it was best for the two of us to keep our distance, particularly after I went out on that very treacherous limb in the hospital parking lot and confessed my feelings for you?" She noted he didn't confess them now. "If my memory serves me right, a few weeks ago, we decided the next move should be yours. Sorry about this phone call, but I needed to see how the kids were doing. The game is 'officially' in your court, Rach."

Did we really decide that? I don't like being in charge, and I don't even like my court, she almost whined aloud. *It's lonely playing singles.*

"Are you still there?" he asked after a moment of silence.

"Yes," she whispered. He mistrusted her, and who could blame him? She wanted what he couldn't give right now—his visits but not his commitment, his attention but not the love and adoration, his company but not his steadfast companionship. How could she possibly have it all the ways she wanted it? She couldn't, and he was right—it was in her court, her lonely little court. Why couldn't life and love be simple just this once?

They talked a while longer, Rachel trying to keep the conversation moving to hold him on the line, enjoying the deep resonance of his voice and his occasional bursts of unpredictable laughter after she told him something Allie had said or Meagan had done. In the end, he apologized for having to cut things short due to a call coming in from his foreman, and that's when she realized how much she didn't want to say good-bye, how much she'd missed him, how intensely she craved seeing him again, and how—heaven forbid—she might even enjoy another one of his kisses. She shook her head in disbelief. *What is happening to me, God?*

Just before suppertime, Ivy Bronson called to invite Meagan to come over and play with Buffy. Naturally, Meagan jumped with glee, not seeming the least bit tired after her long afternoon of play at her friend Lacy Plank's house. Johnny was still asleep, having gone down for his nap later than usual after a full day at the mall with Grandma Roberts and her friend, Mae Gladstone, running in the mall play area and eating snacks.

Having finished spring cleaning the kitchen, Rachel decided to tackle her bedroom, specifically the walk-in closet. This was a job she dreaded because of how many of John's items remained for her to deal with. Oh, she'd repainted the bedroom, purchased new linens, hung new pictures, and even replaced a chair, but the closet still held a carousel of assorted ties and leather belts, a few of his suits and sports jackets, and some of his nicest golf shirts. The only reason she'd held on to them was to walk inside and occasionally lift the fabric of one of his jackets or shirts and breathe in the lingering scent of his favorite cologne. But the time had come to start weeding through his things, and she supposed today was as good a day as any to commence.

By five thirty, she had cluttered the bedroom with folded shirts, boxes of shoes—hers and John's both—an assortment of slacks, jeans, dresses, and sports jackets, and several items she had yet to decide where to put. Johnny's coos from his crib, along with Meagan's return from next door, forced Rachel to leave the room in total disarray until after supper and baths. She sighed and headed downstairs to finalize dinner—for four this time, as she'd invited Ivy to join them. She hoped the kindly neighbor wouldn't mind her worn jeans, old work shirt, and messy hair. At least she had a sparkling kitchen and a large pot of stew simmering on the stove.

"You're so industrious, honey," Ivy said later while helping rinse the dishes after dinner. "Goodness, I don't start my spring cleaning till early May. Something about snow on the ground dampens my desire for such an undertaking."

"Well, it's a bit more than spring cleaning, I guess. I'm finally taking the time to sort through the rest of John's things."

"Oh. That's a big project, then." Ivy paused to look out the window at her own backyard. "When my Frank passed, I dove into that task the very next week. Everyone's different, Rachel. You have to decide for yourself when you're ready. Some people want to move on as quickly as possible, while others just can't bring themselves to think about it for many months. It's difficult no matter how you look at it. One thing is certain, though—there's no right or wrong way." With that, she resumed her rinsing task.

"Thanks for that, Ivy. Sometimes, I feel like all I've done is drag my feet, and there was a time a while back when I felt so lonely and depressed."

"Of course, that's normal."

"My brother-in-law actually helped me get my focus back."

"Ah. I've seen him here a time or two. Seems like a very nice young man. Meagan certainly loves him." She chuckled and rinsed one final dish. "I saw the three of you raking leaves together last fall."

The memory of that day filled Rachel's mind—how Jason had moved about the house doing odd jobs, played with the kids, stayed for supper, and very nearly kissed her later that night—and it wouldn't have been the first time. He'd brought up the matter of that long-ago kiss, and she'd not wanted to discuss it. Looking back, it almost seemed like an eternity ago.

"You're fortunate to have family so close by, dear," Ivy was saying as she squeezed the water out of a dishcloth and proceeded to wipe down the countertops. "I'm sure it's helped greatly in coming to terms with your loss. You've had a long road to travel, and grief is such a rough path to maneuver by oneself."

Rachel watched her kindhearted neighbor make herself useful and thanked the Lord that friendship knew no age barriers. It felt good to know she wasn't alone, that others had walked a similar path and come out looking quite whole. It gave her hope and even spurred her on to finish the job waiting for her in her bedroom.

Later, when Ivy had gone home, the kids were in bed, and the house was quiet, save for the dishwasher humming downstairs, Rachel sorted through a gigantic pile of hangers, tossing the skinny metal ones into a trash bag and saving the thicker plastic ones. Unmatched socks went into the trash right along with the hangers, as did a few old pairs of shoes and some outdated articles of clothing. The remaining items went into bags and boxes intended for charity. She felt a certain sense of satisfaction as she realized the headway she'd made after just an hour into the job. Why, she could actually make sense of her bedroom again, and it felt delightful. She moved to the closet and stood there, taking in all the extra space and planning her next move.

And that's when she saw it—the box containing John's memorabilia. It was the only thing of his that remained in the room, except for the small photo on her dresser of the two of them.

She hadn't touched the box since New Year's Day, when she'd read John's letter, tucked everything back inside, clamped on the lid, and covered the box with John's suits. Today, though, she'd pulled it out in the open to make it easier to access other things. Now, it stood out like a deciduous tree in the desert.

The love letter came to mind, and she suddenly had the desire to reread it. Dropping to her knees, she lifted the lid and took out the neatly folded letter, holding it to her heart. Then, she noticed the black, leather-bound book tucked to one side. It looked to be a diary or a journal and had a thin, gold ribbon sticking out from its silver-edged pages. Before, she'd believed that reading John's private thoughts would be invasive, but now she was overwhelmed with curiosity about its contents. So, after pulling it from the box, she stood up and walked out of the closet, grabbed a pillow from the bed, and then settled against the wall with the pillow behind her and her legs folded beneath her. Once she was situated comfortably, she began sifting through the pages, carelessly and randomly at first, but then paying more heed once she saw the dated entries that corresponded to the days leading up to John's accident.

November 9

Thanksgiving is just around the corner, and I need to figure out where we stand financially. I don't believe Rachel understands the meaning of the words debt or budget. She loves Christmas so much, but purchasing that new van last April and getting a new roof cut quite a hole into our savings. I have to break it to her that she'll need to cut back on her Christmas buying this year, although she'll hate me for it. I'm nervous about the overwhelming responsibility of having another child, let alone overspending at Christmas. I hope I'm up for the task of supporting another child. I know I should talk about these worries to Rachel, but a part of me dreads her reaction. She's like a walking emotional roller coaster these days, happy one minute and crying the next.

Rachel took in the words slowly at first, allowing them to digest a moment before continuing. Their debts had been small by her estimation, and John's life insurance payments were helping immensely. Had they really been so monumental to him as to cause such stress? John had always been a meticulous, careful planner. He hated debt of any kind, even short-term. That's why Christmas had always caused such tension between them. She'd tried buying everything with cash, but occasionally she had gone overboard and turned to the plastic, especially when ordering online. Still, they always recovered by March. His diary entry implied that she routinely overspent, but she'd never seen herself in that light. Heck, she didn't even enjoy shopping all that much anymore. Somewhat confounded, she read on.

November 12

I have not talked to Rachel yet. It's always difficult talking to her about money. She gets so defensive, like I'm attacking her. She is so sweet, I don't know why money always has to be the wedge that comes between us. It still baffles me sometimes that she chose me over Jay. I even wonder if she ever has regrets, but then I hate myself for having such

thoughts, especially since I know God intended us
to be together.

Where had that come from? One moment, he was writing about money, and the next, he brought his brother into
the picture. So, even before they'd argued, he'd battled insecurities about her feelings for Jason? If only she'd known,
she could have reassured him of her love and fidelity. Why
hadn't she ever picked up on it? Anger at the whole situation
welled up inside her, the result of realizing he hadn't fully
trusted her. What more could she have done to convince
him that she loved him? Hadn't she always been faithful
and loyal to him, telling him she loved him, tending to his
needs, and having his children? She swallowed a sob and
scanned the next two entries.

November 15

Tough day at work. At my annual review, Phil said
I have to step up production or I'm liable to lose
my end-of-the-year bonus. I knew I wasn't quite
up to par, but it's been tough getting new clients.
The economy has put a stranglehold on sales. Of
course, Phil doesn't care what's happening elsewhere; he just wants my job. I feel it. The truth is, I
overheard him telling Ray he'd like to hire his nephew
this fall. So, where does that leave me? Lord, I've
been feeling desperate lately. Please help me trust
You more.

November 18

Rachel and I had a huge fight yesterday. I should
have known better than to bring up the whole

money business. Just as I figured, she didn't take it well. I'm sure I said some harmful things about her spending habits, even implying that she'd gained too much weight to wear a certain dress. Sheesh, what's wrong with me? You don't mention anything about weight to a pregnant woman.

Bitter, hateful words passed between us, and before I knew it, she was confessing to kissing my brother just days before we married! What?! Why would she tell me something like that unless she intended to hurt me? Correction—slice me in two! Is there a hidden agenda somewhere? Something I'm missing? Are she and my brother in cahoots to drive me insane so they can finally be together? It's seriously put me on edge. I'm even beginning to wonder if something's been going on between them for a while. I guess anything's possible. Jay's always had a crush on her, as much as he may try to deny it. Well, I'll soon figure it out, but right now, I'm too mad to talk about it. Maybe tomorrow I'll have cooled off some. Lord, please help me see my way through this ugly mess. Thanksgiving is only days away, and then Jay and I head for the mountains.

So, it'd been more than just the money issue and his worries over their growing family; he'd been having troubles at work, as well. Anger heaped upon anger when Rachel realized he'd been too proud to discuss it with her, and his unfounded fears over whether she and Jay were having an affair crushed her to the center of her bones. With her sleeve, she wiped at the tears running down her cheeks and continued reading with blurred vision.

November 24

Thanksgiving went as well as could be expected, considering Rachel and I are still not speaking. I'm sure everyone felt the tension. Shoot, you could have slashed it with a razor blade. I kept a close eye on Jay today, looking for signs that he and Rachel had something going on, but then, wouldn't she have warned him to lie low if they had? Mostly, he just hung out with Meagan, chasing her around the house and making her raise the roof with her joyful shouts. He wanted to discuss our trip, but I just couldn't muster the right mood. I know he's ticked with me, especially since we're leaving in two days. I'll put it to him when we get to Colorado, just ask him point-blank how he feels about my wife. I'll know right off by the look in his eyes if he still loves her, but, oh, dear God, give me grace to contain myself if I recognize that look.

November 25

Rachel took Meagan to visit her mother tonight, so I decided since she went running to Mommy I might as well go see my dad. Wrong move. I told Dad far more than necessary or prudent. Good grief, I even told him about Jason kissing Rachel before our wedding, and he about blew a gasket. He's convinced my brother is a home wrecker, even though neither of us has an ounce of proof. I'm having serious doubts now. I mean, there must be an explanation for all of it. I'm nothing but a big jerk!

Why can't I swallow my pride, apologize to Rachel for my stinking behavior, and then confess that I'm scared to death of losing her, that I love her more than words can say, and that, most important, I'm sorry for doubting her? God, help me be the man I need to be. Forgive me for my faults and short-comings and, most of all, my foolish pride.

She could have swallowed her own pride, she ruled, staring at the blank pages that remained in the journal. She could have been the one to beg for forgiveness first, but no, she'd stubbornly insisted it was his duty to take the initial step. Surely, Satan had laughed all the way to John's grave.

Her fingers skimmed lightly over her precious husband's final words. *Forgive me for my faults and shortcomings.*

"Oh, my darling John, God did forgive you, for He is a gracious, merciful Father who knew you well. He understood your aching heart, along with your worry and confusion, and loved you anyway. I'm the one in need of mercy. Jesus, please forgive me my stubbornness and foolish pride, and, if it's possible, could You tell John how very sorry I am?"

Feeling strangely renewed, she swept away the last of her tears and stood up, suddenly realizing a few things remained unfinished. Downstairs, she methodically selected which photos to remove from the mantel and coffee tables and which to leave. In the end, she selected the one taken of their family before John Jr.'s birth and their wedding photo for display. Neither would be too painful to glance at on a regular basis. The others she made a neat stack of and decided to put in plastic containers to be stored in the basement. Someday, Meagan and Johnny would appreciate having them.

Next, she opened the hall closet and took out John's winter coat and boots, carefully folding the coat and laying it and the boots beside the sofa. Early on Monday morning, she would drop everything off at a local charity. Peace she hadn't felt in some time washed over her like rain—cleansing, cool, and refreshing. It felt good to de-shrine her house of all things John. In fact, it was time. She would never cease to cherish his memory, but she couldn't continue to let her grief keep her from experiencing the wonderful things life still held in store.

Her gaze fell on the coffee table and the Bible Jason had given her for Christmas. She'd been reading from it every morning, taking comfort from its words, words that dared her to step out in faith and take the hand of the One who loved her unconditionally and always had her best interests in mind.

"Thank You, Lord," she prayed. "Thank You for the strength and courage You give. Please give me the patience to wait on Your direction and the discernment to understand Your perfect plan."

Chapter 27

Jason woke with a stiff, aching neck, the result of having lain wrong and being too exhausted to turn his lazy body over. He hadn't been sleeping well lately, and so, once he'd finally drifted off, he'd gone directly into deep-sleep mode. He glanced at the clock and moaned. Seven thirty. What was he doing up so early on a Saturday morning, especially when it felt like he'd just gone to sleep? As usual, thoughts of Rachel drifted in and out of his mind, along with images of Meagan's angelic face and John Jr.'s impish one. He loved all three of them equally—well, almost—and missed them more than the moon misses the night. It had been three weeks since he'd talked to Rachel, and he'd be swallowed whole before he called her again. She knew how he felt about her, so the next move had to come from her. No question.

He threw off the blankets, slid his bare legs over the side of the bed, plunked his feet onto the cold hardwood, and massaged the knot in his neck, contemplating whether to take a shower now or later. He decided to wait. Right now, he had bike ride on the brain. He could live with a little knot in his neck, and, besides, a good, hard ride might work the thing out. Peeking out of his bedroom window, he saw that some snow still remained, but the roads were dry, and the temperatures had been somewhat mild for the last several days—perfect riding conditions. Plus, the sun was already peeping through the blinds, spurring him on. Since getting a seasonal tune-up on his bike, he'd gotten the itch for riding again. It had been a long winter of inactivity, with no downhill skiing, and he looked forward to spring and summer sports—golf with his usual foursome, softball, water sports, and three-man basketball—whenever his work schedule permitted. He'd found ways to keep his body active over the winter, of course, working out in the clubhouse gym and pool, but there was nothing like getting outside in the elements, whether wind, rain, blazing sun, or blinding snow. Skiing truly had been one of his first loves, but would he pick it up again next winter? Perhaps. But would it ever hold the joys it once had?

In the kitchen, he poured himself a cold cup of day-old coffee, put it in the microwave, and set the timer for sixty seconds. As he waited for it to heat, he shuffled to the door to pick up the Saturday paper from the front step, then sauntered back to the kitchen, skimming the headlines mindlessly. He tossed the paper on the counter, unwrapped a loaf of bread, and took out a couple of slices. While he was waiting for the bread to toast, his cell phone vibrated on the kitchen table. He picked it up and answered without checking the caller ID, expecting to hear the voice of his friend and foreman, Todd, or perhaps one of his parents, or maybe even one of his buddies from church. Certainly not his ex-girlfriend!

"Candace! Well, for crying out loud, how are you?"

"You sound happy to hear from me. I was hoping for that. I'm fine. How are you, Jason?"

Did he sound happy? *Shocked* might have described him more accurately, but he didn't correct her. Forgetting entirely about his coffee and toast, he suddenly felt the need to sit down, so he lowered himself onto the closest thing, a barstool.

During the first five minutes of conversation, they exchanged idle chat, discussing the weather, her job at the hospital, his latest building endeavors, and even the guy she'd been dating but recently dumped. "He just didn't have any of the qualities I'm looking for in a husband, you know what I mean?"

Oh, Lord, I don't want to be having this conversation. He muttered a silent prayer for wisdom and compassion. "I'm sorry it didn't work out for you."

"Oh, it's fine, really. It wasn't meant to be. So, are you dating anyone?" she asked.

"No...uh, not really."

"Not really? So, what you're saying is, you are. In a way."

He supposed he should be honest. "No, I'm really not dating anyone."

He heard her let out a slow, deliberate sigh. "Well, what do you know? You're still unattached. What would you say to going out for coffee some night—as old friends, of course? No strings attached."

No strings attached? Candace Peterson carried a ball of string everywhere she went. He could not afford to get tangled up in it again. "I don't think—"

"Oh, come on, Jason. I'm harmless."

As a snake, he wanted to say. "I've been pretty busy."

"I learned to cook!" she announced, passing over his weak excuse. "And would you believe I'm enjoying it?"

"You—what?" He could not help the chuckle that came out. "Really?".

"I've taken some night classes, and they're really fun. I know it's hard to believe, but my domestic skills have greatly improved."

"I should probably go to that class," he joked.

"You should! We could go together. It's on Tuesday nights."

"I just joined a men's Bible study on Tuesday nights." He'd gone to only one session so far, but she didn't need to know that.

"No problem. The class meets on Thursdays, too. You can pick which night is more convenient. I'm flexible. What do you say?"

"I—I'd have to think about it."

"All right, that's fair enough. Now, about that coffee… what are you doing tonight?"

"Tonight?" *Lord, what am I doing tonight?* "I'm—I haven't—"

"Wonderful! What do you say I come by and pick you up around seven?"

"Seven? You'll pick *me* up? That's pretty far out of your way."

"Oh, did I forget to mention I've switched condos? I live in Cadillac now, very close to the hospital. Gosh, I probably live about ten, fifteen minutes from you now. It's great."

"Candace? Um, we broke up, remember? I just don't think it's a good idea—"

"Don't worry so much, Jason. It's just coffee, for goodness' sake—my treat. And we'd be getting together for old times' sake, nothing more. Come on; it'll be fun to see each other and just chat up a storm."

It sounded innocent enough. "Well, I guess it couldn't hurt, but just as friends."

She laughed, and he thought he detected a hint of disappointment or maybe annoyance in her light chortle. But what could he do about it? He had no feelings for her beyond friendship, and even that was sort of stretching it. He didn't want to build up her hopes.

"I've been going to Good Faith Community Church," she said. "It's downtown."

He knew the church. It was one of those "feel good" kinds of churches, the type that didn't challenge you beyond your comfort level or talk about the need for confession and repentance and welcomed every kind of lifestyle into their big, happy congregation, also embracing the philosophy that Jesus wasn't necessarily the only route to God. "That's—uh, good. Have you been reading your Bible?"

"Of course—every chance I get." Somehow, he doubted that. "Okay, then; I'll see you tonight, Jason. I'm excited. We'll go to the Coffee Gallery, if that's all right with you. They have light cuisine, if you happen to be hungry."

"I've been there before. It's a nice place."

After they'd said their good-byes and hung up, Jason sat there staring at his phone for a full minute, wondering what had made him give in and agree to go out with his old flame. He didn't even want to see her. "You dumb weakling!" he chided himself.

Lord, strike me down with a bad flu bug or something— anything to give me reason to cancel this unexpected...was it a date?

He growled with frustration and shoved his phone into his pocket, opting to forgo his cold coffee and toast in favor of beginning his much-needed bike ride immediately. He fumbled to fasten his helmet as he walked to the garage, peeved with himself for being unable to give Candace a firm no.

Brisk winds stung his face like a million pinpricks, and yet he pedaled faster, staring straight ahead, taking in huge gasps of bitter-cold air, which stung his lungs from front to back. Faster. "Lord, wake up Rachel—whatever it takes, wake her up. Open her eyes to Your love and mine. Give her the courage to step out in faith and believe we're meant to be together."

"Seek first his kingdom and his righteousness, and all these things will be given to you as well."

The mental reminder from Matthew 6 gave him pause. He had been seeking God's righteousness first, hadn't he? He pedaled and pondered, pedaled and pondered.

"Lord, I do want to seek the life and plan You have for me. I know in my heart it's the only way to find true peace and contentment." More pedaling and pondering. "Have I been presuming to know Your will without truly seeking it? If I have, please forgive me. Sheesh!" he muttered into the chilly breezes. "Maybe I'm the one who needs a wake-up call!"

As much as he hated admitting that last part, he forced himself to think about it. With fresh insight, he realized he'd been putting his own desires ahead of God's, praying only that God would awaken Rachel's heart to the truth of his love. A hard, painful lump wedged itself deep in his throat. What if the Lord had never intended him to fall in love with Rachel? He tried to recall seeking God's direction for his heart, but all he'd ever done was tell God how he felt. Oh, he was good at telling God things, but those seeking and listening aspects of prayer made him look like a big, fat failure.

Surrender.

The single word pierced him in the heart. "I do, Lord. I do surrender. I know that I'm nothing without You, and that if You want Rachel and me to be together, I must trust You alone to make it happen. On the other hand, if You don't, then please forgive me for rushing ahead of You, declaring my love to her before she was ready to hear it, and insisting that You make her see it. Your timing is perfect, Lord. Mine?" He sniffed the cold air. "Just a bit under par."

Tears moistened the corners of his eyes, but he decided to blame the wind and the fact that he wasn't wearing sunglasses to ward off the bright glare.

At the merge point with West Hobart Street, he glanced over his shoulder but was blinded by the rising sun. So, when he entered the street at full speed, he didn't see the car already in the lane. He heard the screeching brakes, though, and felt the tremendous blow his body took when the car rammed him from the side, sending the bike veering one way and making his body bounce off the hood of the car.

When he made contact with the hood and then slid off and hit the hard earth, unbelievable pain pummeled so many parts of his body at once, he couldn't tell what hurt most. A car door slammed, voices started coming from various directions, someone shouted orders to call an ambulance, and someone else knelt at his side and draped a covering over him. His world started spinning and spiraling. And, just before he slipped into a sea of blackness, he had one last fleeting word for the Lord: "I asked for the flu, God, not this...."

"Okay, you two, hustle, hustle," Rachel said, snagging both kids' jackets from the hall closet and then approaching Meagan, who lounged in her beanbag chair "reading" *Cloudy with a Chance of Meatballs*. When Johnny saw her coming, he dropped his truck and set off down the hall, squealing a plea to play chase.

"Where are we going now?" Meagan asked, obviously put off by the interruption.

"The grocery store. Don't worry; you may take your book along in the car."

"Why do we always gotta go to the store?"

"We don't 'always gotta' go, snuggle-puss, but the fact is, you kids eat like little horses, so I'm constantly running out of food."

"If we had a daddy, he could stay home with us while you went to the store."

In the midst of zipping Meagan's coat, Rachel stilled her fingers and stared for all of five seconds at a tiny spot on Meagan's coat. "That's true," she said, finally bringing the zipper to Meagan's chin and tapping her nose. "But your daddy's in heaven."

"You could marry someone else, like Uncle Jay. Then we'd have a new daddy."

Rachel's heart took a strange leap. "Well, now, how in the world did you come up with that notion?"

"Esther McCormick's mommy got dee-vorced, but then she married somebody else, and now Esther brags that she gots a new daddy. I was tryin' to figure out who I'd want for a new daddy, and I couldn't think of nobody else but Uncle Jay."

"Well, that's an interesting thought," she answered in a noncommittal tone. It'd been three weeks since she'd last heard from Jason, and she'd been getting plain tired of missing him. She decided to call him tonight after putting the kids to bed. She was finally willing to admit that she had strong feelings for him, and the sooner she told him, the better off things would be. Lately, she'd felt like a pressure cooker about to blow its lid off.

Of course, anything could come of her confession. It might be that after three long weeks apart, Jason had reevaluated his heart, decided he didn't love her after all—at least, not in a romantic sense—and had avoided calling her for that reason. Well, it didn't matter. The time had come to bare her heart to him. After purging most of John's clothes from her closet and packing up a number of his personal keepsakes to give to the children later, she felt she'd turned a page, maybe even finished a whole chapter! *Time to move forward*, she'd told herself.

Just then, Johnny burst back into the room, his impish eyes challenging her to a chase. She snatched up his parka. "Okay, you little monster, Mommy's gonna get you." He screamed with glee and took off, and the race to capture her prey and complete her mission was in full swing. This time, Meagan joined in the merriment.

Ten minutes later, Rachel was kneeling just inside the van's backseat, getting her kids buckled into their car seats, when she heard a horn honk in the driveway. She stood up, wiped her brow, and looked out through the open garage to see her in-laws' car slowing to a stop. An immediate sense of doom came over her, whether from the grave expressions on their faces or their unannounced afternoon visit, she didn't know.

"Mom? Dad?" She approached their car as her father-in-law lowered his window, bearing a grim smile.

"What's going on? Something's wrong, isn't it?"

Tom cast Donna a hurried glance, and then Donna leaned forward in order to see Rachel. "Something happened today, honey."

"What?" She went weak in the knees, her stomach instantly tying itself into a hundred knots. *It's Jason. Oh, God, I know it's Jason. Please, Lord, no.* The tears came before she could head them off. "What's going on?" Her voice quivered nearly out of control.

"Honey, calm down," her father-in-law urged her. "Everything's fine, really. Jason was just involved in an accident."

She gasped, covered her gaping mouth, and fought for control, gripping the side of the car to keep from falling over. "What—? Is he—?"

"He'll be all right, thank God," Donna said, still leaning forward, her face tipped up to see into Rachel's eyes. "We just came from the hospital. He was riding his bike this morning, and...well, you tell her, Tom."

For the next few minutes, her father-in-law went on to explain how Jay had been riding his bike and collided with a car. The police had said that his helmet had prevented any major head injuries, although he did have some cracked ribs, several contusions, a fractured elbow, and enough bruises to play connect-the-dots.

More sobs erupted at the conclusion of Tom's detailed account, forcing both in-laws to open their doors and climb out. At this point, Meagan started shouting from the car for attention, which precipitated John Jr.'s loud wails.

"Rachel, take a deep breath," Donna instructed her, wrapping an arm around her shoulders. Tom went into the garage to see the children. "He's not dead. He's not dead," Rachel repeated several times, breathless.

"No, no, honey, he'll be fine," Donna assured her, rubbing her arm.

Rachel heaved several breaths before letting out a long, shaky sigh, then put her hand to her throat. New tears pushed past her eyelids. "I couldn't take it, you know, if something happened to Jay. I just—couldn't take it."

Donna's face went pale. "Nor could we, honey. Thank God, we're not going down that path. Don't even think such things."

She took several more calming breaths. "Is he still in the hospital?"

"Yes, but the doctors are confident he'll go home tomorrow."

"Tomorrow? Will he be able to get around okay?"

"He seems to think so," Tom spoke from the van. The children had quieted, especially with their grandfather standing nearby, except now they wanted to get free. "Mother tried to talk him into coming to our place for a few days, but he'll have none of that, stubborn kid. When he makes up his mind about something, there's no changing it."

"Well, I wonder where that comes from, Tom," Donna said with a smirk.

"Why didn't you call me this morning?" Rachel asked, passing over her in-laws' gentle sarcasm.

"Dad saw no point in upsetting you until we had concrete details. I'll admit, it was a nerve-racking trip to Cadillac. When that call came in from the hospital—oh, my!" Donna's eyes shone bright, revealing her own raw, jagged emotions. Instinctively, the role of comforter reversed as Rachel wrapped her arms around her. "We didn't want to tell you on the phone, so that's why we came straight here from the hospital," she added.

Wiping her eyes, Rachel pulled her shoulders back and looked at her van. "I'll take care of him," she announced.

"What?" Donna asked. "But—how do you—?"

"I'll have to make arrangements for the kids. I'll leave in the morning and come back tomorrow night. Maybe I'll do that for a few days, depending on how quickly he regains his independence. But he'll need someone to cook and clean for him, at least for a while."

Donna brightened. "Tomorrow's Sunday, so it's no problem for me to take care of the kids, unless you want to take them with you."

"I'd get nothing done with them scampering all over the place."

"True. Well, between your mom and me, tomorrow's covered. As for next week, with Arlene working and Tanna in school, I'm your best candidate."

"And I can stop by after finishing my postal route," Tom chimed in from the garage.

"Then it's settled," Rachel said.

"We told him we'd take him to his condo tomorrow and help him get situated," Tom said.

"Please, let me—I mean, if you don't mind," Rachel blurted out. "I'd like to surprise him."

Donna turned her head to look at Tom, and they exchanged flickering smiles. "We sort of thought you might want to do this," Donna said, looking back at Rachel. "Frankly, it puts my mind at ease knowing he won't be fending for himself. He's pretty battered up."

Fresh resolve flowed through Rachel's veins, making her feel exhilarated and almost buoyant. It wasn't the way she'd pictured things—she nursing the man she loved back to health, he having to submit to her orders. And there would be orders. Oh, how she relished the idea of telling him what to do. An unexpected giggle rippled from her chest.

"Now, what's so funny?" Donna asked her, smiling.

"Nothing. Absolutely nothing." She gave her watch a hurried glance. "Goodness, I'd better get to the grocery store before the sun goes down. Please call me tomorrow when you receive word that Jay's ready to be released, and I'll go straight to the hospital."

Chapter 28

It's about time, Jason thought when the morning sun burst through the sterile hospital blinds. Nights spent in the hospital were long and loud, with carts banging, people talking, and nurses coming in at all hours to check blood pressure and temperature and hand out more pain pills. He appreciated the pills, but the rest was a nuisance. He needed to get out of here, the sooner the better.

A tiny rap at the door had him turning his head. He expected to see his breakfast, not his foreman. He pushed himself up with effort. "Todd, come in."

"Wow! Look at you, man. You look like...well, like you got run over by a truck."

"Very funny."

Todd stepped inside, removed his hat, and, standing at the foot of the bed, threaded four fingers through his reddish-brown hair. "How're you doing? Me and a couple of the guys stopped by yesterday, but you were sleeping. We talked to your parents for a few minutes, and then your pastor stopped by."

"Yeah, I heard that. Thanks for coming by. I'll be out of here in no time."

"Is that right?"

"This morning, actually. I'm fine."

"Uh-huh." Todd squinted skeptically and scratched his temple, looking him over. "You're a mess, if you ask me."

"Well, I'm not asking you," Jason groused. Showing his true colors was something he felt comfortable doing with Todd. He hated the inconvenience of pain, and he was feeling plenty of it right now. In fact, he hadn't known it was possible to hurt in so many places at one time.

He relived the bits and pieces of what he could recall from yesterday morning but found most of it sketchy. His last recollection was of the biting chill in the air and yet the piercingly bright sunlight. He still couldn't believe he'd shot directly into the lane and been rammed by a vehicle. The cops said the driver ought to have been more vigilant, but he blamed his own carelessness. He shifted his position gingerly, feeling his bruised, cracked ribs with every breath. The nurses had wrapped a burdensome bandage around his torso, supposedly to secure the rib cage, but he could have sworn it made the pain worse. The first thing on the agenda when he got home would be to loosen the darn thing.

"I hear the doc says you have to rest for a week or so."

"I'll go stir-crazy with no one to talk to and nothing to do. I'll be in on Wednesday."

Todd shook his head. "Don't be crazy, my friend. You took a serious beating. Besides, I've got things under control. Finished the Langston house, hung the trusses on that spec home out at Forest Hills, and even started digging the basement in that next lot over."

"That's good. I was supposed to have lunch today with Howard Baker to discuss a proposal."

"I'm sure Diane's already canceled it."

"Of course—what was I thinking? She knows my life better than I do!"

Then, as if a lightbulb had just exploded in his head, Jason sat up and groaned.

"What's wrong?" Todd asked, leaning forward.

"Oh, no!" he moaned.

"Are you in pain?"

"Yeah, and it's about to get worse."

"What are you talking about?" Todd sounded genuinely concerned as he moved around to the window side of the bed.

"Candace. I missed a date with her last night."

"With Candace? But I thought you two—"

"Yeah, yeah, we broke up, but this was going to be just a casual deal—for old times' sake."

"Casual, huh?" Todd straightened his shoulders and stood tall. "Nothing's casual with Candace. She's out for gold, buddy. She still hasn't gotten over you, you know; might as well face it."

"Sheesh." Jason grabbed his now pounding head. "She probably thinks I skipped out on her on purpose. She'll be so mad."

"So? Maybe she'll get the idea."

Jason looked at his foreman. "It wasn't my intention to purposely hurt her."

Todd shrugged and inhaled a deep breath. "Okay, okay, give me her number. I'll call her."

"Thanks, but no need. I'll do it. She'll want to reschedule, and I'll decline. She'll get over it."

His breakfast arrived at that point, and Todd took his leave shortly afterward. Next, the doctor came in, ran a quick test of his vitals, and handed him a release form, along with a detailed sheet of instructions on caring for his wounds. "Rest," he said, "is essential for healing those ribs and multiple contusions. Stay home from work for the whole week. Depending on how you feel next week, you might consider taking off a few more days."

Fat chance, Jason thought. Todd was good, but not that good.

At eleven forty-five, his parents still hadn't showed, and his patience was growing thin. Hospitals weren't among his favorite hangouts, and he was anxious to get out, even if he had to ride in a wheelchair. He'd asked his parents to pick him up by noon but thought they'd come a little earlier just to get him on his way. He gingerly turned over to stare out the window at the azure sky, and he noticed one puffy cloud drifting past the upper corner of the pane. Today would have been the perfect day to ride his bike—if he still had one. He wondered if his insurance company would pick up the cost of a new one. Chances were, they didn't pay for stupidity.

He dug deep in the recesses of his memory for the perfect passage of Scripture to fit his situation, and the first one that came to mind was a verse from Proverbs he'd read from his *NIV Study Bible* several mornings ago: *"How long will you lie there, you sluggard? When will you get up from your sleep?"* He would have to remember that one!

He tucked a hand under his bruised, scraped cheek and winced. He should sit up, he supposed, but whether he wanted to admit it or not, being vertical made him dizzy. Maybe it was good hospitals sent their patients to the front door in wheelchairs. He hadn't even been able to dress himself without that bossy, gray-haired nurse helping him. Talk about humiliating. He breathed loud and deep, as if that would change anything. Soon, he found himself praying, albeit silently.

Lord, I can't see one good thing about any of this. You say in Romans that all things work together for good to those who love the Lord. Is this Your way of showing me how You have my best interests in mind? I surrendered my all to You yesterday morning, and in the next moment, a guy clobbered me with his car. This hardly seems fair, God. Shouldn't this be a two-way street, with each of us giving a little?

Seek and listen, My son. Seek and listen.

In one fluid move, he flipped over on his back. Ouch! Not only had scorching pain shot up his spine, but also he'd heard the voice of God—and both seared him to the core. Crossing his legs at the ankles and folding his arms across his throbbing chest, he muttered to the ceiling, "There I go again, telling You how things should go. Thanks for that gentle little slap, Lord. I needed it."

A flickering shadow made him glance toward the door. Was he dreaming? "Rachel?" he whispered. In another fluid move, he sat up and slid his legs over the side of the bed, for some reason thinking he had to demonstrate his manly side, ever strong and capable. Altogether the wrong thing to do. Instant nausea overtook him.

"Jason, for goodness' sake, you're turning green. Lie down this instant," she ordered him. He swiftly obeyed, hoping the queasiness would subside before he made a complete idiot of himself. What was she doing here? Where were his parents? She wasn't supposed to see him like this. He was both appalled and thrilled.

"Do you need this?" She thrust a green plastic container under his chin. He quickly shoved it aside, even as he silently acknowledged her wisdom.

That was the only move he made, though, other than to slowly roll his eyes in her direction. She looked gorgeous, her golden-blonde hair catching the light, her blue eyes flashing. He blinked twice. "What are you doing here?"

She smiled sweetly. "I've come to take you home."

"You've what?" He took several swallows, all of them bitter-tasting. Out of the question! His place looked like it'd been burglarized. He couldn't have her walking in there. "You can't—that's not—I can manage on my own."

"Oh, pooh," she said, flicking her wrist. "You can't even sit up without heaving, Jay. I'm going to get you all situated and take care of you for a few days. How's that?"

"What?" Splendid. Amazing. Unbelievable. Impossible. "Rachel, my condo is—"

She leaned forward, her warm breath grazing his forehead. "Yes?"

Licking his dry lips, he peered up at her. "A disaster."

"So?" She raised her eyebrows. "Remember how my house looked last fall when you came barging into my life uninvited? Well, what goes around comes around, buddy." With that, she flicked him lightly on the shoulder.

"Ouch. Just so you know, every place on my body hurts."

"Really?" She scrunched up her nose. "Aw, poor thing." Where did he get the idea she didn't feel all that sorry for him? Furthermore, what kind of game was she playing?

And where were his parents?

❧

"Disaster" didn't come close to describing the condition of Jason's condo. Gracious, had he never been introduced to dusting spray? And no wonder his vacuum looked brand-new—judging by the crumbs, wrappers, and lint in the rugs, it had never been used! Dirty clothes and soda cans littered nearly every room, as did soiled dishes, sports magazines, books, and old newspapers. Was this the same man who'd lectured her last year on keeping a tidy house? The scoundrel!

After two hours of cleaning, scouring, dusting, vacuuming, and mopping, her neck, back, and pretty much every other part of her body ached, but in a good way. She surveyed her progress—the shelves she'd organized, the area rugs she'd shaken out, the emptied trash cans, and the kitchen counters, now cleared of dirty dishes after she'd loaded the dishwasher. She'd even gathered up enough stray clothes around the house for two full loads of laundry. Next time she went up to Jason's bedroom, she meant to ask him why in the world his clothes hamper sat empty!

Helping him get situated had been a chore unto itself. He hadn't exactly welcomed her assistance, and she wondered if he wasn't even a bit perturbed with her for being there. Well, he could just get over it. He obviously couldn't take care of himself, and he'd proved it within his first half hour of being back at home. He'd insisted rather adamantly that he could manage on his own, and so she'd left him to his own devices, only to be called right back into the room to help him get his bandaged elbow past his shirtsleeve and remove his shoes and socks.

"I don't see why you didn't let me help you with this in the first place," she'd scolded him, tucking a blanket around him after he'd fallen back onto his bed in an exhausted heap, his brow beaded with sweat, his breathing labored. She would have been lying to say his nearness wasn't affecting her, but now was no time to dwell on that or divulge her feelings to him. No, there would be time for that later, if and when she sensed God's leading. For now, her mission was to nurse him back to health—with or without his appreciation.

"When did you get to be so bossy, Rachel Kay?" he'd asked, staring up at her, mouth lifted slightly in one corner. His tangled mess of hair had begged to be finger-combed, but she'd resisted.

"When did you get to be such a grump, Jason Allen?" she'd countered.

"I'm not a grump by nature, but, if you'll recall, a giant piece of metal on wheels rammed into me yesterday. That sort of thing tends to put a damper on one's mood and ability to navigate."

"Which is precisely why I'm here. You need help."

"My mom could have come."

"I'm sure you're right, but you're stuck with me."

They'd engaged in a staring contest lasting the better share of a minute, and then he'd blinked and said, "I'm not used to being waited on by such a pretty lady."

Feeling rather bold and sassy, she'd arched an eyebrow at him and said, "Good. Best not get used to it, either." With that, she'd swiveled on her heel and, as she'd opened the door to leave, heard him chuckle ever so faintly.

Giving the condo a critical once-over, she mulled over the furniture arrangement in the living room. Two chairs sat at angles to the flat-screen TV, while the sofa faced a different wall. She couldn't imagine what he'd been thinking when he'd set it up. Why, the entire thing was wrong.

So, while the downstairs filled with the wonderful aromas of ham and potato chowder simmering on the stove and half a dozen crescent rolls baking in the oven, she set about repositioning the living room furniture, including the side tables.

She was certain he would love it.

***

Jason lay in bed, wondering about the racket going on downstairs. First, it'd been the vacuum, then the clatter of dishes, pots, and pans, then the churn of the washer and drone of the dryer. Now, it sounded like she might be trying to move heaven and earth. If he'd had the strength or gumption, he might have walked to the top of the stairs to peer down, but the pain of cracked ribs, bruised, scraped arms and legs, and a splitting headache, along with wooziness induced by pain medication, kept him anchored to his bed. Feeling parched, he reached for the glass of water Rachel had set on his bedside table several hours ago but miscalculated the distance and knocked it over, creating a small puddle on the hardwood. A mild curse came floating off his lips before he had a chance to call it back. While he had a firm relationship with the Lord now, his old habits of the tongue had not vanished entirely.

Why had Rachel come, exactly? He distinctly recalled telling her the next move had to be hers. Is that what this was? Or was she merely playing the part of nice sister-in-law as a way to repay him for helping her during her own time of need? He couldn't let his heart skip all over the place just because she was in his house—not until he'd determined her motives. One thing he'd say for her—she'd tempered her feisty side over the past few months. Could it be that he'd angered her by not calling? Women! Why had God made them so all-fired impossible to figure out?

His cell phone vibrated beneath his pillow. With careful movements, he retrieved it from its resting place. "Hello?" he said groggily.

"Jason Evans, where in the world were you Saturday night? I'll have you know I waited at your condo for an hour, thinking someone would surely drop you off." Candace's high-pitched railing prompted him to hold the phone away from his ear. "I looked through the garage window and saw that your Jeep was there, but you didn't answer your door. If you'd changed your mind about going out, the least you could have done is call me."

"Candace, I'm sorry about that. I meant to call you, I really did, but I've been…well, a bit incapacitated."

"How so?"

"My bike and I had a little run-in with a car."

Rachel lined a wooden tray with a yellow tea towel and loaded it with a set of silverware wrapped in a white linen napkin, a tall glass of ice water, a steaming bowl of stew, and two buttered crescent rolls, then lifted it by the handles and carried it up the stairs. She hadn't peeked in on Jay all afternoon, not wanting to disturb his sleep, but as she approached now, she heard quiet talking.

"Like I said, I'm sorry, Candace. I know I should have called you sooner....Yeah, I'll be fine in no time....What's that?" He gave a light burst of laughter. "You're not kidding. I feel...."

As his voice drifted out of hearing, Rachel dropped her hand from the doorknob as if she'd just been shocked by a live wire. Her heart, once pattering with excitement at the thought of presenting Jay with his supper, now dropped to her toes like a lead sinker. She took a full step back and deliberated whether to go downstairs again, stand at the door until she was sure he'd hung up, or simply write him a note and slip it under the door for him to find later:

Went home, you two-timing skunk. Have a happy life with Candace.

How could he do this to her—tell her he loved her and then, because she hadn't reciprocated the feelings immediately, run back to Candace? And just when had he planned to tell her about it? Gracious, what if Candace were on her way over this very minute? Perhaps the two of them were plotting even now how to get her to go home. No wonder he hadn't been overly thrilled her coming over to help. He'd wanted Candace at his side, instead!

Oh, Lord, what kind of fool was I to think he'd enjoy my barging in on him? She felt her cheeks go hot then cold as her brow beaded with perspiration.

"Rachel?" The sound of his hoarse voice on the other side of the door gave her such a jolt that the water in the glass on the tray nearly sloshed over the rim. She took several calming breaths, gripping the tray tightly, for fear she might drop it in her angst. Pondering how to proceed, she closed her eyes and muttered a hasty prayer for guidance. She figured it would be best not to let him know she'd overheard his conversation and see if he confessed it on his own.

"Rachel?" he repeated. "You down there?"

She silently tiptoed back to the stairs, went all the way down, then retraced her path to his door, making each step count, loud and exaggerated. Swallowing a hard lump, she rested the tray on a forearm and turned the doorknob. "I brought your supper," she said, pushing the door ajar.

"Hey," he said with a smile as she entered. He then winced as he sat up. "Smells great. What is it?"

"Ham and potato chowder."

"Mmm. You've been knocking yourself out downstairs, haven't you? You don't need to do that, you know. You can go home if you want."

There it was—his attempt to casually dismiss her so that Candace could come over. As she lowered the tray onto his lap, she was tempted to feign losing her balance and then dump the contents all over him. But a voice in her head told her how un-Christlike that would be, and so she resisted.

She glanced down and noticed the pool of water and the empty glass on the floor.

"Oh, sorry about that. I spilled." He sounded strangely like Meagan in his admission.

"No problem," she said, turning. "I'll go get a towel."

"No, wait." She paused in mid stride. He waved a hand at her and patted an empty space on the bed. "Why don't you keep me company?"

"Hmm?"

"Here, sit." He shifted his body a couple of inches, so she slowly advanced. "I'm not contagious, you know." Her volatile emotions made it hard for her to keep from screaming. Hadn't he just told her to go home? Men! Why did God have to make them so altogether impossible to figure out?

She lowered herself carefully onto the bed as he slurped a spoonful of hot chowder and sighed happily. "This is delicious. What's in it?"

"Ham and potatoes."

"I guessed that much, silly. What else?"

"Let's see…onions, celery, milk, flour, bouillon, salt, pepper, and, well, that's about it. Do you want the recipe?"

"Do I need it?" he asked, arching one eyebrow.

"I suppose if you want more potato and ham chowder, you do," she said with an edge to her voice.

They stared at each other for half a minute, he chewing, she clasping her hands and squeezing the blood out of her knuckles.

"How come you're not joining me?"

"I sampled enough to equal a meal," she replied.

"Gotcha. I do that when I make macaroni and cheese from the box, one of my staples. By the time it's ready for the bowl, I've already eaten almost every last noodle straight from the pan." He chuckled, but his attempt at humor fell flat for her. Did he plan to break it to her about

Candace or not? She had half a mind to ask him. Instead, she glanced down at the puddle of water.

"Did you know there is nothing on daytime television but soap operas, cartoons, and home decorating shows?" he asked.

"Is that so? I only watch *Sesame Street.*"

"What's an invalid like me supposed to do with himself? And don't tell me to read." He pointed at his beautiful, brown eyes; the left one had swollen shut, and the right one was puffy and bruised, having been smashed with his handlebars. He'd been wearing a helmet, but it had done little to protect his face.

This would be the perfect opportunity to elicit a confession about his conversation with Candace. "Oh, I suppose you could talk to...people. I presume you have your cell phone handy."

With one hand, he lifted a corner of his pillow to reveal his phone, then shook his head. "As you can imagine, it's been ringing off the hook all day."

"Yes, you're so popular, it's almost scary."

He dipped his spoon into his chowder, swishing the contents around and grinning as best as his swollen lips would let him. "Ridiculous, isn't it? Let's see, there was my mom—she called me three times—my pastor, my foreman, another guy who works for me, and Diane, my office assistant." He shook his head. "I'm telling you, I couldn't even get the rest I needed."

She gave a halfhearted laugh and pulled a piece of lint off her holey jeans. How smart of him not to mention his most recent caller. "Well, I'm going to go get a towel to mop up this spill, and then I'll go tidy the kitchen," she said, standing up.

"But we didn't even talk, and all you've been doing is cleaning. You're going to leave me to eat the rest of my supper alone?"

"I'm sure you'll survive just fine. Besides, you have your home and garden channel." She left him to stare at her back when she went to his bathroom.

"Are you mad at me?" he asked when she returned with the towel.

"Why would you think that?" She bent and mopped up the puddle with one sweep.

"Uh, the cold shoulder was the first clue."

"Maybe I'm tired." Until he came clean about Candace, she had no intention of making small talk.

Chapter 29

Things went down a slippery slope after supper. Something definitely had Rachel's dander up; however, she failed to shed any light on what it was. So, he finally came right out and asked her what had her so miffed.

"Nothing," she replied. *Translation: You ought to be able to figure it out, dodo.*

He didn't think she'd overheard him talking to Candace, as he'd been careful to keep his voice down. Besides, she'd been downstairs getting his supper ready, hadn't she? On the chance that she didn't feel appreciated, he made sure to tell her how grateful he was for her help, even told her she could feel free to leave if she wanted to, which is precisely what she did right after cleaning up the kitchen.

"Are you coming back tomorrow?" he asked before she left.

"Should I?"

"If you want to."

"Argh," she spat back, giving her foot a little stomp.

"What? Did I not answer that in the way you wanted? I don't want you to feel obligated. Why exactly did you come, anyway?"

"I wanted to help, all right? It's time I did something for you."

"So, you did feel obligated. Nice goodwill gesture, Rach, paying me back for all the times I looked in on you. But I didn't do it for the payback."

She narrowed her eyes into shimmery, blue slits and stared at him. "Who sounds mad now? I suppose you wish someone else had come in my place. And I'm not talking about your mother."

"What? Rachel, for crying out loud! You're not making any sense!"

"And you are?"

Nothing he said came off sounding right to her, and nothing she said in response satisfied him, so they wound up in a quarreling match of sorts. After she'd left, he was tempted to call her on her drive back to Fairmount, but then his pride stepped in. What was a man to do? Of course, he wanted her to come back, but not if she did so out of a sense of indebtedness. Did she have any feelings for him, or were her affections purely platonic? He'd gone out on a limb by expressing his love some time ago. Wasn't it her turn to express the same—if, indeed, she felt anything beyond a brother-sister bond? How many times did he have to tell her that the ball was in her court?

All day, he hadn't ventured further than the bathroom adjoined to his bedroom; he'd felt weak-kneed, achy, and woozy from the pain meds. He'd tried to resist taking anything stronger than over-the-counter medication, but when his pain had reached a level he couldn't ignore, he'd had to pop a pain pill. Now, at ten o'clock, he was feeling better, almost human, so he pulled back the blankets and sat up, moving slowly so as not to throw off his equilibrium. He got up and walked at a turtle's pace to the door to look down at the living room.

As he did, he got the surprise of his life. Not only did his condo look as neat as a freshly starched shirt, but Rachel had rearranged the furniture. Okay, so he didn't love the new look—he never had been one for major changes—but he did enjoy the smells of polished furniture and scrubbed floors. Even if he practiced for the next five years, he would never master housework at this level. His idea of cleaning was getting rid of clutter, not hauling out all the household products that eliminated grit and grime and made for a sparkling finish. Why, even the fireplace screen glimmered. He decided to venture downstairs for a look at the rest of the house.

The laundry room held the lingering scent of soap, and two stacks of clean, folded clothes lay on the washing machine. Even the tile floor showed no signs of the usual tracks he brought in from the garage, and his work boots, also appearing cleaner than usual, stood together in the corner, a significant departure from their customary positions five feet apart after Jason kicked them off.

In the kitchen, which gleamed and smelled of lemon, he poured himself a glass of orange juice and gulped it down at the sink, then set the glass on the counter and turned to walk away. But then, as if Rachel herself had caught him in the lazy act, he abruptly stopped, retrieved the glass, and wedged it in the top rack of the dishwasher.

Exhausted already, he shuffled back upstairs. Time to swallow his manly pride and call Rachel; forget whose court held the proverbial ball.

She didn't answer, so he left a message. "Rachel, I'm sorry we fought. I do want you to come back in the morning. By the way, my condo looks great, and I like the way you arranged the living room. But how in the world did a little thing like you move that huge sofa? I guess you're a lot stronger than I figured you to be." *Stop rambling*, he ordered himself. "Anyway, if you get this message, just know that I—well—oh, never mind, I'll talk to you in the morning. That is, if you decide to come back."

It wasn't the most convincing apology Rachel had ever heard, but she decided she'd take it, even though he'd still omitted any mention of Candace. She hadn't listened to the message until the next morning, so, after getting the kids up and dressed, she hauled them off to Grandma Evans's place and then headed down the highway to Harrietta, praying about and planning her strategy for putting her feelings out on the table.

Jason lay in bed till 9 a.m., sipping coffee he'd made earlier and watching mindless TV shows. He was alarmed to discover how much he enjoyed the home and garden channel. After about half an hour, he switched the thing off and padded to the bathroom to examine his face. *Bummer*, he thought as he leaned into the mirror. He looked like a poster child for domestic abuse with his eyes still black and the scrape across the whole side of his face still red and raw-looking. On the positive side, he felt stronger and not as achy all over, his ribs weren't as sore, and he hadn't awakened in the middle of the night in desperate need of a painkiller. Shoot, he could probably even manage fine today without assistance, but he hoped like crazy Rachel would still come. He realized he might have to feign weakness for a couple of days just to wheedle the attention out of her. Of course, first, he'd have to figure out what had gotten her so peeved the previous night.

Later, scrounging around in the kitchen for something to satisfy his rumbling stomach, he settled on a bagel with cream cheese. This he scarfed down in a few famished bites, then poured himself a second cup of coffee and stood at the counter, gazing out the window as he sipped it. Just as he took a seat at the table, he heard a car door slam shut. His heart jumped. Rachel! He hobbled to the front door and opened it wide, only to have his soaring heart fall straight to the ground in a heap.

"Candace, what are you doing here?"

"Oh, my gosh, Jason, look at you! You look terrible!" She stood on tiptoe to kiss his cheek—the less bruised one—then waltzed right past him into the condo, the stiletto heels of her knee-high boots clicking on the hardwood, her short, black skirt and the fitted leather jacket over her yellow cashmere sweater accentuating every curve. She always had been a looker, but nothing about her appearance appealed to him today. It didn't help that her showing up unannounced galled him plenty.

She eased out of her coat and draped it over the back of a chair, gave her flowing, dark hair a gentle toss, then surveyed the room. "You've rearranged your furniture. I like it. The other way wasn't exactly conducive to watching your TV or even conversing. This is much nicer."

"Thanks." Suddenly weak, he set his coffee on a side table and dropped into the sofa. Unfortunately, she chose to place herself right next to him. "You haven't told me why you're here, Candace. I don't recall inviting you." He set his hands on his knees and sat stiffly, trying to suppress his anger.

Her lower lip stuck out in an exaggerated pout. "Is that any way to talk to your former sweetheart? I only wanted to check up on you. Can I make you some breakfast? Pour you some juice?" When had she ever lifted a hand for him in the kitchen?

"No, thanks. I'm fine." No way was he about to offer her coffee, even though he had a steaming pot full of it. "Candace, I really don't think it's a good idea for—"

"Does it hurt bad?" she asked, cutting him off and moving a fraction closer before reaching up to touch his cheek. He winced and pulled away out of pain as much as in an attempt to discourage her closeness. She had a streak of determination a mile long; he'd give her that much. "I'm so sorry about your accident," she crooned. "Last night after you told me about it, I just couldn't stop thinking about you."

"Really."

"Yes. I tried to imagine life without you, Jason. It was awful."

"You've had plenty of time to get used to that, Candace. We broke up before Christmas, remember?"

She suddenly snagged his hand between both of hers and squeezed tight, her eyes pooling with tears. She never had been one to show much emotion, and whenever she did, he questioned her sincerity. "And I've been miserable ever since, Jason. Please tell me you have, as well." But when he opened his mouth to deny it, she hurried ahead. "I think you should know, I never got over you. Oh, I've dated other men, but none of them compared to you." She inched closer still. "We had good times, didn't we, Jason?"

"We did," he admitted, "but those were before—"

"What if we just started over?" she asked, sounding frantic and out of breath. "I know I could make you happy this time. Couldn't you give us a second chance? Like I said before, I'm getting downright skilled in the kitchen, and I'm even going to church."

He hated the groveling and felt almost sorry for her. "Going to church is a good thing, Candace, as long as it's a biblically based church and you're going with the right motives. But you should know it's too late for us, regardless of anything you do."

"That's where you're wrong, Jason. It's never too late." Before he had time to react, she reached her hands behind his neck and drew him down to her, planting a hard, wet, unforgiving kiss on his lips.

Upon pulling into the parking lot in front of Jason's condo, Rachel parked next to a red Toyota Camry and cut the engine. She was plagued by the nagging notion that she shouldn't have come, but she pulled the keys from the ignition and dropped them in her purse, anyway. Then, she gathered up the gallon of milk and loaf of bread she'd purchased at the corner market, pulled her purse strap over her shoulder, and slid out of the van, closing the door with her hip. Curiosity made her peek inside the car parked beside hers. On the leather-upholstered front seat lay a yellow silk scarf, an empty water bottle, and several pieces of mail addressed to Candace Peterson. Her heart thudded hard against the wall of her chest, and she sucked in a deep breath for courage before trudging up the walkway.

Lord, give me strength, she prayed. *If Jay has set me up for finding Candace and him together, please forgive me ahead of time for killing him.*

She tried the knob and discovered it was unlocked, so she opened the door and stepped inside. What she saw made her stomach twist, her legs teeter, and her hand nearly drop the gallon of milk. Sitting on the sofa like two snug bugs were Jason and Candace, kissing, no less. Candace's arms were wrapped around Jason's neck, holding him close.

As soon as Jason spotted her with his less swollen eye, he pulled away from Candace. "Rachel!" he exclaimed, standing much faster than she'd thought him capable of doing and causing Candace to tumble backward.

"Rachel?" Candace asked in a stupefied tone, pulling herself up and pivoting on the sofa to stare wide-eyed at her. "Well, well, if it isn't your lovely sister-in-law. What in the world brings her here? And, good gracious, how are you, Rachel?"

"I'm fine, but I—I see I'm interrupting." She hated herself for the tears that sprang to her eyes.

"Indeed, you are," Candace said.

"Actually, you're not interrupting at all," Jason said, his face an ashen gray but turning greener by the second. Then to his girlfriend, or whatever she was, he said, "Candace was just leaving, weren't you, Candace?"

"I was?" She reclined again, this time stretching out her long, graceful arms across the back of the sofa as if preparing to watch a movie. With a Cheshire-cat grin, she said, "I thought we were just getting warmed up, Jase."

"Don't be absurd. That kiss was purely one-sided, and you know it." To Rachel, he implored, "Come in."

"No, I think I'll go." She swiveled on her heel and walked back outside, where the biting air sent chills from the top of her head clear to her toes.

She felt ridiculous still carrying the milk and bread under her arm, so she bent to place them on the doorstep. When she stood up again, Jason nabbed her by the arm and turned her around. "Don't you even think about getting in your car," he said firmly.

"You can't tell me what to do."

"Okay, let me rephrase that." He swallowed hard and took a deep breath. "Rachel, please come back in the house." She gazed past him to see that Candace hadn't moved so much as a hair on her pretty head. If anything, she'd settled in more cozily on the couch.

"Three's a crowd, Jay, or didn't you know? And, by the way, I overheard you talking to Candace on the phone yesterday." This she said just above a whisper. "I suppose you planned this entire event—Candace's coming over this morning at precisely the time you might have expected me to arrive. Very clever."

"What? No! I did not invite her, and as for the phone call, I purposely didn't tell you because I didn't want you getting the wrong idea. She called me, not the other way around."

"Uh-huh. Right. You expect me to believe she came over here of her own accord?"

"I know it hardly seems plausible, but if you knew Candace, you'd understand. She's very assertive, and...well, she still has high hopes for us, even though I've done nothing to encourage her." He turned and looked in through the doorway. Candace still hadn't moved, other than to hold out one manicured hand and inspect the state of her nail polish.

"You're probably going to also tell me she forced you to kiss her."

"That's exactly what I'm going to tell you." He gave a low chuckle. "I had my lips sealed up tighter than a jar of pickles."

"That's very funny, Jason," she said drily, shaking her head. "You told me you loved me, remember? And I was beginning to come to terms with my own feelings for you, but now...this fiasco. What do you want me to think? Good grief, I saw the two of you kissing, tight-lipped or not. If you ask me, you two deserve each other." Blotting her damp eyes, she turned and hustled down the porch steps, intending to jump into her car and speed toward home. But Jason beat her to the car door, albeit out of breath and as pale as a summer cloud, save for his burnt-red cheek.

"Wait a minute. What did you just say?"

She huffed with impatience. "I said, you two deserve each other."

"No, no, before that. The part about coming to terms with your feelings."

"It doesn't matter now," she said as more tears pooled in the corners of her eyes.

He put a palm to the side of her face and gently lifted it. "Of course it matters, sweetheart. It matters a great deal."

"Don't call me that." Her heart thumped past her chest, making it hard to swallow, much less breathe.

"What's going on out there?" Candace asked from the doorway. "Does it usually take this long to tell your sister-in-law good-bye, Jason?"

Jason heaved a sigh and said, loudly enough for Ivy Bronson and her Pomeranian pup to hear, "Candace, get in your car and go home."

"What?" she screeched.

"You heard me. Go. And don't bother coming back; I'm having a conversation with the woman I love."

"The woman you—what? Well, I never!" Her confounded expression aroused a tiny bit of sympathy in Rachel's heart, but it quickly vanished as she watched the tall beauty nab her jacket and click down the hallway in her spiky heels, her mouth pursed in a tight frown that dulled her pretty face. She marched past them and over to her car, eyes on the sidewalk, then stopped before opening the door and peering up at them. "You and your sister-in-law, Jason? Honestly! Isn't that a rather...um, inappropriate arrangement?"

He shrugged and tilted his battered face down at Rachel, grinning broadly. "Uncommon, maybe; inappropriate, no." Then he turned to grant Candace one last look. "Sorry about everything," he called to her. "I hope you find what you're looking for."

"Pfff," she spat, shaking her head in obvious disgust. "You two deserve each other."

She yanked open her car door, climbed inside, and started the engine. Without so much as a glance at them, she backed out of the space and sped off, wheels squealing.

Despite the rather cheerless situation, Rachel and Jason shared a laugh over her parting remark, and it seemed to fuse them together with an unspoken promise of tender vows.

Chapter 30

Back inside his condo, Jason collapsed on the sofa, bringing Rachel with him. Her featherlight body fell into his lap, and he wrapped his arms around her and pulled her snugly to his side. She scrambled to get up, but he wouldn't have it. He'd waited too long for this moment.

"What are you doing, Jay?" she asked, swiveling to look at him, her breath warm and moist on his neck, her lips close enough to kiss. "I'm afraid I'll hurt your ribs. You'd better let me up."

His heart fluttered and flapped as if on butterflies' wings. "Not on your life, honey." Slowly relenting, she relaxed against his chest, where the cloth bandage was still wrapped securely around his torso. Everything about her felt right and perfect. He snagged a lock of her hair and twirled it around his finger. "Did you mean it, Rach, when you said you'd come to terms with your feelings?" He couldn't help the husky quality of his voice, thanks to his nerves.

She didn't answer right off but just sat there in his lap. Her toes didn't quite reach the floor, putting him in mind of an innocent child. She clasped her hands together and touched them to her chin, then nestled in close to his chest. The pressure of her body against his and her shoulder poking into his ribs pained him a little; but the pure joy of it far outweighed any discomfort.

"Well?" he urged her, hungry for her reply, praying for the one he longed to hear. "Want to tell me what conclusion you've reached?"

"You want the fancy answer or the no-frills one?"

He centered his chin on top of her head and rubbed little circles into the upper part of her arm, chuckling softly. "I'm tempted to get right to the no-frills one, but if you want to work your way up to it, that's fine."

"I'll try to keep my answer as brief as possible, but I am a woman, after all." He could almost hear her smile.

He couldn't help himself; he leaned around and kissed her cheek. "You'll get no argument from me about that."

She swallowed and took a couple of slow, methodical breaths. "I found one of John's diaries."

He gently set her back from him to look into her eyes. "Really? Did you read it?"

She gave a slow nod. "I thought I'd feel guilty, but afterward, I knew he would have wanted me to read it. I also found a letter he wrote to me way before the kids were even born."

"You're kidding. And he never gave it to you?"

"Nope." She licked her lips, then pressed them together while weighing her next words. "It's okay, though. It was meant to happen just as it did." She settled against him again, the fit as flawless as a long-lost puzzle piece. "It helped to clear up a lot of things for me."

"Such as?"

"Well, you probably won't believe this, but in that letter, he actually said that if anything ever happened to him, the only person he'd ever approve of my remarrying is you."

This rendered him speechless for several moments. Shoot, he couldn't even move. He stopped rubbing Rachel's arm and stared across the room at a framed photo of him and

John, taken two summers ago at Lakewood Golf Course. Finally, he managed to formulate a sentence. "You're kidding, right? He didn't actually write that. I mean—what in the world could have possessed him to say that, especially when he went so crazy thinking you and I had feelings for each other?"

"He loved and respected you so much, Jay. True, he couldn't bear to think of us being in love, but he also couldn't stand the thought of me ever giving my heart to anybody else if something were to happen to him. It's weird and paradoxical that he wrote that letter, as if he had some peculiar sense of impending doom. I hate to think about it, really, and yet his writing it gave me just the affirmation I needed." She paused for a moment, then went on.

"I think I wasn't ready to give myself the freedom to love again, and particularly not you, knowing that John had argued with you over me in his final hour. But when I read that letter and then his diary with entries leading up to your skiing trip…well, it just set me on a different course and freed me for thinking about…stuff."

Jason resumed gently rubbing her arm, his heart thumping out a hard and fast rhythm. "Stuff, huh?" he asked, kissing the top of her head.

She looked up at him and smiled. "Yes—stuff."

"What sort of stuff, Rachel Kay?"

"Future stuff, Jason Allen."

"Ah." He trailed a few feathery kisses from her temple area down to her jawline. "As in our future?"

"Exactly."

※

Their kisses were lush and dense, as soft and smooth as fine silk. They involved willful gravity that kept them from getting close enough, melding lips and pounding hearts, splayed hands touching every allowable part from backs to napes to hair to waists. Each tender kiss made them long for more, and so when one ended, they drew apart, smileless, only to catch a breath and start afresh, one kiss following another until they all blended together, no ending, no beginning.

"Rachel," he murmured.

"Jay," she whispered.

He broke free first, and, for some time, they merely gazed at each other. It occurred to her that she still hadn't spoken those three tender words, but for the moment, it mattered little.

"I have never known anyone as lovely as you, Rachel."

"And you are the handsomest man on earth, Jason." It thrilled her to say it. They laughed and touched foreheads. "I should probably get off your lap."

"Why?"

"Aren't I hurting you?"

"It would hurt more if you left me."

She stole the next kiss, meeting his mouth and then moving her lips to kiss his less bruised cheek, then ever so gently the other one, then traversing to both eyes. "Poor, poor Jay, colliding with that bad car."

"Oh, it wasn't so bad; it brought me you, didn't it?" he said. "Speaking of, just how long would you have made me wait if that car hadn't plowed into me?"

She put a finger to her chin. "Oh, I don't know. Till a truck came along, maybe."

"What? You're cruel."

She giggled, then quickly sobered. "Actually, Jason, it wouldn't have been long. The Lord's been giving me little signs, subtle but sure. I have no further doubts about us."

He gripped her hands. "You're sure about that?"

"Absolutely."

"Then say the words."

She knew exactly what he was talking about, and her heart swelled with eagerness to say them. Holding her breath and pressing one cheek to his, she ceased breathing. "I love you, Jay."

She felt his eyes close when his lashes brushed her face. They sat unmoving, each reveling in the other's presence.

After a moment, he gently pushed her off him. "Wait here."

"What? Where are you going?"

"I'll be right back." He got up and limped to the stairs.

"Jay, there's a bathroom down here."

He chuckled. "That's not where I'm heading."

"Then what—? Do you need help?"

He took each step with care, then looked down at her and winked. "Like I said, I'll be right back."

True to his word, he reappeared just seconds later, nothing amiss or different, as far as she could see. "What did you do?"

"You're a nosy little thing, aren't you?" he teased as he descended the stairs. "Close your eyes."

"What?"

"And stubborn. Close your eyes."

She obeyed but not without a mountain of curiosity building inside her. "What in the world?" she whispered. "You should know I'm not very good with surprises. I always want to peek."

"Well, restrain yourself, woman."

A spontaneous giggle erupted. At last, he arrived at her side, his musky scent and quiet breaths awakening her senses to his nearness. She kept her eyes pressed shut until he gave her permission to open them after he'd planted himself beside her.

In his hand was a small package wrapped in gold foil with a tiny bow fastened to the top. "Merry Christmas," he whispered, placing it in her open hand.

"What? Christmas? I don't understand. Why didn't you give this to me earlier?"

"I—really couldn't. It was a bit too…um, telling of my feelings."

"Oh." She stared at the pretty box, suddenly feeling jittery. "May I open it?"

He chortled and bent to nip at her ear lobe. "You'd better."

Slowly, carefully, she removed the paper to find a silver box. With shaking fingers, she lifted the lid to reveal a velvet heart-shaped container. "Oh, how beautiful," she ogled, her chest so tightly compressed it almost hurt to take in air.

"Open it," he urged her, his warm breath tickling her cheek.

Hesitantly, she did so, shrieking with pleasure and shock at her first glimpse of two glistening diamond stud earrings. "Jason, this is too much!"

"No, it's not." He pulled her to him and whispered in her ear, "Actually, I'm thinking along the lines of something to fit on your finger next time. What would you say to that?"

She gasped and felt her face go feverishly hot. "Are you—?"

Once again, he got up, but this time he didn't go far, just stood, turned around, and then went down on one knee, albeit slowly and with the tiniest wince. "Jason, you don't have to do this."

"Oh, but I do. It's my first proposal, and I mean to do it up right—well, minus the ring for now, if you don't mind." He sighed and wrinkled his nose. "I'm doing this all backwards, aren't I?"

She giggled. "Oh, my. This is too much. But I love it—and I love you."

"Mrs. Evans," he said, sobering, taking both her hands in his and squeezing, looking at her through his good eye, the other one opening to a mere slit. "I promise to make my brother proud by loving and caring for you always. Would you do me the honor of being my bride, pending the purchase of a ring, which I will allow you to select at your convenience?"

She couldn't restrain herself. Laughter mingled with tears. "Yes! Oh, my goodness, yes!" With the velvet box in hand, she flung her arms around his neck and planted kisses all over his face and neck, taking care to be gentle at the bruised places.

Between fervent kisses, they planned an August wedding, made precious promises to each other, spoke of their future with excitement, and expressed their amazement at the God they served. How incredible that He should orchestrate so fine a plan that would bring them together in this way.

Somehow, the topic of Jay's passion for skiing came up, and Rachel suggested quite by surprise that he ought to go back out. "Next winter," she said. "You need to conquer whatever fears you might have and fall in love with the sport all over again."

She meant it, too, knowing that his return to the slopes would in some way help bring her a certain sense of closure and healing.

"Really?" He squinted at her in disbelief. "But I thought you'd never approve, that the memories...."

She laid a hand on his powerful arm, drawing strength from the mere touch. "I wouldn't dream of holding you back, Jay. I've tasted fear, and it's not of God; therefore, I refuse to let it rule my life. When you decide to hit those slopes again, I will be cheering you on. And"—she put her hands together in a prayerful gesture and looked heavenward—"I can't believe I'm saying this, but if, at some point, Meaggie or Johnny wants to learn, well, I will trust you to teach them."

"Rachel," he whispered, touching his forehead to hers again. "Are you listening to yourself? You've come a long way."

She giggled. "Don't expect me to ever go out there, though. That's where I draw the line. I mean, just the thought of getting on one of those—those things that take you to the top of the hill—"

"Chair lifts," he supplied.

"Uh-uh." She gave her head several adamant shakes. "John always tried to talk me into letting you teach me, but I had no interest, and that hasn't changed. So, please don't start trying to convince me that it's fun to attach your feet to two long, skinny boards and slide down a steep, snow-covered hill."

"I wouldn't dream of it."

"Because I will turn you down again and again."

"I believe you."

"And one more thing."

He couldn't seem to get the silly grin off his face. "I can hardly wait to hear what that will be."

"I would like to have another baby," she blurted out with little premeditation. Yes, she'd been thinking about it lately, but shouldn't she have considered her timing a bit more carefully? He'd only just proposed, for goodness' sake!

First, his eyebrows shot up, his slit of a swollen eye widening a bit, and then his mouth dropped nearly to his knees, stunned silence holding him in its grip. But, suddenly, it all gave way to riotous laughter and a hug so tight that she struggled to breathe. "Rachel Kay Evans, you are a wonder. I can't believe I'm still learning about you after all these years. As for your desire to expand our family, I'm all for it."

"Really?" She let out a ragged sigh as tears of joy trickled from the corners of her eyes. Gracious, she was a see-saw of emotions. "Jason, my heart is bursting."

He captured her and pulled her close. "Mine, too."

And in those heart-bursting, dream-building minutes, two souls made one tender vow to love till their last breath.

A Preview of Book One in the

River of Hope Series

by Sharlene MacLaren
Coming in Fall 2011

Chapter One

May 1926
Wabash, Indiana

"Praise ye the LORD. Sing unto the LORD a new song."
—Psalm 149:1

S moke rings rose and circled the heads of Charley Arnold and Roy Scott as they sat in Livvie's Kitchen, each partaking of steaming coffee, savory roast beef and gravy, and conversation, guffawing every so often at each other's blather. Neither seemed to care much who heard them, since the whole place buzzed with boisterous midday talk. Folks came to Livvie's Kitchen to fill their stomachs, but for many, getting an earful of talk and gossip was just as satisfying.

Behind the counter, utensils banged against metal, and pots and pans sizzled and boiled with steam and smoke. "Order's up!" hollered the cook, Joe Stewart. On cue, Olivia Beckman, the owner, set down two hamburger platters in front of Mr. and Mrs. Waters and delivered them a hasty smile. Her knee-length, cotton floral skirt flared as she turned, mopped her brow, blew several strawberry blonde strands of damp hair off her face, and hustled to the counter. "You boys put out those disgusting nicotine sticks," she scolded Charley and Roy on the run. "How many times do I have to tell you, I don't allow smoking in my establishment? I don't even have ashtrays."

348

"Aw, Livvie, how you expect us to enjoy a proper cup of coffee without a cigarette? 'Sides, ar' saucers work fine for ashtrays," Charley whined to her back.

"Saucers are not ashtrays," stated old Mrs. Garner from the booth behind the two men. She craned her long, skinny neck to train her owl eyes on them, her lips pinched together in a tight frown. Mr. Garner had nothing to say, of course. He rarely did, preferring to let his wife do the talking. Instead, he slurped wordlessly on his tomato soup.

Livvie snatched the next order form from the counter and gave it a glance, lifted two more plates, one with macaroni and cheese and a roll and the other a chicken drumstick with mashed potatoes, then whirled back around, eyeing both men sternly. "I expect you to follow my rules, boys"— she traipsed past them—"or go next door to Zeke's, where the smoke's as thick as cow dung."

Her saucy remark gave rise to riotous hoots. "You tell 'em, Liv," someone said—Harv Brewster, perhaps? What with the racket of babies crying, patrons chattering, the cash register clinking as Cora Mae tallied somebody's order, the screen door flapping open and shut, and car horns honking outside, Livvie couldn't discern who said what.

"You best listen, fellas. When Livvie Beckman speaks, she means every word," said another. She turned at the husky male voice but couldn't identify its source.

"Lady, you got to start goin' to preachin' school," said yet another unknown speaker.

"Yup, yup. She's somethin', ain't she?" No mistaking Coot Hermanson's croaky pipes. Her most loyal customer— also the oldest by far—gave her one of his famous toothy grins over his coffee cup, which he held with trembling fingers. No one really knew Coot's age, and most people suspected he didn't know it, himself, but Livvie thought he looked to be a hundred—ninety-nine, at the very least. But that didn't keep him from showing up at her diner on Market Street every day, huffing from the two-block walk, his faithful black mongrel, Reggie, parked on his haunches out under the awning, waiting for his usual handout of leftover bacon or oatmeal or the heels of a fresh-baked loaf of bread.

Before scooting past him, she stooped to tap him with her elbow. "I'll be right back to fill that coffee cup, Coot," she whispered into his good ear.

He lifted an ancient white eyebrow and winked. "You take your time, missy," he whispered back before she straightened and hurried along.

Of all her regulars, Coot probably knew her best—knew about the tough façade she put on, day in and day out; recognized the rawness of her heart, the ache she carried straight to her bones. She'd talked to him on many a day when business had slowed and he'd hung back, telling her about his sweet Bessie or listening as she spoke in hushed tones about Frank and her deep sense of loss. Almost a year had come and gone since her husband's passing, but she still dampened her pillow almost every night after tucking in her young sons, Alex and Nathan, saddened by how little they spoke of their daddy anymore. It made her frantic to keep his memory alive, so she constantly told them stories—how she'd met him at a church picnic on a hot July day when she was seventeen and he a mere five months older; how he'd loved to laugh and build things with his hands; how he'd thrived on playing baseball and fishing and hunting rabbits, squirrels, and raccoons; how he'd always enjoyed cooking a fine dinner for his family, rare among young men, as most boys his age wouldn't have been caught dead alongside their mothers in the kitchen.

She told them how, from the day they'd met, he'd spoken of his dream to own a restaurant, and how, once they'd married, they'd saved every spare penny to open Livvie's

Kitchen. She had worked in a five-and-dime until Alex was born; Frank had worked in a factory. She relayed his utter joy when they'd cut the ribbon and welcomed their first customers, Coot Hermanson and a lineup of others who would one day become regulars. What she failed to tell them was how hard it was to keep her passion alive in their daddy's absence. Oh, she had Joe Stewart, but he'd just dropped the news last week that he'd picked up a new kitchen job in a Chicago eatery, some well-known establishment, he'd said, and he could hardly turn it down, especially with his daughter and grandchildren begging him to move closer to them. Wabash had been home to Joe since childhood, but with his wife's passing, he had little to keep him here. It made sense, Livvie supposed, but it didn't make her life any easier having to find a replacement.

She set down two plates for a couple she'd not seen before, a middle-aged man and his wife. Strangers were always passing through Wabash on their way north or south, so it wasn't unusual for her not to know them. "You folks enjoy your lunch," she said with a smile.

"Thank you kindly," said the man while loosening his tie and licking his lips. "This meal looks mighty fine."

She nodded, then made for the coffeepot behind the counter, sensing it was time for a round of refills.

Smoke still rose over Charley and Roy's heads, though their cigarettes looked to be nearing their ends. She decided not to mention anything further about their obnoxious behavior unless they lit up again. Those old fools had little compunction and even less consideration for the comfort of others. She would have liked to ban them from her restaurant, except for the revenue they brought in with their almost daily visits. Gracious, it cost an awful lot to keep Livvie's Kitchen operating. She would sell it tomorrow if she had a backup plan, which she didn't. Besides, Frank would bust out of his casket if she hung a "For Sale" sign on the front door. The diner had been his dream, and she'd adopted it with gusto because she'd loved him so much, but she hadn't anticipated his leaving her alone in the thick of it, especially with bank loans yet to pay off and a good profit still to be made.

Oh, why had God taken Frank at such a young age? He'd been thirty-one, married for ten years and the owner of the restaurant for five. Couldn't God easily have intervened and sent an angel just in time to keep Frank from stepping in front of that horse-drawn wagon hauling furniture? And why, for mercy's sake, did the accident have to occur right in front of the restaurant, drawing a huge crowd and forever etching in Livvie's mind's eye the sight of her beloved lying in the middle of the street, blood oozing from his nose and mouth, his eyes open but not seeing? Coot always told her God had her best interests in mind and that she needed to trust Him with her whole heart, but how could she when it seemed like few things ever went right for her and she had to work so hard to stay afloat? Goodness, she barely had a minute to spare for her own children.

She swallowed a sigh, hefted up the coffeepot when it finished percolating, and started the refills with Coot Hermanson.

⋙⊜

Will Taylor ground out his last cigarette with his worn sole as he leaned against the wall of the train car, his head pounding with every jar of the tracks, the whir and buzz of metal touching metal ripping through him. He stared down at his empty pack of Luckies and turned up his mouth in the corner, giving a little huff of self-disgust. He didn't really smoke—at least, not anymore—but when he'd left Welfare Island State Penitentiary in New York City in the wee hours of the morning, one of the guards had handed him a fresh pack, along with what few belongings he had to his name, and he'd smoked the entire thing to help pass the time.

Sharing the mostly empty freight car with him were a dozen or so men, the majority of whom wore unkempt beards, ragged clothing, and long faces. They also stank to the heavens. He figured he fit right in with the lot of them. Frankly, they all looked like a bunch of bums—and probably were, for that matter. Why else would they have jumped aboard the freight car at various stations while the yardmen had their backs turned? Will had intended to pay his fare and had even found himself standing in line at the ticket booth, but when he'd counted his meager stash of cash, he'd fallen back out. Thankfully, the dense morning fog had made his train-jumping maneuver a cinch. If only it had had the same effect on his conscience. He'd just been released from prison. Could he not get through his first day of freedom without breaking the law?

"Where you headed, mister?" the man closest to him asked.

He could count on one hand the number of minutes anybody on that dark, dingy car had engaged in conversation in the hours they'd been riding, and he didn't much feel like talking now, but he turned to the fellow, anyway. "Wabash, Indiana," he answered. "Heard it's a nice place."

Actually, he knew nothing about it, save for the state song, "On the Banks of the Wabash, Far Away," which spoke about the river running through it. He'd only just determined his destination that morning while poring over a map in the train station, thinking that any other place in the country would beat where he'd spent the last ten years. Overhearing someone mention Wabash, he'd found it on the map and, being that it had its own song, set his mind to going there.

He didn't know a soul in Wabash, which made the place that much more appealing. Best to start fresh where nobody knew him. Of course, he had no idea what he'd do to make a living, and it might be that he'd have to move on to the next town if jobs there were scarce. But he'd cross that bridge when he came to it.

His stomach growled, so he unwrapped his knapsack and took out an apple, just one of the few items he'd lifted from the jail kitchen the previous night—with the approval of Harry Wilkinson, the kitchen supervisor. The friends he'd made at Welfare Island were few—couldn't trust most folks any farther than he could pitch them—but he did consider Harry a friend, having worked alongside him for the past four years. Harry had told him about the love of God and convinced him not six months ago to give his heart over to Him, saying he'd need a good friend when he left the Island and could do no better than the Creator of the universe. Will had agreed, of course, but he sure was green in the faith department, even though he'd taken to reading the Bible Harry had given him—his first and only—almost every night before laying his head on his flat, frayed pillow.

"Wabash, eh?" the man said, breaking into his musings. "I heard of it. Ain't that the first electrically lighted city in the world? I do believe that's their claim to fame."

"That right? I wouldn't know."

"What takes you to Wabash?" he persisted, pulling on his straggly beard.

Will pulled on his own thick beard, mostly brown with some flecks of blond, briefly wondering if he ought to shave it off before he went in search of a job. He'd seen his reflection in a mirror that morning for the first time in a week and had nearly fallen over. In fact, he had to do some mental figuring to determine that he was actually thirty-four years and not fifty-four. Prison had not been good to his appearance—there were lines around his eyes from slaving under a hot summer sun digging trenches and hoeing the prison garden. The winters had been spent hauling coal and chopping logs, and while the work had put him in excellent shape physically, the sun and wind had wreaked havoc on his skin, freckling his nose and arms and wrinkling his forehead. When he hadn't been outside, he'd worked in a scorching-hot kitchen stirring kettles of soup, peeling potatoes, onions, and carrots, cutting slabs of beef, filleting fish, and plucking chickens' feathers.

"It seemed as good a place as any," he replied after some thought, determined to keep his answers short and vague.

The fellow peered at him with arched eyebrows. "Where you come from, anyway?"

"Around."

A chuckle floated through the air but quickly drowned in the train's blaring whistle. The man dug into his side pocket and brought out a cigar, stuck it in his mouth, and lit the end, then took a deep drag before blowing out a long stream of smoke. He gave a slow, thoughtful nod and gazed off. "Yeah, I know. Me, too." Across the dark space, the others shifted or slept, legs crossed at the ankles, heads bobbing, not seeming to care about the conversation, if they even heard it.

He might have inquired after his traveling companion, but his years behind bars had taught him plenty—most important, not to trust his fellow man, and certainly never to divulge his personal history. And he'd only invite inquiries of himself if he posed them to others.

After chomping down his final bite of apple, he tossed the chiseled core onto the floor, figuring a rodent would appreciate it later. He wiped his hands on his pant legs and pulled out his trusty harmonica from his hip pocket. Moistening his lips, he brought the instrument to his mouth and started breathing into it, cupping it like he might a beautiful woman's face. Music had always soothed whatever ailed him, and he'd often whiled away the hours playing this humble instrument, having picked up the skill as a youngster under his grandfather's expert tutelage.

He must have played a good half dozen songs—"Oh, Dem Golden Slippers," "Oh My Darling, Clementine," "Over There," "Amazing Grace," "The Sidewalks of New York," and even "On the Banks of the Wabash, Far Away"—before he learned they'd entered the town of Wabash. The shrill train whistle announced their arrival, and another stowaway pulled the big door open a crack to gaze out and establish their whereabouts.

Quickly, Will stuffed his mouth organ back into his pocket and stretched his back, the taut muscles tingling from being stationary for so long. At least his pounding headache had relented, replaced now by a mess of tangled nerves. Or, perhaps "reserved excitement" better described his emotions.

"Nice playin'," said a man whose face was hidden by the shadow of his low-lying hat. He tipped the brim at Will and gave a slow nod. "You've got a way with that thing. Almost put me in a lonesome-type mood."

"Thanks. I mean, for the compliment. Sorry 'bout your gloomy mood. Didn't mean to bring that on."

"Ain't nothin'. I been jumpin' trains f'r as long as I can remember. Gettin' the lonelies every now and again is somethin' to be 'spected, I s'pose."

"That's for sure," mumbled another man sitting in a corner with his legs stretched out. Will glanced at the sole of his boot and noticed his sock pushing through a gaping hole. Something like a rock turned over in his gut. These guys made a habit of hopping on trains, living off handouts, and roaming the countryside. Vagabonds, they were. He hoped never to see the inside of another freight car, and by gum, he'd see to it he didn't—with the Lord's help, that is. He had about enough money to last a couple of weeks, so long as he holed up someplace dirt-cheap and watched what he spent on food. He prayed he'd land a job—any job—in that time. He wouldn't be choosy in the beginning; he couldn't afford to be. If he had to haul garbage, well, so be it. He couldn't expect much more than that, not with a criminal record. His hope was that no one would inquire. After all, who else but somebody downright desperate would hire an ex-con? Not that he planned to offer that little tidbit of information, but he supposed anybody could go digging if they really wanted to know.

He hadn't changed his name to protect his identity, even though Harry had advised him to. "I'm not going to run for the rest of my life, Harry," he'd argued. "Heck, I served my time. It's not that I plan to broadcast it, mind you, but I'm not going to carry the weight of it forever, either. I wasn't the only one involved in that stupid burglary." Harry had nodded in silence, then reached up to lay a bony hand on Will's hulking shoulder. Few people ever laid a hand on him and got away with it, so, naturally, he'd started to pull away, but Harry had held firm, forcing Will to loosen up. "You got a good point there, Will. You're a good man, you know that?" He hadn't known that, and he'd appreciated Harry's vote of confidence. "You just got to go out there and be yourself. Folks will believe in you if you take the first step, start seeing your own self-worth. The Lord sees it, and you need to look at yourself through His eyes. Before you know it, your past will no longer matter—not to you or to anyone else."

The train brakes screeched for all of a minute, with smoke rising up from the tracks and seeping through the cracks of the dirty car. Will choked back the burning residue and stood, gazing down at his strange companions, feeling a certain kinship with them he'd never expected to experience. "You men be safe, now," he said, passing his gaze over each one. Several acknowledged him with a nod, but most of them just gave him a vacant stare. The fellow at the back of the car who'd spent the entire day sleeping in the shadows finally lifted his face a notch. Assessing eyes drilled into him, but Will shook off any uneasiness.

The one who'd first struck up a conversation with Will, short-lived as it was, raised his bearded chin and made eye contact with him. "You watch yourself out there, fella. You got to move fast once your feet hit that dirt. Anybody sees you jumpin' off is sure to report you, and if it's one of the yardmen, well, you may as well kiss your hiney good-bye. They got weapons on them, and they don't look kindly on us spongers."

"Thanks. I'll be on guard." Little did they know how adept he was at handling himself. His years served in the state pen had taught him survival skills he hoped never to have to use in the outside world. When the train finally stopped, he reached inside his front shirt pocket and snagged his watch, which was missing its chain. Ten minutes after seven. Dropping it back inside his pocket, he pulled the sliding door open just enough to fit his bulky body through, then poked his head out and looked around. Finding the coast clear, thanks to a long freight train parked on neighboring tracks, he gave the fellows one last nod, leaped from the car, and slinked off into the gathering dusk, his sack of meager possessions slung over his shoulder.

First thing on his short agenda: look for a restaurant where he could silence his grumbling stomach.

About the Author

Born and raised in western Michigan, Sharlene MacLaren attended Spring Arbor University. Upon graduating with an education degree, she traveled internationally for a year with a small singing ensemble, then came home and married one of her childhood friends. Together they raised two lovely daughters. Now happily retired after teaching elementary school for thirty-one years, "Shar" enjoys reading, writing, singing in the church choir and worship teams, traveling, and spending time with her husband, children, and precious grandchildren.

A Christian for over forty years and a lover of the English language, Shar has always enjoyed dabbling in writing—poetry, fiction, various essays, and freelancing for periodicals and newspapers. Her favored genre, however, has always been romance. She remembers well the short stories she wrote in high school and watching them circulate from girl to girl during government and civics classes."Psst," someone would whisper from two rows over, always when the teacher's back was to the class, "pass me the next page."

Shar is an occasional speaker for her local MOPS organization; is involved in KIDS' HOPE USA, a mentoring program for at-risk children; counsels young women in the Apples of Gold program; and is active in two weekly Bible studies. She and her husband, Cecil, live in Spring Lake, Michigan, with Mocha, their lazy, fat cat.

The acclaimed *Through Every Storm* was Shar's first novel to be published by Whitaker House, and in 2007, the American Christian Fiction Writers (ACFW) named it a finalist for Book of the Year. *Long Journey Home* is a contemporary tale of healing hearts, rekindled faith, and finding love in life's tragedies. The beloved Little Hickman Creek series consists of *Loving Liza Jane*; *Sarah, My Beloved*; and *Courting Emma*. Faith, Hope, and Love, the Inspirational Outreach Chapter of Romance Writers of America, announced *Sarah, My Beloved* as a finalist in its 2008 Inspirational Reader's Choice Contest in the category of long historical fiction. In 2009, she received the same honor for *Courting Emma*.

Hannah Grace, *Maggie Rose*, and *Abbie Ann* compose Shar's latest historical trilogy, The Daughters of Jacob Kane, and in 2010, Shar received yet another nomination from the IRCC for *Hannah Grace*.

In the fall of 2011, Shar's newest series, River of Hope, will release its first installment.

Loving Liza Jane
Book One in the Little Hickman Creek Series
Sharlene MacLaren

When Liza Jane Merriwether rode into the town of Little Hickman Creek, her first thought was, *Oh, Lord, what have I done?* Soon, the petite schoolteacher is beloved by all… including Benjamin Broughton, a handsome widower struggling to raise two young children. Liza Jane's teaching contract explicitly states that she is to have "no improper contact with the opposite sex." Together, they may discover that with God, all things are possible.

ISBN: 978-0-88368-816-8 • Trade • 352 pages

WHITAKER
HOUSE

Sarah, My Beloved
Book Two in the Little Hickman Creek Series
Sharlene MacLaren

Sarah Woodward steps off the stagecoach to find that the man who had contacted her through the Marriage Made in Heaven Agency has fallen in love with and wed another woman. Sarah feels that God led her to Little Hickman Creek for a reason. She refuses to leave until she finds out what that reason is. Rocky Callahan's sister has died, leaving him with two young children to take care of. When he meets the fiery Sarah Woodward, he proposes the answer to both their problems—a marriage in name only. Will Sarah and Rocky find true love from the hand of the ultimate Matchmaker?

ISBN: 978-0-88368-425-2 • Trade • 368 pages

WHITAKER
HOUSE

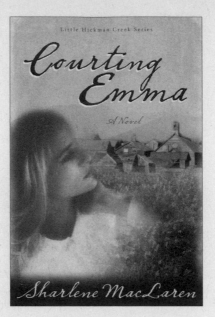

Courting Emma
Book Three in the Little Hickman Creek Series
Sharlene MacLaren

Twenty-eight-year-old Emma Browning has experienced a good deal of life in her young age. Proprietor of Emma's Boardinghouse, she is "mother" to an array of beefy, unkempt, often rowdy characters. Though many men would like to get to know the steely, hard-edged, yet surprisingly lovely proprietor, none has truly succeeded. That is, not until the town's new pastor, Jonathan Atkins, takes up residence in the boardinghouse.

ISBN: 978-1-60374-020-3 • Trade • 384 pages

WHITAKER
HOUSE

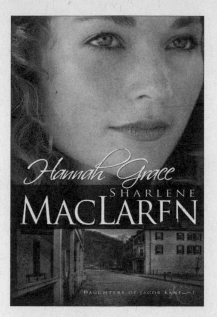

Hannah Grace
Book One in The Daughters of Jacob Kane Series
Sharlene MacLaren

Hannah Grace, the eldest of Jacob Kane's three daughters, is feisty and strong-willed, yet practical. She has her life planned out in an orderly, meaningful way—or so she thinks. When Gabriel Devlin comes to town as the new sheriff, the two strike up a volatile relationship that turns toward romance, thanks to a shy orphan boy and a little divine intervention.

ISBN: 978-1-60374-074-6 ✦ Trade ✦ 432 pages

WHITAKER
HOUSE

Maggie Rose
Book Two in The Daughters of Jacob Kane Series
Sharlene MacLaren

In 1904, Maggie Rose Kane leaves her hometown of Sandy Shores, Michigan, to pursue God's plans for her life in New York City. She works at Sheltering Arms Refuge, an orphanage that also transports homeless children to towns across the United States to match them with compatible families, and comes to love each child. When a newspaper reporter comes to stay at the orphanage in order to gather research for an article, Maggie is struck by his handsome face—and concerned by his lack of faith. Will she be able to maintain her focus on God and remain attuned to His guidance?

ISBN: 978-1-60374-075-3 • Trade • 432 pages

WHITAKER
HOUSE